WINDS OF WAR

BOOK III : HEIRS OF TENEBRIS TRILOGY

BY BRIANNA R. SHAFFERY

Cover and map design by Marcella Thaler

Headshot by Glamour Shots | Photographer: Marko Bulahan | Hair & Makeup: Tatiana Rosa

Publishing Services provided by Paper Raven Books LLC

Printed in the United States of America

First Printing, 2023

Paperback ISBN 979-8-9861732-6-9

Hardback ISBN 979-8-9861732-5-2

For all of the AMAZING teachers in my life: thank you all for your encouragement, wisdom, and friendship over the years.

TABLE OF CONTENTS

MAP OF TENEBRIS
Eurland
Corvus
Sea of Harmony
Shelton Bay
Gossamer
Hart
Woodlane Manor
Covington
Glendale
Caselle
Huntington
Mageffery
Godberd Woods
Union River
Shadow Forest
Halberry
Barrier Plains
Amber Dunelands
Union River
Eurland
Capital
City
Corvus
Fortune Falls
Towns

Indignation

"My shining light," he'd soothed, "we'll get through this, together. I promise."

Astrid hummed, nearly leaning into the warmth offered by the soft-spoken words. Her stomach fluttered, turning into an angry roil she didn't understand. The words faded, along with the soft embrace that had accompanied them. Suspended between the comfort she sought and the pull of her subconscious, Astrid found herself struggling to make sense of anything, let alone maintain her ability to breathe.

Harsh knocking stole Astrid from her troubled slumber. The whispered words of the bitter memory echoed in her ears, keeping time with her heartbeat.

That moment, the day that life had boiled over into pure turmoil, flooded her waking mind like a cold ache in her bones. Acid burned in her blood, eating away at any lingering fondness she might've had for the memory—or any that she'd shared with him.

Casting it from her mind, she bid the person at her door to enter without another thought. She closed her eyes and pressed her palms against them. With each dream she had, the more they began to feel like nightmares. It didn't matter whether true recollections of him haunted her dreams or if they were twisted visions provided by her worst fears; they'd all began to feel the same with each battle Astrid waged to banish them from her conscious mind. She ignored the squeak of the door's hinges and vainly attempted to gather her composure for what the day might place in her path.

"My lady," a man said, entering her chamber, "Tenebris is under attack."

Astrid's blood froze. The fragmented memory and any semblance of sleep finally fled from her mind as she threw back the covers. Springing from the bed, she rushed behind her dressing screen.

"What?"

The floorboards creaked under the guard's feet. "Corvids, my lady. They've infiltrated the country and are mounting attacks at Glenshire and here in Hart."

Astrid pulled her tunic over her head and grabbed her corset. Peeking around her dressing screen, she saw the guard's back to her. Catching sight of the sword at his hip, she recognized him instantly as Fergus, the newly appointed Captain of the King's Guard. Straightening, she fitted her corset over herself.

"How many?"

"Early reports as of a few moments ago said hundreds between the two attacks, but His Majesty fears there may be more waiting to answer their call, if Lord Bailey's reports are to be believed."

"I'm sure they are," Astrid muttered, tugging on her boots. Grabbing her waistcoat, she emerged from the shadows of the dressing screen. "What else? Are they wielding magic? Do they have any weapons? Have there been ships spotted on the coastline?"

Fergus turned around to face her, his brow furrowed. "No ships as of yet, and yes, they are armed and wielding magic to terrorize the townsfolk. Already, they've lit several fires in Glenshire, though they have been extinguished by local Mages." Fergus paused briefly, pivoting to match her movements as she stalked past him to the door of her chamber. "Aren't you going to fix your hair?"

"I think the state of my hair is the least of our kingdom's worries at the moment, Fergus." Astrid yanked open the solid wooden door and strode quickly out into the hallway. Already, the Woodlane Manor was in a frenzy. Servants prepared for a siege, carrying supplies to and fro and raising the different lords and ladies from their slumbers to bring them the sad news. She clenched her jaw.

"I only meant that it would get in your way." Fergus quickened his pace to walk beside her.

"If it comes to that, I'll chop it all off," Astrid grumbled. "What of Cedric and Dinora?"

"No sightings, my lady, only the report of last week."

Astrid's mind turned stormy. The rekindled sting of Cedric's betrayal simmered in her blood. She should've expected something like this would happen when news had reached them of the assassinations of her aunt and uncle. Though she was foolishly reluctant to believe Lord Bailey's reports then, she couldn't ignore them any longer or pray that they were wrong, mistaken, confused. Lord Bailey's network had always been a source of accurate information. And his network also had proven useful in informing the court and his royal majesty of the rumors whispered around the kingdom and beyond.

And this time, his ring of spies were the only reason they had been aware of the threat Cedric and Dinora posed to Tenebris. Cedric hadn't even had the courage to betray her outright, to give her any sort of warning or indication of his plans. He'd snuck away and left her to fit the pieces together, to guess, to mourn, only to realize the truth of what he'd done to her *and* to Tenebris all too late.

Turning sharply, Astrid made for King Harrison's private study. Fergus wrapped a hand around her arm. Taking his cue, she followed him to the main staircase.

As they went, he explained, "They've gathered in the library. It seems that news of the attacks spread faster than anyone had anticipated. Every noble from here to Mageffery has found their way here."

"What? Have they all wisped here?"

"It would appear so."

Astrid rolled her eyes. "Of course they have. I hope they'll prove to be helpful this time around."

Fergus stifled a laugh, coughing. Astrid slapped his arm lightly, glaring at him briefly despite the smile that played at her lips as they turned into the hallway. At the end of the hall, the library doors were thrown open. Astrid raised her brows. During a time like this, she'd expected them to be closed, but looking past the doors, she could see that the room was filled by a rare assembly. It was just as Fergus had claimed: she saw courtiers she hadn't seen since the last feasting days, as well as those who had never left court for very long.

As they approached the looming doorway, the general ruckus of people speaking over each other and holding discordant conversations flooded her ears. Her lips slipped into a grimace she didn't even try to disguise. If she'd been able to look in a mirror, she'd see how her face had pinched into a glower that wasn't all deserved, but Astrid couldn't bring herself to soften her features.

Hardly a season ago, many of these same nobles had disregarded the catastrophic assassinations of her aunt and uncle, the Lord and Lady of Hart, only to hide away in the safety of their estates and ignore the king's call to arms. But now that it was their lives and homes being threatened, it seemed they could muster the effort to appear in this court and stand before their king, ready to offer whatever was asked of them. Astrid's lips turned into a sour purse at the angry rambling of her mind. The phantom touch of arms wrapped around her brushed against her skin. Hardly a season ago, Cedric had held her while she'd cried over her aunt and uncle's deaths. Hardly a season ago, he'd even had the audacity to tell her he'd always be right there, that they'd get through whatever was to come—together.

But he'd lied.

"Ah, Lady Thornraven." At the sound of King Harrison's commanding voice, the crowd parted, and Astrid was able to walk to the front of the room, stopping just under the balcony to stare up at him in all his regal finery. Squinting against the glare of the candlelight and sconces haloing him, she saw the haggard lines of his face hidden beneath the sparkle of his bejeweled crown. "Join me for a moment, will you?"

"Of course, your majesty." Astrid bowed curtly and immediately strode toward the winding staircase.

Fergus made to follow her, but the king held a hand up. "Give us a moment."

Fergus bobbed his head, grasping the hilt of his sword. "As you command it, my king."

Mounting the stairs at a measured pace, Astrid's mind whirled with the possibilities of what Harrison could want from her in this very moment, especially when it was so public. Rumors were already swirling that they had grown closer since the queen's untimely passing—and Cedric's turn toward treason. Astrid had no doubt that an encounter such as this, with all of these witnesses, would only bolster those rumors. People said it was tragedy that had brought them together. Already, the rumors had hooked their claws into the court's intrigue, and every time Astrid passed by a group of ladies hiding behind their dainty fans, she feared that she was the subject of their gossip. Whether Harrison had heard of the rumors or paid them any mind was beyond her. But right now, the last thing she wanted was to be the subject of the room's conversation.

"Lady Thornraven." King Harrison inclined his head before meeting her eyes, motioning for her to follow him through the shelves of scrolls and newly bound books. Once they were far enough from the eyes and ears of those down in the main library, he said, "It's not often that I must admit that I was wrong."

Stopping at the end of the aisle, Harrison turned to face her. Harrison chuckled, running a hand through his lopsided curls. Astrid didn't have a chance to school her face and ease the arch of her brow. "I know. I am the king. I shouldn't admit when I am wrong, but I'd like to think it's what makes me so wise."

"You're wise, all right," Astrid quipped before she could hold her tongue. "I seem to remember you saying not so long ago that the Corvids would do well to remember the Ten Years' War."

"I also seem to remember a wise man once said youth makes a foolish ruler, and yet here we are. I'm surrounded by my peers, and our elders are nowhere to be found."

"I believe they're awaiting your wise words downstairs, your majesty." Astrid eyed the shelves on either side of them. Her mind buzzed, anxious by what Harrison hadn't yet said. "Why did you wish to speak with me?"

"I want you on my war council, as my right hand."

Astrid's eyes flew to his. Shocked by the earnestness she saw shining in his warm eyes, she asked, "You want me to be your right hand?"

"Yes," Harrison said firmly, taking a step toward her and grasping her hand in both of his. "I would've rather Bridget sat at my right hand, but…" He trailed off. His once-steady gaze wavered with the memory of the late queen and the fondness Astrid knew he still had for her even with death between them. "I haven't the head to sift through all of their posturing and endless strategies. I need someone I can trust, who'll take my concerns for the kingdom under consideration aside from their own interests, and fight for Tenebris as fervently as any common person of Tenebrese blood would."

Astrid took a breath and then another. Forgotten were the people in the room below. Forgotten were the rumors spreading like wildfire. Most of all, the broken heart shattered by a foolish man with scarlet eyes and a quiet disposition was forgotten as the king's words echoed in her ears.

"I would be honored to," she said at last. "But I am not of Tenebrese blood like you, however much I wish I was."

"You needn't be," he whispered. "You've already sacrificed a chance for love because of the threat it posed to the kingdom. I don't believe I would've had the strength to do so if our roles had been reversed.

Most people would not have had the strength to do as you have done for this kingdom. I trust you to have the country, to have your *home*, in your heart as you act as my right hand."

Astrid bowed deeply. "I am honored, your majesty. I will, of course, serve my people."

Harrison pulled her up with the gentle hold he still had on her hands. Letting go as she straightened, he flashed her a tense smile. "Then it's decided. May Moerae bless us, else that horde masquerading as nobles mount a mutiny at the news."

Astrid laughed, a dry sound that wasn't at all like the laugh she'd once had. "I'd like to think I'm better liked than that."

"Let us hope we are both better liked than I fear we are at the moment," he sighed. "Declaring war is never a good boost to one's favorability."

"No," Astrid considered. "But successfully leading your people to victory and into peace may yet preserve your legacy."

"I hope so."

Astrid offered him a small smile. "Any longer and I fear they may think we've run off together."

Chuckling, Harrison gestured for her to lead the way. "I see you've heard the rumors too."

"Of course I have," Astrid sniffed. "Courtiers aren't exactly discreet."

"I can't imagine many of them actually fighting, let alone winning the revolution, can you?"

"For all our sakes," Astrid said quietly as they emerged into the visible part of the balcony, "I hope they haven't forgotten how to win."

Harrison nodded. "With you as Royal Mage, I hope we're already at an advantage. Dinora isn't very skilled."

But Cedric was. Astrid didn't dare voice that fact, though. Turning to the king as he came to a stop in the light of the balcony, Astrid said, "Thank you, your majesty."

Bowing, she didn't wait for his dismissal before descending the winding staircase to join the crowd below. She quickly found Fergus leaning against one of the wall-to-wall bookcases along the perimeter of the room and joined him, tuning out the fading whispers as Harrison appeared in the center of the balcony and began to speak.

"Thank you all for gathering here today. As many of you know, our country has been under attack since the tragic assassinations of Lord and Lady Hart," Harrison began, surveying the room with a withering glare. "Though I must admit I am troubled by the delay in our messages to prepare your bannermen for war, I am pleased to see you have all answered our call today. Our country is at war."

A chill silence descended upon the room.

Astrid watched through scrutinous eyes as the gathered nobility squirmed where they stood. She imagined what they could be thinking. She supposed they all shared one single thought as the king's declaration settled in their minds: Tenebris was young. It had only known two decades of peace since its last war. Was it prepared for another? Would their fragile institution survive? Would *they* survive?

As the hurried murmurs and hushed whispers died down, Astrid couldn't help but wonder something more: had the kingdom healed enough to sustain the blows of this war?

Hardly a season had passed since the funeral for her aunt and uncle, and she feared that her grief overshadowed even the turmoil they faced now. Cedric's betrayal weighed down her spirits, especially as he hadn't simply betrayed their love.

All that time, he'd been deceiving her. He'd betrayed her and the country he'd known to be his own since boyhood. Astrid didn't know if it truly mattered how long ago he'd founded his deception, only that that's the path they'd ended up on.

Her own haphazard shouts rang in her ears, yet another recent memory come to haunt her. It hadn't done any good to confront Cedric after the conclusion of the investigation into the deaths—the *assassinations*—of her aunt and uncle had reached her. He'd denied any involvement or knowledge of the plot. Astrid had tried to make him see that this was all his mother's whim, but he'd denied that, and his birth too. Why else would there be a rash of attacks across the country in the wake of Dinora's absence from court and the result of the investigation?

Bitterly, they'd shouted back and forth. She'd begged him to help them, to cast his faith in his mother aside, but Cedric had only shaken his head and denied the truth.

War had come in the night.

And Cedric was to blame for it.

A refugee prince and a vengeful queen, a love so young and fragile, and a woman as wicked as the night was dark. Astrid scoffed. Bitterness flooded her heart. All this time, their enemies had been living amongst them, and she'd freely given her heart to the prince with the timid smile and dim eyes, to the prince who preferred books to people and the early hours of the morning before the estate became a bustle of activity over feast days.

What a fool she'd been—what a fool they all were. Dinora had spun a perfect tale, masquerading as a helpless mother fleeing from the scars of war. And Cedric had done his part too, if not as a boy, then most certainly once he was old enough to enter his mother's confidence—if Dinora was capable of such trust and consideration to others.

But still, Cedric had played his part. A confused man, a man who'd claimed to love her, and a boy still seeking the love of a mother as cold as a stone.

So Astrid would do her part. For her heart, for her country. Whatever might come, Astrid vowed, she would see this war through and do all she could to preserve the country her family and countless others had fought so desperately to form.

Tenebris would not fall, not as she had.

I. A DISTURBANCE IN MAGIC

Shamira's whiskers twitched. Her fur prickled. A sick energy rippled over her senses, distorting the spicy scent of the almost-Harvum air.

Overhead, the sapphire leaves swayed in the stillness. The crackled, ashen trees began to groan. Shamira's bones seemed to quake, but she knew better than to believe it was the result of her nerves.

No, this was anything but.

Something was wrong.

Very wrong.

Shamira? Her brother Talmec nudged her side. She blinked, realizing that she'd stopped mid-step. The assembled pumpkies had stopped with her, openly staring at her with curious gazes. Their anticipation made the already thick air suffocating. *Is everything all right?*

Shamira flicked her tail in time with her thoughts. *No. There's a disturb—*

Before she could even finish her sentence, the earth trembled and began to shift beneath their paws. The quaking intensified with each passing second. Shamira jolted, but not from the violence of the earthquake. Her head pounded, seemingly cleaved open by an axe. Nausea immediately flooded her, burning her throat and stomach.

Shamira! Talmec shouted, jarring her fragile mind.

She whined, leaning into him. *D-Din…Dinora.*

Talmec stiffened beside her, freezing for only a second before he guided her to sit down. Sagging against him for support, Shamira closed her eyes against the assault of the Shadow Forest's dim illumination. Her brows furrowed with the effort it took for her to focus on anything aside from the icy shift of magic wreaking havoc on her body.

Shamira let out a broken whimper. Her body flinched and twisted of its own accord. A sharp ringing sliced through her ears. Her teeth ached. Her jaw clenched tightly against the assault of pain rolling over her body. Minutes, hours, days, centuries could've passed—Shamira wasn't entirely certain how long the agony plagued her body, only that it was a constant thrum of pain, a pain that boiled to a crescendo she didn't think she could survive.

Dinora was definitely doing something horrible on a disastrously large scale. It was the only explanation Shamira could reasonably come to. The only other time she'd sensed a disruption in the balance of magic of this same caliber had been...

Two years ago.

The fire.

The fire that had killed Nyla's family.

But even then, she'd never experienced something this debilitating. Nothing had ever come close to this. Not even the worst natural disaster in her lifetime. The wildfires were like an annoying itch she couldn't reach compared to what she was experiencing now.

The trilled ringing in her ears finally faded. Shamira slowly peeled her eyes open. Blinking, her vision cleared enough to see the shining green eyes of Elder Hecates staring back at her from where he crouched in front of her.

Shamira, he started quietly. *Are you all right?*

Shamira glanced around. The pumpkies had formed a magical shield around them, huddled as close together as the towering trees would allow them. Most pumpkies had their backs to Talmec, Hecates, and herself, watching the Shadow Forest beyond as if they expected something to attack them, and maybe they were right in thinking so. There was no telling for certain what had caused the disturbance she'd sensed, or what it meant for them.

If Dinora hadn't been the cause of it, then what was? And if she was, what had she done that could've caused such a tremendous upheaval in the balance of magic?

Either way, Shamira knew this disturbance would result in nothing good.

I'm fine, she answered weakly. In truth, she wasn't entirely certain. There was a hollowness in her chest that smothered her breath. It was like a longing ache—the kind you only experienced after a great and devastating loss. But she hadn't lost anything. By all means, she was wholly intact, magic and all.

Carefully eyeing her kin, Shamira hesitantly returned her gaze to meet Elder Hecates's eyes.

I think Dinora's stolen a significant amount of energy from the land, she offered, forcing herself to stand on shivering limbs. It was as though this was the first time she'd ever stood in her life, and Shamira found herself forced to sit back down before she fell. Hoping the shrewd Elder hadn't noticed her plight, she continued, *But I can't imagine what she intends to do with it.*

Hecates straightened, attempting to hold her gaze as her eyes shifted with her murky thoughts.

Then we'll have to move quickly, he said, breaking her concentration. Glancing away, he looked at the gathered pumpkies. Shamira assumed an order was given, and as she followed the Brewardt Elder's gaze, she saw four pumpkies break away from their group and step outside the shimmering shield of her kin's combined magics. *They'll track Dinora. For now, you will rest. Once they find her, we'll make haste to fight her.*

Shamira meant to tell him that wasn't necessary, that they could press on now—that they *should* continue on immediately—but Hecates didn't give her the chance to protest. As swiftly as he must've come to her side from where he'd walked beside the few other Clan Elders that had joined their cause, he left.

He's right, sister. Talmec pressed his nose into her neck. *You scared me just now. And don't lie to me and say you're fine. I know you've never experienced something like that before.*

Shamira bobbed her head weakly, surveying the company of pumpkies she'd been tasked with the honor of leading. *You're right, Talmec. I've never been that deeply affected by a shift in the balance before.*

And that's what concerned her straight to her very core.

Just what had she led her kin into? Just what were they to face when they found Dinora? Was it to be more of those creatures Nyla had described? The ones that'd attacked them as they traveled to meet Xander's grandfather?

Or would it be something worse?

Shamira shook her head. Until the trackers found Dinora, it wouldn't do to worry her courage away. She was a leader now. She needed to show those under her charge that she would not be deterred, even in the face of Mordimere's hounds themselves. She would stoke her courage even as the shadows of her mind threatened to consume her. Fear had no place in her bones, and most certainly not in the forefront of her mind.

We should gather some magic, she said, straightening. *We don't know what we will face, but I know we will need all of our energy and more if we are to meet it with an equal force.*

All around her, pumpkies turned their solemn eyes to her or on the Shadow Forest. Shamira met their eyes and held their stares, hoping her gaze showed them a courage she couldn't convince herself to acknowledge, no matter how hard she tried.

We will not be defeated.

At her vow, the pumpkies stomped their paws in a steady rhythm until their beat flooded the surrounding forestland and echoed between the ashen trees and tangled roots of the Shadow Forest. It was this beat, this drumbeat, this steady heartbeat, that Shamira latched onto as she rallied her composure to lead her kin directly into battle even as her unease prevailed.

Nothing had gone according to plan. Not now, not in Nyla's quest for answers about her magic and physical transformation, and certainly not 647 years ago.

She only hoped this time—however much they were caught unawares—that Fate would allow them some small kindness and that things would end differently. Her only regret was that they hadn't acted sooner. That much, she wished, they could've learned from the mistakes of the past.

***

A low growl sounded beside her, the equivalent of a human swear. Shamira wholeheartedly agreed with Elder Hecates's unspoken anger, for the news their trackers brought back was the worst of what she'd expected.

Dinora had raised her army.

Not only had she stolen a detrimental amount of magic from the land, but she'd used it to realize their worst nightmare, to raise her army.

Nyla had been right.

The rock points of the Shadow Forest were the souls of those Dinora had sacrificed to pay the price in her quest for power and revenge 647 years ago. Somehow, for all of these centuries, those souls had remained here, trapped. And now, they were twisted to the whim of the same wicked woman who had damned them.

Shamira's heart wrenched.

They were out of time.

They didn't have time to meet with Nyla and Xander, or the forces they'd gathered in Huntington. They didn't have time to train, to adapt, to learn how to fight side by side with their human counterparts. Dinora had chosen the setting for this battle, and now they had one opportunity to defeat her before she ravaged the countryside with her beasts of stone.

As Shamira weighed their options, she was vaguely aware of the bated attention bestowed upon her by the assembled pumpkies. Most of all, she was aware of Talmec's strong presence beside her. They were foolish to have believed Dinora to be a woman of patience. After 647 years, she was finally free, so why had they believed she would wait a moment longer to exact her revenge?

But there was no time for lamentations or regrets. She needed to make a decision here and now. No matter what decision Shamira made, she was responsible for whatever consequences her brother and her kin would face, whatever might befall the country, and the entire balance of magic.

She knew in her heart what she would do, but to have to make that decision for others? To order them to follow in her path?

Her tail flicked.

That was the hardest burden of leadership. Decisions were easy when made for oneself, when there was little to no consideration of others, when any consequence would burden only the one who'd made it. But to make a decision that would ensnare the lives of others? To bear *that* burden?

That's what stopped her from speaking her mind.

Even if all of these pumpkies had made the decision to be here today, to fight against Dinora and had made their peace with that decision, Shamira knew she was ultimately responsible for the need to face that choice in the first place.

Shamira met the gaze of each and every pumpkie she could. Bowing her head, she said, *The time has come. We must fulfill our most sacred duty and protect Tenebris at all cost.*

The still air turned to static. Turning her gaze over her gathered kin, a small representation of the three clans, pumpkies bowed their heads or bared their teeth. Just as she had made her decision, they'd all made their own. They would follow her, even if she couldn't stomach the idea of ordering them to do so.

Raising her head high, Shamira shouted for all to hear. *We must fight.*

2. SANDS OF ASH

Glaring sunlight reflected off the ash-colored sand, disorienting Shamira momentarily as she acclimated to the new territory. Gone were the trees of the Shadow Forest's heart or the onyx rock of the earth, and in its place was a barren landscape in which she'd emerged after dashing through the forestland's heart at a pace she hadn't thought possible, especially with so large a host to lead through the tangled trees. But they'd done it. They'd raced through the unforgiving heart of the Shadow Forest, and now Shamira was faced with exactly what she had led her kin to fight against. All around her, pumpkies ground to a halt at the edge of Dinora's chosen battlefield where the trees stopped in a jagged line without warning. Catching her breath, Shamira narrowed her eyes against the harsh glint of the sun's rays.

Shock struck her as violently as a lightning bolt.

Far across the barren sands, magic shot up from the earth, writhing and wavering in the air. It shielded whatever lay beyond it, but if Shamira had to wager a guess, she'd say Dinora conducted the energy to her whim from behind its wrath.

Shamira's ears twitched. A low, groaning howl permeated the utter silence of the desert.

Be ready, she warned, knowing her kin understood just as well that danger lay before them.

A single figure emerged from behind the curtain of skyward magic. Sunlight caressed the sleek, jagged creature, hunched over on all fours with an awkward bend to its sharp limbs. Shamira tentatively reached her magic out toward its essence. Her magic immediately recoiled, but still she managed to gather an inkling of the creature's essence. It was exactly as Nyla had described: familiar yet ancient with an anger that buzzed in the undercurrent of its energy. But there was something more, Shamira realized, pressing her senses to glean what it was. Something vile, something bitter. Something not unlike the impression Dinora's magic had left on her memory.

The stone creature let out a piercing wail.

Hundreds more stepped forward.

Shamira's fur prickled.

The creatures wailed in unison, and before she could utter a word of command, the battalion of stone beasts surged forward. Sand flew into the air behind them, creating a cloud of dust on their heels.

The only way to kill them is to shred through their aura! Shamira warned. Her lips curled into a snarl. *Brace yourselves! We hold our line!*

Her kin offered up a roar in response. No matter how much Shamira's courage swelled at the battle cry, her heart shuddered against her chest.

There were too many creatures. If the humans didn't arrive soon, Shamira feared Tenebris would fall, and the damage to the balance of magic would become irreversible.

Shaking herself from her stupor, Shamira growled. The first of the creatures were a mere fifty yards away now.

Steady, she said, more to herself than to anyone else. She pulled on her magic, gathering it up within her. *Ready your magic!*

The air crackled with the distant clap of thunder. It was a steady beat as sure as her own heart. A light breeze blew across the sandy field, bringing with it the scent of freshly fallen rain and a crisp snowfall or the wind off the highest mountaintops.

Shamira's heart stopped. Any order she'd meant to convey to her kin died with the realization of what was headed their way.

Raverins.

Hold your ground! Hecates's firm voice ordered. *Strike!*

The thunder—the *raverins*—drew closer.

On either side of her, her kin unleashed their individual magics on the advancing creatures. Their shrill cries clawed down Shamira's spine as the pumpkies' magics tore into them. Ice flooded her veins, freezing more than just her blood.

Shamira! Talmec shouted. *Shamira, what's wrong?*

Raverins, she said, blinking away her daze. The fur on the back of her neck stood on end. Static filled the air. Shamira unleashed her magic on the nearest of the stone beasts, crouching low to the ground. A loud, resounding boom ricocheted through the air. Shamira's ears swiveled in the direction the blast had come from. She peeled her eyes away from the horde of creatures still advancing in droves to find the source of the thunderous blast.

Relief wove its way through her gut, finding a group of humans surrounding a large piece of artillery, working quickly to reload it as more and more humans appeared throughout the battlefield, joining in the fight to slow the tide of stone creatures. Their metal armor gleamed in the muddied sunlight as they hurried to reload their cannon. *At least the humans have found their way here. I feared we would not be able to fend off both Dinora's creatures and the raverins.*

Shamira cast her magic on a pack of stone beasts bearing down on her. Talmec's amber-colored magic joined hers to help destroy the creatures before they could reach them. As they fought, the large shadows she'd so feared loomed overhead. The shadows stretched over the uneven dunes, dipping over the mounds of sand in time with the thunderous snaps of their great tails. Shamira glanced up. A sharp caw rang through the air. More screeches resounded as a lone raverin led several more over the battlefield, their tails coiling in the air behind them.

The lead raverin dove.

Shamira made to yowl, to warn the group of humans some measure away from her and her kin of the coming attack, but any sound she could've made died in her throat.

Talons outstretched, the lead raverin tore through a stone creature, ripping its head from its body as a second raverin dove in after it and snatched up the still-squirming body.

A relieved huff left Shamira's lips. She couldn't explain their presence here, nor did she care to at the moment. They had come to their aid, and that was enough to quell her curiosity.

As a result of the aerial attack, the stone creatures began to scramble. Fending off the nearly endless wave of stone creatures as they scattered and magic blasted, Shamira didn't have any time to face the confusion swirling in her mind.

Bursts of magic flashed as the cannon blasts became a steady addition to the piercing wails of the fallen and injured rock creatures amongst the din of battle. Shamira did her best to drown out the creatures' screeches and ignore the wrench of her heart whenever her ears caught a sharp whine, a garbled cry of pain, a gasp of air that choked off inexplicably. Somewhere in the grim recesses of her mind, Shamira knew that for as many creatures as they put down, it wouldn't be enough to curb their own losses or prevent them all together.

Both sides would see loss, but she knew only theirs would be conscious of that grief.

As selfish as it was, Shamira found herself praying that she wouldn't know it too personally, already seeking out Talmec for the subtle assurance that her brother was all right. Finding him amongst a crowd of humans and pumpkies, Shamira went to join them.

One after another, the human soldiers and Casters dispatched small groupings of the stone creatures, breaking their haphazard lines, with the cannons. Their guns broke shards off of the creatures where they were struck, creating ghastly beasts with missing chunks that the Casters and pumpkies ultimately finished off with their magic.

The raverins had flown to the far reaches of the onslaught, picking the beasts off and shredding them apart limb from limb. Shamira's nostrils burned from the sharp haze that clung to the battlefield from the discharge of the humans' weapons. The cloudiness was made thicker by the wispy tendrils of smoke released with each creature the combined forces defeated.

There could only be one explanation for these ghostly apparitions. As her mind settled on it, Shamira growled from deep within her chest.

Six centuries. These souls had been trapped in the depths of the Shadow Forest—in the rock points—for six long and horrible centuries. All those lives Dinora had taken to pay the sacrifice for stealing so much magic from the land during that fateful battle had been trapped here, on this plane, in the rocks of the justly dubbed "haunted forest," only for her to manipulate for her own gain once again.

Even if the souls trapped within these beasts of stone were once human, they definitely weren't anymore. Shamira couldn't discern whether they were merely trapped within, an energy source for Dinora's dark musings, or if they had been warped into these creatures and their humanity destroyed in the transformation. There was no way for her to study them, as they dissipated into a fleeting wisp of smoke each time their physical embodiment was destroyed.

She chose to believe that the smoke was a physical representation of the soul gaining its freedom from the creature, and that whoever they once were could finally find some peace in their unjust death.

All she could be certain of was the metallic taste of overexertion sitting on her tongue. She didn't know when or how it'd happened, but the pumpkies had joined the fray alongside the foot soldiers and Casters as though they had always fought together, combining physical assaults with their magic as their energies waned. The creatures had grown agitated, becoming a frenzy of mass confusion as they didn't know where to target or how to combat the opposition they faced between cannons and guns, magic and claws, or swooping raverins and *thwacking* tails.

But they didn't stop.

For every creature they defeated, Shamira swore another took its place. She didn't know if Dinora could regenerate them, or if it were even possible to do so.

If the horde of creatures didn't thin soon, Shamira feared that they wouldn't be able to survive this battle. Her head pounded from the steady use of magic, or from the lack of it in the land, or perhaps both.

But she didn't stop.

She and Talmec worked together, as many of her kin had paired off instinctually. It was as if they had never stopped being a class of warriors, the guardians of Tenebris.

It almost made her wonder if the clans had spent any time preparing for this battle in the wake of her absence, or if the training they'd each completed through adolescence to protect their territory had proven to be more than a silly pretense of duty.

Heart thundering, Shamira's whiskers twitched violently. Her eyes widened with the spark that shot through her as one essence in particular caught her attention.

An energy she'd hoped she wouldn't find on the battlefield, but had looked out for nonetheless even as she faced screeching creatures with jagged teeth and the careless discord of combat, appeared with the slight ripple of the wind.

Talmec! Shamira shouted. *On me!*

Shamira's sage-colored magic faded with the defeat of yet another creature. Her chest heaved. Panting freely, she took half a second to swallow a gulp of air before darting off through the field with her brother on her heels. Her only thought was for Nyla.

She'd been dreading the moment Nyla's essence would tug at her senses, but there was no stopping her from participating in this battle.

It was all Shamira could do to vow to keep her safe. After all, people and pumpkies far older than Nyla had abstained from fighting this battle.

And if she could rely on her instinct for anything, it would be that if she could sense Nyla's presence on this battlefield, Dinora and her nightmarish stone creatures could too.

Shamira, your left! Talmec warned, surging forward and jumping over her to tackle a creature she hadn't noticed as her gaze fell upon a flash of silver hair and lilac-colored magic in the fray up ahead.

As Talmec grappled to pin the creature down, Shamira summoned her magic. She unleashed it in a hellish fury, shattering the creature with ease. Talmec's paws landed on the bloody sand. With a scowl, he glanced back at her.

I had it handled. He bared his teeth.

I know, but we haven't the time for this, she hissed back. She nodded her head in the direction she'd last seen Nyla. The silver-haired girl hadn't moved from the spot where she'd been wisped in by the powerful Caster beside her.

"Ingrid!" Nyla's shout reverberated down Shamira's spine. Her ears twitched, tilting toward the single word as she watched a stone creature lunge for the dark-haired Caster.

Shamira's heart clenched. She didn't wait for Talmec or give him any indication of her movements before she forced herself to move as quickly as she could with her leaden limbs, barreling toward Nyla and the woman she'd called Ingrid.

A flash of fur whizzed by her. Shamira's eyes widened, her whiskers flicking as Talmec launched himself at the stone creature, colliding with it midway through the air before it could even come close to Ingrid. Her brother growled, tumbling with the stone creature and working furiously to pin it down.

As if she suddenly remembered herself, Ingrid unleashed a delicate-colored magic on the creature. Shamira lunged.

Wrapping her mouth around the creature's neck to hold it in place, she stomped her paw down on its flailing limb, its jagged claws poised to attack. Talmec's amber magic shone through the growing cracks, splitting the creature apart in chunks and pieces.

Nyla! Shamira huffed, too exhausted to express the relief flooding her veins. She eased to standing tall as the onyx-colored remnants of Dinora's pawn turned to smoke. She studied Nyla with a grim expression, noticing a bitter tang wafting from the girl.

She was terrified.

Those lilac eyes that Shamira had seen so many different emotions in over the few weeks she'd known Nyla were marred by fear as they struggled to focus or observe the chaos around them. And Shamira didn't know how to help her, not in this moment, anyway, and certainly not in the next. All she knew for certain was that Nyla was terrified and disoriented. Any resolve she'd had about defeating Dinora had fled from her signature.

And that's what scared Shamira most of all.

3. SO IT BEGINS

Nyla blinked against the glaring sunlight. Explosions thundered in her ears. Screeches and *caws* rounded out the cacophony of the battle raging around her as she struggled to gain her bearings. As Nyla turned on her heel to steady herself on the sand shifting beneath her feet, the hair on her arms stood on end.

"Ingrid!" Nyla shouted, drawing a sharp intake of breath.

Before Nyla could react further, a blurred mass of fur collided with the stone creature leaping at Ingrid. The creature wailed, flailing beneath the pumpkie. Nyla's heart pounded in her chest, her eyes wide as her gaze flew to Ingrid. The dark-haired woman's mouth dropped open. The stillness between them lasted for only a second before Ingrid nearly growled and summoned her blush-colored magic.

Another pumpkie rushed into the fray, barely avoiding Ingrid's attack on the creature as the pumpkie wrapped its jaw around the neck of the thrashing monster to pin it in place.

Amber magic glowed through the forming cracks. Seconds later, the creature burst, its remnants turning to smoke before Nyla could even blink.

Nyla! Shamira's gritty voice floated over her mind, jarring her from the void that'd consumed her mind at the harried sight of raverins and creatures and soldiers and pumpkies. *Nyla, you need to gather yourself!*

"Shamira!" Nyla breathed in relief, nearly snapping out of the daze that had utterly overwhelmed her conscious mind. Shaking her head to clear away the rest of the fog, Nyla glanced around them, noticing for the first time that several pumpkies had gathered around them in her momentary incapacitation. As war waged across the sandy plain, smoke curled in the air with each expulsion of the army's munitions. Energy magic burst like lightning bugs, flashing here and there. Raverins cawed, flying overhead and swooping over Dinora's army. The rock creatures wailed, a piercing cry that would no doubt shatter her eardrums if they didn't stop anytime soon.

Already, there was a soft ringing in her ears. But Nyla didn't care, not as her gaze refocused on the aurora bursting up from the ground in the middle of the ashen battlefield.

Dinora.

Gritting her teeth, Nyla said, "We have to get to her."

Lead the way, Shamira huffed, coming to stand by her side now that the stone creature who'd nearly attacked the Mage General had been destroyed. *We'll keep these beasts from your path. Conserve your energy.*

"I'll gather some Casters to help," Ingrid offered, reaching a hand toward the sky and letting her magic flare. The light pink magic burst, shooting high into the sky and piercing through the haze of smoke and grit. "Take Shamira's advice and conserve your energy. You'll need every ounce of your magic if you want a proper chance at defeating Dinora."

"What about the raverins?" she asked, trying to ignore the lick of anxiety curling in her blood at Shamira and Ingrid's instructions. They couldn't really mean that, could they? Did they truly expect her to stand by and watch as people protected *her*? That hadn't been her intention when she'd decided to defeat Dinora, but maybe…maybe they knew better, from experience.

We'll leave them to do as they please, Shamira said. *They're on our side from what we've gathered, but otherwise, our kind do not interact with one another due to grudges as old as the war itself.*

Nyla nodded, overlooking the allies gathered around her. Doubt wove its way into her gut. She swallowed hard. Maybe it was her ambitious vendetta that had fueled her confidence enough to take this path, or maybe it was her righteousness, but either way, she didn't know if she could survive this in any sense of the word. But damn it all if she wouldn't try, and by Helpet's blessing, she might even be able to save everyone she cared about and all those who she didn't know but cared for all the same.

As the last of Ingrid's Circle wisped to them, Nyla was shuffled to the middle of the assembled pack as Ingrid explained that she was the one who had inherited Astrid's magic, and could very well be their only chance at winning this battle and stopping Dinora. Finding Shamira on one side of her and Ingrid on the other, a grave realization hit the pit of Nyla's stomach. They truly intended to sacrifice others for the sake of protecting her—her magic, Astrid's magic. She clenched her hands into fists to stop their shaking.

"Ready?" the Mage General asked.

"No," Nyla said honestly, "but does that really matter?"

Shamira chittered, a sound Nyla hadn't heard before, and offered a smile that was all pointed teeth. *I suppose it doesn't, but know that we're right here beside you.*

"Then that's all that matters." Nyla prayed her words were true, taking one step forward and then another. Her heart beat like an ominous drum in her ears.

With each step the group took across the ash-colored sand, Casters and pumpkies alike threw magic at any creature that dared threaten their path. Soldiers clad in tattered indigo cloaks joined their ranks, as did those marked by the tunics of the Tenebrese army over their gleaming chainmail. Their guns and primitive weaponry stalled the creatures barely long enough for the magic users to shred into them. Every time

Nyla made to gather her magic and aid someone in taking down one of the onyx-colored creatures, Shamira or Ingrid stopped her with a stern word to conserve her magic, to let them handle this so she could face Dinora with every bit of her strength intact.

But the farther they traversed across the battlefield at this agonizing pace, the less Nyla was inclined to listen to them. With each grunt, groan, or pained cry of the people and pumpkies fighting to protect her that fell on her ears, the harder it was for her to keep her magic at bay or ignore the wrench of her heart, begging her to do *something*.

Acrid smoke burned her nostrils as it swept across the battlefield. The clash of metal against stone had ceased to make an impact on her ears the more accustomed she became to the battle raging around her. Keeping her eyes focused on the dusty world surrounding her, Nyla caught glimpses of the battle beyond her gathering of protectors. The flare of magic, the spark of a cannon, or the diving shadow of a raverin caught her eyes every so often, but for the most part, she saw only the shoulders and the backs of the people tasked with protecting her, the person they knew only as Astrid's heir, as their dim hope of defeating Dinora because she knew how to wield her magic in a similar fashion and had fought her before—and *survived*.

From the corner of her eye, Nyla saw the hulking shadow of a stone creature lunging for a soldier. Without so much as a second for consideration, Nyla shoved Ingrid and the soldier aside. The creature loomed over her, its faceless body stretching through the air with a clawed hand just a hair's breadth away from her. Lilac-colored magic burst from the instantaneous cracks that fractured the tip of its clawed hand. The cracks ruptured along its awkward limb, just as she'd pictured them doing in her mind's eye.

The agonized wail of the creature pierced the air, cutting off as abruptly as it had started thanks to the cracks splintering its torso and the lilac magic that shredded the creature to pieces of lifeless stone.

Nyla didn't have time to revel in the way the chunks and shards of stone turned to smoke and dissipated before Ingrid was yanking her back into the center of the group.

"What were you thinking?!" she shouted, forcibly turning her so they were face-to-face. Nyla opened her mouth to answer, but the woman never gave her the chance. "Do you want to die, Nyla? Do you not understand that I've been tasked by nearly everyone to keep you safe, to keep you from doing something reckless in the name of your country? Have you ever stopped to consider how devastating it would be to *me* if you were to die? No, of course you haven't. You've been too busy—" Ingrid paused just long enough to send a blast of magic over the shoulder of an injured Caster on the other side of the group. "—too busy fighting to make your own choices and get revenge on Dinora to notice! You're a child, Nyla, and I for one am not going to let you die for the vain thought that you're the only one who can defeat Dinora!"

Nyla inhaled a sharp breath, ignoring the squeezing of her heart as Ingrid's blazing eyes held her gaze. "I'm no more a child than you are. My youth was stolen from me, and we all know it. If Fate didn't want me here, then I wouldn't be, but that's not what's happened, is it? I inherited Astrid's magic for a reason, and while I'm sure there are plenty of people who *think* they can defeat Dinora, what will it cost them? What will it cost Tenebris?"

"Then let me help you! Let me get you to a place where you can defeat Dinora without losing your strength!" Ingrid snapped. "Can't you see that extending yourself now, that rejecting our protection, will put your goal—*our* goal—in jeopardy? You might be Astrid's heir, but you are not invincible—none of us are!"

"I won't let anyone die just to protect me! If Alexander and the Heirs, if the royals, if the government, if *you* didn't want me here because you think I'm too young, you should have just left me then!" Nyla hissed back, her blood boiling. Out of spite or in honor of the silent oath she'd made to her own heart, she shattered another creature before the soldier it charged could even fire their weapon. They shot her a bewildered glance before turning back to the chaos around them. "But we all made our choices, didn't we?"

As if Ingrid was remembering how she'd allowed Nyla to see Cedric with the hope of tricking him into believing she was Astrid or how she'd adamantly supported Nyla's right to make the decision to fight Dinora for herself, Ingrid's nostrils flared. Nyla pressed her lips into a grim line as Ingrid's eyes cleared of whatever memories her question had brought to her mind.

"I suppose we did."

Neither said another word, turning away from each other. The group continued on, fighting their way through the endless horde of stone creatures bearing down on them from all directions. Ever so slowly, the varied group of pumpkies, Casters, and soldiers maneuvered their way across the battlefield, hardly moving an inch at a time as the creatures seemed to flock to them. Nyla began to doubt that it was a coincidence, remembering the attack on their carriage, wondering if they could sense her presence here or if there was some other reason why this fear came to her. Nyla wouldn't be surprised if Dinora had targeted them, was targeting *her* specifically. But for what, Nyla couldn't say.

Surrounded by the humanoid creatures on all sides, the group was forced to a halt, fighting desperately to keep from being overwhelmed. Nyla's hand flitted over the wand in her pocket. She hadn't had the time to practice with it, let alone ask about its purpose, but Astrid had told her what mattered.

The only question left in her mind now was—would it make a difference?

Nyla's head snapped in the direction of a harsh grunt. Her eyes hardly registered the sight of an onyx-colored creature tearing the throat out of a flailing Caster. A red mist sprayed through the air, but that was all she saw before someone had grabbed her and she was jostled behind a new shield, another protector she didn't know, forced to stand between her and the converging threat.

The line of Casters and soldiers had scattered when the creature pounced and advanced on the opening it had created, leaving a gap in the defenses that had scrambled to form around her only moments before. Nyla couldn't hear the shouts and frantic communication happening around her over the thundering of her heart between her ears. But she knew one thing: the creatures *were* drawn to her.

Shamira! she called telepathically, unable to find neither whisker nor tail of her friend in the fray. *We can't keep going like this! We can't move. We're not getting any closer to Dinora so we can stop this!*

Then what do you want to do? Shamira grumbled.

Nyla conjured a shield to fill the gap left by the fallen Caster and broken formation scrambling to push back against the tide of creatures swarming there. Their defenses were broken. Nyla didn't know how any of the unlucky group ordered to protect her were still standing, given how haggard they looked. Grime and sweat clung to their exposed skin. Blood crusted or gushed from where they'd sustained injuries, but not once had she heard any complaints or grumbling.

I want to end this! she answered.

Nearly growling, she shoved her shield against the creatures clawing at her magic. Elbowing her current protector away, she forced herself to take a step forward and then another. As she shoved her shield against the horde of creatures, the Casters and soldiers closed their ranks. But Nyla didn't stop shoving through the crowd or forcing the creatures back with her magic.

Gritting her teeth, Nyla called upon her power in full. Staring down the shrieking creatures on the other side of her magical barrier, Nyla let her shield shatter and rained its sharp fractals upon the creatures.

A chilling chorus of screeches cut through the air. Nyla didn't stop, unleashing a slash of magic to cut the creatures down where they stood. Tears prickled her eyes.

No one else was going to die for her.

4. Helpless on the Homefront

Xander blinked, dazed. He knew wisping was instantaneous, that it was like disappearing in the exact timing of a blink, but he hadn't expected the empty static that would consume him by watching Nyla and Ingrid disappear.

A warm hand tugged on his. Glancing down, Xander met the worried eyes of his cousin Meredith. Quietly, as if she were afraid to speak, she asked, "Do you really think Nyla will be okay?"

Xander swallowed against the lump in his throat. He knew he should lie, that he should assure Merry she needn't worry, but he couldn't find it in his heart to do so.

Instead, he said, "I don't know, but I hope so."

Merry's lip wobbled. Xander wrapped her in a hug as she began to sniffle again. He wasn't sure what to do. In the distance, he could hear shouting, but the words were indiscernible. He didn't know what was going on around Pemberly, not with the earthquake or the sudden preparations for battle, but he knew somewhere beyond the utter stillness of his mind, life had sped up inconceivably fast. He didn't know how it had come to this.

For all of their planning this morning and afternoon, none of it mattered. Dinora had forced them into haphazard action. Any belief he had that they could easily defeat her fled his mind. Especially if that earthquake was any indication of what those who'd gone to battle were about to face.

"Xander! Merry!" Their grandfather's voice shattered the odd calm of the back garden. Merry peeled away from him and sprinted toward their grandfather, throwing herself into him and wrapping her arms around him. "You're both all right!"

Xander wiped his cheeks, unaware of when those tears had been shed, and forced himself to join his family where they stood.

"Nyla's gone with Ingrid," he said, though his choked throat made it difficult to speak.

His grandfather nodded. "This isn't at all the circumstances we'd all hoped for, but I have faith in us and our abilities."

Xander raised his brows. "How can you say that when we're not the ones fighting?"

Merry squeaked, clutching a hand to her chest and glancing between them. Instant regret wove its way through his veins.

Their grandfather cleared his throat. "In all my years, I've learned that if nothing else, you cannot worry so much that you doom yourself."

Xander took a shaky breath and forced the tension to fall from his body. Unable to accomplish the latter, Xander at least managed to loosen the worried grip on his mind and find what he hoped was an appropriate response. "You're right. I'm sorry. I just…all I can think about is…"

He didn't know what he'd meant to say. His mind was jumbled beyond coherent comprehension. Fragments of thoughts and half-realized sentiments flooded him instantly until all that was left was this tangled mess he couldn't decipher.

"I understand." His grandfather laid a hand on his shoulder. "You have never faced something like this before. Neither of you have, and while I am grateful for that, it doesn't help you now. You aren't equipped to understand how to navigate a situation like this, and I am unfortunately needed elsewhere, or else I would shield you from this too."

"What are you doing that you can't stay with us?" Merry asked with a frown.

"I need to help direct people. We're trying to set up a healing ward and find places for people to rest in relative comfort when they return from the battlefield. There are communications to be sent, repairs to be made, and a whole mess to clean up. This is our home, and I wouldn't entrust it to someone else."

Xander nodded grimly. "Go on ahead. I'll look after Merry."

"I don't need to be looked after!" Merry protested.

"I'll look after Merry." All eyes turned to Moretta, Pemberly Hall's head cook, as she hurried down the cracked steps of the damaged estate.

Merry opened her mouth to protest further, but Moretta didn't give her a chance to before she was speaking again. "Come with me," she said. "We need your help in the kitchen with boiling water and preparing Healers' tonics for the Casters and soldiers."

"You need *my* help?" Merry asked doubtfully.

"Yes." Moretta nodded, steering Merry toward the steps she'd only just descended herself. "An extra pair of hands is always welcome in my kitchen."

Merry cast a glance over her shoulder, catching Xander's eyes. He nodded in what he hoped was a reassuring way and tried to offer her a smile but to no avail. He only hoped it wasn't a grimace.

"Xander, could you see that the Healers and medical teams have everything they need?" his grandfather asked. "Geraldine will be in charge of the operation, but we are still awaiting her arrival, but for now, someone needs to show these people where we keep things."

Xander toed the dirt beneath his feet. All he could think about was Nyla and what might be happening to her. "I can try."

His grandfather put a hand on his shoulder. Glancing up, Xander watched as his grandfather gave him a stern look, one that usually was accompanied by some difficult advice or a request.

"Lord Huntington!" a voice interrupted. His grandfather muttered under his breath, but ultimately turned to face the frantic page running toward them. "George and Geraldine Remington have arrived!"

"About time!" his grandfather huffed. And just like that, the page was off again, running toward the next message they would be tasked to relay. His grandfather patted his shoulder, the expression of pure authority still intact as he said, "Take some time, Xander. Gather your composure and then join us when you are ready. Geraldine will handle things, though I'm certain she wouldn't mind the help if you're up to offering it, or you may join us in observing the battle. The choice is yours, though I personally find idleness and helplessness to be inescapable when forced to watch a situation unfold outside of your control. I'm sorry I can't offer more support to you in this time of great need."

"I know," Xander said. Taking a deep breath of resignation, he added, "I'll only be a moment."

But Xander knew—a moment could mean anything.

Nodding thoughtfully, as if he too realized the ambiguity of "a moment," his grandfather walked back toward the once stately home.

Xander let out a shaky breath and tilted his head back, closing his eyes. Warm sunlight kissed his skin, but the feeling only left him with a deep emptiness that crowded his chest.

Nyla had really gone to defeat Dinora.

Dinora had really raised an army, or gathered the power necessary to pose a grave threat.

The legends people told of the Shadow Forest, of the evil sorceress who once wielded unnatural power, were more than stories. And they were certainly more than nightmares. The legend was a fact, a hidden truth, and a history that had encroached upon their present, that now threatened all of Tenebris. And salvation rested on an ill-prepared force at best, or the shoulders of a young woman—the woman he inevitably had come to love—to save them all.

Xander cursed, dragging a hand through his hair. There was nothing he could do, and it gutted him almost as much as the thought of his friends, of all those trained soldiers and Casters—of Nyla—facing Dinora while he did nothing to help.

There had to be something he could do, but what? All he was was an archer, and he doubted arrows would be of any help against Dinora's stone creatures. So what? What could he possibly do to make himself helpful or at least keep himself busy enough to stop the worry from eating through his gut? It wasn't like he could help Gerri much, for he knew very little about medicine and treating battle wounds. He would only get in the way if he were to try and help her in the makeshift infirmary.

Xander dragged a hand through his hair once more, pacing the width of the walkway. All he could think about was the fact that there was a battle raging somewhere, and he hadn't the slightest idea where or how severe. A heavy sigh fell from his lips. He ran his hand through his hair again.

Maybe he could find someone to wisp him there. Maybe he could fight, be of some help in defeating Dinora instead of sitting behind a shield of relative safety.

A chill raced down his spine.

Was anyone really "safe?"

What if they lost? What if Dinora…what if she—

Xander shook his head furiously. He couldn't think that. He couldn't dare to finish that thought because if he did, it would give it an air of possibility. If he finished that horrible thought, it would validate his deepest fears, and he couldn't bear to do that.

His hand lifted, and just as he was about to run it through his hair again, a voice called, "If you keep doing that, you won't have any hair left at all."

"Edwin!" Xander burst, turning on his heel. Nearly frantic, he hastily closed the gap between them, jumping up onto the step beside his friend, and grasped him by the shoulders. "I need you to take me to her! I have to be there!"

Edwin frowned at him. Brushing his hands aside, Edwin said, "I can't. Nyla asked me to keep you and Merry safe at any costs, and frankly, I'm not inclined to spite her after that duel with Frederick."

"Edwin, please," Xander pleaded, "as your oldest friend, I need you to do this for me."

"And as *your* oldest friend, I'm telling you I can't." Edwin shook his head and took a step back. "Even if Nyla hadn't already asked me to keep you safe, I wouldn't bring you to that battle, no matter how much you begged me to or came to hate me for not bringing you."

Xander glanced away, clenching his jaw. He bit the curse burning on his tongue. Tensely, Xander forced his shoulders to drop and shook his hands out at his sides. "I'll respect that, but I'm still angry."

Edwin laughed. "I wouldn't expect anything less." Edwin gripped his shoulder and squeezed it. "They've set up an emergency healing ward in the ballroom and main dining hall. Gerri's taken full control of the situation there. With both Sir Hubert and Lady Ravencroft on the battlefield, the Heirs of Tenebris and a few high-ranking members of Lady Ravencroft's inner Circle and Sir Hubert's command are working cohesively to manage things here. Your grandfather's study is the main communications quarters until we need a bigger space."

Xander quirked his brow. None of that meant much of anything to him. Or rather, it didn't seem to be of much importance given how his mind was plagued by other matters.

"It means they've set up viewing glasses," Edwin explained.

"Ah." Xander nodded, swallowing thickly. He wasn't so sure he'd want to see what was happening on the battlefield through the eyes of the enchanted glass, especially since he couldn't do anything about what he might or might not see through their magic. Forcing himself to mount the steps and put one foot in front of the other, he asked, "And Nyla? Do you know…do you know where she is?"

"Commander Howards has a crystal ball specifically monitoring Nyla set up. She's taken it upon herself to watch over Nyla for the entirety of the battle," Edwin said, following beside Xander as he numbly ascended the few short steps and stepped over the rubble-strewn opening where a pair of glass doors had once resided. "Violet says she'll drag Nyla back here yowling like a hellox if it means getting her out of that battle safely. No one's going to let her get hurt, Xander. I promise you that. Ingrid is still with her, and Shamira's there with the pumpkies too."

Xander's breath stuttered. "Shamira's there too?"

Edwin bobbed his head, sidestepping a chunk of plaster in his path. "Based on the initial reports of the first Casters on scene, the pumpkies were already there when our forces started to wisp onto the field."

Xander nodded. His throat went dry. Between the confirmation of both Nyla and Shamira actually being on that battlefield and his first look inside Pemberly Hall since the earthquake that must've accompanied Dinora's successful attempt to raise her army, his mind couldn't form a response.

Taking a long breath, Xander willed his eyes to ignore the destruction of his ancestral home and only focus on the path ahead of him. He didn't dare let the cracked walls or the bits of plaster from the ceiling or glass from the windows shattered against the carpeted hallway impose themselves on his mind. Xander didn't know how they were going to fix any of this. He didn't know how they'd remedy the insecurity seeping into his veins, a feeling he'd bet every single person here today recognized in themselves. He only hoped his younger cousin would be able to recover some sense of childish ignorance again, no matter how long it took. She was too young to have that carefreeness stolen from her.

At least Merry was safe with Moretta. If anyone could offer her some comfort while keeping their own wits from fraying, it was Pemberly's head chef. There were few people, Xander had found, in this life who seemed to be as strong as the impression they gave. He was only grateful that Moretta had chosen to become a close family friend, and not someone who would seek to sell their secrets for a small boon.

With so many people over the years who'd only gotten close to him and his family for their own gain, Xander couldn't begin to recognize how grateful he was for the people who'd remained in his life simply because they wanted to. Without an ulterior motive, without ambition, just simply because they wanted to. Love, friendship, whatever the case might be, there were so few people in his life like that, that he found himself thinking about Astrid.

Briefly, he wondered what had actually happened between Astrid and Cedric all those centuries ago. With so many of the old legends pieced together now, the only gaps left to fill were the things neither history nor fable had deigned to immortalize.

An answer hadn't come to him before they reached the doors of his grandfather's study, askew from the earthquake.

The usual quiet and stuffiness of the office had been disrupted by a general disorder and cacophony. Explosions and the routine discord of battle echoed from the viewing glasses. Their frames rattled where they stood around the room. Heirs of Tenebris, members of the Caster Corps, and soldiers of both the Royal Guard and national army gathered around each viewing glass in small groups, observing the battle unfolding within their smooth panes.

Taking in the disarray and messengers bustling to and from the different parts of the estate, Xander came to a complete stop just inside the broken doorway. All around him, the war room revolved in a sensation of movement and incomprehensible noise. The long table that resided in the center of his grandfather's study was covered in maps and alight with magical projections of the battle. High-ranking officials from all sects were gathered around the oval table, monitoring the battle and grumbling amongst each other with furrowed brows, pointing to different areas along their maps. A messenger skirted around him, jarring him from the momentary daze that had forced him to a grinding halt.

"Ah, Xander, Sir Maffis," his grandfather greeted, glancing over at them from where he stood beside a shorter woman with brown hair and a deep concentration marring her face. "What news have you brought us of the dungeons, Edwin?"

Edwin strolled forward. "The dungeons are intact, and Cedric remains quiet. The guards checked in on him after the earthquake, but he wouldn't respond to them."

Xander's grandfather nodded solemnly. "At least there is that small consolation in all of this."

Xander turned to glance at Edwin, but his friend was already turning away and strolling toward the closest viewing glass.

"Xander," his grandfather started, "I'd like for you to meet Commander Howards. Commander, this is my grandson Alexander, a close friend of Nyla's."

"Pleasure to meet you, Lord Alexander," she said without taking her eyes from the crystal ball in front of her.

Xander swallowed against his dry tongue. "Is that the crystal ball you're using to monitor Nyla?"

"Yes." His grandfather motioned for him to join them. "Come and take a look. Nyla is fine, though she seems a little disgruntled. Ingrid keeps telling her to conserve her magic, and I assume Shamira has told her the same."

Xander gingerly came to stand beside the pair and glanced into the depths of the glass sphere. Within the smooth pane of the orb, he had an astoundingly clear view of Nyla and Shamira. Ingrid was on her other side, and beyond the three of them was what looked like a circle of soldiers, Casters, and pumpkies working diligently to keep Nyla safe as they traversed the length of the battlefield.

Between the shoulders and shields of those around her, Xander could just make out the hazy battlefield beyond the closed-rank group. The sight of the smoky landscape and brief flashes of magic coiled the worry in his gut, a feeling that was only made worse when one of those stone creatures like the ones that had attacked their carriage on the way to

Covington leapt through the thickening haze, its clawed limb ready to slash through Nyla's protectors.

Xander's heart wrenched as he saw Nyla shove the soldier in front of her away, facing the creature head-on just as it was ready to slice through flesh and bone.

The claw cracked. The line rippled up its arm, glowing with a bright light. Xander's breath hitched as lilac-colored magic erupted from the growing cracks forming over the creature's torso and odd limbs, shattering the creature to pieces. Nyla's magic.

"The Mage General isn't going to like that," Commander Howards murmured.

Xander bobbed his head distractedly, fighting against the nightmare that threatened to take hold of his mind. The dual image of the stone creature leaping at Nyla and the hellhound that had lunged at his sister clashed together in his mind's eye, churning the simmering acid in his stomach to the point where Xander pulled at his collar, vaguely wondering if he'd be sick. "Nyla won't care."

As the words left him, Ingrid's voice pierced through his eardrums, reverberating from the crystal ball. Ingrid's words were lost among the chaos of battle, as was Nyla's response. Xander only managed to catch a few snippets of the heated exchange as the two glared at each other, but when Nyla's voice cut through the static of the battle song, it bit just as deeply as Ingrid's initial barb had.

"But we all made our choices, didn't we?" Nyla's sharp words echoed in his mind, rattling his failing disposition.

Not waiting to hear Ingrid's response, he asked, "Do we know what their plan is, or if they even have one?"

"They're going to confront Dinora," Commander Howards said grimly, her voice quiet.

Xander's jaw dropped. It took all of his willpower to close it and square his shoulders.

"And then what?"

"We don't know."

At Commander Howards's words, the world stood still. The messengers racing back and forth between the command center and wherever their messages brought them froze mid-sprint. Words, fragments of Xander's inner thoughts, sputtered out. His own breath stilled in his lungs.

So that was it then? There wasn't any plan at all? The only plan they had was the vague idea that they needed to stop Dinora? That *Nyla* was going to stop Dinora because she'd inherited Astrid's magic, because she'd asked to defeat Dinora herself?

As the fact became a tangible thought in Xander's mind, he found himself marveling at the lack of how, or when, and who was involved in the notion. They had to stop Dinora, and that was all anyone knew.

"I think I'll go and see if Nan needs any help in the infirmary," he muttered, knowing he should probably find Gerri and see if she could give him something for the nausea burning in his gut. He'd probably end up getting sick long before he ever reached the ballroom.

Swallowing hard, Xander didn't wait a second longer to take his leave. He practically knocked over a messenger in his haste to flee from the stifling room. He didn't know where he was going, not in any realistic sense, but he wondered if the ballroom was a good idea or if he should keep away from the war effort all together.

Xander's lips twisted into a grim line. He couldn't hide away. He *wouldn't* hide away, not when so many were willing to fight against such a formidable threat as the evil sorceress of legends written long ago.

5. THROES AND WOES OF LEADERSHIP

Gather the pumpkies, Nyla said as Shamira's fur prickled at the energy she'd expelled—and from the sheer horror of the creatures' joint call. *We'll move faster if it's just us. I'm running with you.*

What are you saying? Shamira called back. *You want us to escort you to Dinora? Without the humans?*

We'll move faster, Nyla repeated.

Considering her words, Shamira finished off the creature she fought. Ensuring it was slain, she turned on her heel and started for Nyla. Roaring aloud, she telepathically called the attention of the pumpkies she'd gathered to their ranks.

To the heir, to Nyla! she ordered. *We're going to escort her to Dinora, as quickly as we can.*

What about the humans? Elder Hecates's voice skirted over her mind.

Shamira's whiskers twitched. *Nyla thinks we can move faster without them.*

Do you believe that? Talmec asked, coming to run by her side.

Maybe, she said, *considering their progress across the battlefield or lack thereof so far. With the way they've come together, yes. Their formations aren't conducive to movement, not at this scale. Our goal is to stop Dinora, not die at the claws of her beasts. And the sooner we stop Dinora, the sooner the creatures will stop, or so I hope. Nyla is right. Stopping Dinora as quickly as we can is the only path to survival.*

Nyla broke through the cluster of people gathered around her. Ingrid's furious voice called after her, but Nyla didn't even give the woman a backward glance as she sprinted to meet them, knocking aside a creature meaning to tackle her from the side with her magic. The creature's head shattered, though Shamira didn't see the projectile that had managed that feat. There wasn't any sign of magic that she could see either as Nyla raced past her. Shamira followed her, keeping pace with her as the assembled pumpkies fell into a formation around them.

I think they're drawn to me, Nyla said, her voice wavering with panic. *We'll have to be careful.*

Shamira nodded her head, turning swiftly as Nyla veered off in the immediate direction of the pulsing aurora where they believed Dinora to be. The pumpkies moved with them as Shamira and Talmec silently flanked Nyla. A few pumpkies broke away from the pack, moving ahead of them as others dropped behind them to make sure any threats coming from the rear wouldn't reach Nyla.

I imagine Ingrid isn't very happy with you? Shamira risked a glance at Nyla.

The girl let out a ragged huff, barely even a breathy laugh. "I wouldn't know. I couldn't hear her as I was running away."

Shamira's lips pulled back in a smile she didn't think was possible at the moment. *So much for being the Mage General. Astrid would be proud of you.*

Nyla didn't respond, but the air around her changed. The girl's energy swelled with the savory scent of pride, Shamira knew how much her words had meant to her, even as the musty tang of mournfulness joined the undercurrent of Nyla's emotions.

They were going to defeat Dinora. For Tenebris, for the pumpkies lost 647 years ago, for Nyla's family, and for the future, Dinora would not see the smiling dawn.

***

Nyla's chest burned. Her ragged breaths seared the fragile tissue of her throat, but she didn't care. She didn't care about the blood pounding in her temples, or the emptiness clawing at her stomach. She didn't care that every now and again, Ingrid's voice flashed across her mind expressing her displeasure and worry, but Nyla knew that the woman was far behind them now.

All she cared about was the fact that the pumpkies had fanned out around her and were tearing into any stone beast who dared to threaten their path. Nyla didn't have time to marvel at their physical prowess or the way they wielded their magic in tandem with their physical attacks. All she had time for was ensuring she never slowed her pace. She had to keep her footing, no matter how heavy her limbs were becoming or how difficult it was to trudge through the coarse sand beneath her feet or how the shadows looming above them as the raverins passed overhead frightened her as much as the snaps of their tails.

All that truly mattered was getting to Dinora and stopping her. All that mattered was protecting the sunny future she'd briefly glimpsed upon breaking the bond between herself and the Woodlane Manor. She grasped at that freedom, at the promise of what her life could offer her, and used that memory to propel her forward.

Helping Shamira shatter a creature who had gotten closer to them, the pumpkie she'd introduced as her brother Talmec diverted another creature that lunged for them. In this fight, Nyla found that the courage she'd had during her duel with Frederick and the resolute certainty she'd had during the war councils was growing inside of her once more.

Her determination had cowered somewhat upon seeing the battlefield for the first time, but it hadn't wholly left her. She didn't find their mission to be any less daunting, but her courage was slowly turning into a roar.

With each stone creature they slayed, and the mistier the battlefield became, Nyla grasped onto that unwavering confidence and resolved to stoke it as goosebumps erupted along her skin. The mist had an energy that buzzed, that gave the battlefield an air of anticipation that threatened to drown her. But the sensation didn't drown her nearly as much as the sight of the faces that flooded her mind's eye from the far reaches of her memory, and rather than add to the quiet whispers of her inner fears, the faces bolstered her.

They were all there. Each and every person that meant something to her.

Her mother, with her kind eyes and gentle hands. Her father, with his easy smile and captivating stories. Her oldest brother, who was nearly the spitting image of their father but had the curious and hungry mind of their mother. Westley, her twin brother who shared her round face but had Pa's curly hair. Lydia, the youngest of them all with an infectious giggle and a sparkle in her eyes that made everyone she'd ever met forfeit their world to her.

Then there was Xander, the boy who'd scared her half to death when his hand had appeared, clawing at the entrance to the cave she'd taken shelter in all those weeks ago. The man who'd traveled through the heart of the Shadow Forest with her as they sought the fabled waters of Fortune Falls. The friend who'd encouraged her to find the answers to the questions she'd had about her newfound magic and had gone with her despite owing her absolutely nothing. Xander, the person she wanted to share her future with, who her mind had taken to include in every hope and dream for her future even though her rational thoughts couldn't quite comprehend why.

Merry, George, Nan, her neighbors—anyone who'd touched her life in any way flooded her mind, and the memory of them made her knees wobble.

In her heart, Nyla knew they were the reason why she'd chosen this path, and why she had to be here today, why she had to be the one to defeat Dinora. Nyla knew it had little to do with inheriting Astrid's magic and everything to do with them, the people she loved and cared for and wanted to protect. It was because of her family and the time that had been stolen from them that she wanted to be the one to kill Dinora.

Their memory gave her strength and weakened her resolve all at once.

Nyla had promised them. She'd promised her family, she'd promised Astrid, she'd promised Xander that she would live and make a life for herself, that she'd survive.

That blooming resilience was the key to surviving this, to getting back to all the things—all the *people*—she was fighting for. But with every creature they defeated, Nyla found herself wondering just how many creatures were left, or if Dinora had been generating more of them this entire time.

Could she do that?

Nyla's lips pressed into a thin line. Grim uncertainty trickled into her blood as she knew no answer could present itself to her now. The time for answers had passed. The only way to help those fighting alongside her on this battlefield was to kill the source of it all.

She had to kill Dinora.

***

Xander's gut twisted at the sight of how many injured Casters and soldiers were already spread throughout the space. The battle had only just begun, but already the ballroom was packed. Stunned, all Xander could do was stand in the doorway and observe it all like a specter. Pemberly's servants hustled to and fro, stopping at different cots and depositing bandages or pails of clean water. Healers and doctors worked silently over patients, sharing a quiet word when necessary with any of those assisting them. An oppressive metallic tang burned his nostrils. A low symphony of moans, grunts, and groans filled the room.

Xander swallowed thickly, nearly choking on the acid rising in his throat. He fought to keep his breath steady as he stared out across the ballroom.

Gathering his resolve, Xander forced himself to weave through the room with a confidence he didn't feel. He didn't know if his appearance mattered to those lying on the cots under the influence of their injuries or to the doctors and Healers attending to their patients in varying states of injury. But maybe it did, he realized, as people paused and glanced at him briefly as he passed by.

He started offering small smiles and a couple nods to anyone he happened to look in the eye. Sometimes they nodded back. Sometimes they only stared at him long after he'd gone, the weight of their gazes burning into his shoulder blades.

Xander couldn't stop the questions from consuming his mind. How many of these men and women would make it home? How many would return home, but not quite like themselves? How many had already died on that battlefield?

He shook the thoughts from his mind, feeling them sink their icy claws into his already wavering resolve. There would be time to mourn later. Right now, he needed to find Nan.

"Xander!" a weathered voice chirped. He didn't have time to respond as the woman wrapped him in a fierce hug.

"Nan!" he breathed, hugging her back just as eagerly. Pulling away from each other much too soon, he asked, "How are you doing?"

"As well as anyone can right now." Nan eyed him keenly for a moment and then shook her head as she gave him a quirky smile. "It helps that I'm doing the only thing I can do: helping people. How are *you* doing, Xander?"

Xander's gaze slipped from hers. He rubbed the back of his neck. "Not great. I just keep thinking…" He stopped as the words caught in his throat. He couldn't dare speak his deepest fears.

Nan nodded as though she understood. "You are welcome to take refuge here. We could always use an extra set of hands here, or supply runners."

"What do you need most?" he found himself asking.

"'What do we need most?'" Nan's eyes sparkled, her lips turned up in a wry smile. "A miracle. But I think a morale boost would do us all a little good. Talk with them, Xander. Calm them down so the doctors and Healers can do what we can for them. You're good with people."

Xander blinked. "You really think whatever I could say to them would really be of any help?"

"Anything would be of help. A friendly face and a distracting conversation means the world in a situation like this. We can't do everything—treat people, calm them, hold their hand—but we can heal them or care for the worst of their injuries. We can't soothe their souls, though."

Xander nodded. "I'll try."

Nan nodded. "Good." She grasped his hand and squeezed it reassuringly. "Come and find me if you need anything. Merry's running supplies for us too, so you may see her about." As she turned to walk away, Xander found himself reluctant to let her go. As if sensing this, Gerri paused and added, "I have no doubt that we will win this battle, Xander. Nyla will survive this as she has survived everything else Fate, the gods, this sorceress—whatever you want to attribute her suffering to—has dealt her. Nyla will come back to you."

"I hope so," Xander said with a wobbly smile. Though he and Nyla had never spoken about it—about what might be between them—the words they had shared on the balcony and just before Ingrid had wisped her away to the battlefield came to him. Xander prayed that whatever sentiment Nyla had toward him wouldn't find itself a casualty of the battle. He prayed that whatever sentiment Nyla had toward *herself*, her life, her future, wouldn't become a casualty of this battle.

A fresh wave of fear flooded his bloodstream. Nan smiled at him reassuringly, but offered no word of comfort before she walked away, surely needed elsewhere. Xander stood, watching after her for a moment, growing numb to the world around him as this newest prospect of doom engulfed him.

Maybe the patients all around him weren't the only ones in need of a distraction, of something to focus on other than their pain. Maybe Nan had been right. Swallowing thickly, Xander hesitantly approached the nearest cot and offered the battle-weary soldier there a small smile. At the sight of the soldier's sweat-drenched face and the dried blood staining his temple, Xander's tongue went numb. So much for being a distraction, for either of them. Xander prayed that wherever Nyla was, and whatever she was doing, she'd prove more successful than he was.

6. COWARDICE AND COURAGE

Slowly, Xander moved from cot to cot, chair to chair, table turned recovery bed, to yet another recovering patient. At first, he hadn't known what to say or do. Sometimes he'd introduced himself, only to be met with the bewildered eyes of the Caster or soldier. They didn't care who he was, not while they were in the sort of pain he would probably never be able to describe.

But the more people he sat with, the easier it became. He asked them about their homes, their families, and he told them about the places he'd been or pulled a funny story from the far reaches of his memory. As he chatted with them, doctors or Healers performed their duties, administering medicine or using their magic to heal their patients' injuries.

Xander didn't bother the surgeons and tried to avoid the foyer all together. He doubted he'd ever look at the entryway the same way again. Though he'd only caught glimpses of it as he made his rounds through the ballroom, he'd heard the pained cries or screams of those recently returned from the battlefield by way of wisping before someone managed to sedate them or they were healed.

Bidding the woman he was speaking with well wishes for her recovery, Xander gravitated toward the broken doors to the ballroom's patio. The ballroom had become stiflingly hot. Not to mention the overwhelming stench of blood and sweat that burned his nostrils. Xander didn't know if he could survive one more second in the large room before he was at risk of fainting.

Stepping out onto the cracked flagstones of the patio, Xander took a gulp of fresh air. The late Hugony air held spicier notes than he remembered it had. He welcomed it, knowing the alternative was the stuffy atmosphere of the ballroom.

Risking a glance at the spacious room behind him, Xander felt his eyes go wide.

He'd known there were a lot of injured Casters and soldiers—his raw throat more than proved it—but he hadn't realized just how *many* there were.

His heart clenched at the sight of people hurriedly maneuvering around cots and blankets laid on the floor—the best they could offer now that they'd run out of cots and tablespace for people to rest—of doctors and surgeons and Healers standing around those same cots or blankets, working diligently to save as many people as they could.

Xander's hands clenched into fists.

He'd seen the ballroom crowded before, but this? How had he navigated through all of this and not realized how packed the room was with the injured or the dying?

How many more would come to fill this room?

Xander shook himself from his stupor. Something needed to be done, before they were overwhelmed—that was, if they weren't already.

Not bothering to work his way through the ballroom once more, Xander drew the attention of a supply runner, telling them he was taking some leave if anyone asked for him, before he headed for another of Pemberly's many entrances.

Hurrying through the halls, Xander wove a path to his grandfather's study. Hovering in the doorway for just a moment, Xander's eyes swept over the room. His gaze landed on his friend, and as if Edwin could sense the attention on him, he turned, breaking his intense study of the viewing glass before him.

Catching Edwin's eye, Xander nodded his head toward the door. Edwin broke away from the small group clustered around the crystal ball, and Xander knew his friend would follow behind him. Leaving behind the crowded study full of devastating viewing glasses, Xander stopped a little way down the empty hall.

"There has to be something we can do to end this sooner rather than later," he said desperately.

"Like what?" Edwin asked.

"I don't know," Xander admitted, "but I have an idea."

***

"You realize this is an awful idea, right?" Edwin asked once more.

"He has to know something. *Anything* that could help Nyla," Xander insisted, following Edwin through the courtyard's maze of hedges. Eyeing the shrubbery on either side of him, Xander considered whether Edwin was leading him astray, stalling until he'd found a way to convince him of how horrible this idea truly was.

"Do you know how many people have tried to get answers from him?" Edwin went on, whirling around. Xander nearly collided with him thanks to the abrupt halt. "Nyla herself—"

Xander's hands clenched into fists. "What do you mean, 'Nyla herself?' Nyla saw him?"

"That's the rumor, anyway," Edwin sighed, pinching the bridge of his nose as he made to turn. "Are you sure you want—"

"Where did you hear that rumor?" Xander grasped Edwin's shoulder, preventing him from continuing on down the lane.

"Harper, another Caster," Edwin said, turning to him with furrowed brows and a deep frown. "I also overheard it from a few of the king's men."

"So you think it's true? Nyla saw Cedric on her own?"

Edwin shook his head. "They all say the Mage General was with her, so no, I don't believe Nyla went alone."

"But otherwise," Xander amended, glaring at his friend, "you believe them?"

"Do I have to answer that?" Edwin asked, cringing away from Xander.

"I suppose not." Xander clicked his tongue. Why hadn't Nyla told him about this? When had she gone?

Guilt immediately flooded him, making his lip quiver ever so slightly.

It was Nyla's choice, or so he hoped. He didn't doubt that the physical similarities between her and Astrid would've been tempting to someone desperate enough to wring a few answers out of Cedric, but…he knew Nyla. Nyla could've easily wanted to see Cedric for her own reasons, whatever they were. If it was Nyla's choice, then he had to believe she would've told him as soon as she was able to. Perhaps she would've, but she hadn't had the time to, thanks to Dinora and the earthquake.

Xander pressed his tongue to the roof of his mouth.

Everything had happened so quickly. They'd hardly had a moment's rest upon their arrival at Pemberly before the talk of war had turned into fighting a full-scale battle. Xander still couldn't wrap his head around all of that, let alone the fact that all their planning had been for naught with Dinora's unexpected attack.

And between all of that, he felt like he hadn't seen much of Nyla. The only time they'd been alone recently was on that balcony, and that moment seemed like a lifetime ago.

Xander forced himself to fight the rocks threatening to crush his windpipe.

Maybe he should've told her then. Maybe he should've taken that moment to let her know how much she meant to him because as things stood now, he wasn't so certain he'd get another chance to.

He couldn't help but think that in the few minutes he and Edwin had been away from Pemberly Hall proper, so much could've happened. For all he knew, Nyla was dead.

Nyla could already be dead, and the army that'd meant to save her could be fighting for their lives right at this very moment, and he wouldn't be the wiser.

Pursing his lips, Xander followed after Edwin. He wouldn't give those thoughts any mind. They were only wicked imaginings conjured by his fears.

And after all, weren't fears the opposite of truth—or, at the very least, the opposite of reality?

Xander wiped his hands against his pants. Fear couldn't have a place in his mind or in his heart right now. He chose to believe that Nyla was fine. In fact, he knew it. Xander had seen her wield her magic before. He'd seen her fight before. She'd obliterated an ogre before she even knew she had magic. She'd destroyed stone creatures before any of them truly knew what they were up against.

Nyla was fine. For if she wasn't, surely the universe would offer some sign. Surely, the world would go dark if Dinora had triumphed over Nyla.

Xander let out a slow breath. He kept repeating the phrase that Nyla was fine over and over again in his head as Edwin led him farther into the hedge maze of Pemberly Hall's estate. The silence of the courtyard's far reaches seemed to pulse in time with Xander's heartbeat. He didn't have any idea where Edwin was leading him and could only hope that Pemberly's dungeons weren't too far off now. Even if he'd convinced himself that Nyla was still okay, he couldn't help but feel the hands of time closing tightly around his throat.

Finally, Edwin came to a stop before a hedge. Xander raised his brow. Why was Edwin stopping here? Was this where he intended to stall or make him reconsider this desperate decision?

As Xander's mouth dropped open to ask, Edwin lifted a hand. His silver-colored magic emanated from the gesture as Xander looked on in confused silence. The stone pavers of the garden path shifted. Panic surged in Xander's chest. Was this another earthquake?

His eyes landed on the hedge, or rather the gap opening in the earth where the hedge had once stood. Stone grated against stone as the pavers shifted and the hedge slid back, revealing a secret entrance to Pemberly Hall's dungeon—an area Xander hadn't known existed until yesterday.

"H-how…how did you do that?" Xander sputtered in disbelief.

Edwin grinned mischievously, glancing over at him as he began to descend the roughly hewn steps down into the earthen dungeon below. "Magic."

"Right, of course," Xander muttered. "Magic is the vague answer that explains everything."

Edwin snorted, a steady flame dancing in his palm, giving light to the dimness below. Swallowing hard, Xander followed after the man he was grateful to call a friend. As soon as he'd gotten a few steps down into the dungeon, the dimness tackled him like a fiend. The cool air tickled his nose, forcing a shiver down his spine that wasn't fear-induced for the first time in what felt like an eternity.

Just as they'd gotten a quarter of the way down the earthen stairs, the grating of stones filled the air. Xander didn't dare look back, not wanting to see the only exit he knew of sealing itself closed against him.

He really hadn't thought this idea through. How was he supposed to get out without Edwin?

In actuality, the likelihood that he'd be leaving without Edwin was slim at best, but the concern plagued him far longer than it should have.

Stepping down onto the main floor of the dungeon, Xander and Edwin were met with two sets of eyes staring at them. Xander made sure his posture was perfect. He wanted to be the young lord the pair probably believed him to be. Hopefully, the belief in the power his status wielded was enough to gain them entrance to Cedric's cell.

"Hello, Abraham, Luce." Edwin bobbed his head by way of greeting.

A Caster with short ginger hair nodded back in reply while a portly Royal Guard stepped forward.

"I'm sorry, Sir Maffis, Lord Huntington, but we've been prohibited from allow—" Abraham began.

"I understand your position and orders given the circumstances," Xander interrupted, "but this is important. I believe Cedric has answers that can save Nyla."

Abraham and Luce shared a look.

A crystal ball sat on the wooden table where the guards had previously sat, displaying fragmented views of the battlefield, switching its perspective every few seconds to give Luce and Abraham a changing view of the battle unlike the fixed scenes of the viewing glasses inside. Xander's hands itched as he tried to keep them still. He fought the urge to snap his head in its direction, desperate to see what was happening on that lonesome battlefield.

A slight tremble started in the tips of his fingers. So many things raced through his mind, from the steward who'd brought Pemberly the news of his parents' deaths, to seeing Issie's gruesome murder at the jaws of a hellhound, to the speckle of red against Nyla's lips as she'd lain on the stone steps of the Woodlane Manor.

And though that last memory was different from the others for the sole reason that Nyla had survived that day, that memory—that *nightmare*—ignited something in Xander he'd never felt before. It buzzed in his chest. It caused the tremors in his fingers. It caused the urgency in his blood that he couldn't fight against. He knew whatever that crystal ball could show him, it wouldn't dissuade the nightmare replaying before the forefront of his mind, just as it had haunted him more and more since he'd met Nyla. Inhaling slowly as he fought to banish the memory of his recurring nightmare from his mind, Xander found his voice again.

"I—we—need to see Cedric immediately," he said authoritatively. "It could mean life or death for Nyla."

Abraham and Luce stared at him for a moment. As Luce turned to glance at Abraham, Xander was nearly vibrating with the effort of restraining himself from wrestling the keys away from whichever of them had them, and seeing Cedric himself. He'd fight a thousand people if it meant the slightest chance of finding a way to help Nyla.

"All right." Abraham nodded, more to Luce than anyone else.

"We'll let you see Cedric," Luce said, "but only if you'll allow me in the room with you both."

Xander wanted to protest, but he didn't know why. It was a sound condition, so why was his immediate reaction to argue?

"Of course," Edwin said into his silence. "Please, lead the way."

Luce started for the dim hallway behind them, leading them away from the lone table and the pair of chairs in the entryway. Abraham followed behind them, the keys jingling in his hand. They hadn't traveled far when Luce stopped before a large metal door etched with different sigils across its front and down its crossbars. The door was fastened with multiple locks and bolts. Xander supposed the sigils were a type of magical warding to prevent Cedric—or whoever the unlucky prisoner was—from escaping. He supposed they prevented Cedric from using magic too, though it was more of an assumption than a fact.

He should've asked Edwin about that before they'd come all the way down here. It wasn't likely that they'd allowed Cedric the ability to wield magic, but Xander knew better than to count that as a guarantee.

The red-eyed man had proven himself to be just as ruthless as his mother when he'd tried to kill Nyla during her unwanted astral travels. Xander needed to be prepared for any eventuality, or at the very least, he should've prepared some sort of plan.

"Ready?" Luce asked, turning to them. Abraham slid the key into the final lock.

Xander nodded, his lips pressed together grimly.

Edwin responded as Abraham turned the key in the lock with a resounding clank, "I've met worse people in my life."

Xander nearly choked. Glancing over at his friend, Edwin shot him a self-assured look before he returned to the picture of bored composure.

"You have visitors," Luce nearly sang, stepping into the cell first as Abraham heaved the thick metal door open. Abraham motioned them both inside, with Edwin following after Luce in Xander's momentary hesitation. Xander forced his feet to move, if not for himself, then for Abraham, so he wouldn't have to keep the door open much longer or potentially allow Cedric an opportunity to escape.

As he stepped into the cell, Abraham closed the door behind them. Blinking and hoping his eyes would adjust to the dim light of the cell quickly, Xander's heart thudded in his ears with the clank of the locks sliding back into place behind him.

"What do you want now?" Cedric asked, not bothering to look at them from where he sat huddled against the far corner with his head turned toward the wall.

"You seem better off than I'd heard," Xander said. "They said you were waiting to die."

Cedric slowly picked his head up. His scarlet-colored eyes sparked with recognition. "You're that boy."

Xander's stomach clenched. Of course Cedric knew who he was to Nyla. Nyla had mentioned to him once or twice that she'd felt like she was being stalked, and how the visions given to her by Fortune Falls' waters had confirmed her intuition. She'd told him that Cedric had been watching her through a crystal ball, but she didn't know for how long. For all they knew, he'd been watching Nyla throughout her whole life.

"Forgive me," Cedric started. "I've forgotten my manners. Most people don't like it when they've had no introduction. It must bother you that I know yo—"

"It's only fair," Xander said, taking a step farther into the cell but not daring to get too close to where Cedric sat. "I know a lot about you too. I know that you tried to kill Nyla, that you helped your mother transfer the curse to Nyla, that—"

"It wasn't a curse," Cedric muttered, turning his head away and scratching at the wall with a finger as though he had better things to do with his time. "It was a bond."

"If you knew it was a bond, how come you didn't free your mother? What kind of son lets their mother suffer that sort of thing?"

Cedric shrugged. "Didn't suit my interests."

Xander glanced at Edwin. His friend made a face and shook his head, as if to say this sort of interaction was normal for Cedric.

"Then I wonder what does." Xander licked his lips. "What if I told you your mother was dead?"

"Then I wouldn't be speaking to you, would I?"

Xander cursed silently. He kept the flicker of defeat in his blood from showing on his face, aiming for an expression of boredom, of someone wholly unbothered. "Who else would care to bring the news to you?"

"That woman, the stern one who only ever wants answers." The red-eyed man didn't even spare him a glance, still picking at the stone wall as if he could chip it away bit by bit if time allowed him to do so.

Cedric must've meant Ingrid. That was the only woman who fit his given description that Xander could think of who would've been granted permission to question him.

Edwin stepped up beside Xander, staring down at Cedric coolly. "I see you're doing better. Did you decide you have something more to live for? More misery to spread?"

Cedric stopped scratching at the wall, sparing a glance at Edwin. "No."

"Then what? Wasting our time yet again?" Edwin rolled his eyes. Folding his arms over his chest, he looked over at Xander. "I told you he wouldn't be helpful."

"You're right," Xander said, matching Edwin's stance while never once taking his eyes off of Cedric. "I suppose it's a good thing we're not reliant upon his help."

Edwin agreed, "Nyla's just about killed Dinora anyway."

Cedric watched them with a keen interest now. "What about the girl?"

"Who?" Xander asked "Do you mean Nyla?"

"Astrid's heir, yes." Cedric nodded.

Xander's lips curled into a mirthless smile. "She's just fine."

The tension eased from Cedric's shoulders. Any interest that had shone in his eyes dimmed. He returned to poking and scratching at the wall as if ignoring them would get them to go away, but Xander wasn't leaving. He couldn't, not just yet. They had to get something useful out of Cedric.

"Though I suppose that's not welcomed news to you," Edwin guessed. "After all, when Nyla kills your mother, there's nothing left to distract us from your crimes."

Cedric didn't acknowledge him.

Sharing a look with Edwin, Xander's heart sank as his friend shrugged his shoulders.

The metal door groaned open. Xander turned his head to glance at Luce, but she seemed just as confused as he and Edwin were. Abraham's pale face could just barely be seen from where he stood mostly hidden by the shadow of the metal door.

"Time's up," he uttered.

Xander raised his brow. Neither guard had said a word about a time constraint.

Something must've happened, Edwin said, his voice floating across Xander's mind. At his slight cringe, Edwin added, *Sorry.*

Xander almost didn't hear him over the panic thrumming in the heartbeat pounding between his ears.

"Well, that's certainly never happened before," Cedric drawled. "Either you aren't someone of importance or—"

Before Xander could stop himself, he was across the cell despite the protest of everyone behind him. Grasping the rough fabric of Cedric's collar, Xander hauled him to his feet and shoved him against the wall.

"Tell me how to stop her, or I'll kill you right now," he seethed.

"Lord—" Luce's reprimand was cut off, but Xander didn't dare look over his shoulder to see what'd happened to her or why Abraham had gone silent too. He could only pray that Edwin had somehow gifted him the time to threaten Cedric and get some meaningful answers. He fixed Cedric with a deadly scowl.

"I take it Nyla isn't doing well then," Cedric coughed, blinking hard. Grasping Xander's wrist, Cedric's eyes seemed to focus after a second, and he stared straight back at him. Calmly, he whispered, "Let me go. I can kill Dinora."

"Do you honestly think I'd believe a statement like that from you?" Xander jerked him against the wall as if he could throw Cedric through the stone. "Tell me. Now."

Cedric shook his head. "Nyla won't kill her."

Cedric couldn't know that. No one could know that—and yet… Xander knew he wasn't wrong. Even after all the evil Dinora had done, especially the acts in which she specifically targeted Nyla, Xander had always known Nyla wasn't that sort of person.

Nyla couldn't kill anyone.

No matter how badly she wanted revenge against Dinora, Xander believed Nyla wouldn't actually kill her in the end. Not because Dinora deserved that mercy, but because Nyla herself did.

As if sensing his agreement, Cedric added, "I'll take a blood oath, anything you ask, and all I ask in return is the chance to finally do the right thing. Let me end this, for all of us."

"Xander," Edwin said, his hand landing on Xander's shoulder. "Don't listen to him. There's a horde of people waiting for permission to do just that."

"Then why haven't they?" Cedric asked. "They're afraid, aren't they? Everyone's heard the stories of the evil sorceress, so of course they'd all be afraid to."

Xander glared at him. "If you wanted Dinora dead all this time, why didn't *you* kill her? Why set her free from the Woodlane Manor in the first place with that potion?"

Cedric shook his head vigorously. "That's not what the potion was for, and I didn't set her free. She did that all of her own accord. I guess she finally had the motivation to do it herself." Tilting his head, something flicked across Cedric's eyes like recognition. "Or the means."

"What was that potion for then?" Edwin asked. "What means?"

Cedric's eyes flicked to him. "It was…a transfer potion," Cedric admitted, rushing to add, "but not of the sort you think! It was…I wanted to…" He closed his eyes and tilted his head back as much as his current position would allow. "*Mortis tradsmagique.*"

"A bequeathment potion?" Edwin asked in disbelief. "You made a potion to bequeath your magic, and you want us to believe that it wasn't for Dinora's benefit?"

Nyla's account of the fight flitted through Xander's memory. She'd told him that Cedric had shown Dinora a potion, but from what Xander remembered, Dinora never received it before Nyla had collapsed the ceiling in on them.

The only time either of them had used the potion was when Cedric had grabbed her in the hallway as she'd run past.

"Why did you attack Nyla on the astral plane?" Xander tried to put the pieces together, of why Cedric would've created a bequeathment potion and why he'd made sure to get it on Nyla and not Dinora.

Or had he been too disoriented during the fight upstairs to notice?

No, that didn't make sense at all. Nyla had made it seem as though Cedric hadn't ever been physically close enough to Dinora, that Dinora had left him behind in the foyer as she'd followed Nyla upstairs when she'd gone to find Shamira. Nyla had said that Cedric had grabbed her as she'd run by, and then she'd shoved him using her magic.

"I needed her blood, for the potion."

"Why?" Xander pressed, his fingers gripping Cedric's collar tighter.

"Because bequeathment potions need a piece of both magic users for it to work," Edwin murmured. Shaking his head, Edwin asked, "Then why attack her as viciously as you did?"

Cedric snorted. "Dinora has her ways. I thought she would've had a means to monitor the astral plane. And if you're referring to that day at the manor, I never attacked Nyla. In fact, she nearly killed me. I'm only alive today because of my spell."

Xander realized that that's how they must've stayed alive for so long. The implication that they'd cursed themselves with something like immortality explained how Cedric and Dinora could still be standing here today to wreak such havoc. It would've been the only way they could've outlived their natural lifespan and extended their lives for six long centuries. Cedric and Dinora had used a spell to stay alive; that must be what Cedric was talking about now. Xander tucked that information away in the back of his mind for another time, knowing that the matter of how they'd kept themselves alive all these years was of little consequence right now.

Xander eased away, but didn't let Cedric pull away from the wall. Scowling, he said, "Well, congratulations. You're either the best liar I've ever met, or you're just that desperate to pretend you're a hero."

Cedric blinked. A flash of irritation reflected in his eyes. "Try and find someone who's willing to do what's necessary. I doubt you'll find anyone willing who can actually succeed."

"I can think of plenty of people who could."

"So could I," Edwin added.

"Maybe, but can they get close enough to Dinora without dying first?"

Xander considered him for a moment. Edwin shifted beside him.

That may be the only valid argument he's made, Edwin admitted.

Xander clenched his jaw. "I'm sure we'll manage."

Jerking his hands away, Xander took a full step back. Edwin hesitated a second, allowing Xander to back away toward the door, and the apparently indisposed guards Edwin had left in a heap by the doorway.

"Your wards are weak," Cedric called just as Xander had stepped over Luce's outstretched leg.

Behind him, Edwin's echoing footfalls stopped. Xander turned around. Edwin stood in the middle of the cell, his face nearly murderous. He remembered that Edwin had been ordered to improve the warding when Ingrid and her Circle had first brought Cedric here for holding. His friend had always prided himself on his magical talent, especially when it came to his attention to detail.

"They're good, by today's standard of magical practices," Cedric continued from the corner of the cell. He hadn't moved an inch since Xander had let him go. "But they could be better."

"What are you saying?" Edwin nearly hissed, turning around slowly. "That you could escape? That the spell binding your powers is ineffective?"

"Yes."

Magic crackled at Edwin's fingertips.

"Let me end this," Cedric begged. "Please."

"Why the change of heart?" Xander asked, leaning against the doorframe and crossing his arms.

Edwin was right. This was a horrible idea, and not for any of the reasons Xander had feared.

Cedric's lips twitched into a small smile Xander hadn't thought the man to be capable of. He'd even dare to say that the smile held a hint of fondness, if not outright adoration. "Astrid," he explained slowly, "She told me once, 'it's much crueler to betray someone who loved you,' so maybe it's time I finally acted faithfully, even if it's toward a love I no longer have or deserve. None of this should be happening now, and if I'd only had the courage to act sooner, none of it would've happened in the first place. At any point, I could've stopped it, all of it, the beginning, the centuries that have passed since, and the very thing that drove Nyla down this path. But I didn't because I was selfish and desperate and weak. This should not be Nyla's burden to bear. It is mine, just as it always has been."

Xander considered him for a moment. Casting a lingering gaze toward Luce and Abraham's slumped forms, he began to turn away from Cedric.

"Come on, Edwin," he called without looking back. "There are plenty of people capable of killing Dinora."

"Myself included," Edwin muttered, presumably following after him.

"But will they be safe?"

At Cedric's question, Xander stopped just outside the doorway of his cell.

"What?" he asked, glancing back. Edwin's eyes urged him forward, his lips twitching impatiently. "What do you mean 'will they be safe?' Of course they won't be. None of us will be unt—"

"If Nyla and Dinora are dueling each other, will the bystanders be safe from the backlash of Nyla's magic once Dinora's is no longer pushing back at hers?"

Xander's eyes slid to Edwin's.

Possibly not… Edwin admitted. *But would that matter to you if Dinora was defeated?*

Xander didn't respond, knowing both his own answer and, in his heart, knowing what Nyla's would be too, though he couldn't very well say it aloud in front of the red-eyed man.

It would certainly matter to Nyla.

And Cedric knew it too.

Spreading his arms in a passive gesture, Cedric made what Xander considered to be a last offering. "If Nyla inadvertently hurt someone while trying to stop Dinora, I don't think she'd be able to forgive herself, however accidental. Either that or she is nothing like the woman whose magic she possesses. It wouldn't matter to anyone if I died in the backlash, least of all to Nyla. I can help her defeat Dinora, and no one else would have to die in her quest for vengeance."

No matter how sound Cedric's argument was, it didn't change the fact that this was a horrible idea.

"I'm sure there's another way." Xander turned and hauled Luce up, throwing her arm over his shoulder.

As he stepped into the hallway, Cedric's voice followed him. "You don't sound so confident."

Xander doubted anyone was ever confident in war, but he didn't say that as he nudged Abraham's legs out of the way for Edwin to shut the thick door of Cedric's cell.

Placing Luce against the wall opposite, he watched as Edwin slid the bolts into place and clicked the padlocks closed. The sigils etched into the metal glowed silver for only a second before Edwin was turning to him with a dark look.

"Well?" Edwin asked. "What are we going to do?"

Xander let out a long-suffering sigh. Before he could say anything, Edwin said, "Please don't tell me you're considering letting Cedric go."

"No," Xander said, his voice firm. He definitely wasn't considering that, but rather what he'd said last. "He's right, though. If Nyla and Dinora's battle today is anything like what happened before…anyone who tried to kill Dinora in a surprise attack would more than likely die from the backlash of magic."

"Unless…" Edwin started, clasping his hands behind his back as he began to pace. "If Nyla knew someone was coming, we could time it."

Xander nodded, beginning to pace himself. "Yeah, but who?"

His eyes darted toward the end of the hall where the entryway was—that and the crystal ball that sat on a lonesome table, hopefully still displaying images of the battle happening so far away from here.

"Before we do anything, we have to know what's going on," he said, shifting toward the hall. His gaze flicked to the pair of unconscious guards. "We should…What *did* you do to them? They're okay, right?"

Edwin flashed him an irritated frown. "Of course they're fine. It's a sleeping spell. I could wake them now, or they could come out of it naturally in an hour or two."

Xander nodded. "I guess we'll just leave them here then." Starting down the hall with Edwin beside him, he said, "We'll see what's going on first, especially with Nyla, and *then* we'll figure out what to do."

"Agreed."

The glowing light of the enchanted sphere filled the entryway. At the sight of it sitting in the center of the table, Xander's heart began to pound in his chest. While they'd been in Cedric's cell, he was able to forget that an outside world existed. Cedric had goaded them. No matter what his motivation was—whether he genuinely wanted to kill his mother or if he was only trying to distract them and waste their precious time—Xander couldn't say.

Watching the flicker of different battle scenes flash inside the crystal ball, Xander was instantly reminded of the urgency that had prompted him to seek out Pemberly's lone prisoner in the first place.

All too briefly, the images changed, and Xander caught a glimpse of Nyla. The soldiers and Casters that had previously surrounded her were nowhere to be seen. An icy trickle of desperation flooded his bloodstream. The urge to do *something* overtook his mind as the memory of Dinora's escape consumed his mind. But this time, he feared the scale of the battle—that the creatures they faced—were skewed from Nyla's favor.

He whirled on Edwin. "Take me there. Take me there right now."

Edwin narrowed his eyes at him, unaffected by the frantic plea. "What? No, that's crazy! You can't—"

"Then who, Edwin? You? Ingrid?"

Edwin pursed his lips. "If we brought this plan forward—"

"We'd be wasting time!" Xander hissed.

"And what are you going to do when we get there, huh?" Edwin asked, thrusting his finger against Xander's chest. "You're unarmed! And, not entirely beside the point, I promised Nyla—"

"And Nyla promised me she wouldn't do anything reckless!" Xander turned on his heel, throwing his hands up. "I don't care about who made which promises—I just want to save Nyla!"

"And Nyla wanted to save you."

Xander glanced over his shoulder at Edwin. The words knocked aside his urge to fight. Nyla really would ask someone to watch over him in her final moments before heading off to battle, wouldn't she? After all, he'd have done the same if their roles were reversed. Almost ruefully, he said, "What a match we make, huh?"

Edwin snorted. "Truer words have never been spoken."

Xander ignored him, his mind already racing with potential plans to save Nyla and end the battle before she lost her control over it. Dragging his fingers through his hair, Xander shifted through his mind for any spark that might present an actionable plan.

"Okay, so we definitely need a Caster," Xander said, shifting on his feet. His fingers touched the ring sitting against his chest, eager to twist it and the chain between them as his mind worked through their situation before he ultimately let his hand fall awkwardly at his side. "Let's assume that's you. And we need someone to basically sneak up behind Dinora and kill her. We need a weapon—"

"Or two Casters…" Edwin muttered.

"Right…I guess," Xander amended. "I still think it should be me."

"With what weapon?"

"My bow?"

"And where's your bow?"

Xander scowled at him. "You know damn well it isn't on me."

"You're both overcomplicating this."

Xander's blood froze in his veins. Sharply turning toward the opening on the other side of the entryway, Xander's vision swam from the whiplash of his movement. Beside him, Edwin cursed.

"I tried to tell you the warding could be better." Cedric strolled into the torchlight of the guard's station. "But you can work on that later. Right now, I think it's best to focus on killing Dinora, don't you?"

Xander opened and closed his mouth. Every fiber of his being seemed to vibrate, flooded with an adrenaline that had no escape. He found himself grasping for a weapon he didn't have, stuttering out the only thought his mind could form. "How?"

Cedric raised his hands placatingly. Uncertainty swam in his eyes. "I just want to help," he said quietly, like a plea.

"Haven't you done enough?" Edwin hissed. Before Xander could even blink, a bolt of his friend's silvery magic slashed through the air, headed straight toward Cedric.

A shield of scarlet energy burst around the red-eyed man, though he never wavered. He hadn't even moved to conjure his shield. By all means, the only movement Xander had noticed from Cedric was the slight downturn of his lips. As if he shouldn't have been surprised by their opposition to his desire to help.

"If you think," Xander started, a dangerous edge to his voice, "that I'm letting you anywhere near Nyla, you're sorely mistaken."

It was lucky for Cedric that Xander didn't have a drop of magic in his blood, or a weapon of any sort on hand. If he had, Xander had no doubt that the man who'd tormented Nyla from afar and who was to be blamed for her short bond to the Woodlane Manor would be dead.

Cedric's frown deepened. Another of Edwin's magical attacks crackled against his scarlet-colored shield. His voice was soft, almost earnest-sounding if Xander could believe him capable of any shred of honesty. "I have no intention of hurting Nyla. All I want is for this to be over. I just want peace."

"If you wanted peace so badly, you should've done something sooner!" Xander clenched his fist as though he could actually punch Cedric. Perhaps he would've tried, if it wasn't for Corruptio's contemplation forcing his hand to stay beyond his will.

"I suppose you're right," Cedric said, bobbing his head in what might've been a silent decision. "I should've done something much sooner." Cedric paused, glancing at each of them in turn. Xander's heart quickened as the shield of scarlet magic wavered and then faded altogether. "I should've done something before my decisions led us here, but I see my path now, and this time I will not hesitate to follow what I know to be right."

The man's words turned over in Xander's mind. Before he could reply, to keep Cedric talking as he stalled for some miracle that wouldn't come, Edwin shoved Xander behind him, unleashing a wave of his silver-colored magic just as Cedric's power began to emanate from his hands.

"I am only sorry that we cannot walk it together," Cedric said.

His magic overtook Edwin's, sweeping under and above it as though it didn't exist. The scarlet glow blinded Xander, forcing him to look away.

His head spun.

"I am truly sorry about this." Cedric's voice rattled in his skull. "But I will not sit idly by as I have done for all my life. For the first time in my life, I've found the courage to fight for what's in my heart and all that I should've held dear but let slip through my fingers instead, chasing after a boon I would never earn. Far too late, I'll admit, but it's something, and I will not let her pay for the mistakes I have made time and time again."

Xander's eyes fluttered. He swayed on his feet, bumping into Edwin in front of him as his friend began to tremble with the effort of fighting back against the scarlet tidal wave. The wave of magic grew stronger. And with it, so did the fatigue invading Xander. He blinked hard, trying to clear his mind. He saw Nyla in his mind's eye and grasped at the realization that quickly followed.

He couldn't let Cedric escape. He couldn't let him get to her.

Edwin collapsed. His friend hardly let out a whimper before his magic failed and he fell forward, smacking against the stone floor.

Xander barely managed to lock eyes with Cedric through the haze of the bright scarlet energy filling the room. He forced himself to take a step forward. Wobbling, Xander's eyes drooped as he staggered backwards. His chest heaved, unable to catch his breath in the wake of Cedric's magic. He tried to block out the light, bringing his arms up as if he could sufficiently shield himself, that his fraying willpower alone was enough to combat the magic, but before Xander knew it, he was falling backwards.

His head cracked against something hard. Through the flickering of his gaze, Xander just barely saw Cedric's shadow move above him. A curtain of darkness eclipsed his vision, though he could feel Cedric doing something, hear him saying something. Xander didn't know what exactly, could hardly keep his eyes from falling shut, but he knew Cedric had grabbed his hand and had uttered something about a vow, that he would do everything in his power to end it. Beyond that, Xander understood nothing. And then he was gone. Xander tried to follow the red-eyed man with his eyes, but he couldn't even move his head. Blinking against the darkness, Xander just barely saw Cedric mount the staircase only feet away from where he lay on the cold stone floor.

There was nothing after that, not even a tremor of the panic that had flooded his veins only a heartbeat earlier.

7. THE MOST DESTRUCTIVE FORCE

Her mind spun faster than she could comprehend. Nyla hadn't known what to expect of the battle, or of her haphazard idea to immediately target Dinora, but a spiraling mind wasn't one of them. She'd expected a numbness to consume her, a sort of all-encompassing focus as had bewitched her during her fight with Dinora and Cedric back at the Woodlane Manor. But that hadn't happened.

Instead, her mind was a flurry of thoughts, of concerns, of reminders. Thoughts about how to defeat Dinora, concerns for those fighting alongside her, and reminders of what it was exactly she was fighting for—or rather, *who* she was fighting for.

Nyla, Ingrid's panicked voice flashed before her mind, *where are you? With the—*

This is serious, Nyla! Cedric's escaped, she hissed, *I'm coming for you right now.*

Nyla's blood turned to ice. Her feet slipped against the sand. Her arms pinwheeled frantically as she tried to keep herself upright. Cedric—he'd escaped?

Recovering from her near fall, Nyla managed to ask, *Do we know where he is?*

He's here, and I'm bringing you back for your own safety!

Nyla's gaze swept over the battlefield. Every second she didn't know exactly where Cedric was, she was in danger. The scar across her shoulder and collarbone pulsed as though it was freshly cut. The ballroom scene flashed before her memory, of how Cedric had managed to disappear and reappear throughout the room until he'd gotten close enough to her to strike.

"Shamira?" she rasped, breathing heavily. "Cedric's escaped."

What do you want to do? she asked, slowing to match Nyla's pace.

Nyla gulped down some air, slowing down even more so she could speak without straining her voice. "We need to find him. If he hasn't already joined Dinora, he could be anywhere."

And Ingrid is looking to take you back, Shamira added.

"Yeah, and that."

I don't disagree with her, Shamira admitted.

"I—" Nyla cut off, noticing a large shadow drift overhead. Tilting her head back, Nyla watched a raverin glide through the air. Following it with her eyes, she saw a burst of scarlet energy some ways ahead of them. Chunks of the onyx-colored stone the creatures were made of flew in every direction, as well as sand. Nyla's breath hitched. Though she couldn't see through the scores of pumpkies, creatures, and human soldiers in her path, it looked to her like Cedric was doing the unthinkable. "Is he…fighting with us?"

Her gaze landed on Shamira in time to see the pumpkie's whiskers twitch. *It appears so. He's just taken out a whole grouping of creatures bearing down on some Royal Guards according to Myra.*

Nyla didn't know which pumpkie was Myra, but clearly, the pumpkie had an unobstructed view. "And Myra's certain?"

Quite.

"Then…" Nyla trailed off. The words to convey that they might not have anything to worry about stuck in her throat. The battle wasn't over yet. But there was still *plenty* to worry about.

Ingrid? She reached out hesitantly. The only indication Ingrid had heard her over whatever other telepathic conversations she was having was the slight spark of worry emanating from the other woman. *The pumpkies think Cedric's fighting with us. I'm staying the course.*

Silence. Nyla's heart thudded in her ears. Still, she watched the raverins circling over where Cedric must've stood. They swooped and dove and tore creatures apart in midair with their sharp talons. Still, she could see the sparks of Cedric's scarlet-colored magic, and she wondered just how much she could trust her own eyes. Were they seeing things properly?

Be safe, Nyla, Ingrid said at last, her voice full of resignation. Nyla blew out a relieved breath. *That's all I ask.*

Nyla swallowed the emotion sitting in her throat like a sob. *You too.*

Focusing her attention back on the battle around her, a hulking shape caught Nyla's eye. Her head whipped in its direction, but it was too late.

"Talmec!" she gasped in an attempt to warn him. Her eyes widened, watching as a creature tackled him to the ground. Shamira swerved to her brother's side, yowling in a way Nyla had never heard before. Instinctually, Nyla threw a bolt of magic at the gruesome thing. As the creature was knocked aside, Nyla rallied her magic to tear it apart, but the sight of glowing fractures stopped her. The creature burst in a spark of scarlet-colored energy. Nyla whipped her head in the direction she'd last known Cedric to be in. Nyla had barely caught Cedric's eye across the distance between them before Shamira's cry tugged her attention back to Talmec. Had he truly destroyed the creature on her behalf, or had he missed *her*? Nyla couldn't explain his intention or just what he'd meant to hit with his magic, but she hadn't the time to contemplate it any further as she focused on Shamira and Talmec.

Everything came to a grinding halt in Nyla's mind. The pumpkies converged around them, battling any stone creatures in their immediate proximity with ruthless efficiency. Numbly, Nyla conjured a shield of shimmering lilac magic and wrapped it around Shamira, Talmec, and herself as she came to crouch down beside the pair.

Talmec whined low in his throat, staring up at them, at Shamira, with pain-glazed eyes. His forepaw twitched, reaching out to Shamira weakly. Blood seeped into the ashen sand from the gaping wound in his torso. A trickle of heat flooded Nyla's chest and down the back of her neck at the sight. Shamira let out a guttural chitter that cleaved Nyla's heart into pieces.

Weak sage-colored magic pulsated around Talmec's wound. Nyla watched as Shamira's magic spread over the injury, wavering and flickering as if she couldn't concentrate enough or couldn't summon the power necessary to heal him.

Laying a hand on Shamira's back, Nyla eyed the wound and urged it to heal beneath her gaze, hoping her intention was enough to aid in Shamira's effort.

A light touch of lilac energy blanketed the wound. A sick prickle buzzed against her magic, snapping at it as if it had teeth. Nyla pursed her lips, willing her magic to stay and heal Talmec even more desperately. The vile energy of the wound grew stronger, licking at her magic and hissing against it. Her magic recoiled against the wound. Nyla narrowed her eyes, praying that one last effort would prove more fruitful.

The wound would not heal.

T-the m-ma… Shamira's voice hiccupped in Nyla's mind as she turned her murky green eyes on hers. *W-we can't h-heal him.*

Nyla's fingers curled in her fur. "Can you wisp him to Pemberly?"

Shamira blinked. *Wisp?*

I can, a tawny pumpkie said, stepping forward. *I will bring them both.*

Nyla bowed her head. "Thank you." Glancing back at Shamira, she said, "Take care of Talmec. I'm sure they'll have a way to heal him at the estate, and don't you dare think of coming back here just for me. You should stay with your brother."

Shamira blinked up at her, her eyes vacant. *Thank you, Nyla. I'm sorry I can't be here for you.*

"Don't be. I'd never forgive myself if I took you from your family when they needed you," she said. "Now go. Save Talmec."

The pumpkie with tawny fur placed a paw on both Shamira and Talmec, and in a blink, they were gone, leaving only a static that kissed her skin.

Nyla exhaled a tense breath. The remaining pumpkies had their eyes cast to the ground, either out of respect or from the realization that they couldn't be healed if wounded by the creatures, Nyla wasn't sure.

But then a single pumpkie lifted their face to the sky and let out a low howl. Goosebumps erupted along her skin as each and every pumpkie near her joined in their call until the battlefield was filled with a chorus of howls.

Her hands curled into fists against her legs.

They couldn't stop Dinora if they couldn't combat her creatures. They needed to somehow find a way to destroy the creatures once and for all, something that wouldn't deplete their energy. Maybe they were going about this all wrong. Maybe she'd been wrong to think stopping Dinora would stop the creatures too, but she didn't see any other way.

Nyla got to her feet. Quickly, she glanced around, searching for Cedric, but all she could see were the distant flashes of his scarlet-colored magic amidst all the other bursts of magic, of the flashes of discharged cannons and rifles. Nyla pressed her lips together, surveying the field one last time before she turned her attention to the pumpkies around her.

A pumpkie with gray eyes and a stockiness Nyla hadn't expected of the pumpkies stepped forward. *I am Elder Myra of the Zeldher Clan. In the wake of Shamira and Elder Hecates's absence, I will be leading the pumpkies.*

Nyla pressed her lips into a grim line, nodding numbly.

What is your course, Nyla?

"My course hasn't changed," Nyla said. "We have to stop Dinora."

Myra's lip curled back, exposing sharp teeth, sharper than even Shamira's. *Then we will follow you.*

8. EDWIN'S BANE

Xander's eyes blinked open only to fall shut once more at the sharp slice of pain that stabbed his temples. Slowly, he cracked his eyes open so as to shield himself from the immediate assault of light. A blurry figure hovered over him.

"Alexander!" a harsh voice said.

Xander nearly groaned, vaguely recognizing the tone as a reprimand. His fear was only confirmed as his vision cleared, revealing the pinched expression on his grandfather's face as he knelt beside him. Xander turned his head, searching for Edwin. Propping himself up on an elbow, Xander's eyes landed on Edwin speaking quietly with an angry-looking Luce and Abraham.

"You'd better have a good explanation for all of this," his grandfather said gruffly.

Xander scrunched his nose, rubbing the back of his head with a wince. "I do."

"Are you hurt?"

"Nothing serious," Xander assured him, finally meeting his gaze. "I just wanted answers."

"Your actions have allowed Cedric—"

Xander shook his head. "He would've escaped anyway, if he wanted to."

His grandfather raised an eyebrow, silently pushing him to explain his meaning. Xander took a breath and tried to gather his thoughts despite the pounding headache behind his eyes. Slowly, he pulled himself into a sitting position. "He said that the wards were weak. It sounded like he was only indulging us with the idea that he was our prisoner."

"I see," his grandfather said almost coldly. Sighing heavily, he added, "Xander, I wish you hadn't done this, but you must understand that there has to be a consequence for your negligence. I have no choice but to place you under guard until Lady Ravencroft returns and we can deal with this infraction properly."

Xander nodded. "I know, and I accept that. I knew the risks when I…when I *ordered*—Edwin to bring me here. Don't worry about my feelings, Grandfather. I only care about Nyla's safety right now and ending this battle. Do we know where Cedric is?"

His grandfather's face darkened. "On the battlefield, last I saw."

Xander's gaze flicked to the crystal ball sitting on the lonesome table in the room. Glowing, it still showed the image of the battlefield. Xander didn't know if he had the strength to look. He didn't know if he could bear to watch the catastrophic result of his act of desperation. For all he knew, the very scene he'd been trying to avoid was playing out, but this time, he'd be forced to know which of the two Casters would survive the blast of scarlet- and lilac-colored magics colliding.

"There's been reports that Cedric is fighting against the stone creatures, but the general consensus is that he is not to be trusted. A team is making an effort to remove him from the battlefield as we speak."

Xander didn't respond. So Cedric had meant it then, that he wanted to kill Dinora. It was the only explanation his addled brain could provide him with for the reason why Cedric was fighting *with* them instead of *against* them. But he couldn't find the words to explain it all to his grandfather.

He winced as his fingers curled into his palm. Glancing down, Xander saw a slice against his palm, the blood crusted around the length of the cut and down the side of his hand and wrist. Furrowing his brows, Xander wondered what it meant, and if it had anything to do with what Cedric had said as he was losing consciousness. Before he could ponder over it any further, his grandfather spoke again.

"In that case," his grandfather said softly, "I'll leave you and Sir Maffis in Abraham's and Luce's capable hands." Turning to the guards in question, his grandfather added, "Don't let these two out of your sight. And furthermore, they're restricted from—"

"Talmec!"

Xander's blood turned to ice at the desperation in Nyla's voice echoing from the crystal ball. His breath quickened. Forcing himself to his feet, Xander stumbled toward the table to watch the scene unfolding within the curvature of the crystal sphere. His entire being buzzed with the urge to do something. But what was he to do? He wasn't there; he didn't possess the magic to stop what was happening or the ability to turn back time long enough to change their current circumstances.

There was absolutely nothing he could do but watch and send up a desperate plea to any god or goddess that would listen to him.

His lungs burned, unaware he'd been holding his breath. A familiar-looking, scarlet-colored magic shredded into the stone creature leaping toward the pumpkie Nyla had called out to by name. With each chunk that fell from the main body of the warped humanoid-figure, they turned to a wispy smoke that reminded Xander of the trail of smoke that had led them to Fortune Falls. But no other sign of Cedric came, and all Xander could do was watch as Nyla stood, seemingly frozen for a moment before she burst into action at someone's—at *Shamira's*—yowl. His heart raced, twisted over itself as Shamira raced toward the fallen pumpkie.

Were they close? The curious question flashed across his mind with the harsh assault of Shamira's yowl echoing in his eardrums. Already, he knew that cry would haunt him for the rest of his life.

Magic flared in the crystal ball.

The wave seemed to cut off as a dome of lilac magic came into focus, wrapping around Shamira, Nyla, and the fallen pumpkie. Dinora's creatures had the pumpkies and Nyla surrounded.

As the pumpkies battled the stone creatures threatening their perimeter, the figures within the safety of the lilac-colored dome went utterly still. Despite the chaos of the battle raging around them, the three figures seemed to be completely frozen in a rare moment of tranquility, like a painting.

As Edwin and the pair of guards came to join Xander and his grandfather around the crystal ball, a pumpkie with tawny fur approached the dome and entered it with ease. Xander furrowed his brow. Leaning closer to the crystal ball, he hoped to get a better look at what was transpiring within but to no avail.

"What do you think they're doing?" Luce asked.

"I don't know. Maybe they're trying to heal the other pumpkie?" Xander offered, remembering how Shamira had healed Nyla after Dinora had nearly killed her that day at the Woodlane Manor.

"I don't like this," his grandfather muttered. "I need to return to my study and convene with Commander Howards now that we know how Cedric managed to escape. Nyla should be extracted. It's too dangerous for her there."

Xander's hand floated to the ring he wore on a chain hidden beneath his shirt. Pinching it, and the soft material of his shirt, for just a moment, he tried to consider what Nyla would want. Begrudgingly, he said, "Nyla chose to fight...but maybe we should, just until—"

The shield of lilac-colored magic dissipated.

Shamira, the fallen pumpkie, and the pumpkie with tawny fur were gone.

The pumpkies let out a long, haunting howl that chilled his bones and made goosebumps appear on his skin.

After a moment, Nyla stood and seemed to square her shoulders. Xander cursed.

Even with all the miles between them, he knew that look. He'd seen the power of her grit and determination the very same day Dinora had nearly killed her.

Nyla wasn't giving up.

Edwin's sharp intake of breath broke Xander's daze. "Shamira. She's here, and from the sound of it…she's panicked."

Xander's head snapped in his friend's direction. "What?"

"Shamira's here, and—"

"Lead the way," Xander demanded, already rushing toward the stairs that would lead them back to the surface.

"Alexander!" his grandfather said, grabbing his arm and stopping him in his place.

Xander wrenched his arm from his grasp. "I will gladly accept any punishment you deal me in the future, but right now, my friend needs me."

His grandfather's jaw twitched. "You realize Lady Ravencroft is likely to make an example of you both?"

"You could disown me, and it wouldn't change a thing to me right now," Xander said dangerously, taking a step back. Bringing his hands up to try and negate the severity of his words, he added, "My friend needs me."

Shaking his head, his grandfather waved his hand. "I will allow it, but as soon as your friend is seen to, Luce and Abraham will escort you both to my study where I can keep an eye on you."

"Thank you, Grandfather," Xander breathed.

Without a second thought, Xander raced up the stairs with Edwin following closely behind him. Over the pounding of his own heartbeat and footfalls, Xander barely heard him say that Shamira and the other two pumpkies were in the makeshift healing ward. A bright light flooded the stairwell as the hidden entrance opened at either Luce's or Edwin's command. Xander didn't stop to consider whose, already weaving a path down the hedge-lined trails of the garden maze. Footsteps echoed behind him, following in his wake, but Xander didn't care enough to see if they'd all managed to keep pace with him. Ahead, the hedge-lined path opened up to the courtyard beyond.

Sprinting across the patio, Xander entered Pemberly Hall through the first opening he saw and into the back hallway. Passing through it in a blur, his eyes trained on the sight of the ballroom mere yards away.

Bursting into the brightly lit room, Xander halted just inside the doorway. Surveying the room, he tried in vain to find Shamira amid the bustling room.

"This way," Edwin panted, hardly coming to a stop beside him. "When did you get so fast?"

"Have you met my friend Nyla?" he replied dryly. "She could outrun a pollipes."

Edwin huffed, stepping into the room and forcing Xander to follow him deeper into the ballroom-turned-hospital. Xander needed to get to Shamira and see that his friend was as well as she could be.

Sweeping his eyes over the room, Xander quickly found Nan. Weaving his way toward her, Edwin and the pair of guards entrusted with keeping them from making any more trouble followed after him.

"Xander!" Nan said, her eyes studying the four of them. Her gaze lingered on Luce and Abraham, though if she had questions about why he'd come with a pair of guards, she didn't ask them, too focused on him and him alone. "Where have you been? People have been looking for you!"

Xander rubbed the back of his neck. "It's a long story. But I'm here now, and I heard a friend of mine was here."

"Who?" Nan asked, her eyes going wide with concern.

"Shamira, she's a pumpkie," Xander quickly explained, beginning to search the room again.

"Ah." Nan nodded. "This way. I've been tasked to see to the injured pumpkie as the senior surgeon here. Now come along. I could use an extra pair of hands."

"If you're certain," Xander said. "I'm not sure how much help I'll be."

"Nonsense." Nan waved her hand dismissively, turning away to lead him through the bustle of activity in the room. "The only way someone could be unhelpful at a time like this is by remaining idle. You too, Edwin. I hope you've been practicing your healing skills."

"Always," he replied, puffing up like a proud raverin. Xander rolled his eyes. Edwin would never cease to be the prized pupil.

"Good." Nan nodded, leading them through the ballroom's splintered doors and onto the courtyard's veranda.

Xander took a deep breath of fresh air. His eyes immediately landed on Shamira. Her shoulders slumped as she sat completely still and nearly bent over the fallen pumpkie. Xander shuddered, nearly stopping dead in his tracks. He'd never seen Shamira less than composed, so to see her like this…Xander swallowed, reminded once again of how terrible the odds were that those fighting faced. His eyes flicked toward the pumpkie with tawny fur who stood just off to the side, looking on as Shamira seemed to forget the world surrounding her.

Xander's blood simmered in his veins. He hadn't the slightest idea of what he could do. Sitting with strangers and people he'd met in passing over the years or during the war councils had been one thing, but to find himself needing to comfort a friend?

"All right, let's see," Nan said, breezing past him and breaking him away from his worried thoughts. He watched as she crouched down beside the injured pumpkie. "Edwin, come around and help me."

Healing magic hasn't worked, the tawny-colored pumpkie offered. *We haven't been able to figure out why.*

Nan furrowed her brow. "That shouldn't be."

Uncertain of what to do, Xander kneeled beside Shamira and put a hand on the back of her neck. "Shamira, this is Gerri, a good family friend of mine. She's one of the best doctors you'll ever find."

Shamira blinked slowly, turning her bleak sage-colored eyes on him. *I don't know what to do.*

"It'll be okay." Xander tried to sound reassuring, but there wasn't much he could say. None of them knew anything for certain, especially since he'd seen tens of people being healed just earlier today. What made this pumpkie any different than them? Was it the fact that the others had been human, or was it something they'd yet to encounter, a new horror fresh from the mind of the evil sorceress? "Nan will figure out what's wrong. And even if we can't heal…there's always surgery. Nan was one of the top surgeons in the country before she retired."

Nan? Shamira returned her gaze to the scene unfolding over the unconscious pumpkie. Both Nan and Edwin were examining the gray-and-black-striped pumpkie as the tawny one stood vigil. As Xander studied the injured cat-creature, he realized how similar he and Shamira appeared, right down to the splotch of burnt orange fur on his forehead. *Is this the woman Nyla had seen in Caselle? That Nan?*

"The very same." Xander nodded. "Nyla told you about all that?"
Not all of it, she replied, *but she told me about Nan.*

Xander smiled to himself. She'd probably raved about Nan's banana cake. Sometimes, during the thankfully brief time Nyla had been bound to the Woodlane Manor, Xander would find her sitting outside on the veranda, looking to be deep in thought. Sometimes she wouldn't say what she was thinking about when he'd ask, though she'd usually mutter something about the curse and just being tired, adding a vague assurance that she was fine. But other times, when he'd ask her what she was thinking about, she'd turn to him and answer him very seriously with the simple explanation of "Nan's banana cake."

"Can I ask you…" Xander started slowly. Shamira's ears flicked in his direction, but otherwise, she didn't start at or acknowledge his words. "Can I ask you how Nyla seemed? On the battlefield?"

Shamira was silent for a moment before her strained voice skirted the forefront of his mind. *Nervous, but angry. When she first appeared on the battlefield, she seemed helpless, but as her daze seemed to wear off, she became more confident.* Shamira paused, her mouth opening and closing once before she added, *I think she can do it. I think she can defeat Dinora.*

Xander's heart missed a beat. Several memories flashed through his mind, from the fight in the Woodlane Manor's courtyard to the glimpses of the battle he'd gleaned from the viewing glasses and crystal balls to the scene that played out in his nightmares of the two Casters embroiled in a terrific duel—a duel that he knew with an unshakeable certainty left one of them dead.

Beside him, Shamira shifted slightly. *You smell of a blood oath.*

Xander's heart spasmed. He glanced down at his sliced palm, mystified. "A...a blood oath??"

How did Cedric escape? she asked, turning clear eyes on him.

"It's a long story," Xander replied hesitantly, carefully curling his fingers into his palm to hide the cut as if it could stop Shamira's line of inquiry. "I ordered Edwin to take me to him, and in the end, he managed to break free. He said the wards were weak."

And the blood oath? Shamira asked. Her eyes narrowed in suspicion. *How did that come to be?*

"I wish I knew," Xander muttered. Was that what Cedric had been doing as he'd lost consciousness as a result of his attack? Had he really sworn a blood oath?

Shamira didn't press him any further, turning her attention back toward the injured pumpkie. Xander tried to push through the haziness of his last waking memory before he'd lost consciousness. Cedric had murmured something about a vow, about ending the battle perhaps? What were the terms? Xander wracked his brain, trying to piece together a possible truth, but all his mind could supply him with was the unverifiable plea Cedric had made to set him free so he could kill Dinora.

"You're certain?" Xander heard Nan ask Edwin. His eyes snapped to the pair, finally returning his attention to their assessment of the fallen pumpkie.

"Yes." Edwin sat back on his heels and glanced over at Shamira. "We'll need to do surgery. I think there's a piece of the creature inside the wound that may be preventing us from using magic to heal…"

Talmec, Shamira offered, *my brother's name is Talmec.*

The instant tension in the air was palpable. Xander swallowed around the rock in his throat, exchanging a brief look with Nan.

"We'll do our very best," Nan assured them both, though her caring eyes were fixed solely on Shamira. "You couldn't ask for a better team than myself and Edwin."

I'm sure, Shamira said. *Nyla spoke very highly of your skills.*

"Oh, she did? Well." Nan was flustered, smiling as she began to unpack her surgical instruments. "Nyla is an amazing young woman, wouldn't you say so, Xander?"

Xander hummed in response. "She's truly something."

In truth, Xander didn't know what to tell Nan. He couldn't disagree, but at the moment, he'd found that his worry for Nyla greatly outweighed any admiration he may have had for her. He didn't know whether she was following a path set before her by the fickle hand of Fate, or if she felt that it was her solemn duty as Astrid's heir to defeat Dinora on her own. No matter what was motivating her, Xander knew he'd never be able to forgive himself for being unable to help her in this battle, to share at least some of the burden with her.

Biting the inside of his cheek as Nan began to examine Talmec's wound, Xander hoped this wasn't a sign of what was to come. He hoped that this wasn't any indication of how the battle would go or that Nyla would meet a similar end.

Glancing over at Shamira, he noticed her observing the scene with glazed eyes as Nan began to line up her surgical instruments.

"Edwin," Nan said, "hold Talmec steady."

Xander gulped, wholly unprepared to witness what would come next, just as much as he was unwilling to helplessly stand by and watch the battle unfold through a viewing glass.

But he didn't have a choice. In either case, Xander knew his mind wouldn't allow him the luxury of choosing avoidance or ignorance. He would be here, for both of them—Nyla and Shamira—however much his helplessness threatened to destroy him.

Clarity

Astrid studied the map spread out over the long table with a furrowed brow. Dinora's forces had certainly moved throughout the kingdom quickly, wreaking havoc as they went. There didn't seem to be any strategy behind the destruction, as no advantage given by the path they cut could be discerned by even the most experienced of their war council. At first, Astrid had believed there was some strategy, but now? It was nearly impossible to link their movements to a cohesive thought, let alone a discernable reason.

"What do you think, Lady Thornraven?" Fergus asked, drawing the room's attention to her.

"There is no reason," Astrid began, clicking her tongue. "At first, I believed they were targeting places of significance, either because of their strategical advantage to us in battle or their sentiment to our people, but now?" Astrid shook her head. "Even when taking into consideration the battles of the Ten Years' War, there seems to be no tangible reason to Dinora's attacks. But having known her, I believe these attacks are meant to demoralize our people and cause as much damage to our infrastructure as possible. They aren't meant to be strategic because of where *or* what they are. Dinora wants revenge, and that means inflicting as much pain as she can unto us and our people.

She wants to see our kingdom destroyed, and if she can divide us, she knows there will not be a war."

The gathered military commanders were silent for a moment. Astrid's heart beat fiercely in her ears, her cheeks warm at their unwavering attention on her.

"You believe," the eastern commander, Sir Locke, started, staring at her with hardened eyes that had seen both war and reconstruction, "that Dinora's plan is no plan at all? That she only seeks to cause chaos and demoralize our people?"

Astrid nodded. "That's what it seems like, yes."

Sir Locke pursed his lips, leaning his fists on the table and studying the map behind furious brows. "All of this destruction, all of these lives lost, and you claim it was for no tangible reason?"

"Seeing as we have yet to unravel the reason behind the Corvids' movements, it's the only explanation we haven't considered yet. Wars have been lost because they were ceased to be believed in."

"Let's entertain this idea, then," Lady Rowan of the South said in the momentary lapse Sir Locke had allowed. "If what Lady Thornraven says is true, it would explain why engaging the Corvids in direct combat has been near impossible. They aren't looking to combat us, but to destroy us. Every counter we make is met with ghosts, and yet the casualties of their attacks are devastatingly obvious. Destroyed towns, mourning loved ones, and bitter glares from survivors who feel as though we've failed them. And haven't we, if we can't stop the Corvids? If we can't protect them? Already, the people are deserting the fight. Our bannermen are returning home against their orders, and no threat of punishment for desertion seems to prevent them. So what if we are not fighting a war, but, rather, what if we are fighting to keep the unity of our kingdom in the face of those who would tear us apart?"

Sir Locke slowly glanced over at her. "Is it not still war then? Wouldn't we still have to confront those who would seek to tear our kingdom apart from within?"

"It is, but it is a different sort of war than we scrambled to prepare for," Lady Rowan insisted.

Sir Locke sighed heavily. When he pushed himself away from the table, Astrid found her nerves writhing in her gut as his gaze landed upon her once more. Though he wasn't but ten years older than her, the age between them seemed far greater than it was in the lines etched upon his face from many a sleepless night these last several weeks. "Then what do you propose we do?"

9. TO FIGHT

"Then what do you propose we do?" Nyla huffed, blasting another stone creature into oblivion.

Beside her, Myra growled, slinging her pale yellow magic at another leaping beast. Its jagged mouth parted in a silent screech as it shattered. *You need to press on. The creatures will follow, and we will destroy them. It will give us enough of a reprieve to catch our breaths.*

"Shamira wouldn't like that, and Ingrid most certainly won't," Nyla said between ragged breaths. The emptiness in her stomach twisted painfully. She should've packed some snacks in her pockets, if not for hunger, then to keep up her energy at least. She didn't know how much further into the well of her magic she could pull before there was nothing left but sparks. Conjuring a shield for herself, she uncorked one of the foul-tasting potions that she'd taken to stashing in her pockets after her duel with Frederick. Shuddering as she drank the thick liquid, Nyla closed her eyes, imagining the meal she would eat when this was all over.

It's a good thing Shamira isn't here right now then because that may be our only option. Myra leapt over another pumpkie, colliding with the rock creature in midair and knocking it to the ground as the pumpkie she'd jumped over conjured their magic into a concentrated ray of dazzling orange. Nyla instinctually curled away from the splinters of onyx-colored rock that threatened to rain down upon her as the creature was destroyed, turning to nothing more than gentle tendrils of smoke.

The shards sizzled against her shield. Letting out a relieved huff, Nyla shoved the empty bottle back in her pocket and let her shield drop. Still feeling the stinging exhaustion in her bones and the droop of her eyelids as she stared at the fray of pumpkies and stone creatures around her, she hoped the potion would take effect soon.

Out of the corner of her eye, Nyla saw a burst of scarlet energy. She hadn't realized how close they'd come to where Cedric was, but now she could see burst after burst of his magic flaring in between the dipping shadows of the raverins diving to pluck stone creatures from the sands.

Mesmerized, she watched his magic, trying to make out what was happening through the disarray of creatures, soldiers, and pumpkies in the stretch of battlefield between her and Cedric.

It almost seemed like the creatures were converging on *him*, as if Dinora realized what he was doing. Whether or not she knew Cedric was here was beyond Nyla's ability to confirm, but she was certain of one thing: Dinora had to know that there was someone more powerful than her on this battlefield, someone capable of wiping out her creatures faster than she could create them.

Nyla jumped. Goosebumps erupted down her arms and legs at the shrill shriek of a raverin. Her heart pounded in her ears. An involuntary chill raced down her spine, watching as a raverin dove haphazardly into the fray just beyond her sight. She couldn't see what was happening, only that the constant flare of Cedric's magic had stopped. Nyla licked her lips, forcing herself onto the tips of her toes in an effort to see. Her blood thrummed and rushed in her ears, her heartbeat pounding as the raverins became frenzied. The thought of asking Myra if she could see crossed her mind, but the question would not form.

"Nyla!" a voice shouted. Nyla's head had half-turned in the direction the voice had come from, only for a harsh weight to slam into her, knocking her off her feet.

"Oof," she wheezed, her eyes squeezing shut at the sharp jarring of her bones against the sandy ground and the impact of armor hitting her square in the chest.

A horrible screech pierced her ears. Flinching, Nyla's eyes flew open. A sticky warmth trickled down her neck, seeping into her shirt.

Nyla! Myra's silky voice shouted in her mind.

Blinking, Nyla's vision focused on the sight of blonde hair in her peripheral vision. But, most importantly, on the jagged onyx teeth snapping at her. Nyla's hand shot out, her lilac-colored magic jumping from her open palm like a bolt of lightning, blasting the creature right in its featureless face. Shards of rock rained down upon her and the person sprawled on top of her, slicing her face as she turned her head away in vain before they turned to smoke.

Heaving a breath, Nyla watched dimly as the creature continued to move, though it seemed confused without its head, starting one way and then whipping around to take a few steps in the other direction. Myra and another pumpkie combined their magics to reduce the rest of the creature to smoke.

Blinking some more, realization slowly seeped into Nyla's mind as much as the sticky pool of red oozed along her skin. Crying out, Nyla scrambled to shove the stilled body off of her. Her throat burned from the acid swimming up from her simmering stomach. Barely managing to sit up, she turned over onto her hands and knees in time to empty the contents of her stomach.

Nyla, are you all right? Myra was instantly by her side. A dome of rippling yellow energy like sunbeams formed around them. Wiping her mouth with the back of her hand, Nyla's eyes cut to the body she'd had to push off of herself out of a morbid curiosity she couldn't deny. Sir Ian's unblinking eyes stared back at her.

Nyla!

Breaking her gaze away, Nyla opened and closed her mouth. The image of Sir Ian commanding the crowd of betters after her duel against Frederick flashed before her mind.

"No," she said weakly, shaking her head in a daze. "No."

Come on. Let's get you up and away from here. Myra nosed her arm, managing to maneuver Nyla's limp arm over her head and around her neck. Standing to her full height, Myra hardly got Nyla to sit up on her knees, but still she pushed at Nyla's side, urging her to move. *Come on, Nyla. We have to move!*

Blinking, Nyla eased herself to her feet. "I knew him."

We all know somebody, Myra said, pushing Nyla to take a step away. *That's just a fact of life and death.*

Myra's words were harsh despite the soothing tone of her voice, but Nyla grasped onto them in the attempt to numb herself to the losses she couldn't afford to feel at the moment. Nyla glanced in the direction that had almost cost her her life. The distraction that had cost Sir Ian his. Resolutely, she turned away. Whatever had happened to Cedric, and the raverins, was no longer any of her concern. She focused on the bright flare of magic erupting from where she guessed Dinora was. It seemed more vibrant than it had moments before, leading Nyla to wonder just what had happened mere seconds ago as the clap of the raverins' wings grew distant. Nyla reminded herself of the dangers all around her. She forced her mind to understand that mourning would have to come later, once Dinora was defeated. Only then could they mourn in peace.

Shaking her head in an effort to clear the fog still flooding her conscious thought, Nyla forced herself to take another step. She took another step, feeling the numbness fall away from her limbs. Myra's eager pushing fell away from her side as Nyla took another step on her own. Taking a deep breath, Nyla began to move faster. Staring over the battlefield, her eyes focused on the shimmering aura wavering in the sunlight, blocking what she could only imagine to be Dinora from view.

And before Nyla knew it, she was running. No longer did the shadows of the raverins fall over the sand as they traveled overhead. There was only the endless ash-colored sand before her.

She was running for all her life with a singular goal in mind. And though there was a weariness simmering in her blood, her eyes stung from exhaustion, and her bones cried out with each and every movement for a minute's rest, Nyla ran.

Just as Myra had said they would, the stone creatures turned to follow her. It was like they were drawn to her and fought with the others in their path to get to her. As Nyla wove her path over the battlefield, dodging abandoned cannons and fallen weapons, the creatures followed her. It was their mistake, for their distraction gave the pumpkies and any human fighters near them the chance to set their magic loose upon them, shattering them into the smoke they once were.

They were still fighting.

She was still breathing.

Dinora hadn't won, not yet.

Nyla's heart swelled. Her legs burned from the effort of running, and she chose to focus on that instead. If she focused on the bubbling emotions in her chest hard enough, she feared they would choke her. The memories they invoked would choke her. And if she focused on those memories hard enough, Nyla worried she might find her family watching after her in despair. It was that thought that she couldn't bear.

Of all the promises she'd made and kept or had broken over the years, breaking the promises to her family—to Astrid—was the worst of them all. She'd meant every word of them, of her vows to live and to strive for happiness, and that's what stung the most.

But sitting by and allowing her mind to consume her was something she'd never be able to forgive herself for. It was why she was on this battlefield to begin with. If she had any chance of keeping those promises, she needed to do this.

She had to do this.

"*I want to live,*" she'd told Xander only a night ago.

"*Then let's live,*" he'd replied, the weight of their promise in his warm eyes.

Tears pricked her eyes.

"I will live," she murmured. Her words burned in her throat. The puff of air that had fled her lips with those words burned just as much. Panting as she ran, she said them again, louder this time so Fate would hear her vow too. "I will live!"

Impulsive

Astrid threw the doors of King Harrison's chamber open. She couldn't believe she was really doing this, and yet she couldn't stop herself. Fergus stopped midsentence at her intrusion and stared at her from his place beside their sovereign's desk as both the king and his manservant turned to look at her.

"Astrid, what are—"

"They're stealing magic from the land," she fumed. "If we don't stop them now, Dinora may become too powerful for us to—"

"Slow down," Harrison said, stepping away from the frazzled manservant helping him dress. Silently dismissing him, Harrison grabbed for the article of clothing the man had set aside upon his departure.

Astrid averted her gaze as she only now realized how her friend was only in his long tunic.

"I apologize. I should've waited for a more reasonable—"

"You really couldn't have, even if you'd tried," Fergus said from the other side of the room.

Astrid's eyes flashed to him. He only shrugged under her glare. "It's true," he continued, "and you know you cannot deny it."

Harrison chuckled. "Fergus raises a valid point, Astrid. You're rather… eager? Yes, eager, when it comes to stopping Dinora and Cedric."

Astrid rolled her eyes. Turning her back to the room, she crossed her arms over her chest. Fabric rustled behind her. Glancing up at the ceiling, Astrid fought the writhing embarrassment that wove its way into her gut.

"All I'm trying to explain is that we have a fleeting moment of opportunity to end this war before it gets worse. Our people are suffering, and we could end this now."

"And how do you propose we do that?" Harrison asked. Metal clattered together. Astrid assumed it was his sword and dagger clanking together on his belt as he pulled it on. "She has an army—"

"Ah," Astrid started, smiling wryly. "Her army is growing restless. They want to go home, but she keeps promising them victory and glory. They may not be as demoralized as ours, but they're homesick, something just as devastating to an army as low morale."

Astrid's skin prickled as if she could hear the mute communication passing between king and commander. Slowly, she turned around to face them both. Sure enough, she caught the two sharing a silent conversation held only by raised brows, shrugs, and the quirk of a lip as their only thought indicators.

"Well?" she asked, glancing between them.

"How do you know this?" Fergus asked. "My scouts have different reports."

"The raverins know everything."

At the mention of the holy bird, Harrison began to fiddle with the royal seal on his finger. Pacing, the king pursed his lips, studying the floor. After a moment, he asked, "The raverins spoke to you?"

"Not exactly," Astrid explained. "I spoke with the pumpkies. The Brewardt Clan intercepted a messenger raverin used to communicate between Dinora and Cedric." Withdrawing the miniature letter carrier tube from the folds of her dress, Astrid extended it to Fergus to examine for himself. As he read it with furrowed brows, Astrid added, "The pumpkies have pledged their support to our cause. They will join us in battle to defeat Dinora, but we must act now, for they fear the balance of magic is in peril."

Harrison froze, staring at her with wide eyes. "The Brewardt Clan has pledged their support? What of the Zeldher and Reyhart Clans?"

Astrid grinned, a rare sight, she realized, these days. "Was I not specific enough? I did say the *pumpkies* have pledged their support."

"All of them?" Fergus asked.

"All of them," Astrid confirmed, grinning even wider. "Oof."

She staggered backwards as Harrison tackled her in a bone-crushing hug. Sheepishly returning it for a second, Astrid managed to pull away. As she did, she gently placed her hands on his forearms to keep him at bay.

Blinking, Harrison took several steps back, rubbing the back of his neck. "Sorry. I just…I forgot myself." Swallowing, he glanced toward the portrait hung over the fireplace of Astrid's cousin, the late queen Bridget.

His mouth dropped open as if he meant to continue, but Astrid interrupted him before he could ever begin. "It's all right. Favorable news has been rare since…since Dinora's attacks began. We could all use a bit of hope right now."

Harrison nodded. "Indeed. Hope had been in short supply, but the pumpkies' support will mean a great deal to everyone. Fergus," Harrison said, an air of authority dripping into his voice that had the commander standing to attention, "gather the war council immediately."

"Yes, my liege," Fergus said, offering a single bow to both of them. Harrison frowned at the title. Astrid bit back a laugh as Fergus left them.

Harrison eyed her with a withering look. "I'm glad to see you've maintained the ability to laugh, even if it is at my expense."

Bowing her head and offering a low curtsy, Astrid said, "For who else would balance your ego but Fergus and myself, my liege?"

"I think there's an entire council of our elders who would like to claim that duty," Harrison sighed. "And we're about to face them all."

Astrid hesitated, meaning to follow after Fergus before the king's words had stopped her. "But this time we have news that none of them could have procured themselves."

Harrison offered her a small smile. "And that is why I chose you to be my right hand. No one else has maintained our relationship with the pumpkies with the same reverence as you have."

Astrid swallowed. "I am honored to have your confidence, but I fear it may be wasted if even this advantage cannot save our kingdom."

Harrison *tsk*ed. "Such grave worries," he said, grasping the handle of the other door and opening it for them both. "Let's just relish this moment of hope before we lose it."

Astrid slipped out into the hallway. The king followed beside her. As she and Harrison walked down the candlelit passage, she said, "Then let us pray we use this moment wisely."

10. TO LIVE

Focusing on the harsh landscape ahead, a sick tremble worked its way into Nyla's bones. Streaks of crimson soaked the ash-colored sand. Weapons lay scattered across the landscape, forcing her and the pack of pumpkies flanking her to weave around the bigger artillery pieces. Her mind raced, trudging just as hard as her feet tried to carry her across the blazing sand.

What had happened to the people that were supposed to be responsible for these weapons? Where were their operators? Were they dead? Alive? Wounded or out of ammunition?

Sir Ian's still face flashed before her mind. She feared the image of his glassy eyes would forever be imprinted in the shadows of her memory, forever haunting her.

But her own reluctance to acknowledge the deaths that had surely befallen their forces wasn't strong enough to stop her from wondering where the bodies were. Surely, for as many streaks of red intermingled alongside the gray flecks of sand, there would be plenty of soldiers and Casters and pumpkies strewn throughout the battlefield. So why hadn't she passed any?

A chill ran down Nyla's spine. Her knees threatened to buckle as the air was knocked from her lungs with the theory that struck her mind.

If Dinora had resurrected the rock points because they were the souls of those she'd killed and had subsequently trapped in the Shadow Forest during her quest for vengeance 647 years ago, did that mean she was using their fallen comrades to fill her army too?

Nyla's stomach roiled.

Ingrid! Nyla shouted desperately, flinging her magic out across the battlefield in search of the Mage General's steady presence. *Ingrid, please!*

Nyla! Are you all right? Where are you? I'll take you bac—

The bodies. I think she's using the bodies of our dead!

Silence rang between her ears. Ingrid's presence across the battlefield turned still. Nyla cringed at the trickle of disbelief that ebbed its way into her mind as it seeped into Ingrid's essence, not far at all from where Nyla had initially left them in favor of maneuvering with the pumpkies.

Ingrid's voice stuttered. *What?*

Nyla desperately tried to explain her theory. *Do you see any bodies?*

Ingrid's magic tickled her skin. Nyla imagined that if she focused her eyesight enough, she'd see Ingrid's delicate magic sweeping over the battlefield in search of the dead, but Nyla didn't dare to waste her energy on that. Just as suddenly as the subtle hum of electricity had licked at her skin, it vanished.

Out of the corner of her eye, Nyla saw a burst of pink energy erupt in the sky. Spraying like a blooming flower, Ingrid's signal burned bright through the haze hanging over the battlefield from the discharge of cannons and gunfire—and slain rock creatures.

Everyone fall back, now! The heir and I believe Dinora is creating a constant stream of creatures—we need to regroup and better assess how to combat Dinora's actions. Ingrid's voice was harsh against Nyla's skull. As her message registered with each and every one of their forces spread over the sandy plain, the blasts of magic skirting through the smoke sputtered out. The cannon blasts and gun fire quieted. Everything stopped until there was nothing but a ringing silence that pierced through Nyla's ears, almost making her miss the clap of the raverins' wings that had long ago disappeared, along with signs of Cedric's magic. Nyla's brows furrowed, wondering what Ingrid's intentions were.

Coming to a slow stop, Nyla and the pumpkies drew closer together. Working together, they conjured a shield of protective magic, all converging into one glimmering dome that kept the creatures at bay.

The humans are retreating? Myra asked, her storm cloud-colored eyes blinking up at Nyla in confusion. *Why?*

"There're no bodies," Nyla breathed, panting as she doubled over with her hands on her knees. She gulped down a full breath of air, swallowing against her parched throat. Grimacing, she straightened, pressing a hand to her ribs. "There aren't any bodies, so I told Ingrid, and she ordered everyone to fall back. I think Dinora's transforming the bodies into more stone creatures."

Myra's eyes widened for only a second. Her low growl made goosebumps erupt along Nyla's skin. She looked every bit like the fierce creature Xander had feared the pumpkies were when they'd first met Shamira. Myra's lips curled back in a snarl. *Then we'd better kill her before the day is lost.*

Nyla swallowed, biting her lip. She couldn't deny having the same thought, but hearing the words uttered aloud made the reality of their conviction sink into her mind.

"Nyla!" a voice hissed. A looming shadow appeared beside them, a vague figure in Nyla's peripheral vision. Nyla flinched at the sound of the gruff voice, whirling to face them. Her lilac-colored magic sparked at her fingertips before the energy fizzled out. Nyla let out a relieved sigh, glad to see the disheveled woman beside her. Ingrid's eyes went wide at the sight Nyla must've been. "Are you all right?"

Nyla nodded her head. Relief washed over as she took in Ingrid's form. Grit coated Ingrid from head to toe. Her dark hair clung to her sweat-drenched face where it had come loose from her braid. Nyla imagined she looked much the same, maybe worse. A wild thing. A person of tragedy. A warrior in need of rest.

"We're returning to Pemberly," Ingrid started, reaching out to grab Nyla's arm. "Let's go."

Nyla shook her head, stumbling back a step. Ingrid reached for her again, scowling. Again, Nyla stepped back, batting her hand away. "No. I'm staying."

"Nyla, be smart about this," Ingrid said. "You need to rest, you need to eat, and we need to regroup. We need to know if your theory is fact or not."

"Wherever I go, these creatures will follow me. I'm staying."

Ingrid's eyes flashed pleadingly. "Nyla—"

Nyla squared her shoulders, drawing herself up to her full height, her chin held high. "I am staying, and *that* is final."

Glaring back at the dark eyes flashing with indignation and something she saw only as disappointment, Nyla refused to waver. She knew that she was right. The creatures would follow her to Pemberly, and that wasn't something she would be responsible for. She wouldn't put the people she cared about in danger's direct path.

Regret unfurled in her gut. Quietly, Nyla added, "If I go back with you, I'm afraid it will only bring more danger to everyone. I *have* to end this, here and now, but I can't do that if everyone's worried about me and if I'm worried about everyone else. I can't let our fears and anxieties leash me anymore. I have to do this, Ingrid."

Clicking her tongue, Ingrid bobbed her head. "What should I tell the others, then?"

"Tell them…" Nyla considered her words carefully, licking her lips. Her heart sputtered. Never in her life had she felt so gutted.

Maybe that wasn't entirely true, she realized. The memory of fresh lilacs heaped high in front of the burned remains of her home flashed before her mind's eye. She'd known this feeling before now, but this time, she knew what it was to overcome it. She looked toward the strength she'd found lurking inside of her and that had carried her through the journey to the Woodlane Manor, to this point in her life. Taking a deep breath, Nyla corrected her posture and straightened once more. "Tell them that I expect cinnegals and ponanchkas and cake when I get back."

Ingrid blinked at her. The beginnings of a sad smile twitched at the corners of her lips. "Anything else?"

Nyla hesitated, glancing toward the shimmering aurora flaring up from the earth in the center of the battlefield. "Tell Xander I'm sorry for breaking my promise."

Ingrid arched an eyebrow. Shaking her head the slightest bit, she asked, "And you're sure about staying?"

We'll be here too, Myra interrupted. *Nyla will never be alone.*

Nyla took a shuddering breath, turning to the pumpkie. "Actually…I think you should all go. It's…it's not safe here for all of you."

And you believe it'll be safer for you if we go? Myra shook her head, growling. *We're staying.*

"No," Nyla said firmly, shaking her head. "The more people or pumpkies on this field, the more…Dinora would only use our fallen against us if any more die."

So you'll risk yourself—

"No—yes." Nyla shook her head, squeezing her eyes shut to gather her thoughts. The protective magic wavered with a slight *ping* as the stone creatures outside its barrier began to ram into it, growing agitated now that there was nothing else to presumably distract them from getting to Nyla. "Astrid's magic surfaced in me for a reason, and whatever that reason might be, it puts me at an advantage to defeat Dinora. And the more people here, the more potential for Dinora to create new creatures, the less safe I am or the less likely I'll actually be able to reach her in order to kill her. I need you all to be safe, so that I can finish this. That's the only way we're going to defeat Dinora."

Her companions fell into silence. Nyla reluctantly glanced between them, expecting the worst. A look passed between Myra and Ingrid. Nyla wondered if they were communicating with each other.

Shamira won't like this.

"Neither do I, and nor will anyone else, especially the Huntingtons," Ingrid added, grumbling. "Do you really believe you're fated to defeat Dinora alone?"

Nyla bit her lip. "I had hoped it wouldn't come to this, to just the two of us, but I don't think there's any other way. I can't help wondering why *me*? Why has Astrid's magic surfaced in me, of all her descendants, why now?" Meeting Ingrid's gaze and then Myra's, Nyla offered them a sad smile. "I can only think of one answer: it must be Fate as much as my own desire for revenge."

Ingrid nodded slowly, her eyes withdrawn in thought. Nyla saw the moment she accepted her explanation in the purse of her lips. Without a word, Ingrid patted her pockets and produced three small glass vials. Handing them to Nyla, she said, "These two are energy drafts." She pointed to the sludgy-looking potions and then to the one that shimmered like gold. "This one is a healing tonic. I think you should take the energy potions now. If you're truly unharmed, save the healing tonic for in case you need it."

Nyla grimaced. "Maybe this time I'll be able keep them down."

"Hopefully one day soon, Sir Maffis will manage to produce a new blend that tastes better."

"If Fate is kind," Nyla muttered, uncorking the first energy potion and drinking it quickly. Cringing, she swallowed thickly, eyeing the second tonic in her hand with contempt. Sending up a silent prayer to Helpet and Corruptio both, Nyla downed the second with a shudder. "I guess this is goodbye for now."

"Good luck, Nyla." Ingrid gripped her shoulder tightly, her voice nearly as tense as her grip. Nyla noticed her blink away the excess water in her eyes—unshed tears—and take a breath before speaking again. "We'll drop the shield when you're ready. Myra, the pumpkies, and I will take care of these creatures while you run directly for Dinora. We'll dispose of as many creatures as we can before wisping us all to

Pemberly. We have only seconds to work with before we have to leave. Can you handle that?"

Nyla's lip wobbled, though she fought the urge to bite it. Nodding, she gathered her conviction and banished the uncertainty pooling in her gut. "Yes."

"Good. Then it's decided: Fate will have Its turn." Before Nyla could blink, Ingrid rushed forward and wrapped her in a bone-crushing hug. "Astrid's magic chose *you*. That must mean something more than we all know. If nothing else," Ingrid said under her breath, "have faith in yourself."

Nyla squeezed her back. "I will. I'll see you when I get back...though I guess you'll have to come and get me, huh?"

"I may not be the first one, but I'll be here," Ingrid said with a thin smile, though her eyes studied the magical dome fraying around them. "Something tells me Shamira or Xander will be here first when they learn of your plan. I suppose it will be my task to keep them from wisping here the moment we return."

Nyla laughed, wiping her eyes. "You're probably right."

Take care, Nyla. Myra's tail curled around her paws. *We'll do what we can for you now.*

"Thank you," Nyla turned in a slow circle, taking in the pumpkies surrounding her, "all of you. Just...thank you."

Taking a deep breath, Nyla eyed a path with fewer creatures. As she got into position, Ingrid's voice sounded behind her. "Ready?"

"As I can be," Nyla murmured.

The magic withdrew.

Nyla's heart pounded in her chest.

Their shield fell.

II. THE SURGEON AND THE MESSENGER

A tense concentration consumed the three companions hovering near Talmec as Edwin and Nan worked on his wound. The clatter and clamor of the ballroom behind them faded into the background of his awareness as Xander measured the minutes ticking by with the beating of his heart. In that time, Xander had learned that the tawny pumpkie with the keen green eyes was an Elder of Shamira's clan. Glancing quickly at Shamira, Xander saw that she hadn't changed. Her eyes still remained vacant, fixed unblinkingly on her brother, and he wondered if she were seeing anything at all. The vacancy in her eyes unnerved him. He imagined he'd had a similar look in his eyes when Issie had died from a hellhound attack right in front of him, but no words of comfort came to him. Realistically, he knew there wasn't anything he could say to dispel her worry. When Issie died, anything anyone had said to him fell upon deaf ears. All he'd heard was the echo of his own shout, the blood pumping in his veins in time with his heartbeat in that moment, and the howl of the wind as he'd cradled Issie.

But Xander knew one thing for certain: he could be here to offer Shamira his support, and that was what mattered most of all. After Issie's death, that was all that had mattered to him, and that had stuck with him to this day.

Watching as Nan sat back and pulled off her stained gloves, Xander held his breath. Depositing them into an awaiting bucket, she said to Edwin, "All set. Try healing him now."

He sat up a little straighter, watching as Edwin hovered his hands just over Talmec's wound. Silver magic emanated from his hands. The magic spread over the wound. Talmec's torso expanded with a deep breath, the sort Xander hadn't noticed before. His forepaw twitched, nearly kicking out if Nan hadn't put a gentle hand there to hold him in place. Edwin's brow furrowed, twitching as his eyes fell shut.

Amazed, Xander watched as the jagged wound began to close. Before his very eyes, cells and tissue began to knit themselves back together again under the careful urging of Edwin's magic. Beside him, Shamira sat up, nearly leaping from her place.

"Just a little more now," Nan whispered, observing Edwin's work. Hair began to grow where the newly healed skin had sealed itself shut until it stood even with the rest of Talmec's fur. "There."

Edwin peeked open his eyes. Retracting his hands, Edwin slumped back on his heels. "Talmec is completely healed. There's no trace of the stone creature left within him, but because of the blood loss and his body's rejection of the foreign magic, it'll take some time for him to recover."

Every sensation Xander hadn't realized he'd lost rushed back to him. Conscious once more of the orders being shouted inside and the moans or cries of the injured, Xander took a deep breath. Relieved, he glanced over at Shamira, hoping to find her in better spirits now.

Shamira blinked. *Thank you.*

"We'll get him inside where he can rest," Nan said reassuringly.

Actually, Hecates started, *the best place for Talmec to recover would be out here. Is there a quieter place where we could move him to?*

Nan paused. "I'm sorry. I didn't realize. Of course…Xander?"

Xander wracked his mind for an answer to what was asked of him. "There's a bit of privacy down that pathway there," he replied, gesturing toward the courtyard. "That's the best place I can think of where you wouldn't be disturbed and that would still be intact after the earthquake."

A noise of distress came from Edwin. Xander's eyes darted to him. Edwin's face paled.

"What?" Xander asked, staring at his friend. Unease flooded his bloodstream.

Behind him, a wave of silence descended upon the ballroom. Xander didn't dare look around, fearing what he might see. He hadn't known how loud the clamor of the makeshift medical facilities had been until the buzz of complete and total silence had left only a vacuum in its place. Now, with only his heartbeat pounding between his ears, Xander wished for all the world that someone might scream in pain or a page might come running in to shout the news of their victory for all to hear.

But neither occasion happened. Instead, there was only that deafening silence and a static in the air.

"Tell me," he begged, his heart seizing from all the devastating possibilities flitting through his mind. At the memory of Nyla sprawled out across the front steps of the Woodlane Manor, blood speckling her lips, her chest falling with what could've been her last breath, Xander's voice broke, barely allowing him to croak out, "Please."

"Ingrid's given the order to retreat," his friend said absently. "Commander Howards just told me."

Xander's throat went dry. He opened his mouth to speak, but no words came. One single thought consumed him. That concern overwhelmed him until it was all he could see. His fingers trembled. A flash of silver hair crossed his mind, replaced only by the blinding light of lilac and scarlet magics colliding and hiding the world from view behind their brilliance.

And Nyla? Shamira dared to ask the question that Xander assumed had crossed all of their minds. *What of Nyla? Or Cedric and Dinora?*

Edwin's hands curled into fists against his lap, an old habit that

Xander knew meant nothing good. "Nothing was offered about Cedric, but Nyla's staying behind to defeat Dinora."

With whom? Hecates pressed.

Edwin shook his head. His eyes met Xander's, glinting with grief. "Alone. Ingrid and the pumpkies are the last to leave. They're—"

Xander didn't hear the rest. He didn't even know if he'd heard Edwin correctly. They were retreating? Without Nyla? Nyla had…she was staying behind?

Xander couldn't hear anything over the roar of his own blood pounding between his ears. Panic and desperation were like a tsunami, flooding him. A numb tingle traveled down his arms, raising goosebumps in its wake.

He'd heard wrong. He was mistaken. Nothing was horribly amiss, nothing at all.

"Xander!" Nan's voice sounded as though she was a million miles away from him. Maybe even as far as a different plane of existence. "Alexander Huntington!"

Xander blinked. The power of his full name broke through his daze. A trickle of heat bloomed along the back of his neck. Glancing behind him, Xander noticed quite a few people—doctors, Healers, the injured, soldiers, Casters, pages—looking their way. Sad downcast eyes, eyes glazed with tears, the twist of an embittered face all met his gaze.

"Lord Xander?" a quiet voice asked. A soft touch to his shoulder made him flinch. Turning his head, he found Luce staring down at him with unshed tears in her eyes. "Your grandfather would like for you to join him in his study."

Xander nodded weakly. Memories of his parents' deaths, of Issie's death, flooded his mind. Rather than the anger and bitterness he'd felt standing in the Woodlane Manor's front courtyard, he felt that same empty, gutted desolation buzzing in his chest that had come with the finality of his family's deaths. Clenching his fist against his knee, Xander forced himself to his feet. He didn't think it was possible, and yet he managed. And then he managed a step, two steps, three steps.

Xander found his breath again. The world began to turn, or to crumble around him, or rebuild itself. He wasn't altogether certain, but he knew one thing: Ingrid and the force they'd gathered to fight Dinora were retreating without Nyla.

The weight of it and the murmurs of the prayers people had begun to whisper throughout the ballroom settled itself on his mind. Urgency overtook the numb panic in his veins until his whole body buzzed with adrenaline.

Xander began to sprint, uncaring of the guards behind him, of the people looking on, or of the helplessness his hurry might have displayed. He bolted through the crowded ballroom, dodging doctors, Healers, and patients being helped to cots by their fellow warriors, as his mind focused on only one thing: Nyla.

He didn't care about the pretense of calm and stability he'd tried to offer the injured earlier in the afternoon. If the mournful atmosphere choking the ballroom meant anything, then they all knew what was happening now, that Ingrid had given the order to retreat and that Nyla was about to be left on that cursed battlefield all alone. Surely, they all understood the panic he felt now—if they didn't feel some of it themselves.

Xander gritted his teeth. She'd promised not to do anything reckless, that she'd try her best to come back. She'd said that she wanted to live.

Had Nyla known all this time that she was going to sacrifice herself just as Astrid had? Had she really intended to follow in her ancestor's footsteps, or was it an effect of the battle, of seeing its unrelenting impact that had led Nyla to make this final stand on her own?

Xander didn't think he'd find an answer anytime soon.

Bursting into his grandfather's study, Xander paused in the doorway. Nearly every person who stood motionless around the room—Casters, military commanders of the Royal Guard and the Tenebrese army, messengers, people who'd claimed to be Heirs of Tenebris—turned to stare at him with solemn eyes.

Xander kept his grandfather's gaze.

Sadness shone in his eyes. His proud shoulders slumped with—Xander swallowed. It wasn't disappointment, he knew that, but he wasn't sure what weighed them down. Dejection wasn't something he thought he'd ever associate with his grandfather, but it was the only feeling that accurately encompassed the frown and furrowed brows of his grandfather's face, the slope of his shoulders, and the dull gleam in his old eyes.

"It's what Nyla wanted," Commander Howards whispered. She didn't quite meet his eyes, and Xander wasn't certain if it was out of shame or the grief they all felt for the young girl—the young woman—who'd made this difficult choice. "They're about to let the shield down."

Xander took a long, slow breath. He forced himself to cross the room, watching the image reflected in the surrounding viewing glasses from the corners of his eyes. Each viewing glass displayed the same heart-breaking image. He almost considered walking straight past where his grandfather and Commander Howards stood and out onto the balcony, but his feet wouldn't let him. Against his own selfish need for air, for the freedom of an open space, Xander found himself stopping beside his grandfather. He was vaguely aware of Luce falling in beside him as the glow of the crystal ball consumed his attention. Transfixed, Xander stared into the crystal ball, unable to look away as he finally registered all that was happening. He saw Ingrid and Nyla hugging as if it would be the last time they saw each other. As the pumpkies looked on, so too did everyone standing around his grandfather's study. Xander watched, forcing his body to remember to breathe, to ignore the anxiety buzzing in his chest, as Nyla and Ingrid exchanged a few words that were too low for the viewing glasses to transmit.

It was as though sound had ceased to exist. The only noise at all echoed from the viewing glasses. The slight *ping* as the stone creatures hurtled themselves at the wavering dome of magic, the distant screeches and whines of the creatures, all mixed with the stiff silence of the wood-paneled study.

Xander's breath caught in his throat as Ingrid and Nyla pulled away.

"Ready?" Ingrid's voice echoed from each viewing glass.

"As I can be," Nyla said, her quiet voice sinking like an anchor in Xander's chest. At her words, it was like the room held a collective breath, watching helplessly as the shield around the last group of warriors faded and the stone creatures eagerly advanced on them.

Before the last of the dome had even fallen, Nyla was gone, running faster than Xander knew she could over the sandy landscape. It was all he could do to fight the idea that she was running toward what could only be her certain death, and it still wasn't enough to overpower the panic that had wholly consumed his mind.

12. BORROWED MAGIC

Shamira blinked her shock away. *What do you mean they're going to drop the shield and then retreat?*

"Violet said that their plan was for Nyla to run as soon as the shield was dropped, and in that small window of time, they were going to destroy as many creatures as possible before retreating. They think Dinora is turning our fallen into more of those creatures, which is why Ingrid gave the order to retreat," Edwin huffed, running a rough hand over his face. "We've been giving her an endless army!"

It was the most anger Shamira had ever noticed wafting off of him. Edwin was a fairly consistent human emotionally. Any emotion he'd previously expressed had been calm and steady, but this was uncontrolled. Raw. Vibrant.

For someone so passive, Edwin certainly had a lot of anger to spare over Ingrid's order to retreat. And Shamira couldn't damn him for it, for she agreed with him.

Would Myra truly abandon Nyla? she asked Hecates. His green eyes were already on her.

If it's what Nyla wanted, then I believe she would unless one of us ordered her otherwise. His whiskers twitched. *You know Nyla best, Shamira. What should we do?*

"If it were up to me," Edwin seethed, "I wouldn't let Nyla sacrifice herself, Astrid's heir or not."

"Neither would I," Nan whispered, tears sliding down her face. "And neither would Xander or George or Alexander. No one would."

No one, Shamira said, taking a keen interest in her paws so she wouldn't have to see the effect of her words, *but Nyla herself.*

The air rippled with a bitter static, the manifestation of her companions' displeasure.

"So you're going to let her?" Edwin asked.

Shamira remained silent. Was she?

The silence radiated throughout the ballroom, spilling out on the patio where they sat until there was nothing left but the flitting of Shamira's own thoughts to fill her ears. The news had spread instantaneously. Everyone knew what was happening, and if the shifting of the air crackling in her ears was any indication, they were losing time to make a decision that could save Nyla from herself.

Shamira's fur prickled with the fizzling of the magical energy around her as the warriors from the battlefield had begun to return. The biting tang of humiliation and helplessness assaulted her nose. The dry static of exhaustion sat on her tongue.

No one was willing to let Nyla sacrifice herself, but no one was going to stop her either.

Snarling, Shamira said, *There has to be something we can do to help her. What if we set up a Cooperative Circle?*

"That's a fantastic idea," Edwin said. "I'll pass it along to Ingrid when she returns, but for now, I'll gather the Casters and see how Lord Huntington would like us to go about setting it up. Can you gather the pumpkies in the courtyard?"

Of course, Shamira assured him. *If this is the only way Nyla will allow us to help, then we will all gladly do our part.*

Edwin nodded, quickly getting to his feet. She watched him as he set off through the teeming ballroom before her eyes fell to her brother once more.

"Go," Nan said. "Talmec will be just fine. I'll make certain of it, dear."

Shamira bowed her head. *Thank you, Gerri.*

"Just help bring Nyla home safely," she pleaded.

Shamira nodded as best as she could, her throat too tense to do much of anything. Even her mind had ceased to find the words to comfort the older woman. Beside her, Hecates shifted, standing on his paws now.

We will, he said.

Shamira prayed his vow could be kept.

***

"Is Nyla all right?"

Xander jumped, whirling in the direction that the new voice had come from. Battle-weary and marred by sand, blood, and grime, Ingrid took a step closer to him. Her eyes were desperate and her face harried in a way Xander hadn't known possible. At the sight of her, Xander's blood turned cold. They left Nyla alone on the battlefield that had left Ingrid, the Royal Mage and Mage General, looking like *that*? Xander's breath hitched as his panic nearly choked him. Somewhere in the recesses of his mind, he knew he needed to regain control of his own mind, but all common sense and rational thought had left him.

"Nyla? Is she all right?" Ingrid asked again, her voice stronger than it had been only seconds earlier.

Blinking away his surprise at her sudden appearance beside him, Xander managed to say, "Look for yourself."

Shifting slightly, Xander motioned for her to join himself, his grandfather, and Commander Howards around the crystal ball. In the minutes that had passed since Ingrid's and the pumpkies' departure from the battlefield, he'd had about nine near heart attacks. He didn't think his chest could take anymore of Nyla's recklessness before his heart would burst.

He let his eyes fall shut, forcing himself to take long slow breaths through his nose in an effort to regain control of his own mind. Maybe if he didn't know what was happening, he'd be able to get a hold of his scrambling mind. Tamping down on the whispers of his own fear, Xander felt the tension in his chest loosen after a moment.

"What's happened to Cedric? Do we have any word of him?" Ingrid asked no one in particular. At her words, Xander opened his eyes and studied her rather than glance at the crystal ball, afraid whatever sight it beheld would only undo the ground he'd gained over his anxiety. Now that the shock of Ingrid's appearance in the cramped study had eased along with his panic, Xander was able to fully take in the blood and grime dusting her skin, her clothes, and the sand strewn through her disheveled hair. Averting his gaze before his mind had any time to conjure theories of how Nyla might look in person if the Mage General's appearance was any measure to go by, Xander willed himself to pay attention to Commander Howards's response, having never once wondered what happened to Cedric once news of Ingrid's order to retreat had reached him.

"I've already dispatched a team to look for him," Howards explained. "Some of the pumpkies also offered to help them, but so far they haven't been able to trace him. The pumpkies are attempting to follow the raverins now, and Alistair is leading a team to search through the looking glasses to see if the memory of the battle thus far may hold any clues."

The Mage General merely sighed in reply, offering a noncommittal utterance of her approval. Xander's full attention returned to the crystal ball.

Silently, they all watched as Nyla ran. Xander held his breath, uncertain of her plan or the outcome it would produce. The image consumed each and every viewing glass throughout the room, making her desperate flight inescapable.

His heart panged, threatening to cave in on itself.

Alone, weary, but alive and determined.

Surrounded by creatures, Nyla didn't falter, much to Xander's amazed relief. Danger wholly trailed after her and pressed in on her from all sides, but still Nyla ran. The sole focus of the viewing glasses, Xander could see the fire in her eyes where he'd feared there'd be exhaustion. But even witnessing Nyla's own grit and determination wasn't enough to squash the fear brimming and boiling over in Xander's chest.

"Do you really think those are the souls Dinora took 647 years ago?" Xander asked.

"I couldn't say," Ingrid replied, crossing her arms over her chest and staring with a furious intensity into the crystal ball. "But if the legends have been right thus far, I don't see why they couldn't be telling the truth about the souls haunting the Shadow Forest too."

Xander nodded. Everything always came back to those legends. He wondered if Nyla would ever escape them, if defeating Dinora would really be the end of it or if there would still be more to come.

"The boldness of youth with the resolve of someone beyond her years, I do not doubt Nyla," his grandfather smiled ruefully, "but I wonder, do you think she has a plan?"

"Yeah," Xander muttered. "Defeat Dinora."

"Ah, well, at least she's thought this through."

Off to the side where he watched the scene unfold from a viewing glass, Sir Hubert laughed bitterly. "She did say she'd defeat Dinora at any cost."

"But are we prepared for her to pay that price?" Ingrid uttered, deflating as she closed her eyes in defeat.

A shudder ran through the room at the woman's words.

Xander certainly wasn't willing to let Nyla be the price to save all their lives, but what was he supposed to do?

"Lord Huntington!" Edwin's voice carried throughout the room. Xander's eyes snapped to the doorway in time to see Edwin come to an abrupt stop. His friend's eyes surveyed the room, landing on their small group huddled around the crystal ball Commander Howards had set up. "Ah, Lady Ravencroft, you're here!"

All eyes turned in his direction as he stopped just inside the door. Abraham was only a step behind him.

"What is it, Sir Maffis?" Ingrid asked, her voice tight with irritation.

"Shamira wants to establish a Cooperative Circle. She's gathering the pumpkies in the court—"

"Any Casters that can be spared are to report to the courtyard *now*," Ingrid commanded, already stepping away from their weary observation and toward the door herself. Edwin bobbed his head in a nod before retreating elsewhere as quickly as he and Abraham had come. Helpless to do anything but watch, Xander raptly paid attention as Ingrid hesitated, turning to his grandfather. Bowing her head, Ingrid said, "With your permission, Lord Huntington, I would like to create the strongest circle we can to help channel magic to Nyla." Pausing for only a moment, Ingrid added, "It would mean carving sigils into your courtyard's paver stones in order to—"

"Do what you must," his grandfather interrupted. "Just bring Nyla home safely."

Relief trickled into Xander's bloodstream even though his grandfather's words had been heavy. With a sharp nod, Ingrid rushed confidently from the room. His body sagged as the tension eased from his limbs. Maybe Nyla wouldn't be facing Dinora alone after all. There was a way to help her, and everyone was determined to do everything they could, even at the sake of Pemberly's stately appearance. Perhaps it would be enough. Perhaps it would give Nyla the advantage she needed to defeat Dinora, if she even needed one to begin with.

For the first time all afternoon, Xander was beginning to truly believe the battle was not lost, and neither was Nyla.

13. NYLA'S SACRIFICE

Nyla's heart beat impossibly hard against her chest, thumping like it was counting down the seconds until she was utterly alone on the battlefield. She'd started sprinting across the sand before the shield had entirely faded, knowing every second counted.

The moment the magic began to recede, the stone creatures began their vicious attacks. Their screeches clawed down her spine, but Nyla didn't dare let their haunting wails pierce her mind. Pumpkie growls and snarls met high-pitched shrieks in battle as the pumpkies unleashed their magic alongside the lone Caster who'd stayed behind. Nyla couldn't think about any of that. Nor could she think about the clench of longing in her heart that called out in vain to remind her of the future she'd started to plan, the one surrounded by her friends, of people she'd come to consider family, and of the man she didn't want to lose.

Instead, she focused her efforts on keeping her balance on the slippery sand. Wind had blown the ashen sand across the empty plain, heaping it in mounds that made it difficult to traverse as her feet sank deeper in some places.

She and Xander had learned several weeks ago that when magic was drained from the land, it left behind only sand and an ashen landscape. Whatever was here before, it was only sand now. It wasn't even a dried tangle of remains, a shadow of its former self like the patches they had traversed after leaving Caselle.

Nyla thought back to the map she and Ingrid had scried over. She couldn't imagine that this used to be a part of the Shadow Forest, least of all somewhere in its dark heart. But she'd seen where the crystal point had landed on the map Ingrid had spread over the table. It'd shown them that Dinora was in the heart of the Shadow Forest, though it looked more like the Amber Dunelands now. And it was just as vacant.

When she and Xander had come across those few patches of drained land on their way to the Woodlane Manor, she'd suspected Cedric had done so intentionally. She'd thought that he knew of their path and had wanted to leave them with an impression of the threat he and Dinora had posed. Nyla couldn't have known then how right her theory was. Though neither she nor Xander had known the greater of two evils was waiting for them at the manor, Nyla still couldn't comprehend where her decisions had led them all. Had she known then what she knew now…she would've crossed an endless sea to escape the terror she'd unwittingly unleashed upon the world.

No matter how much she wished she could change the not-so-distant past, Nyla knew that the only way to fix things was to go forward.

She'd never outrun these creatures, however many of them remained. They would catch her, and they would attack her, but Nyla was ready. For whatever might come, Nyla would be ready for it no matter how badly her body yearned for rest, no matter how her mind sought comfort, and no matter how her heart longed for a life she couldn't have. She would fight them—she would fight *Dinora*—no matter the cost.

Her cheeks stung with the heat of exertion. She'd ceased to feel her legs. The burning of her limbs had turned numb. She didn't know how much longer her body could withstand the tax on her energy stores.

A shadow loomed over her, morphing with her own. Nyla feinted to one side, stumbling over the sand. The sharp claws of a creature raked across her calf.

Crying out, Nyla fell to her knees. Her hands flew out, pushing against the sinking sand to force herself up, but the creature pounced, holding her down.

Conjuring a shield between herself and the creature, Nyla urged her magic to pry the creature away from her, picturing it flying into the air from the force of her magic.

The creature wailed as it was sent arcing through the air.

Nyla gulped down a lungful of air.

Blasting another creature away, she stumbled to her feet, a hand clasped around her calf to staunch the flow of blood. A horde of creatures circled her like the easy prey they believed her to be.

There wasn't anyone to hold her back anymore. There wasn't anyone but herself now.

Danger couldn't touch the ones she cared about, and neither could she. She could be just as wild and untamed with her magic as these creatures were with their viciousness.

Smirking through her exhaustion, Nyla eyed her adversaries as more stone creatures joined the outskirts of the circle surrounding her. Nyla conjured a ring of razor-sharp energy, igniting it like a ring of fire around her. Writhing and licking, the tongues of her lilac-colored magic leapt at the creatures. Snapping their jaws at it, any creature who dared try to break through her magic cried out in pain. Chips of their jagged stone fell to the ground below like teeth.

Nyla's fingers flitted over the wand in her pocket.

The rigid line offered her the comfort of Astrid's words, and of the wisdom Nyla hoped had been passed down to her by her ancestor. And with that wisdom, Nyla hoped that she could learn from Astrid's mistakes of 647 years ago. She wouldn't let Dinora live.

She wouldn't let the scars of this war live on to haunt future generations, to allow itself to renew its fervor again.

Nyla would end this, once and for all.

Grasping the wand in her hand, Nyla pulled it free from the confines of her pants. She raised her arm toward the sky. The warm metal was heavy in her hands, as if she were brandishing a sword.

Maybe if she'd used it sooner, Sir Ian would still be alive. Countless others could've been saved too. But in truth, she'd been afraid. Nyla hadn't the slightest idea of what she was doing, or what the wand was capable of. And she certainly hadn't remembered it when she'd first wisped onto the battlefield, consumed by the smoke and the daze of overstimulation. But when she had, when her fingers had brushed against it in her search for the energy potion she'd kept stashed in her pocket, Nyla began to wonder if it could change the course of this battle. But the thought had quickly fled her mind in the wake of Sir Ian's sacrifice for her. After that, she'd only known one thing: survival.

But now?

She remembered the stories people told of the Shadow Forest. She remembered the evil sorceress who'd survived centuries upon centuries beyond the knowledge of those storytellers.

Nyla remembered the trails of smoke people claimed haunted the Shadow Forest and the storyteller who'd said that there were those who believed the ghostly trails were the souls taken by the evil sorceress in her quest for power. The storyteller had said that people believed the spirits were cursed to remain trapped in the Shadow Forest until the great wrong committed against them had been righted.

Until this very moment, Nyla believed the only way to do that was to kill Dinora.

But what if it wasn't?

What if, trapped inside these stone creatures, were the actual souls of the people Dinora had killed in her quest for power? What if the stone points of the Shadow Forest weren't just mere representations of these souls, but the actual souls themselves, trapped where they might've once stood?

Focusing her sight until she could see the writhing auras and magical essences around her, Nyla now believed that she had to test her theory that these rock creatures were the onyx-colored stone points of the Shadow Forest, and that those points were the physical representations of the souls Dinora had taken in her greed, if not the souls themselves.

If she were right, Nyla hoped she would be able to separate the magic fueling the creatures from the auras of the damned, thereby freeing them from their torture.

If she were wrong…Nyla gulped. She couldn't give life to that prospect just yet.

Watching as the bleak battlefield morphed into a blinding array of color as she focused her vision, Nyla began to pull the magic from the creatures nearest to her. Sapphire and gray, black and amber, all of the colors she'd come to associate with the Shadow Forest gravitated toward the clear crystal point jutting from the star fixed to the top of Astrid's wand.

As it did, the creatures began to dissolve. Their limbs faded first. The irregular oval shape of their heads sharpened as their jagged teeth disappeared. Silently, the creatures stretched, standing on their hind legs as if rearing up like a sagittarii. The position didn't last long as their awkwardly bent legs morphed into a singular base on which the reformed rock point rested on, nestled in the ashen sand.

The familiar sight made Nyla's heart swell. She never thought she'd be so happy to see the haunting stone points of the Shadow Forest. The sight of them clustered by the Union River used to make her uneasy.

Now, she'd never been more grateful to see a sight such as them in all her life.

More magic flooded the wand in her hands. Glancing up, Nyla's breath hitched as the magical energy began to pool into the sphere embedded in the base of the wand's crescent moon. The emeralds in the metal vines and leaves wrapped around the golden wand glowed, pulsing in time with the magic being consumed by the clear quartz point jutting from the tip of the star molded to the top of the wand.

With a heavy breath, Nyla stopped the flow of magic and lowered her arm. She let her own ring of magic fade. Turning in a slow circle, she created a shield around herself, knowing that more creatures prowled closer to her from the far corners of the sandy plain. Her eyes swept over her surroundings.

Where the creatures had once snapped their stone jaws and clawed at the air between them with their jagged extremities now stood gleaming rock points of the darkest stone.

Heart pounding, Nyla stared at the wand resting in her palm. Magic swirled inside the gemstones, contained for now. Nyla relished in the fact that her theory had been right. The creatures could be stopped if the magic that had brought them to life no longer fueled them.

Staring at them, Nyla realized there was still more to be done. If these rock points remained here, Dinora could just as easily reanimate them. She had to destroy them. As soon as she tended to her leg and regained her breath, she vowed to do just that.

Reaching in her other pocket, Nyla grabbed the healing potion and prayed it would work on the slash across her calf. Her pant leg stuck to her skin uncomfortably, becoming itchier the more her blood dried against the material.

Uncorking the vial, Nyla quickly drank the potion, shuddering as the thick liquid slid down her throat, simmering in her gut. Nyla immediately felt the effects of the potion as a cold tingle trailed down her leg. Twisting around, she gasped as the magic worked to heal the harsh wounds. Nyla squeezed her eyes shut as the potion renewed her.

Relieved, Nyla turned her attention back to the rock points. In the brief time she'd had her eyes closed, a handful of stone creatures had inched their way closer to her. She watched them for a second before tightening her grip on the glowing wand still in her hand.

Focusing on the rock points and the creatures, Nyla was amazed to see the different auras haloing each and every point. Every obelisk had a different aura, whereas the creatures were masked by that writhing energy her magic couldn't stand to touch. Raising the wand up high,

Nyla cast her gaze out to the battlefield beyond. As the magic exploded from the wand at her command, Nyla felt a single tear trail down her cheek.

Taking a deep breath, she whispered, "I hope you find peace."

"There must be something we can do!" Astrid said, whipping her magic at any opponent who crossed her path.

"Like what?" Harrison asked through clenched teeth. His sword clashed against his opponent's, his body shifting against hers as they stood back to back.

Astrid whirled around, sidestepping to get a clear view of Harrison's adversary. Lightning erupted from her hand, racing toward the man's chest. His scream filled the air, shuddering down Astrid's spine like it was the first time she'd ever killed a man. She'd tried to reconcile the feeling, but each and every time she found herself on another battlefield, the more her resolve whittled away.

"Anything," she called over the din of battle, turning to face her king. Her eyes drew to movement over his shoulder. Without hesitation, she zapped the Corvid soldier bearing down on Harrison from behind. "We just have—"

Searing pain blazed through her temple. Astrid pressed a hand to her forehead as her vision flashed white. Harrison's shout was lost to her as the earth shifted beneath her feet. Swaying, Astrid slammed into something hard. Gripping at the metal links of his armor-clad arm as it wrapped around her waist, Astrid gasped, collapsing into the embrace.

Blinking furiously, she attempted to clear her vision.

"Astrid!" Harrison shouted beside her ear.

Breathing heavily, Astrid fought to find some clarity. Her own blood roared in her ears. The commotion around her faded from her mind as the paralysis consumed her.

"T-they're…t-they're s-steal-ing…" she tried to say, but the breath was knocked from her lungs. Her teeth chattered uncontrollably.

Usually, she could still stand. Usually, her body was still her own whenever there was a shift in magic, but this?

This was unlike anything that had ever happened to her before, and Astrid didn't know what to make of it as the cramping in her stomach grew worse. Acid burned in her throat. Somewhere in the far reaches of her mind that had managed to remain her own, she feared she might become sick.

Forcing herself to gulp down air, Astrid closed her eyes. Breathing deeply, she clung to her friend and the stability his presence offered her. Her ears cleared after a moment, though the frantic orders called out to those nearest them were lost to her as one single realization consumed her.

Her eyes burst open. Shouting over the clamor of battle, Astrid gathered her magic. "Shield!"

Uncaring of who stood among those closest to her, Astrid crafted a dome of her lilac-colored magic as large as she could manage in the hopes her magic alone would be enough to save them. Already, she could see all the colors of magic being pulled to a focal point in the distance.

As her call rang out across the vicinity, more Mages added their energy to her shield, fortifying it against the draw of magic being swept from the land.

Her mouth dropped open as she watched the horror unfolding on the other side of their magical fortress. Soldiers and Mages wasted away. Their auras joined the myriad of colors sweeping over the battlefield, their life force drained. Where muddy and blood-stained grass once carpeted the earth was only sand as the last of the sapphire energy faded away, consumed by where she could only assume Cedric and Dinora were gathering it.

"*Sek guds…*" a voice murmured behind her. Astrid cast a glance over her shoulder, finding a Corvid soldier had fallen to her knees, a look of unmasked horror on her face. Tears shone in her fear-struck eyes.

Faintly, Astrid understood the Corvid phrase, through the pounding of her temples and the magic roaring in her blood, and she wholeheartedly agreed with the terrified woman, and the sentiment behind her words. Only by the gods and their grace were any of them going to survive this.

Glancing around the relatively small area of their magical dome, Astrid realized there was a fair mix of Dinora's forces intermingled with their own. Her eyes found Fergus. He watched the destruction on the other side of her magical shield with a grim purse of his lips, his jaw clenched tightly as he stood several feet from her.

"What are we to do now?" Harrison's voice was quiet, barely even a murmur.

Astrid turned her gaze back to the drained landscape outside of their dome. "We pray to whatever gods will listen to grant us mercy."

"You can't mean that," he said.

Astrid bit her lip. She didn't have a better answer for him. None of them, least of all her, had ever seen anything like this before. And if Dinora and Cedric could contain the amount of magic they were gathering…

None of them would see the next sunrise, no matter how strong this shield was.

The world outside stilled. The parade of color seemed to shudder, frozen in place.

Her brow quirked, her mouth agape.

In the distance, the magical energy flared like a flash of lightning. She blinked. And when she opened her eyes only a fraction of a second later, her bones went cold.

"BRACE YOURSELVES!" she shouted over the howling of the wind.

Too much magic.

There was too much magic.

Already, Astrid could see their shield splintering against the assault of magical energy hurtling toward them. Without thinking, she slipped her wand from its sheath at her hip. Nodding to herself as her rational mind caught up with her subconscious actions, Astrid prepared herself for the brunt of the tsunami's impact.

Raising her wand arm, she took a deep breath. The world seemed to slow as she readied herself. Picturing a small hole forming in their defenses, the shield melded to her whim. Reaching out to the wave of magic cresting over and consuming the barren landscape of the battlefield, Astrid guided the energy that found its way into her siphon to her wand.

The crystal quartzes at either end were quickly filled. She hissed but grit her teeth. The wand burned hot in her hand.

Taking a shuddering breath, Astrid closed her eyes. Drawing the energy into herself, Astrid's free hand shot up, expelling the excess magic into their shield and strengthening it against the unending assault.

Slipping across the grass as the recoil of magic traveled through her, Astrid dug her heels into the ground beneath her. A firm hand pressed against her shoulder, helping to keep her upright. Her skin buzzed, unaccustomed to the amount of magic coursing through her veins.

Astrid staggered backwards. As abruptly as the tide of magic had turned on them, so it came to a grinding halt. Saved from falling only by the quick action of the person beside her grabbing onto her, Astrid panted.

Their shield fell with her collapse, exposing an unfiltered view of the world before them. Astrid couldn't focus, still reeling from the magic demanding to burst forth from beneath the surface of her skin.

"I need…I need space," she breathed. "Too much…too much magic."

"Clear the area!" Fergus shouted.

"Y-you too," she grumbled, her head swimming.

"I'm not going anywhere," he said.

Astrid didn't have time to reply, her heart racing too fast, too hard.

Screaming out, Astrid unleashed wave after wave of magical energy into the air against her own volition. Fergus's arms tightened around her. She tried not to hurt him as the magic fled her body, but she had little control over her own breaths, let alone the excess energy simmering in her veins.

Shuddering as one final burst of magic exploded from her body, Astrid sagged against her friend.

Breathing heavily, Astrid uttered, "Fergus?"

He only hummed.

"Thank you for staying."

"Of course," he said. "No one deserves to be left behind, especially not when they just saved everyone they could."

"It wasn't enough," she whispered.

Fergus shifted beside her. His rough hand cupped her cheek, tilting her head ever so slightly to look him in the eyes. "It was. Dinora and Cedric did this, not you."

Tears filled Astrid's eyes. "I should've known something like this could happen."

"You couldn't have. No one could have." Fergus shook his head.

Astrid took a shuddering breath.

"Can you stand?"

"I think so."

Fergus helped her to her feet. "We should check for survivors."

Astrid didn't dare to tell him that there wouldn't be any. Instead, she turned her blurry vision on the battlefield around them and waited for her vision to fully clear. It took several blinks, but when her vision finally did clear, Astrid's breath caught in her throat.

Her eyes widened.

Where once a grassy field had been, there was a rich forest of dark trees with crackled bark. Indigo and navy leaves danced in a gentle breeze. At her feet, where their shield had been, was scorched earth and a perfectly round clearing where the forest did not touch.

"Are you all right, Astrid?" Harrison's voice sounded from behind her. She turned slowly, seeing that the survivors had clustered together on the farthest side of the clearing. The energy of the shield they'd constructed to stand against her expulsion of magic lingered as they let it fade, realizing she'd unleashed everything she'd absorbed from Dinora's attack. "Astrid?"

Nodding absently, Astrid couldn't muster the words to say so.

None of this was here before. The trees, the leaves, the sheet of dark stone beneath their feet…

Just what had Dinora and Cedric done? Was this their intention? Astrid licked her lips.

No. This couldn't have been Dinora's intention.

She'd lost control.

14. SO IT WILL END

A potent silence blanketed the courtyard.

It was as though the world had stopped, frozen from the moment Nyla's voice had echoed from the viewing glasses the Casters had set up in the courtyard at Ingrid's request while they'd all worked to set up and enchant the Cooperative Circle. The glasses had since been removed to help promote a concentrated environment, but echoes of Nyla's prayer replayed itself in Shamira's mind.

"I hope you find peace."

Those words were like the cue they'd all needed to channel their magic, lending it freely to Nyla. It was the only way she'd allowed them to support her in the effort to defeat Dinora.

Myra's report had proven that Nyla was correct in thinking that the stone creatures—the rock points and trapped souls of the Shadow Forest, Shamira reminded herself—were attracted to Nyla specifically.

It was Nyla's hope for those souls and that single realization that had reaffirmed the need for the pumpkies and Casters to gather in the courtyard. Quietly, the magic sigils were etched into the flagstone pavers of the Huntington family's estate, and they'd each taken their place around the circle like spokes on a wheel.

Ingrid had said that Xander's grandfather granted them permission to do whatever was necessary, that he cared only about saving her. Shamira hoped it was a feat they could manage. She didn't know how much she believed in Fate or Its fickle whims, but she knew one thing: Nyla had taken Astrid's magic to heart. And more than that, Nyla had taken this fight, this battle, her role as Astrid's heir, and her quest for vengeance to heart too.

Again, Nyla's words echoed in Shamira's mind. She wondered if the words echoed in anyone else's mind, or if lending their magic to Nyla was simply another order for them.

Peeking open her eyes, Shamira glanced around the vast courtyard. The aura of the conjuring circle glowed dimly. That was good. It meant that Nyla was still alive, that the connection between them had been established, and now all they had to do was gift some of their energy to her and pray that it would be enough.

Beside her, Hecates was utterly still. Glancing to her left, Myra was like a statue. All the pumpkies were.

Across the way, Shamira spotted Ingrid, but she couldn't make out the woman's face.

A few of Pemberly's staff had stationed themselves around the courtyard, on the outskirts of the circle.

She wondered if Xander was among them, or if he'd stayed with his grandfather. Wherever he was, Shamira hoped he was all right. He hadn't seemed in the best of states when Edwin had broken the news of the retreat to them after Talmec's surgery. Xander's panic had rolled over her ten times worse than his bitter grief had when he'd thought Nyla had died battling Dinora at the Woodlane Manor. It hit her worse than when she'd found him speaking with that man outside of the Woodlane Manor's bounds, in the field of tangled weeds and six stacked-stone markers. Whatever he felt for Nyla had amplified his worries and fears since then, but there was nothing she could do to help him except to maybe bring Nyla home safely, and even that Shamira knew she couldn't guarantee anyone, least of all herself.

Shamira? Talmec whined, his voice threatening her concentration.

I'm here, she said. Her tail curled tighter around her paws. *We've set up a Cooperative Circle. Nyla's alone against Dinora.*

Panic overtook Talmec's delusion. *I—*

No, Shamira interrupted sternly. *You will do nothing. You are to heal and listen to Gerri. I will visit when I tire.*

Talmec grumbled, *I can help.*

You've done all your duties and then some, Shamira assured him. *The goddesses will understand, as will Nyla.*

Submission quietly tickled the forefront of her mind. *If you so wish it.*

But Shamira didn't. She wished Talmec was well enough to join them, that he hadn't been so close to death, but she couldn't bear to put him in harm's way again. Not at the expense of himself. She couldn't bear the thought of losing anyone else in this war. It was already enough of a burden on her mind that she *didn't* know and couldn't estimate who they'd lost on that battlefield already. There hadn't been time to gather, to regroup, to assess before the battle or after their retreat. There hadn't been time for anything at all, not even strategy or mourning, for she'd seen the streaks of crimson staining the ashen sand.

Shoving aside these distractions, Shamira dug deeper into her well of magic. She'd give everything to stop Dinora. And that was her choice.

Nyla had made her choice. Talmec had made his. They'd all made decisions over the course of Dinora's short freedom and the threat it posed for all of them. Shamira supposed it was only fitting that Nyla wasn't the only one willing to sacrifice themselves to stop Dinora.

She could only hope her vow was enough to at least save Nyla.

***

"Dinora!" Nyla shouted, turning sharply to face the wall of magic some thirty yards away from where she stood. The wand pulsed in her

147

hand like it was keeping time with her heart. "I thought you've wanted to spill my blood for centuries, but you've yet to show your face!"

Squaring her shoulders, Nyla's eyes narrowed into a glare. The aurora of magic writhed, bursting up from a deep fissure in the earth she hadn't seen before. But then, she hadn't been this close to it before either.

The wall of magic flared as if in response to her words.

Nyla raised the wand once again. Taking a deep breath, she prepared herself to siphon the magic from Dinora's shield.

The magic crackled before she could even begin to pull the fine threads of energy from the wall of raw magic.

Nyla stiffened. She didn't want to know why the wall of energy was moving. As a tendril of magic hurtled toward the wand, Dinora's voice echoed all around her, no doubt amplified by the excess of magic she was wielding.

"Why go to you when you so willingly came to me?" she said.

Ice raced down Nyla's spine.

The wand seared her fingers, burning impossibly hot as she willed it to absorb the magic, unwilling to wait and see what Dinora would do. Nyla's lip trembled, her arm shaking from the effort of remaining steady. All the gemstones, from the crystal point to the emeralds embedded amongst the raised metal carvings to the spherical quartz nestled snugly in the crescent moon, were glowing with magical energy.

You need to expel that magic, Nyla. Someone's voice skirted the forefront of her mind. It could've been Ingrid's, Astrid's, or Shamira's, though she wasn't entirely certain.

Panting, Nyla pulled one of her hands from the wand. Keeping her palm parallel to the ground, she prayed with every fiber in her being that the magic she was about to embrace wouldn't kill her. She gulped at the fear, but didn't balk from it.

Letting the energy flow through her, Nyla accepted it as if it were her own. As she opened herself up to receiving the magic from the wand, she set it free with the hopes that it would return to where Dinora had taken it from—and that it would stay there.

Acting as a conduit between the magic she expelled and the wand that continued to funnel energy through its crystals, Nyla fought to keep her breaths steady. She fought to ignore the chills racing up and down her arms and legs, the buzzing of her veins as the power flooded her. Even as the wall of Dinora's stolen magic crested over her and tried to smother her, the wand consumed the energy in her path as she managed to successfully control it.

"You think you can take from me what I've earned?" Dinora cackled.

"No," Nyla ground out, "but I can certainly return what you've stolen!"

The wall of magic advanced on her with vigor. Nyla's fingers tightened around the wand as she braced herself for the impact of the imposing wave of energy.

"All I need to do," Dinora mused, "is overwhelm you, and you will crumble."

Nyla huffed, glaring at the wave. "That won't be—"

The crystal point at the tip of Astrid's—of *her*—wand cracked. The fracture grew larger, traveling up the length of the wand. The magic coursing through the wand and into her own bloodstream buzzed, growing volatile as the emeralds burst.

Nyla barely managed to form a shield, dropping the wand, before the whole thing exploded. Sharp bits of metal and jagged shards of crystal flew in every direction. The splinters *hissed* against her shield.

The wave of magic cast Nyla in shadow, looming above her. Wide-eyed, Nyla stared up at it for only a second before curling into herself, as if she could shield herself if her magic failed. A trickle of fear wiggled its way into her heart. Nyla stubbornly ignored it, forcing herself to focus on her survival instead.

With what little remnants she'd retained of the absorbed energy from the wand, Nyla channeled it into her shield, strengthening it against the magic crashing down upon her.

Her breaths stuttered. A weight sat on her chest, preventing her from taking in air. Her muscles vibrated from her efforts. A low hum buzzed in her veins, pressing against her mind almost like a telepathic connection, reminiscent of when she'd speak with Shamira across a long distance.

Falling to her knees, Nyla cried out as her magic began to sputter. Her shield shrank, collapsing in on itself under the pressure of the onslaught raining down on it.

She was going to die.

Nyla shook her head. No, she was only going to die if she couldn't think of something to save herself.

With her shield closing in around her, her mind desperately tried to form a coherent thought. The hum consumed her mind, though Nyla found it wasn't unwelcome. In fact, she realized, opening her eyes, it was actually pleasant. Nyla concentrated on it, letting it consume her as the buzz in her bloodstream began to crescendo.

A rush of energy caressed her senses like a cool breeze. Nyla closed her eyes, savoring the feeling like she would a hug. Power sparked inside of her. A surge of energy flooded her, as did the familiar connection of those she cared about.

Nyla's eyes shot open.

We're with you, Nyla.

Shamira.

Her breaths came in short, harsh gasps. Unable to wholly understand the rush of magic flooding her, Nyla forced herself to her feet, growing her shield as she did. Her hands clenched into fists at her sides.

"I will *live*," she seethed. "I will fight."

Taking a deep breath, Nyla let her shield drop. Raising her arms to either side of her, Nyla tilted her head back and let the magic wash over her. She absorbed everything: the magic Dinora tried to smother

her with, the magic flowing into her like a gift, all of it. It renewed her, it gave her a moment to catch her breath, it gave her the sensation of having wings.

But only for a moment.

All too quickly, her body felt like it would burst from the excess of all the magic brimming in her blood.

Energy rippled through her veins, her bones, her very essence until she thought it would tear her apart.

But rather than be afraid, or letting the panic of the mousy voice in the back of her head consume her, she gently guided the energy through her chest.

Redirecting it to either side of her, Nyla pictured it traveling through her body and to her arms. She would be a conduit for this magic, absorbing it only to return it to the universe. It was all she could do. Nyla knew she wasn't strong enough to do anything else with it. She couldn't redirect this amount of magic at Dinora or absorb it for herself to use.

So returning as much of it to the land was the best she could do for now, reserving the magic gifted by her friends and her own to use against Dinora.

The flood of Dinora's magic slowed. Nyla opened her eyes, blinking against the setting sun. Her arms fell, hanging limply at her sides. Observing the crimson trickle flowing toward her, Nyla smirked. This, she absorbed for herself.

"Is that all you can do?" Nyla taunted, throwing her words like an assault across the stretch of sand between herself and the woman whose display of power had failed. Finally able to see the wretched woman, Nyla met her eyes with an unwavering determination. "Do you even know how to wield magic?"

Dinora glared at her. Nyla grinned back at her, watching the woman breathing heavily from atop a raised dais of onyx-colored rock. For as pristine as Dinora seemed, Nyla saw only a tired old woman too weak to wield the magic she'd summoned from the earth rather than the terrifying sorceress her mind had conjured. The dais seemed to have a rippled surface like the frozen waves on a lake, just like the ground in the heart of the Shadow Forest.

Dinora sent a bolt of magic at Nyla.

Nyla raised a hand, waving Dinora's magic away dismissively.

Stalking forward across the now-pebbly sand, Nyla diffused Dinora's haphazard attacks as they came.

Just as she came to stand several yards away from her, fire erupted from Dinora's hands. Nyla halted, watching the flames lick up Dinora's arms.

"You think you can defeat me?" Dinora sneered, straightening to her full height. Her ragged hair framed her face, windswept and as haggard as Nyla had always imagined the centuries-old sorceress to be. "A girl with no family, no training, and nothing to live for, against a queen?"

"I don't see a queen," Nyla said. The spark of her magic flooded her chest, bolstering her resolve. Magic curled around her arm, licking at her fingers. Lifting her chin just a fraction higher, she added, "I see a wretched woman playing games for her own vanity."

Dinora cried out in frustration. Her fire hurtled toward Nyla in a fierce column. Nyla jumped back, bringing her arm up at an angle and forming a shield of magic as if she had a shield of old strapped to her arm, turning her face away.

The heat of the flames blazed across her skin. Sweat beaded along her brow and down the back of her neck. But her shield held. Nyla turned her head to face the flames beyond the barrier of her magic. The flames collided endlessly with her shield, flattening against the surface of her magic and spraying out on all sides.

Nyla pressed her free hand against the shield. Gritting her teeth, she kept her hand there no matter how badly it burned her flesh to do so. Breathing in, Nyla hesitantly reached out to the flames with her magic.

The energy was still there.

Smiling softly, Nyla took the energy like it was the hand of a friend and guided it to herself.

Across the sandy plain, Dinora howled like a deranged cerbertes.

The column of fire shoved against Nyla's shield. Her feet slid across the sand, but she remained standing, widening her stance to better brace herself against her shield. As Dinora's attack strengthened, it increased the amount of energy Nyla was able to harvest from it.

As the magic she'd consumed began to press against the underside of her skin, Nyla relented, knowing any more would make her lose control of it.

Shoving her shield back against the onslaught of fire, Nyla conjured a fierce wind, wrapping it around the column of fire. Pressing her wind down on it from all sides, Nyla smothered the flames.

The fire blinked, wavering. Her brows drew together in concentration. She doubled her efforts to extinguish the fire.

This isn't a duel, Nyla. Do well to remember that. This time, Nyla knew it was Ingrid speaking to her. *Don't be afraid of doing what you must in order to win, to survive. Fight and come home to us, Nyla.*

As the flames sputtered, Nyla realized Ingrid was right. She shouldn't be trying to dispel Dinora's attacks and counter them. This was nothing like her duel with Frederick—this was war. It was for all of Tenebris and all of magic.

Peeling her wind from the fire, Nyla urged the flames to life again, certain of her control over both the wind and the flames. Immediately, she recognized Dinora's bitter and restless energy fueling the flames once more.

Nyla's lips curled victoriously.

Rearing her wind back, the flames erupted wildly. Leaping and dancing on the wind, Nyla created a gust that swept under the pocket of air she'd been manipulating. The fire fanned, bursting vigorously. Tendrils of flame curled back, hurtling toward Dinora as Nyla intended.

Dropping her shield, Nyla thrust her hands out, throwing the wind against the flames to keep them pressed against Dinora. Staying her magic, she fought against the woman's effort to squander the blazing fire.

As her wind faded and the tail of the flames joined the wall surrounding Dinora, Nyla was met with the sight of smooth glass where there had once been sand.

Rallying her magic and guiding it down into her leg, Nyla stomped down on the glass. A crackling shatter traveled up the length of the aisle, producing shards of glass in the wake of where their magics had melted the sand and cooled the earth.

In her mind's eye, Nyla picked up the shards of glass with her energy. The jagged pieces floated in the air, outlined in her lilac-colored magic. Poised to strike, Nyla admired the shimmering shards and the light fractals within them. She nodded sharply. The glittering glass soared forward, sailing through the dust and flames.

Dinora cried out. Nyla's attack had found its mark. Her lips twisted in a sinister smile.

The flames shrank. With their heat extinguished, Nyla took a breath of cool air. She gathered her magic and unleashed it in a fury upon Dinora, not giving another thought to the tatters of the woman's clothes or the splashes of red slashed across her face from Nyla's previous attack.

Crimson energy met her strike.

The two magics collided, pushing against each other to no avail. As one magic gained an inch, the other doubled their efforts and reclaimed their place. Locked in a formidable battle, the two magics reached a stalemate, with neither Nyla nor Dinora willing to surrender.

Nyla's spine flashed with a sharp pain, replaying the memory of her last fight with Dinora. The jarring pang at the memory of striking the stone steps at the Woodlane Manor made her skin crawl. Jitters ran up and down her arms and legs as if she were bound to the manor and all its inhabitants once again.

Nyla clenched her jaw, her lips twisting in a determined frown.

This time was different. *She* was different.

Grunting, Nyla searched for every scrap of magic within her being. Her mind sought out the connection between herself and those who were so generous to join Ingrid and Shamira in lending her their magical energy.

Nyla called upon that magic and held it just beneath the surface of her skin. Her muscles shook with the effort of standing the longer Dinora's magic shoved against hers. Breathing heavily, Nyla's magic began to slip. Dinora's energy overtook the ground between them.

Nyla licked her lips, panting as her muscles tensed. She let her magic slip, allowing Dinora's magic to overtake it. The heat of Dinora's attack brushed against her skin, barreling toward her. Instinctually, Nyla's hands fanned out in front of her, her fingers splaying like a spark. Her magic and that of her friends' flared up inside of her, just as she'd intended it to. The crimson tide stopped, shuddering for only a moment. Nyla breathed out.

She pictured her magic hooking into the tidal wave like fingers and began to pry it apart. Cleaving it in half, Nyla's arms moved of their own accord. She ignored the worried whispers of her mind and leaned into her instincts. Nyla grunted from the exertion. Seeing Dinora in the space she'd created down the middle of the ray of magic, Nyla flicked her hands. The magic splayed to either side, dissipating as she tossed it aside.

Growling, she whipped a fierce attack at Dinora. Dinora conjured a quivering shield. The fierce plum-colored energy slammed into the so-called queen's flimsy means of protection. Shattering upon impact, Dinora was left bare to Nyla's attack. The evil sorceress stumbled back a few feet as the magic slammed into her.

Nyla inhaled a sharp breath. She unleashed another blast of her magic.

Scarlet energy erupted against hers with a renewed fervor. Magic erupted from the ground, flaring up behind Dinora and casting the world in a dim shadow. Nyla tilted her head back, watching the magic waver and dwindle.

Her feet began to slip back against the sand.

Sucking in a breath through her gritted teeth, Nyla reached the trembling threads of her magic out toward the energy and eagerly began to collect some of it for herself.

She wouldn't let Dinora defeat her like this. She wouldn't let herself be killed. She would live, she would fight, she would find happiness again.

Dinora would not win.

Vengeance

Astrid slammed her fists down on the wooden tabletop. "You all need to leave, protect the other villages. The Corvids are on a rampage, and with the magic she stole from the land, it will be nearly impossible to defeat her."

She leaned forward, bearing her weight on her hands. Unable to meet the eyes of those around her, least of all Fergus and Harrison, Astrid fixed her gaze on the heaps of scrolls and parchments covering the majority of the solid table.

Tension filled the air until it seemed to sit like ashes on her tongue. She watched as those gathered for this desperate war council glanced at each other, murmuring a few words under their breath to those nearest them, before the static silence returned.

Astrid's heart pounded against her chest. Unshed tears stung her eyes.

This was the only way as far as she could see—as far as the Brewardt Clan's High Seer Rhigul had seen before his death.

"And you, my lady?" Sir Huntington asked.

"I will stay here and try to stop her." Raising her gaze, she met the eyes of one of her most trusted friends, knowing exactly the task she would burden him with. She could only hope she'd gotten the spell right, having never tested it before, and that it wouldn't leave her dearest friends with any adverse effects.

She'd never had a reason to use the spell before. Until now.

When—*if*, she tried to convince herself—if Dinora and Cedric killed her, a select few would receive a vision. In that mental projection of herself, Astrid pleaded the case for a society to keep watch over Tenebris, to keep it safe should Dinora and Cedric ever free themselves from their bond to the Woodlane Manor should she fail to eliminate them.

"You'll die," Lady Remington said grimly.

"You'll all die if you stay here," Astrid breathed, nearly pleading with them now. "If I can stop her in her tracks, and save the rest of Tenebris, even if I lose my life in doing so, then so be it. That is the oath we've all taken, and I will not let any of you remain here, only to be killed for vengeance. We all know why she is doing this, why Corvus is. Let's not make more bloodshed than there has to be." She straightened, hoping she could convey some semblance of the resolve she couldn't quite muster for herself.

Meeting the eyes of each and every one of the people she considered to be her dearest friends, Astrid held her breath. Exhaling slowly, she forced herself to meet Fergus's eyes and then Harrison's.

They'd all lost so much already, the three of them especially. She'd lost the man she'd wanted to spend her life with, the man who she'd preemptively assumed wanted the same thing. Fergus had lost countless men throughout this war, and Harrison…

Harrison had lost his one true love, and was on the verge of losing his country—and his crown.

Lord Bailey was the first to nod his head solemnly. As her words seemed to take root in each of their minds, his nod was passed onto the next until they'd all in some way acknowledged their acceptance of her plan.

Silently, they all filed out of the room.

There weren't any words to dispel the weight of the burden Astrid had bestowed upon herself, or the burden that came with being aware of her plans—albeit, a small part of them—in the case of the others.

She followed them through the barren halls of the Woodlane Manor and all that was left of its splendor now. Whatever hadn't been moved to the new capital would have to remain at the Caradels' secondary estate forever or be destroyed. Whichever consequence would come to pass first.

They'd intended to leave today anyway, Astrid reminded herself. Though little did the others know she'd never intended to go with them to safety.

Watching sadly as Sir Huntington and Lady Remington stopped to pick up their bags from the pile they'd made beside the door, Astrid lingered on the grand staircase. Fergus and Harrison joined them, neither quite looking at her for too long. Astrid understood their indignation. She hadn't warned them of her plan. She hadn't asked permission, and she certainly hadn't asked their opinion of it.

"Safe travels," she called as the first of her friends waved from the door and left, a fragile smile on her face. Slipping her hand into her pocket so Harrison and Fergus wouldn't see the tremor there, she gripped the banister even harder. Realizing the king and his guard were lingering, she offered what bare hope she could muster, no matter how dishonest it was. "I'm sure we will meet again."

Harrison turned, meeting her eyes with a fiery gaze. "I pray we do."

Astrid bobbed her head, clutching the vial in her pocket. Forcing herself to take a step down the stairs, and then another, she slowly approached her king.

Quietly, she said, "I'm sorry, Harrison. But we both knew this would happen eventually."

"Did we?" he whispered harshly. "I don't think self-sacrifice ever crossed my mind."

Her eyes flooded. She blinked away her tears, twisting her lip to keep it from wobbling. "It hadn't crossed mine until recently."

"Endpoint," Harrison said in a tone that was decidedly not an inquiry, but Astrid nodded anyway. Endpoint, indeed. She would make certain that cursed battle was the end of this all, however it might damn her. Gripping her shoulders, he leaned closer to her, his eyes warming earnestly. Desperation shone through his vigorous concern. "We can find another way. You don't have to do this. We—"

"That's just the thing," Astrid whispered, her voice a choked rasp. "'We' can only sacrifice so much before we've lost everything. If…if I can stop them here, today, then it will all be over. The kingdom will survive."

"Or they could win, and you'll have died for nothing."

"Or I will succeed and buy the kingdom time to live." Astrid took his hands in hers. "You could live. All of you."

Harrison pursed his lips. His eyes held hers, intently studying her gaze for something Astrid wasn't certain of. Giving her hands a firm squeeze, his hands slipped from between her fingers.

Cradling her face gently between his hands, he said, "I'll make certain you are always remembered."

Astrid cracked a small smile. "I never cared much for what my legacy would be. I cared only for making it."

"Consider it made then." Harrison smiled back. "A most formidable woman, a woman to fear not because of her strength, but because of her fierce love."

"You make me sound godly, like an epic hero of legend," she murmured.

"You are." His thumbs swept over her cheekbones. "If your plan works, you've more than earned that status, and I'll make certain to immortalize your actions in legend."

"That really isn't necessary," Astrid tried to argue.

"Perhaps not in your mind, but mine's made up." Harrison's gaze swept over her face. "I wish you victory."

"I wish you a long reign, my liege."

Shaking his head, Harrison chuckled. His fingers slipped from her cheeks as he took a step back. "There were days I bitterly regretted ever making you our Royal Mage, and then my right hand, but in my heart, I know including you in this court, and in our confidences, was one of the soundest decisions I have ever made as king."

Astrid laughed. "I'm glad to hear it. I only hope that this last act hasn't disparaged that opinion."

"No," Harrison shook his head solemnly, "it's only reaffirmed it."

Any response Astrid could've uttered caught in her throat. Biting her lip, she glanced away. She said the only thing that was left to say. "You should go, before the kingdom is without its king too."

"Should there be lilacs at your memorial?" Harrison asked, turning away from her and starting for where Fergus waited by the towering oak doors. His voice was tense, as though he could barely find the strength to speak anymore. "It is one of your traditions after all."

Fergus snickered, the tension breaking from his posture.

Astrid scrunched her nose. "I've always hated them."

"Then we'll have forget-me-nots, if it pleases you," Fergus offered, closing the short distance between them as Harrison shouldered his pack.

"It does," Astrid said, accepting the commander's hug. Squeezing him maybe a little harder than necessary, she whispered, "Take care of him, will you?"

"It'll be harder without you," he whispered back, "but I'll try. No one could replace the queen, or your friendship."

Astrid pulled away. "I don't believe that."

Fergus shrugged in response, stepping away. Tears brimmed in his eyes, though he vainly tried to blink them away. Nodding firmly as if to assure himself of his own strength, he said, "We'll see."

Astrid swallowed the sob sitting in her throat. If they exchanged any more words, if she gave in to the impulse that begged her to reach out to the two people she'd come to hold most dear just to avoid the inevitable any longer, she would change her mind. She had no choice but to follow through with her plan, and there was no breaking that resolve.

Watching them walk through the door made her chest cleave open. Slowly, Astrid forced herself not to follow them, watching as her friends and allies strolled into the dazzling sunlight of a changed world.

Taking one final glance to immortalize the glow of the sun's rays over the new plum-colored leaves of her home and a changed kingdom, Astrid reluctantly retreated back to the staircase. Sitting heavily upon a step, Astrid's shoulders sagged. Withdrawing the vial from her pocket, she murmured the fateful words that would make her body the vessel of a great burden. Even as she did so, she hoped beyond her ability that her bequeathed magic would never be needed, that the future would have a better world, a world of peace and prosperity, and of love returned.

Closing her eyes, Astrid drank the potion. Shuddering at the thick, slimy texture, she added "better potions" to the list of things she hoped waited for the future. Deflated, Astrid took a deep breath as she pulled herself to her feet.

She didn't know how much time she had until Cedric, Dinora, or the both of them would come to claim their victory here, and there was still much for her to do. She needed to act on the rest of her plan, or else none of this would be worth the effort.

Calling upon her magic, Astrid stood in the middle of the foyer. Her eyes fell shut. A pulsing orb of plum-colored magic grew between her hands. As she spread her arms wide, the magic grew. She pictured it wrapping around the manor, spreading it through each and every crevice. She didn't dare extend the weaving tendrils out into the courtyards, not wanting to allow Dinora and Cedric more free rein than they deserved.

By binding them here if she couldn't defeat them, Astrid hoped it allotted Harrison, Fergus, and the others the time they needed to find a permanent solution. She'd be sure to cast a power suppressant too, so Dinora and Cedric couldn't continue to steal magic from the land.

Smirking, Astrid's magic surged. She'd devise a spell so strong they wouldn't be able to draw on the depths of their magic.

She'd make it so her spell was stronger than even the wrath in their hearts. Surely, that intention would make the bond between them and the manor, as well as the power suppressant, nearly unbreakable. Cedric and Dinora would never plague this earth again. She would make certain of it.

As Astrid's thoughts rallied her will, her magic unfurled around her. Her energy penetrated the very essence of the Woodlane Manor. Astrid could feel the tickle of its tiny inhabitants—the insects, mice, and webkers within its walls—as if they crawled along her own skin. The breeze against the manor's frame raised goosebumps on her arms and legs.

Vaguely, she wondered if this added torture was perhaps too cruel.

In answer, her mind supplied her with the memory of the colors of the land's magic flowing toward the Mage calling to it, stealing it from where it belonged. The wave of magic recoiling from whichever of her enemies was foolish enough to steal it crashed over her mind next. She remembered how Dinora and Cedric had stolen the life from those outside her shield, how even the Corvids weren't safe from their quest for power and victory.

Astrid gritted her teeth. Nothing she could do would be as wretched as what had happened on that battlefield.

Let Cedric and Dinora know discomfort. Let them know humility. Most of all, let them know a fraction of the suffering they had caused.

Her magic crested, rising to the topmost floors of the Woodlane Manor, save for her workroom. She would conceal it and charm it with the strongest protection magics she could muster, but she wouldn't dare let them—let *him*—near that room ever again.

Perhaps she should just burn the contents of her workroom, as that seemed to be the surest safeguard. But for now, she needed to complete the bond. When that was done, Astrid would…

She would think of some way to safeguard her wand and the memories archived in her looking glass so they couldn't be used against

Tenebris, against the desperate feats of enchantment she was attempting here today.

Astrid stumbled as her magic flared. Shivers wracked her body. The tickle of the manor's unseen inhabitants had grown to an itch that she fought against in vain. Her magic finally receded back to her. Astrid's chest heaved. She fought against the buzzing haze over her mind, knowing her work wasn't yet done. There was still the talisman to make that would transfer the bond from her to the pair of enemies she expected to arrive at any moment. Astrid shook her head. Slowly, the buzzing subsided, and she was able to focus again.

The bond between herself and the Woodlane Manor was complete.

Dinora and Cedric might deserve this punishment, but as Astrid drew the transfer sigil on her skin—turning her body into a talisman of its own—with a delicate hand and a cool magic like ice, she hoped no one else would ever suffer a torment such as this.

15. A HALO OF POWER

Nyla's legs burned with the effort of leaning against the magic threatening to overtake her. It didn't matter how much energy she consumed, how much she was given by the winds of a gentle grace bestowed upon her thanks to the scores of Casters and pumpkies lending her their magic. All of that energy flowed through her, caressing her bones, and with the rate of her waning energy, Nyla feared their strength was the only thing keeping her upright against the force of Dinora's attack.

Crying out in frustration, Nyla coiled her muscles. She gave herself a split second to think this through, knowing she couldn't withstand this attack for much longer. So she did the one thing she knew could save her in this moment. Diving to the ground, Nyla let her magic drop.

The blast of Dinora's magic soared over her as she rolled to the side and onto her knee. She thrust her hands out. A fierce wave of energy erupted from her hands. Her magic burst forth like lightning and barreled under the current of Dinora's sustained attack.

Looking through the flash of her magic, Nyla watched as it struck Dinora, knocking her from her stone pedestal and sending her flying through the air.

"I will live," Nyla muttered to herself. The words echoed in her mind until it became a chant, rallying her blood and her courage, her strength and her magic. It rallied her fear too, and the hatred she'd reserved for Dinora and Cedric until she was utterly consumed by a power she'd thought had waned. "I will fight for this life, for mine and for all the lives of those you've destroyed. I will never stop fighting for them!"

Her shout rang clear through the empty battlefield. Heaving herself onto her feet, Nyla's heart pounded against her ribs. Her chest heaved. Her magic didn't stop, and Nyla didn't attempt to leash it. She let it pound into Dinora, hoping for all the world that this would be the end of it.

Forcing herself to remain steady even as those breaths didn't feel like enough, Nyla carefully made her way over the scorching sand, closing the distance between herself and Dinora.

A wind licked at the sand, whipping it up around them as she focused on her attack. Wisps of her hair swept over her face, catching on her eyelashes and irritating her eyes just like the fine particles of sand flying through the air.

Nyla stopped mere feet away from Dinora. She lay exactly where she'd fallen, unmoving and undisturbed. Stopping the flow of magic, Nyla coiled the energy around her arms, weaving it around her fingers to keep it at the ready, untrusting of what her eyes were seeing.

This couldn't really be it? Dinora wasn't really dead?

Relief unfurled itself in her gut and wove its way through her limbs. The tension that had carried Nyla for so long began to crumble. At her feet was the solution they'd all been praying for. But why did she feel so empty? Why had it brought her nothing but an empty relief? Nyla cast her senses out, watching the wavering essences of the land's magic. Her eyes stuttered over the aurora of magic jetting up from the long fissure in the ground. Doubt curled in the pool of her stomach.

If Dinora was dead, why was the land's magic still so agitated?

Dread tensed Nyla's limbs. Something was definitely wrong. Turning her head, Nyla surveyed the ashen landscape, squinting against the harsh sunlight reflecting off of it. Maybe killing Dinora wasn't enough to appease the magical energy of the land? Maybe it needed to be tamed or returned to where it belonged before things could feel more final, before the world could return to normal and breathe a sigh of relief again?

The wind whipped furiously. Magical energy still wavered throughout the landscape, writhing and ebbing with no apparent direction that Nyla could discern. Nyla's brows furrowed.

It shouldn't have been so easy. Or maybe she just hadn't expected it to be? Nyla wracked her brain for some sort of assurance, but found nothing other than disbelief. If Dinora was truly dead, she believed something inside of her would feel more settled, that everything would feel at peace.

But still, Nyla couldn't explain what was happening now, why there was an inkling of disbelief pulling at her gut and pounding in her temples.

Nyla's gaze returned to the form of the woman at her feet. Nyla's eyes widened. Dinora's body faded, disappearing into a wavering stream of scarlet-colored smoke. Nyla haphazardly conjured a shield as the illusion ceased to exist.

Harsh magic collided into her side, shattering her forming shield. Nyla gasped, the breath knocked from her lungs as she went flying backwards from the force. She didn't even know she'd fallen until the soft sand began to burn her nose from accidentally inhaling it as her breaths sputtered at the harsh landing, nearly gagging from the pain of being blasted by Dinora's magic.

Nyla groaned. Her eyes closed against her will. Wheezing and coughing, Nyla knew she needed to overcome her disorientation, but the pain searing outward from where she'd been hit flared and throbbed like a burn. Twisting against the sand, Nyla laid a careful hand where she'd been struck.

"Ah!" she huffed. Her skin stung to the touch. A ripple of agony flooded her. She couldn't move a muscle. No matter how much the itch, the urgency in her mind screeching at her to move, to call her upon the magic lying beneath the surface of her skin, Nyla couldn't move. She peeled her eyes open. Frozen by pain or by the daze of finding a ragged Dinora with sand in her frazzled hair and dried blood across her face staring down at her, Nyla couldn't move a muscle.

"What happened to fighting?" Dinora asked with a sick tease in her voice despite the rasp Nyla hadn't noticed before. "I thought you'd never stop?"

Looming over her, Dinora watched her with a sneer that couldn't quite hide her pain or exhaustion.

Nyla struggled fiercely, or at least she wanted to. She couldn't so much as wiggle her fingers, let alone roll over or leap to her feet.

Dinora must've bound her as she'd frozen Shamira that day in the courtyard. Panic began to flutter in her throat. Helplessness threatened to sink into her bones.

"I would say it's a pity," Dinora said, glaring down at Nyla, "but it's quite all right. I always knew I would get what I needed in time."

Utterly powerless, Nyla could do nothing as the earth rumbled. The sand quaked and shifted beneath her as a ring formed around them. Dinora called the magic up from the earth below. The dazzling energy surged upwards from the newly formed cracks in the ground, dancing angrily as Dinora fixed her concentrated gaze on Nyla.

Nyla's mouth ran dry. Her breath caught in her throat.

A stab of ice shot through her veins, clawing at her insides. It raced through her bloodstream, furiously collecting the magical essence within her and draining it from her body. A numb vacancy clawed at her insides, shredding muscle and tissue as her magic slipped from her, stolen by the icy force sweeping through her.

Her eyes rolled to the back of her head. A white flash consumed Nyla's vision, plunging her into a blind state. That prickle of ice sliced through her weak attempts at guarding her magic, blasting through her meager defenses and shattering them. An aching throb pounded in her temples. Her breaths became shallow. Her lungs labored futilely for even the briefest reprieve of air. Nyla thrashed against Dinora's magic holding her in place. She fought against the force creeping through her body, but to no avail.

All the magic being funneled through her, and all the magic that was hers and had been bequeathed to her from Astrid, was being consumed by the ice.

Dinora was stealing her magic.

And there was absolutely nothing she could do about it despite the fists pounding against her mind, the fight she so desperately wanted to put up.

Nyla. A smooth voice, a determined voice, a voice full of a conviction her addled mind couldn't remember, skirted over her consciousness, parting the haze of pain. *You can fight this. You* must *fight this!*

She gasped. Nyla's vision burst with a bright light like a spark. Her sight cleared, and all too suddenly, she was aware of the magical essences all around her, though her mind couldn't comprehend the new clarity she was presented with, still consumed by the icy grip of Dinora's thievery.

Live, Nyla. Remember to live.

The voice was like a lifeline, pulling her from the depths of the ice drowning her in a void of where her magic once was.

Nyla closed her eyes in concentration.

The empty numbness that had consumed her turned into a slow tingle in the tips of her fingers. The tingle grew stronger, traveling up her arms until the power buzzed inside her chest.

Nyla let it consume her until the power flooded her veins, pushing back against the ice.

Power surged inside of Nyla.

She latched onto it, letting it pull her up. Sand fell from her as she rose, haloed in the glowing light of the magic. As Nyla rose into the air, magic crackled around her, sparking and fizzling from the raw intensity of it.

Opening her eyes, Nyla's smile glowed with confidence. Lilac-colored magic radiated from her hands. "Did you really think you could steal my magic and I wouldn't do anything about it?"

Nyla didn't let the infuriated woman answer, unleashing the surge of magic upon her, scorching the sand and the spot where Dinora stood.

Dinora batted her magic away, rearing up for her own attack. Nyla struck her, throwing bolts of her magic one right after another.

Nyla gritted her teeth, throwing a shield up and shooting her magic around it, striking at Dinora's legs now.

Dinora sent a tidal wave of magic at Nyla. It loomed, imposing its will over the waning daylight until it was all Nyla could see.

Exhaling, Nyla's feet found the ground again, sinking into the sand. She brought her hands up, fanning out her fingers. Inhaling, Nyla moved her glowing hands to the side, picturing the wave of magic curving around her. Swishing it around her body as she gained total control over the crimson energy, Nyla flung it right back at Dinora, using her own momentum against her.

With a growl, Nyla added her own force to it.

A sandy haze billowed up from the earth. An unforeseen consequence of the disturbance caused by the magic flowing over the landscape, Nyla squinted in an attempt to peer through the dust.

Nyla extended her awareness, sharpening her senses until she could see the fine whirls of magical energy surrounding them—and the energy fueling Dinora's attacks.

She focused most of her efforts on stealing the energy from Dinora's attack. As she did so, the intensity of Dinora's magic weakened, the column of power growing thinner.

Dinora howled. A surge of power rippled through Nyla as she consumed Dinora's power to rekindle her own attack. Nyla pictured that energy cycling through herself, her body becoming a conduit for the essences once more. As she consumed the energy, ripping tendrils of it from the agitated crimson magic, she channeled it back into her own counterattack.

Dinora sent a long, chaotic burst of flame toward her. The heat of the flames kissed her skin, but Nyla redirected her magic to form a shield against both assaults. The flames hissed and crackled against her shield.

Nyla fought to take another step forward.

She leaned against the magic pushing against her like a fierce wind, struggling to stand her ground. Another step, and her hands clenched into fists.

Through the wind and distortion of her shield, Nyla could see Dinora smirking victoriously.

"No matter how much you steal from me, there will always be more," she half-cackled.

"No more," Nyla seethed, clenching her jaw.

Nyla wouldn't let her steal any more magic. She wouldn't let her devastate the land like she'd done 647 years ago. She wouldn't let the evil sorceress from the legends destroy the lives of those who dared to exist in her path for vengeance. She wouldn't let Dinora ruin more lives, more families, or entire countries all for the sake of an undeserved revenge.

Nyla's shield faded at her whim. Opening her arms, Nyla embraced the magic for what she knew would be the last time.

Dinora cackled. "You think that's going to work? Aren't you tired of trying the same old strategy?"

"No." Nyla smiled. Walking calmly forward, Nyla consumed the energy in her path, sending it through the connection that had formed between herself and the Casters and pumpkies who'd lent her their magic. "I'm only getting started."

Dinora raised her brow, snarling at her.

Nyla jerked her chin, sending Dinora flying. The sorceress's attack stopped. Nyla severed the connection between herself and the Casters gifting her their magic.

Thank you, she said to them. *But I no longer need it.*

Dinora scrambled to her feet just as Nyla stopped before her. The sorceress's wild eyes met Nyla's, but she didn't falter, watching as the haggard woman attempted to scramble back. Not allowing her the chance to move, Nyla bound her limbs in shimmering bonds of magic. They glowed with all the colors of the land. Sapphire, indigo, scarlet, emerald, rust. There was the color of the sky and the most delicate shades of gray and amber. There was light the color of a rare sunbeam, and black, the color of the onyx-colored pebbles and forest floor in the heart of the Shadow Forest. There was orange the color of a fiery sunset, much like the one blazing low in the sky now. But there was lilac too, and plum, the color of Nyla's magic—of Astrid's magic—the color of her strength and the ferociousness of her intent.

"I don't know what you expected to happen here today," Nyla said, her voice echoing with the raw power she'd held onto. "But I always knew I would kill you."

Resignation

Astrid folded her arms against her middle, drawing her legs up to her chest. Maybe she'd been wrong. Maybe they weren't targeting the Woodlane Manor and had changed their course to where the others had fled, believing she was among them. Her stomach clenched with worry at the thought. If that were the case, all of the energy she'd expended here had gone to waste. But that wasn't like Dinora.

She wanted power, and Astrid had it.

She was quite possibly the only one who could stand against her, and Dinora knew it too. She wouldn't change her course, not unless she had something to ensure her victory—something Astrid highly doubted the wicked woman had obtained. Staring out across the front courtyard, she shifted against the stone pillar she sat beside.

If something didn't happen soon, she would undo the bond and reconvene with the others. It didn't do to sit here and wait while countless others could be suffering at Dinora's hand.

Forcing herself to her feet, Astrid stretched and turned toward the towering steeple doors of the manor. The air fizzled. Stopping as the static rippled over her skin, Astrid found her hand curling into a fist at the discomfort flashing across her bones. Astrid turned slowly. Her breath hitched in her throat. Cedric appeared in the courtyard, but the sensation of him wisping onto the manor's grounds had felt like she'd been stabbed in the gut.

Quickly regaining her composure, Astrid straightened her shoulders and stood proudly, her chin held high. Stalking down the steps, she pinned Cedric where he stood with a glare. Every ounce of hatred, of contempt, of bitterness she had for him burned in her chest.

"So you've come at last," she drawled, stopping several yards from him. His face was cast in shadow, the setting sun not daring to bless him with its rays. But as she took in the look on his face, Astrid wanted to scream. She wanted to scream, to order him to fight her. She wanted to throw wave after wave of magic at him until there was nothing left of him to have existed at all just so she could finally do something about the betrayal burning in her heart, and the hate that had sprouted where once she'd held love. He had no right to look at her—at anyone—with such painful sorrow on his face. "Where's Mother Dearest? Don't tell me you've come because she's abandoned you."

"What are you doing, Astrid?" Cedric asked quietly.

Her fingers curled into fists at her sides. Folding her arms over her chest to hide her rage, she said, "What I've always done."

Cedric glanced around then, as if he expected others to be lurking in the shadows, waiting for the perfect moment to strike.

"This isn't an ambush," Astrid said. "I'm not you, or Dinora. I wouldn't stoop so low."

"I know," he said.

Astrid narrowed her eyes, watching him curiously. Where was Dinora? Had they planned to attack separately? Was she off destroying the new capital while Cedric distracted her?

Even as the thought crossed her mind, Astrid wanted to ask him if this was what he'd intended to happen, if he'd earned his mother's love or if all the awful things he'd done for her admiration still wasn't enough, if he was still a failure in her eyes. Astrid wanted to know if his betrayal had hurt him too.

But instead, she shoved aside her personal feelings and gathered up her sense of duty.

"Well?" she started, raising a brow and tapping her fingers against her arm. "What have you come here for? To kill me? To steal my magic? To take the Woodlane's?"

Cedric nodded slowly, as if in hesitation. He opened his mouth to say something, but Astrid didn't dare let him, unwilling to see if he was capable of telling only lies.

The words 'were you ever true' formed on her tongue, but she swallowed them.

"Go on then," Astrid called instead, spreading her arms to either side of her, "kill me."

Cedric clenched his jaw. Taking a step forward, his voice cracked as he asked, "Why didn't you leave with the others?"

"And miss the opportunity to say hello?" Astrid scowled. "Now that's just rude." She let her arms fall against her sides. She couldn't keep her hatred for him from speaking for her. The longer their encounter dragged on in this seemingly endless fashion, the more Astrid realized she needed to free herself from her lingering feelings. It wasn't just Cedric she hated, but herself as well.

She hated herself for having loved him as deeply as she did. She hated how her mind couldn't discern what might have been treachery and what might have been genuine. She hated the fact that she'd made him her apprentice, teaching him everything she'd learned of magic from her predecessor, for sharing secrets most Mages would never know existed.

But most of all…she hated the part of herself that still loved him, and wanted him to come back to her, to beg for forgiveness and desperately explain his betrayal. She hated how there was a part of her that hoped he'd come and promise to show her what she'd meant to him even if there wasn't a chance at all that she could love him again.

Astrid took those feelings and let them slip into her veins as surely as her magic did. She channeled them into her words as her magic rallied within her. Grabbing hold of all she'd ever wanted to say to him over these past seasons, she snarled, "Although I suppose it's much crueler to betray someone who loved you! It's cruel to use them and deceive them and use what they've taught you to hurt innocent people!"

Her heart pounded in her ears as she hurled a bolt of fierce energy at him. Startled by the attack, Cedric conjured a translucent shield of his scarlet-colored magic. From behind its radiance, she saw him frown. His eyes flashed with a mix of condemnation and offense.

"You want to talk about betrayal and innocent people?" His shield vanished completely. "Fine, let's talk about it then! What about Corvus? What about us?"

Astrid gritted her teeth. There wasn't any sense of comradery in the memory he tried to invoke, as they were both children during the rebellion that had granted Tenebris and Eurland their independence from the Corvid Empire. She'd heard Dinora say similar words before, and wondered just how many of them Cedric believed in himself, or if he were only echoing his mother's sentiment in an effort to be a son worthy of her pride.

She whipped another attack at him, begging the question, "And waging this war is supposed to fix that?"

This time, Cedric met her attack with a weak show of magic. Why was he practicing restraint? Why not attack her outright?

The tender brush of his fingers tucking her hair behind her ear ghosted her face as if he was really standing before her to do so. Astrid clenched her jaw. She had no desire for her mind to betray her too by replaying their times together, of the kisses they'd shared or the dances spent laughing at something the other had said, whispering secretly to each other as the orchestra played in the background.

Gathering the bulk of her magic for a bigger attack, Astrid froze. The air rippled, making her feel as though she'd been stabbed. Dinora appeared beside Cedric.

Astrid's lungs heaved with the breath she took. The world stilled. Raw energy radiated off of Dinora, her aura filled with energies that didn't belong to her.

"What have you done?" Astrid seethed. She knew exactly what Dinora had done, that she'd stolen more magic from the land, but it didn't stop the tremor of outrageous disbelief from simmering in her veins. Her hands balled into fists at her side. "Do you have any idea the fury you've unleashed upon the land?"

Dinora clicked her tongue. "Oh, how cute. You think I care. Did Tenebris care what they unleashed upon the Corvids?"

Astrid knew the previous war had seen its atrocities. She knew it had been bitter and abhorrent, but this? What Dinora and Cedric had done? Her blood boiled. Nothing could ever come close to the horrors they'd committed.

"And stealing the land's magic, killing innocent people, going *against* Corvid law, you can justify that?" she shouted, her voice rising in volume and severity the more she argued. "Convince yourself you're not doing exactly the same things, worse things, than what happened during the Ten Years' War?"

Dinora rolled her eyes. "As lovely as this has been, Astrid, dear, Cedric and I have places to be." She tossed her hair over her shoulder and made to turn around.

Astrid's nostrils flared. Taking a deep breath, she thought about the spell, invoking the words that would activate the transfer of the bond between herself and the Woodlane Manor. The sigil she'd drawn on her skin pulsed in time with her heart, burning as though it were aflame.

She sent her magic, and with it the bond, at the pair on a gentle wind. It was enough to draw Dinora's attention to her, for when Astrid unleashed her second attack a heartbeat later, Dinora met it with a force of crimson-colored magic that knocked the breath from Astrid's lungs.

She'd known conjuring that bond and creating those spells and the wards protecting her workroom had drained her, but Astrid didn't know just how drained she was until her feet began to slip against the stone pavers.

Whining low in her throat like a growl, Astrid turned her face away from the bright light. Attempting to regain her stance, she shoved against the torrent of magic. The column of energy cracked. All the colors of the land's magic burst, filling the air.

Blinded by the light, Astrid attempted a shield.

Something hot struck her in the chest, knocking her off her feet. Her eyes burst open. She couldn't breathe. Gaping, Astrid's vision sparked and wavered. Groaning silently, one single thought crossed her mind, the final part of her plan, the phrase that would bind their magic for good.

As the final word crossed her mind, her lungs sputtered, and the world beyond her vision faded.

16. WISPS OF SMOKE

Xander couldn't breathe. In fact, it was highly possible that there wasn't any air left at all. The walls of his grandfather's study closed in on him. An oppressive heat made beads of sweat form on the back of his neck, which only trailed down his spine and added to his discomfort despite the chills running down his arms and burning his hollow chest.

"What happened to fighting?" Dinora's snide voice echoed from the crystal ball. Beside him, Commander Howards shifted. Xander could almost hear the debate that was undoubtedly whipping through her mind, as it was likely the same urge flitting through his. If he had magic, Xander would've already wisped onto that battlefield and launched every last bit of magic he had at Dinora, no matter the cost to himself. "I thought you'd never stop?"

Xander didn't want to watch as Dinora loomed over Nyla. And yet he couldn't tear his eyes away from the crystal ball, too frozen by the fear in his mind as the memory of Issie's death and his own helplessness in the present moment warred for his attention. Caught between the battle raging over his mind, Xander couldn't help but watch through a numb haze as Dinora stood over Nyla. He didn't know what she was actually doing to her, or how it affected her, but to him, all he could see was the subtle twitch of Nyla's fingers, her limbs, her body. She was trying to fight; he just knew it. Fighting against whatever Dinora was doing, Nyla hadn't given up. And if she hadn't given in, then Xander needed to believe in her. They *all* needed to believe in her.

"Maybe I should…" Commander Howards started. Seconds ticked by after she'd trailed off before Xander realized she wasn't going to finish her thought. Part of him wished she had, if only to know he wasn't the only one who wasn't willing to sacrifice Nyla no matter how much she seemed capable of fighting.

"I would say it's a pity," Dinora's voice came again, "but it's quite all right. I always knew I would get what I needed in time."

Xander's hands clenched at Nyla's weak scream. He couldn't quite make out what all was happening within the crystal ball, but he'd seen enough. He couldn't imagine what Dinora was doing to her, or the pain she must be in, only that the torture seemed to go on for an eternity. As Nyla's body jerked this way and that against the magic Dinora must've been attacking her with, he turned his head away.

But no matter where he looked, his eyes were met with the same image. Every viewing glass displayed the same heart-wrenching image of Nyla's struggle against Dinora.

Glancing back at the crystal ball, Xander set his jaw. His throat tensed, nearly choking off the too little air he managed to inhale. Watching as the magical energy shifted around Nyla and Dinora, he saw Nyla's eyes roll into the back of her head. Xander flushed at the sight. Dread filled his gut as emptiness wholly consumed him.

The whispered prayers of those spread throughout the room fell on his ears. Xander had never been very faithful, but he too found himself praying to any god who would listen. He found himself praying to Fate, an entity he didn't wholly believe in until he'd met Nyla and had witnessed her journey to this very moment firsthand.

His heart thundered in his ears. He prayed the Cooperative Circle Ingrid and Shamira had established was keeping Nyla alive. He prayed that that magic would save her and give her the strength to fight whatever this was.

He begged, and prayed, and he pleaded with his own life, but still, Nyla didn't rise.

She'd gone utterly still by the time his mind had gone silent.

"Commander Howards," his grandfather murmured. "I think it's—"

A harsh gasp rattled from the crystal ball. Nyla's eyes burst open. Or so he'd thought. From her eyes, a brilliant light flared. Bright and dazzling, that light consumed the crystal ball, sparking. Panic trilled in his heart. Unable to explain what was happening, Xander could only watch as the light faded. And as it did, the unveiled scene made his heart stutter.

Goosebumps trailed down Xander's arms and legs. His knees went weak, watching Nyla take another breath, a calmer breath, a steady breath.

As though the breath was knocked from his own lungs, Xander watched as power flared around Nyla and she rose into the air. Crowned by a halo of magic, Nyla's eyes opened. Her lilac-colored magic pulsed from her hands. Confidently, she said, "Did you really think you could steal my magic and I wouldn't do anything about it?"

At her words, Xander sank to his knees in relief. Letting loose a breath, he tried to ease the burning of his chest, nearly panting as his whole body went slack from the sheer hope overwhelming him. Nyla was alive. More than that, Nyla had power.

Nyla was going to win. Really and truly, Nyla was going to defeat Dinora. There could be no other outcome, Xander hoped.

Dinora unleashed a torrent of magic at Nyla that she returned in kind. Locked in a furious battle, Xander could only watch and hope that Nyla could withstand Dinora's attacks and remain unscathed, especially as the tide of crimson magic turned to scorching flames.

But Nyla stood firm against it. A shield of lilac-colored magic was the only thing keeping her alive. Xander didn't know how she'd remained standing, let alone how she managed to keep her shield intact as she fought for every inch she traveled across the stirring sand.

Unable to stand, Xander found himself leaning closer to the glass orb as if it could absorb him and bring him to the scene unfolding before his eyes. As if sensing his anticipation, Xander's grandfather laid a hand on his shoulder, but Xander didn't dare take his eyes from the crystal ball. Inch by inch, Nyla drew closer to Dinora. Inch by inch, his heart pounded against his chest, watching as the person he cared most about faced impossible odds.

Inch by inch, Nyla battled against the force of magic slamming against her shield.

Xander gasped, losing his breath. Nyla's shield disappeared.

It hadn't faded, nor had it broken. It simply vanished.

A foul curse fell from Xander's lips. His heart plummeted, spiraling in a freefall he couldn't stop. Realizing that Nyla had made the conscious decision to let her shield fall, Xander watched as Nyla lifted her arms to either side of her and seemed to accept the stream of magic just like she'd done during her duel against Frederick.

Dinora's cackle clawed at his ears. "You think that's going to work? Aren't you tired of trying the same old strategy?"

"Nyla," he breathed, "please, please, *please* have a plan."

Xander didn't know whether he was begging her or praying. Absently, Xander reached for the chain around his neck. His fingers found the ring he kept there, twisting it as his eyes remained fixed on the final confrontation. There was no mistaking it. He knew it, Nyla had planned it, and Fate had no doubt orchestrated the whole thing.

"No," Nyla said calmly as she took a steady step forward, easily wading toward Dinora as if the ferocious stream of magic were nothing but a gentle breeze reviving her. "I'm only getting started."

A mist crept over the landscape as Nyla progressed across the sand. It whirled and seemed to reach out to Nyla, though she paid it no mind. Xander wondered if she even noticed it. He couldn't explain what it was, or whose magic was causing it, if it was even their magic to blame for it.

Dinora's stream of magic wavered, crackling and fizzing. Slowly, Xander watched in wonder as the ashen sand began to turn to onyx. His lips twisted, fearing the worst as his mind thought of Dinora's creatures.

But as twigs—saplings, he realized—began to sprout from the ground, breaking through what he could only imagine was a sheet of the darkest stone, Xander knew.

Nyla was doing this.

She was absorbing the magic of Dinora's attack and redirecting it back into the land, exactly as she had done during her duel with Frederick. While she'd been working with Ingrid, and before the earthquake and the orders had been given to prepare for battle, Edwin had explained to him that redirecting magic was risky, and that it was very easy to be consumed by the energy you were absorbing if you didn't expel it in equal proportion. It was difficult to find that balance, especially in battle when most people would think to absorb and hold some of the energy they were consuming.

It was about timing, he'd said.

Xander hoped Nyla knew this. But as the heart of the Shadow Forest came to life around her and she closed in on Dinora, Xander could only assume that she did.

Power radiated around Nyla, ebbing and flowing like the tide. Brilliant and steady, Xander watched as she came to a stop. Bands of magic wrapped around Dinora as Nyla stood before her. The Shadow Forest flourished, and all was still except for the tendrils of shadows weaving between the newly grown trees, encircling Nyla and Dinora.

Xander swallowed hard. This was the moment he hadn't realized he'd been dreading all day long.

This was the burden he knew had plagued Nyla, the revenge she'd sought since breaking the bond between herself and the Woodlane

Manor. But still that voice in the back of his mind insisted Nyla wasn't that sort of person. Nyla wasn't like that.

Xander held his breath, afraid of the question his mind posed next: was she?

A chill raked down his spine at the words Nyla spoke next. "I don't know what you expected to happen here today, but I always knew I would kill you."

***

Magic rushed back to her, buzzing through her veins. Shamira's eyes flew open. The fizzing air of confusion wafted up her nostrils. The Cooperative Circle flared, glowing brighter with each passing second.

Thank you, but I no longer need it.

Shamira poked at the bond between Nyla and the circle, only to find it fading.

Nyla had reversed the flow back to them and was closing off the connection, but why?

"SOMEONE GET ME A VIEWING GLASS!" Ingrid shouted as the magic sparked before it cut off completely. The circle went cold in an instant.

Servants and soldiers wearing indigo cloaks or plain chainmail rushed to fulfill her request, but all Shamira could think about was Nyla, now wholly alone on that battlefield.

What should we do? Hecates asked. *Do we go to her?*

Shamira blinked, staring but ignorant of the courtyard before her until his voice had skirted over her mind. *I don't know.* Her eyes landed on the fountain. *But I'm not waiting for that viewing glass.*

Slowly shifting to her feet, Shamira wavered. Blinking against the faintness that threatened to collapse her, Shamira took a tentative step. Stars winked in her vision. She pressed on. One slow step at a time, she pressed on until Shamira reached the fountain in the middle of the courtyard.

Staring into its depths, relief wound its way through her heart. There was still water in its basin. She could imbue the water with magic and achieve the same effect as a viewing glass, or a looking glass if she so desired. The only real difference between the two was the intention of the one enchanting it, and, in this particular instance, all she wanted was to see Nyla with her own two eyes.

Raising a heavy foreleg, Shamira gently laid her paw against the surface of the water. A sage glow swirled through the water, causing gentle ripples throughout the basin. A golden-brown magic joined hers next. Hecates stood beside her, adding his magic to her efforts. The water clouded over with their magic.

Shamira held her breath. Soon enough, the water cleared and, in its place, was the image of Nyla consuming the vast amount of magical energy Dinora was actively blasting her with. Or rather, *trying* to blast her with.

Is she...? Hecates uttered in disbelief. *She is.*

More pumpkies joined them, crowding around the fountain. Shamira glanced to either side of her, noticing how servants, soldiers, and Casters had all gathered around behind them, standing on the tips of their toes to see into the fountain.

Scanning the courtyard, her eyes landed on Ingrid. The woman hadn't moved from her spot in the circle. A gray twinge had overtaken her aura. Shamira wondered just how much magic she'd given to Nyla, and if she was even able to stand from the drain of all that she'd expended.

Ingrid didn't notice her stare, too consumed by the scene most likely playing before her eyes as her sole attention was fixed to the hand mirror clutched in her hands.

Shamira had thought the courtyard was silent before, but now?

Now it was as though sound didn't exist. It was as though the whole world had shuddered to a stop and was holding its breath, waiting for the battle raging so far away and yet all too close to home to end.

***

Lifting her chin, Nyla raised her hand. Her magic glowed a dark plum. In the last rays of light cast by the low-hanging sun, she could just make out the wavering aura of the land's magic and all its colors on the fringe of her magic. She stared at it for a second, realizing the weight of what she was about to do before she shoved the notion aside.

Nyla had known it would come to this. Everyone had.

She couldn't afford to wait a heartbeat longer. She couldn't afford to make the same mistakes that were made 647 years ago.

Pressing her lips into a grim line, Nyla set her magic upon Dinora. Nyla shredded her aura, ripping her magical essence away in tatters just as she'd torn apart the creatures. The wisps of magic faded in the air just as Dinora's creatures' essences had.

With each tendril of her magical essence Nyla tore from her aura, Dinora let out a howl, struggling against her bonds. Hissing and spitting like Nyla imagined a cornered pyrosa would, Dinora thrashed. Her shrieks grew louder and more gut-wrenching with every fiber Nyla ripped from her aura.

"All these centuries," Nyla said, her voice echoing with the raw power humming inside of her, waiting to burst forth. Licking her lips, Nyla began to release the magic she had accumulated, giving it to the land beneath her feet. A shadow loomed in the corner of her eye. As her gaze flitted to it, Nyla was overwhelmed by a sense of gratitude, of peace, of wholeness. She watched as each tendril of Dinora's essence she ripped from the wicked woman's aura gave life to the barren landscape. Delicate sprouts grew and blossomed into young saplings; buds bloomed and displayed flowers Nyla had never seen before as she began to dispel the magic she'd consumed alongside Dinora's magic. Around her, the Shadow Forest began to bloom anew. Her gaze flicked back to Dinora.

"All these centuries, and all you've done is stew in your bitterness." The more magic she released, the less her voice echoed like an almighty being's. "You've been so focused on reclaiming the past, on gaining power, that you've completely missed the chance to live. Do you ever regret that?"

Dinora didn't answer. Nyla hadn't expected her to as she finally went limp in her magical bonds. Nyla let the bonds fade, watching the glow of Dinora's aura dim and sputter as she ripped into the core essence of it now. Splotches of writhing darkness recoiled away from Nyla's magic. Gritting her teeth, Nyla concentrated harder. A dark indigo now, her magic persisted.

With each wisp, Nyla released the burden on her shoulders.

Chest heaving with each breath, Nyla conducted her magic furiously. Dinora's whimpers didn't register as such to her ears. All she heard was the roar of a fire long since extinguished, the terrible rush of wind from a vision granted to her by magical waters, and the voice of the woman who'd asked her to live for her country.

She heard the voices of her siblings arguing over the rules of a game, the accent in her mother's voice as she sang, and the mystique dripping from her father's voice as he told them of his adventures when he'd return home after a long journey.

Nyla heard the screeches of the tormented stone creatures and the haphazard orders shouted over the tumult of battle.

She heard the quiet assurance of a friend and felt the promise of a gentle kiss to the top of her head as she'd fallen asleep. The sincerity of a promise that they'd be stuck with each other all their lives flooded her memory next.

Most of all, she heard the pounding of her own heart racing and leaping, thrumming with energy even as her shoulders ached and her legs burned from the effort of even standing. Sweat drenched her skin, making her clothes stick to her uncomfortably, but none of it mattered as the sickly aura shrank with each wisp of Dinora's life force she peeled away.

A strange eagerness consumed her. Fueled by rage and indignation, Nyla's magic tore into Dinora's essence with a fervor she didn't think was entirely her own design. Something curled in her blood like possession, like she was empathetically affected by the anger and a thirst for vengeance belonging to another being. Its rage simmered in her blood, its hatred shadowed her heart, and its righteousness guided her magic.

Nyla didn't know what to make of it.

That was until a cool mist kissed her skin.

It called her attention to the forestland around them. Smoke wavered and billowed between the dark, crackled trees of the regrown Shadow Forest. Tendrils weaved their way toward her. Before they could reach her, they faded. The smoke seemed to flood the space between the trees in the renewed Shadow Forest around them.

Taking it all in, Nyla understood. All this time, she'd been right— and so had the legends.

The Shadow Forest was haunted. Not by vicious souls, but by the victims of an evil sorceress who'd stolen magic from the land and indiscriminately stolen the essences of those who'd opposed *and* supported her.

The people who'd believed those souls needed to be freed were right. But Nyla knew now that this was the only way to free them, to set right the great wrongs that Dinora had committed against them.

Nyla jumped, startled by a cool touch of air landing on her shoulder like a hand might. She didn't dare turn to look, not when she was so close to destroying Dinora's aura. Just a few more slices of her magic, and Dinora would be nothing but a grim nightmare in her memory.

Taking a deep breath, Nyla envisioned the final ember of Dinora's essence flickering out like a smothered flame. As her mind commanded, so it became before her very eyes.

The last of the smoke hiding in the shadow of the trees faded as the last light of Dinora's aura extinguished. Nyla heaved a sob. Exhaustion flooded her all at once, nearly bringing her to her knees if it weren't for the immediate shock of feeling the cold hand tightening its grip on her shoulder.

Turning sharply, Nyla's breath hitched. The magic crackling at her fingertips faded. Tears flooded her eyes.

"Astrid?" Outlined by a pearly aura, Nyla couldn't stop the tears from falling as she took in the ghostly sight of her family—Astrid and the family she'd known and loved and lost to that cursed fire—standing behind her.

Had they been there this whole time? Had they watched as she'd… Nyla's mind couldn't form the words to say what she'd done.

She'd wanted to kill Dinora. She'd wanted to kill Dinora that day at the Woodlane Manor and had been nearly prepared to do so when she'd thrown her knife at her, but today?

No matter how prepared Nyla had thought she was to kill Dinora, she couldn't stomach the actual consequence of doing so on her conscience. Destroying Dinora's aura might have been a despicable thing to do, but it seemed about the only thing Nyla could do that didn't make her stomach completely rebel against her.

She'd only wished now that she had been the only witness to the darkness of her soul, that her family had been spared from seeing her do something that had already begun to haunt her mind—and her heart.

Warm tears freely trailed down her cheeks. Overwhelmed by grief, pained by the sharp exhaustion grating against her every move, and plagued by the weight still settled on her shoulders, Nyla wavered. She didn't know if she would ever be able to let go of her family if they were truly here with her right now.

They couldn't be real, but still her heart clenched.

"Our darling girl," her mother said, reaching her arms out to her. Nyla desperately desired to run into her embrace, to feel the comfort of her mother's arms wrapping around her, but knew she couldn't. And even if she could, she didn't think she should, not after what she'd done. A shudder wracked through her body with her sobs. Her knees buckled. The weight of this seemingly endless day finally crashed down upon her. Nyla took in the faces of her family as a horrid numbness consumed her. Numb from exertion, from her tragic deed, from the weariness of her heart, Nyla couldn't comprehend how her family stood before her now.

Her hysteria was broken halfway through by a sob.

"I'm sorry," she murmured, her voice strained. "I didn't—"

"Shh." Her father hushed her soothingly, coming to crouch down beside her. Nyla's lips trembled as he laid a gentle yet weightless hand on her shoulder. They were real. Gone, but still present. A physical manifestation on this earth, but intangible and untouchable. "We know. You were very brave, Nyla, and no matter how terrible it may seem, we will never reproach you for it. We understand. More than anyone perhaps, we understand."

Nyla stared back at her father. His eyes shone with a pained expression that sent a pang through Nyla's heart. She understood that his pain wasn't because of what she'd done, but because of why she'd had to do it—why she'd had to kill Dinora. And just as he understood why she'd done as she had, Nyla realized why there was pain in his eyes now. No parent wanted to see their child face such terrible trials, no matter the outcome. No *loved one* wanted to witness someone they loved face something so burdensome, especially on their own.

Nyla's gaze shifted to the rest of her family. Derek offered her a solemn nod. Lydia's eyes were made even brighter by the opalescent sheen of her ghostly presence. Westley stood just apart from the others, as if he'd meant to take a step toward her, but had decided better of it. As their eyes met, he gave her a sad smile that twisted the guilt in her gut, remembering their last encounter when he'd given her the clue to find Astrid's journal at the Woodlane Manor.

Observing her family through tear-studded eyes, Nyla didn't know what to do or say. She didn't know what to think, only that she never wanted this to end, even if she had to forfeit her soul to keep this moment, to keep them by her side for only a little while longer before it was time to say goodbye.

"I know that look," Astrid said. "But we cannot stay, Nyla. We will fade, but know we will never be far away from you."

"We'll always be right here," her father said, caressing the back of her head with a cool hand, "and here." At this, he laid his other hand on her heart, as he cupped her cheek with the other.

"I know," Nyla whispered, swallowing against the bile rising in her throat as he pulled away to return to Ma's side.

Lydia began to fade. Nyla's lips twisted, threatening to let another sob break free as Lydia stared at her with tears streaming in her wide eyes. "I don't want to say goodbye yet!"

"Oh, Lydia," Nyla murmured. "It's not goodbye. It's...see you later."

"Promise?"

"Does a niphony sing?"

Lydia grinned, a sight that twisted Nyla's heart just before her sister faded away.

"We'll always, always, *always* be here for you," her mother said. "Remember that, Nyla. Love is for forever."

"I will," Nyla whispered, curling her hands against her knees and taking a deep breath despite the tension in her throat.

Pa and Derek waved at her, fading quickly.

"Promise me you'll live a good life, so that when the time comes, and you join us, you won't be upset when I reclaim my Harvum crown?" Derek asked, grinning despite the dash of sorrow in his eyes.

"I have my whole life to practice," Nyla said. "That crown is mine."

Derek faded, though his laugh lingered in Nyla's ears.

Ma's body began to waver. Seeing his wife begin to fade as well,

Pa wrapped his arm around her shoulders and pulled her into a side embrace. Nyla watched them fade away with soft smiles on their faces.

"I love you!" her mother called, blowing her a kiss.

Nodding solemnly, her father said, "You've grown up so much. You should be proud of yourself, our darling girl."

Nyla numbly raised her hand to wave goodbye. Sniffling, she wiped at the tears staining her face. Her eyes flicked to Astrid and Westley. As she met her twin's gaze, Westley offered her a small smile that wasn't altogether sad.

"I'm sorry I can't stay longer," Westley said, finally coming to kneel before her.

Nyla studied his face. They'd had the same eyes, once upon a time anyway. But their face…Nyla smiled, hoping the battle and the exhaustion and the stress of the last few weeks—of the last two years since the fire—hadn't changed the one thing she and her twin had in common.

"It's okay," Nyla whispered hoarsely. "I didn't know…I didn't want you to see that, but I'm glad to see you all."

"I'd never let you go through something like this alone. You know that."

"I know," Nyla breathed, remembering how often Westley would begrudgingly join her schemes or console her when she needed it. "It's just been so long, and with everything that's happened…I have no idea what to do now."

"You can do anything," Astrid said. "Just as you always could have."

"Yeah." Westley grinned. "You have a whole life to fill with happiness and memories and…actual adventure! Even if you do nothing with your life, try to be happy, and live for us."

"I'll try," Nyla cried earnestly, sniffling as Westley wrapped his fading arms around her. "That's a lot of pressure to place on me, though."

"It really isn't," he laughed, "not after this. This will be the worst thing you ever face. I just know it."

The cool air of his hold faded. Nyla sat back on her heels, watching as he faded away, bowing slightly to her and flashing her a bright smile. "Don't let your life slip through your fingers, foolishly waiting for your time to bask in the sunlight. You'll be waiting forever if you don't seek the sunlight out."

Nyla nodded, her throat too tense to speak.

"But most of all," Astrid said, crouching in front of her and taking both of her hands in hers in a way that almost felt real and solid, "be selfish. You were wholly prepared to sacrifice yourself to stop Dinora, and you nearly did. Reclaim your youth, Nyla, and lose yourself in its ignorance."

"I don't think I can," she sniffled, her nose stuffy now that she'd stopped crying. The air rippled behind her.

Astrid's gaze shifted for a second before fixing her eyes back on hers. Her eyes sparkled. "I think, with a little help, you'll remember what it's like to be young."

Nyla opened her mouth to ask what she'd meant by that, but Astrid disappeared in a blink. It was as though she'd chosen to return to the realm beyond, unlike the rest of their family, who had faded against their wills.

Her heart sank at the thought. Caught up in the memory of times not long past, Nyla didn't hear the desperate shuffle of footfalls behind her.

"Nyla!"

Nyla gasped. Glancing over her shoulder, she found herself tearing up all over again. Her heart swelled at the sight of him, beating faster than she thought possible. She barely had any time to look at him and convince herself that he was real before he was steps away from her. Xander was here, and that was all that mattered to her fractured mind right now.

"Xander!" Her body started with the spark of her mind, stumbling over herself to get to her feet. Barely managing to do so, she jolted forward and threw herself into his ready embrace. Burying her face in the crook of his neck, her legs collapsed, wholly depleted of the strength to remain standing. But it didn't matter.

She was safe.

17. A Quiet Jubilation

Xander tried to catch his breath, watching as Nyla's power withdrew and Dinora slumped to the ground. A chill ran down his spine at the scene displayed in the curvature of the crystal ball. Six figures stood behind Nyla. If he had to wager a guess, he assumed—no, he *knew*—it was her family. They glowed with the same translucent opalescence as Issie had when she'd appeared to him as a ghost at the Woodlane Manor. The mist of the Shadow Forest cleared, vanishing as easily as it had come, and in its place was a clarity Xander hadn't realized was missing from the world.

It was over now. Nyla was safe, and Dinora was finally defeated. They could—she could…What were they going to do now?

Xander found himself frowning at the question.

After all these weeks, and all that they hadn't known, this question seemed to gut him the most.

Ever since he'd met Nyla in the outskirts of Halberry in the middle of a thunderstorm—a storm that didn't seem so bad, now that he thought about it in comparison to the threats they'd faced since then—and she'd pulled him to safety, riddles were all they'd known. From trying to decide if they could trust each other to the visions Fortune Falls had shown her to the discovery of her magic and their travels to the Woodlane Manor, there had always seemed to be a path laid out before them.

But now?

Xander focused his attention back on the crystal ball. Only two figures remained beside Nyla now. A boy with curly hair and a round face, and the woman with silver hair who'd tried to end this threat all those centuries ago. His heart clenched, watching Nyla with her brother and Astrid. He wanted to be there with her—he wanted to be there *for* her.

"Please," he begged, addressing no one in particular. His eyes landed on his grandfather. "Let me go to her. Please."

His grandfather and Commander Howards shared a glance before fixing their gazes on him.

"You understand that you have yet to face the consequences for letting Cedric escape?" his grandfather said.

Xander's mouth went dry. He knew he and Edwin still had to face the punishment for the circumstances that allowed Cedric to escape, but he would've thought his grandfather would understand. Numbly, Xander nodded his head.

"For Nyla, I will let you go," his grandfather said slowly, "but know this. I will not protect you from whatever punishment Lady Ravencroft deems fit for your and Sir Maffis's negligence."

"Thank you." Xander bowed.

His grandfather clapped his shoulder. "Bring her home, Xander."

Commander Howards raised her hand, but Edwin stopped her. "Let me."

A silver glow emanated from Edwin's hand as he raised it. Turning to Xander, Edwin said, "Tell Nyla I'm glad she's all right, if you find the time."

Xander opened his mouth to ask what he'd meant by that, but couldn't get the words out before his body flushed and seemed to pull itself apart, only to fuse back together seconds later. Blinking harshly, Xander stumbled. Glancing around, he found himself in the heart of the Shadow Forest. Turning on his heel, Xander's eyes landed on the two women across the way. His heart thundered in his ears.

Astrid noticed him first and seemed to smile. With Nyla's back to him, he couldn't make out if she were all right, only that her clothes were dusty and that her hair was in tangles. Blood crusted her clothes, making his throat tighten.

"Nyla," he breathed. Astrid disappeared. Beginning to run toward Nyla now, Xander called out her name. Stumbling over the slippery sheet of onyx-colored stone, he'd practically flown toward her thanks to the grace of Balmae's blessing.

At the sound of his voice, Nyla straightened and glanced over her shoulder at him. When her eyes met his, his chest loosened with relief. As she scrambled to stand, Nyla's silver hair shifted, catching the waning sun's rays in way that made it appear darker. "Xander!"

In the few precious seconds it took Nyla to get to her feet and for him to get within arm's reach of her, Xander was able to get a good look at her. Grit and blood painted her torn clothes. Sand speckled her hair. But the thing that most concerned him about her disheveled appearance was the torn side of her shirt, and the oozing gash he barely caught sight of as Nyla lurched toward him. Xander braced himself as Nyla threw herself at him. Carefully, Xander wrapped his arms around her, his heart pounding against his chest at finally being able to see her safe and sound—though not unscathed. Her hands fisted in the material of his shirt as she buried her face in his shoulder. As if she couldn't hold herself up any longer, Nyla collapsed against him, sobbing into his chest. Xander smoothly followed her lead, allowing her to slump against him as he lowered them both to the hard ground.

Shifting ever so slightly, he made certain his hands were nowhere near the nasty gash on her side. His lips pressed together tightly at the thought of it, and all the other injuries she might have sustained that he hadn't noticed, and at the realization that he was utterly incapable of doing anything to help her in this moment.

Incapable of all but one thing.

"I'm here," Xander murmured against her hair, cradling her gently.

Nyla sobbed, heaving. She didn't say anything, though Xander didn't expect her to. He only let her sob, staring across the dim landscape at the crumpled body mere yards away.

Xander didn't know if it was his imagination or if it was actually happening, but Dinora seemed to be shrinking, or disappearing.

Nyla stiffened in his arms. As Xander soothed her again, Ingrid and Sir Hubert appeared in front of them. More Casters appeared throughout the woodland. A handful knelt around Dinora's body, obscuring it from view.

"Nyla?" Ingrid asked softly. Approaching them, Ingrid crouched down and reached a hand out. Hesitantly, Ingrid pulled her hand back, never touching Nyla. "Nyla, are you all right? Do you need a Healer?"

Nyla shook her head. Her sniffled words were muffled against his shoulder. "I'm fine."

Ingrid squinted. Her eyes raked over Nyla slowly before meeting Xander's. Concern shone in her grave eyes. Xander shook his head slightly.

"Just…give us a minute?"

Ingrid nodded curtly. Straightening up, Ingrid turned away from them. Xander watched her as she briskly strode across the onyx-colored rock and exchanged a few words with one of the Casters examining Dinora's body.

Ingrid turned back around. Her face had turned grave as she surveyed the assembled crowd. Her gaze landed on him, on Nyla.

"Dinora Kashar is dead." Her voice carried through the grove. "Her body will be enchanted so that the proof of her death does not fade like the centuries that have passed since her natural lifespan and the excess of magic she has exerted."

Silence pierced the Shadow Forest. No one cheered. Instead, Xander noticed their gazes turn toward the woman hiding from the world in his arms. An air of mournfulness rippled through their gazes before Ingrid ordered them to carry on about their business.

As the general shuffle of movement happened around them, Nyla took a deep breath, calling his attention back to her. Slowly shifting, she pulled back just enough so he could look at her. Exhaustion marred her face. Her eyes, normally so bright and full of life, were dull. Xander delicately brushed some sand from her forehead. His mind spiraled as he vainly grasped at something he could say to help ground her, to assure her that she was safe, that it was over. But nothing came to mind except his own need to make certain that she was at least okay.

"Nyla, are you—" Xander's gaze flitted back to her face, studying her a little more closely.

Shock struck his core.

Brushing back Nyla's hair, he ran a gentle hand over the tangled strands. "Your hair!"

"What about it?" Nyla whispered, her brows knitting together as he cupped her face.

Xander shook his head, smiling softly. He brushed away specks of dirt and tears, explaining, "It's turning auburn."

A light flashed in Nyla's eyes.

"There you are," he murmured. "I was starting to get worried."

Her lips twitched. "I'm still worried."

"Are you hurt?" he asked, already knowing the answer, or at least what it should be. His gaze drifted back to her side.

"A little..." She cringed. Her eyes fell shut. Quietly, she added, "I just want to go home."

Xander froze, uncertain what she meant by 'home.' "As soon as you're healed, I promise I'll help you get home, wherever that is."

Nyla blinked open her eyes and smiled softly. "Could I...do you think your grandfather would mind if I stayed at Pemberly for a while?"

"I don't think anyone would mind at all." He smiled back.

Nodding weakly, Nyla swayed. Carefully readjusting them, Xander let her lean against his chest as he pulled her into his lap. Closing her eyes once more, Nyla said, "I'm really glad you're here, Xander."

"I thought we've been over this," he replied softly, tucking her against him more securely but being mindful of her injuries. "Neither of us is about to be rid of the other any time soon."

Nyla hummed, melting against him. "Wake me up if anything important happens?"

"Sure," he lied, already planning on cutting down anyone who dared to disturb Nyla from her rest.

Watching until her breaths became even and deep, Xander let out a shaky breath. Ingrid strode over to them again, glancing over Nyla and meeting his gaze.

"We should get her back to Pemberly," she whispered. "Let me look at that gash. I want to make sure it wasn't inflicted with infected magic."

Xander slowly moved his arm from around Nyla's waist, granting Ingrid permission to observe her.

With pursed lips, Ingrid knelt in front of them. Closely examining Nyla's wound, she said nothing. A soft, rosy glow emanated from her hand. Nyla turned her head into Xander's shoulder, but otherwise didn't wake.

"There," Ingrid said under her breath. Taking one last look at Nyla, she whispered to Xander, "No Healer necessary, though she'll still need plenty of rest and food to counter the magical drain of today."

"I'll see to it," he vowed.

Ingrid smiled. "I expected nothing less. Now, I'll send you both back to Pemberly. We'll take care of things here. You just focus on Nyla's care."

Xander nodded, unable to form a word of assent as his own energy began to wane.

Nyla was safe. She was safe, and she was going to be all right.

Danger had passed her by. Now all there was to do was figure out what came next. For her, for him, for them—if they chose to stick together, that was.

Staring down at Nyla, Xander hoped that they did. He couldn't imagine a bright future without her in his life.

Standing, Ingrid waved her hand. Her blush-colored magic sparkled in the air between them. Xander closed his eyes against the tilting of the earth beneath him, still unaccustomed to wisping.

As the ringing of his ears faded, the gentle crackle of a fire washed over him. Opening his eyes, he found that Ingrid had wisped them into the Lavender Room. Nan and his grandfather stood beside the stripped bed, prepared as though Nan had expected the worst upon Nyla's return to Pemberly.

A sharp gasp had Xander turning his head to find Merry jumping to her feet where she sat in the seating area of Nyla's room. Her hands covered her mouth. Tears gleamed in her eyes.

"Nyla's okay, Merry," Xander whispered. "Ingrid healed her before sending us here."

"Still," Nan said quietly, creeping over to where Xander knelt on the floor with Nyla still in his lap. She laid a gentle hand on his shoulder. "I'd like to examine her myself, to be certain. Place her on the bed for me?"

Xander nodded. Hooking an arm under Nyla's knees and the other around her back, he slowly shifted to sit up on his knees. Agonizingly slow so as not to disturb her, he forced himself to his feet. Nyla didn't stir. Her chest rose and fell peacefully.

Stepping up onto the raised platform of the Lavender Room's bedroom space, he carefully made his way to the bed. Nan followed silently behind him. As he laid Nyla down gently upon the plain sheet of the bed, he noticed Nan's gleaming surgical tools on the nightstand alongside the portrait of Nyla's family in the bronze frame.

As Xander stood back to let Nan examine Nyla, his grandfather laid a hand on his shoulder. "No matter what, Nyla is going to be fine. We'll make certain of it."

"I know." Xander nodded. His hand found the ring hidden beneath his shirt. His fingers itched to pull the chain free so he could feel the smooth metal of the slender band against his skin.

"Come," his grandfather said soothingly, "let's give Gerri room to work before you begin your endless vigil over Nyla."

"It wouldn't be endless," Xander grumbled. "She's going to wake up…hopefully soon."

Merry nodded, making a spot for him beside her on the couch. She twisted a handkerchief between her hands. "Yes, soon."

Settling onto the cushion beside her, his cousin's words echoed in his mind. Already, the seconds passing by were lost on his mind as Xander became consumed by the events of just the past day, the past week, the past season.

***

The clock on the mantel ticked relentlessly. The long hand moved so slowly, Xander worried the mechanism had shifted out of place during the earthquake. When he'd asked his grandfather if that could be the case, he'd only chuckled and assured him that the Lavender Room was one of the few rooms to have been fully repaired in the short time following the battle. He'd said that once it was apparent Nyla would triumph over Dinora, some of the Caster Corps had aided in the efforts started by Pemberly Hall's staff to repair the essential portions of the estate, such as the kitchen and the makeshift medical facilities set up in the ballroom.

Xander straightened in his seat, noticing Nan coming over to them while she wiped her hands on her apron.

"All right," she sighed. "Nyla is fine, though I'd like to get her into clean clothes. Do you know where I might find those?"

Xander nodded, sweeping the room with his eyes for Nyla's bag. "If she hasn't unpacked, they'd be in her bag. Merry, could you check the drawers and the armoire please? I'll look in the washroom."

"Of course," Merry said eagerly. Hopping up, she strode toward the dresser and pulled the first drawer open before Xander could even cross the room. Her quiet call seemed like a shout in the otherwise silent room. "I found them!"

"Perfect," Nan said, beginning to shoo at Xander and his grandfather. "Now, both of you, out so I can change Nyla. Merry, dear, pick something comfortable, cottons or something loose-fitting, any loungewear you can find."

Shooting a worried glance toward Nyla on the bed, Xander opened his mouth to protest.

Nan *tsk*ed at him. "It's only for a minute, Xander."

Bobbing his head, he cleared his throat. "I know. I just…"

"You're allowed to worry," Nan said, "and I'm sure Nyla will appreciate your overprotectiveness when she wakes, but for now, you need to let me do my job."

Xander nodded, turning away and following his grandfather out of the Lavender Room's double doors before his worry could overwhelm his rational thought.

Closing the doors behind them, his grandfather hesitated before moving to face him. "We'll, of course, have to discuss the matter of you and Sir Maffis visiting our prisoner and his subsequent escape." A strike of fear stabbed Xander's gut. Eyes twinkling, his grandfather continued, "Though I suppose that can wait until later. Lady Ravencroft is still recovering from her own bout of magical drain, as are most of the Casters and pumpkies. For now, just stay with Nyla. Be there for her when she needs you to be."

"Thank you, Grandfather." It was all Xander could think to say in response.

"I am glad to see that Nyla is all right," his grandfather added, as if he didn't want to let the utter silence of the estate consume them just yet. "Ensure that she knows she is welcome here as long as she wishes to stay."

"I'm afraid I've already made that promise," Xander admitted, rubbing the back of his neck. "She told me she'd like to go home, eventually, and that until then, she'd like to stay here."

His grandfather smiled. "Pemberly is your home, Xander. You

needn't ask my permission to invite someone like Nyla to stay with us indefinitely." Shifting on his feet, his grandfather continued, "Just don't share that with the rest of the family. They are not quite as good a judge of character as you."

Xander's chest swelled. For so long, he'd feared what his grandfather might've thought of him and what their confrontation would bring. But each time his grandfather entrusted him with his confidence or reminded him that Pemberly was his home, Xander was flooded with an immense pride.

Perhaps *pride* was the wrong word, but stunned as Xander was, there was no other way to describe the satisfaction, relief, love, and immense gratitude these interactions brought him. Especially not as he still found himself at a loss for words when the doors of the Lavender Room creaked open behind them.

"Nan says you can come back in now," Merry said softly, a mournful note in her voice.

Xander wilted under the weight of emotion pressing down on his chest. Nyla was fine, according to both Ingrid and Nan, but the knowledge didn't stop him from worrying. Nyla had seemed so small when she'd curled herself against him on that battlefield. Xander had rarely seen her so withdrawn. There was the day she had astral projected and had told him the whole truth of Fortune Falls' visions and the deaths of her family.

But there was that day—or night, rather—when he'd found her in the study. Alone and crying, that was the night he truly realized how the burden of Dinora's escape and being bonded to the Woodlane Manor had weighed on her mind. In front of him and Shamira, Nyla had presented a false courage even if her impatience to break the bond between herself and the Woodlane Manor had been apparent in her shortened temper.

But neither of those times compared to this. For as much power as

Nyla had displayed on that battlefield, for as triumphant as she was, she seemed so small in this moment. It nearly broke him.

Swallowing hard, Xander braced himself for the hours and days ahead of keeping vigil over Nyla. He prepared himself for a lifetime of being by her side if she allowed him, because after everything they'd been through together, Xander knew people like Nyla were a rarity in life.

He understood now what his grandfather had meant earlier when they'd spoken on the balcony. There were people who came into your life and, in an instant, it's like you'd known them forever.

Nyla was one of those people to him, and he'd do anything to show her how much her friendship—her genuine friendship—meant to him.

So with a valiant heart, he carried a stiff chair over to her bedside and sat heavily down upon it. Nan had pulled some blankets up around Nyla and lined up a few dozen potion bottles on the nightstand beside Nyla's framed family portrait.

Catching his stare, she said, "Those are for when Nyla wakes up. They're energy potions to help counter the effects of magical drain. And I've also left some nutrient drinks in case she can't stomach solid foods or…isn't interested…"

"Thanks, Nan," he said earnestly. "I'm sure Nyla will appreciate that."

Xander watched as Nan packed up the rest of her things and shut her bag. Walking around the bed, she leaned down to hug him. "Promise me you'll take care of yourself too, dear."

"I promise." He half stood, squeezing the woman he'd come to consider like another grandmother to him back as tightly as she did to him.

Pulling away after a moment, Nan patted his shoulder and nodded approvingly. "Good." Turning to his grandfather, she said, "And you'd better make certain these two do what they're supposed to."

"I will. I most certainly will," his grandfather replied in assurance. "Come, I'll walk you out. Merry, come and say goodbye to Gerri."

Merry pouted, but didn't argue.

And then it was only him and Nyla and the silence of the Lavender Room.

***

Shamira would never forget the ripple that had nearly rendered her unconscious when Dinora had slumped in her bonds. If it hadn't been for Hecates's and Myra's quick reflexes, she would've collapsed from the assault on her senses as Dinora met her end.

As the image of Dinora's death had seemed to resonate with those strewn throughout the courtyard, Shamira had found herself expecting something to happen. She'd expected some sort of reaction, but all there was was that all-consuming silence, an empty vacuum that had blanketed the world.

It was as if the Casters and soldiers were waiting. Waiting for Dinora to rise again, waiting for some cosmic consequence, waiting for a sign that the battle was most definitely over. They hadn't felt what she had felt. No one here likely had.

A lone pumpkie had howled, low and steady. Others joined in, a haunting tone that grew until every one of their legion was howling but her.

That's when the world had started again.

Magic sparked in the air, bursting. Whether it was a signal or purely celebratory, Shamira didn't know. But as their howl persisted, so joined the cheers and applause of Casters and soldiers.

The world might not have known what service Nyla had completed on its behalf, but each and every person and pumpkie here did.

In the hour or so that had passed, she'd already overheard rumors of a celebration to be held here at Pemberly. Servants whispered about it as they passed by the place where she sat beside a sleeping Talmec. Soldiers and Casters discussed the pending repairs to the estate.

But mostly, the humans kept their distance from her and the

206

pumpkies now that they—humans and pumpkies alike—had all found a place to rest, to recoup, to debrief. Her own kind kept their distance from her and Talmec. She knew this was out of respect and to allow him the privacy to heal. But the humans surprised her. She would've assumed they'd be eager to meet with them and to learn their ways.

Shamira knew she really should've went to Nyla, but she hadn't the strength to. After she'd rested a bit, Shamira promised herself, she would find Nyla and Xander to see how they both fared. She couldn't imagine what either of them were feeling. She'd barely been able to sort through her own emotions in the wake of the battle. And in truth, Shamira hadn't even processed her time on the battlefield, let alone all that had happened after that, and just what Nyla had faced on her own.

She was so young. To have known a burden such as this was one thing, but to have triumphed over it was another thing entirely. Even at her age, Shamira didn't know how to compartmentalize the events of the last twenty-four hours. If she couldn't, how could Nyla?

Was it easier for a species to live and process things when they knew their time was short? Or was it easier to know that one had centuries ahead of them to live still?

Shamira didn't know. She thought both realities seemed bleak, if for different reasons. While shorter, a human lifespan came with the guarantee of urgency. But then there was its brevity to consider when compared to a species like theirs or the ursas, who were said to live longer than even the pumpkies. In a long life where one faced centuries to fill with memories and some sort of meaning, there was also the prospect of feeling unchanged even as the world evolved around you and, with it, the fear of being unable to adapt to it.

You look pained, sister, Talmec said, stirring beside her.

I am not, she assured him. *I am merely worried.*

About Nyla? he asked.

Yes.

Then you should go to her.

Shamira studied him, narrowing her eyes.

Go to her, he urged, *before your stare burns right through me. I'm all right, truly.*

Shamira purred, nodding her head. *Then I will return later.*

Talmec closed his eyes again, turning his face to the moonlight. *And I shall remain here, comfortably asleep.*

Shamira rolled her eyes. Even as he'd healed, Talmec remained unchanged. Facing death had left him unbothered, or so he appeared to her. Ever since he'd awoken, he'd done nothing but assure her of his health.

Secretly, Shamira appreciated him for it.

She'd never been so overwhelmed by her own emotions before that it completely drowned out the energies she could sense. It wasn't that she couldn't recognize her own emotions over the abilities of her empathetic awareness; it was only that she'd never been left entirely to her own emotions before. It was new and strange and overwhelming in a way she hadn't expected it to be.

Was this what people meant when they expressed what it was to be consumed by something, like worry or love? Was it this utter stillness in their mind, a void of anything other than that one feeling—for better or worse?

Shamira shook her head. She couldn't answer that. She didn't know if anyone could actually explain what it meant to be consumed by one singular emotion. For all anyone knew, that was truly hyperbole and nothing more. How could one singular emotion overcome all others and all reason or logic?

It simply couldn't.

And yet Shamira realized that the overwhelming majority of the last few days had been marred by a tension that broke in the span of a single breath.

She wondered what Kasand had thought of it, the moment of Dinora's death. She wondered if the Elders and High Seers knew of all that had happened. Shamira imagined they'd gathered at the shores of the Terrive and watched as the battle unfolded. Hecates had mentioned to her as they'd made their camp on Pemberly's estate that he would contact High Elder Florence and make his report. Shamira hadn't the mind to face the Brewardt Clan High Elder, let alone report to her all that had transpired since she'd led the pumpkies through the protective barrier and into the human territory.

Shamira could barely face Nyla now that she'd found herself staring at the dark wood panels of her bedroom door. Nosing at the air, she sensed Xander's protective presence and another similar, though distinct, presence beyond the door. Nyla's was there as well, tame, though still bursting with the energy Shamira knew to be the motivation for all of the girl's movements. Her essence was as wild as Shamira imagined her to be as a child.

But who was the third? It couldn't be Edwin, as there was no relation between him and Xander, and she doubted it was Lord Huntington for the sole reason of what Nyla had told her of him after their first meeting. She wracked her brain for a possible answer, but Nyla hadn't told her much more than that the last time they'd spoken. She'd barely managed to warn Nyla against dueling Frederick…and give her a few tips to help her in her endeavor. There just hadn't been enough time for pleasantries or banter, a problem Shamira hoped would vanish now that Dinora was defeated. Now, she hoped, they had time for everything they so desired and could fill their lives with happiness. After all, hadn't they—hadn't *Nyla*—earned that with all they'd faced and fought against?

Bowing her head, Shamira knew the longer she hesitated, the worse she would feel. Summoning the courage to open the bedroom door, Shamira's sage-colored magic wrapped itself around the handle and quietly pushed the door open.

Her nose hadn't even crossed the threshold before a quiet gasp made her ears stand on edge.

"A pumpkie!" an excited voice whispered. Shamira's eyes landed on a young girl with loose curls in her hair and a sparkle in her eyes. The third essence, the one with a tempered wonderment. "You must be Shamira!"

Shamira's eyes darted to Xander, though he hadn't moved. Slumped in a chair, his sole focus was on Nyla sleeping soundly in the bed.

I am, she replied, *and who might you be?*

"Merry," she said, standing and giving Shamira a prim curtsy. "I'm Xander's favorite cousin, though he won't say it aloud for fear of the others becoming jealous."

Shamira laughed, *I suppose that could pose a problem…for the others.*

Merry beamed, nodding her head. "Well, in any case, I'll leave you to visit. Here, you can take my seat."

She offered the cushioned seat with a small smile. Turning to Xander, Merry said, "I'll be back later with snacks."

"Thanks, Merry," he whispered, finally turning to look up at his cousin and then at her. The girl gave a light shrug and a nod in reply, but said nothing more as she made her way to the door on quiet feet. Xander followed her with his gaze, straightening in his chair and twisting around. His eyes sparked as if he'd only just noticed she was there. "It's good to see you, Shamira. How's Talmec?"

Fine, thanks to Nan and Edwin. He should be recovered in no time at all now. Gesturing with her head toward Nyla, she asked, *How is she?*

Xander sighed, falling back against his chair. The candlelight glinted off of something as he leaned back. Shamira noticed a ring worn on a chain around Xander's neck that she hadn't ever seen before. But if he wore it frequently, it explained why she'd often catch him touching a hand to his chest before he realized what he was doing.

"She's going to be fine," Xander explained. Years, if not centuries, of exhaustion filled his voice. "Ingrid healed her before wisping us back here, and then Nan examined her. By then, Nyla had already either fallen unconscious or decided to rest on her own. I'm not really certain, to be honest."

Shamira watched as Nyla's chest rose and fell with her steady breaths.
Perhaps a little of both.

Xander hummed in agreement.

And so began their silent vigil over Nyla.

18. FOR EVERY ACTION

Xander's ears pricked. He didn't bother to look over his shoulder, knowing it was only someone to come and sit with Nyla. It was probably Merry again, as she'd gone down to eat breakfast with their grandfather and the Remingtons. He knew he should've made an effort to appear at breakfast too, especially since he'd promised to visit Nan and George again, but he'd decided that they'd all understand his absence given the circumstances.

After all, each of them had at some point joined his silent vigil in the Lavender Room.

Merry and Nan had even played a game of cards on the coffee table before going to bed last night.

"Grandfather asked for you to join him in the parlor," Merry said softly as the quiet footsteps came to a stop beside him. "He said that he wanted to talk to you about something."

Xander glanced up at her. Resignation settled like a yoke on his shoulders. "I…" Sighing heavily, he braced his hands against the arms of his chair. "Come and get me—no, *send* someone—to get me if Nyla wakes while I'm gone, okay?"

"I promise." She smiled. "Now go. The sooner you meet with Grandfather, the sooner you can get back to Nyla."

Kissing the top of Merry's head, Xander thanked her before quietly moving toward the door. Taking one last look at Nyla and then Merry as she settled herself into the seat he'd given up, Xander forced himself to open the door.

Stiffly stepping over the threshold, he silently pulled the door to the Lavender Room shut behind him. Exhaling a long, slow breath, Xander strode down the hallway to his room, delaying the inevitable. Merry might not have known what their grandfather wished to speak to him about, but Xander certainly did. And he wouldn't be surprised if Edwin had been summoned as well.

Xander prayed his friend wouldn't get into too much trouble on his behalf. Edwin was barely a newly minted member of the Caster Corps. With any luck, Xander would take the brunt of the blame—as it *was* his idea to see Cedric anyway—and Sir Maffis could remain undisciplined. Xander had heard unpleasant rumors about the sort of consequences members of the Caster Corps could face. *Anything* was possible. Magical illusions to force them into reliving the event until they'd found a solution to it that was considered acceptable. Physical labor. Imprisonment. Xander's mind raced with all the possibilities his mind supplied him with thanks to Edwin's tales of the punishments the Caster Corps were rumored to administer when the occasion called for it.

Shuddering as he quickly changed into fresh clothes, Xander banished the thought from his mind. Maybe if he reported what Cedric had told them, his grandfather and the Mage General would be less inclined to punish them and better interested in sorting the truth from Cedric's lies.

No matter what happened, Xander knew they needed to be made aware of what Cedric had claimed, particularly about the bequeathment potion and Shamira's assertion that Cedric might have promised a blood oath. If anything, they needed to look into the potion for Nyla's sake.

***

Xander shrank under Ingrid's undivided attention. "Well…we—I persuaded Edwin to take me to see Cedric because I was hoping he might be able to tell us something that would end the battle sooner."

"But instead," Edwin continued, picking up where Xander had left off, "all he did was try to get us to free him so he could 'kill Dinora' and 'do the right thing for once' in his life.'"

"Obviously, *we* didn't let him go, but he managed to break free anyway. He claimed that the wards were weak, and…well, that isn't all that important when you consider what he said before his escape," Xander added. "I've been trying to make sense of his claims since then, but I don't think there is any. He claimed to have…what was it called?"

"Cedric claims he performed a *Mortis tradsmagique* to benefit Nyla," Edwin finished.

"Is this true?" his grandfather asked in bewilderment, his brows shooting up as his eyes flicked to Edwin.

"Yes, my lord," Edwin answered.

His grandfather slumped back in his fireside chair, looking utterly defeated.

Ingrid studied them through narrowed eyes. "Anything else?"

Xander glanced toward Edwin. His friend only shrugged, shaking his head. Licking his lips, Xander answered her question, "That's the most pressing. When I saw Shamira while Edwin and Nan—I mean Gerri—were healing Talmec, she said that I smelled of a blood oath, and there's this cut on my hand," Xander held his hand up, continuing, "but I don't remember much about how it happened."

Ingrid's gaze fixated on the scabbed-over cut across his palm, her lips pursed. "You truly remember nothing of it?"

Xander let his hand fall, rubbing the back of his neck. "It's all pretty hazy. Cedric hit us with this wave of magic, but I sort of remember him talking before he left. Something about not letting her pay for his mistakes, but I'm not all that positive I heard him correctly."

Ingrid hummed in acknowledgement, sitting back in her chair. Her eyes flicked between them one final time. "Anything else?"

"Aside from some other explanations of why we should trust him to kill Dinora and that he'd been trying to foil Dinora's plans without raising her suspicions, I don't think there's anything else that's of great importance to you," Edwin concluded.

Ingrid nodded her head slowly. Her eyes withdrew as she considered their tale. "Very well." Ingrid pressed a hand to her temple, rubbing away what Xander could only guess was the onset of a massive headache. "We had better summon the council. I fear the day is about to be much longer than I had anticipated."

"Already taken care of," Xander's grandfather assured her. "We will be meeting later this afternoon."

"Good." Ingrid nodded. "Now about your punishment."

At her words and sharp gaze, Xander found himself swallowing uncertainly. Beside him, Edwin flinched, freezing with his shoulders back and the tense air of someone caught unexpectedly. Xander found himself hoping the couch would swallow him whole.

Ingrid continued, "Lord Huntington has given me his blessing to punish you as I see fit too, Xander. Now I understand that you're concerned about Nyla, but I assure you she will be in the most capable hands possible. She will not be alone. I promise you that. But I cannot allow the two of you to go unpunished. And as such, I have decided that you will both be locked in the dungeon until you can break my new wards."

Xander arched his brow. "Until we can break *your* wards?"

"Yes," Ingrid said. "I've tailored some new wards, and I'd like to test them. I hope it doesn't take long for Sir Maffis to break them. It would be a pity if you were both subjected to spending the next few weeks in the dungeon, if not the next season. I imagine Nyla will argue with me to set you both free, though I will deal with that when it comes to it."

Xander glanced at Edwin. His friend was utterly still, his face completely slack.

"Right," she said, standing from her chair and looking them each in the eye, "now that that's all settled, I suppose we had better put this matter to rest. The sooner you begin your punishment, the sooner you might be able to break my wards, and then, Xander, you can resume your vigil over Nyla."

Edwin didn't say a word in response. Xander tried to catch his eye, but his friend was completely withdrawn. The only sign that he wasn't completely shell-shocked was the furrow of his brows. If Xander had to guess, he would say that Edwin was already contemplating how to break the wards Ingrid had put in place in order to help shorten the length of their punishment.

Dread coiled in Xander's gut. But he had to ask the question churning over in his mind. "Does that mean…You want to lock Edwin and me in the dungeon, *now?*"

"If not now, this may have a ripple effect on my authority. I cannot delay this punishment, and I sincerely doubt you would want to either, because the longer you do, the more you risk missing Nyla upon her awakening or having to serve this punishment after she regains consciousness. Is that what you want? For her to wake up and then immediately have to leave her side?"

Xander licked his lips. He wanted to fight Ingrid. He wanted to convince her to allow him just a little more time—a *day*—to make sure Nyla was all right and that she wasn't in immediate need of anything.

He would've fought, and was about to argue with her, but Ingrid carried on.

"I will watch over Nyla until you and Edwin have completed the terms of your punishment," she explained. "And if, for whatever reason, Nyla's condition worsens, I will put a hold to this punishment, and you and Edwin can go free until such a time as you might resume it."

"Xander," his grandfather prompted. Xander's eyes flicked to him.

"You should accept these terms and be done with it. There are plenty of people here to watch over Nyla and ensure her safety. No one will let anything happen to her or allow her condition to slip. Gerri has already promised to watch over her as well. Nyla will be safe."

Xander's heart pounded desperately against his chest, beating hard enough he feared it would break through his flesh and bone. His lips parted slightly, as if a part of him still intended to persuade Ingrid otherwise. Xander forced himself to digest what the pair had said, to consider the terms Ingrid had laid out to him and the promise offered to him by his grandfather. His shoulders sagged. "All right. I suppose there is no other choice then."

Ingrid smiled thinly. "Then let us get this over with, for all our sakes."

Xander swallowed the retort threatening to slip past his lips. The only worry Ingrid needed to fear was what Nyla might say if she found out about this, but aside from that, he couldn't imagine what had caused the tension in her pinched face. Following the example set forth by his grandfather and the Royal Mage, Xander got to his feet. Edwin still seemed dazed, as if he hadn't accepted their punishment quite yet either. For his own selfish hope, Xander prayed his friend would regain his senses soon, knowing that Edwin and his magic was the only way he would get to see Nyla anytime soon.

One last desire to fight Ingrid and his grandfather simmered in his blood. Maybe it would've been worthwhile, but Xander tamped it down and allowed them to lead the way to the dungeons and the doom he suspected lay in wait for him and Edwin there.

19. THE SURVIVOR WITH THE AUBURN HAIR

Nyla woke slowly. The first thing her barely conscious mind realized was the weight and feel of her body, of her limbs stretched across the soft warmth beneath her and the one wrapped around her. The next was the devastating ache in her gut, begging for food so desperately it was as though she hadn't eaten for an entire season. Nausea roiled through her stomach despite the obvious rumble.

Most of all, as Nyla pulled herself to a sitting position, she noticed the unbearable ache in her bones and the tension in her muscles, the tug of pain that pulled at her one side. It was like a giant bruise had formed over her entire body, weighing down her limbs and barking in pain anytime she moved.

"Take it easy, Nyla," someone said. "You have severe magical drain and need to rest."

Nyla raised her brow, glancing toward the voice. Ingrid and Merry were seated beside her bed. Her brows furrowed. Willing her head to move once more, Nyla spotted Shamira and Talmec lying by the fire, staring at her with matching, unblinking eyes.

"Ah," Nyla said dumbly. Her body went limp against the pillows, unable to support her any longer. Murmuring, she asked, "Where's Xander?"

Her heart beat between her ears at the silence that answered her question. Forcing her heavy eyes open once more, Nyla saw Ingrid staring at her with a crumpled expression that wasn't altogether a frown. If Nyla didn't know any better, she would say that the Mage General looked guilty, but she didn't think the woman could feel fault on such a personal level.

"Ingrid imprisoned Xander and Edwin in the dungeons," Merry gushed, "because they inadvertently let Cedric escape during the battle and Grandfather let Ingrid punish them both and now they have to break her wards or be stuck there forever."

Nyla blinked. She hadn't the slightest idea what Merry had said. Her fatigued mind could hardly follow the jumble of words that had come tumbling out of the girl's mouth. "What?"

Ingrid let out a long sigh, straightening in her chair. "Thank you, Lady Huntington. I'm sure that's precisely the first thing Nyla wanted to hear upon waking."

"Well, *someone* had to answer her," Merry muttered, folding her arms. "No sense tangling the snicket any more than necessary."

Nyla finally managed to process all that Merry had bombarded her with. Her eyes drifted back to Ingrid. "You locked Xander in the dungeon?"

"Yes…" Ingrid said, "but I imagine Xander is already nearly done with digging a hole through the floor if Edwin hasn't unscrambled the first layer of my wards in the last few hours."

Nyla shut her eyes against the light of the bedroom. A sharp ache pounded in her temples. "Do you think it'll take them long?"

Another beat of silence answered her question. Nyla didn't open her eyes, hoping she needn't ask again.

"I should hope not," Ingrid answered at last. "I'm rather confident that they should be free sometime tomorrow or the day after if Sir

Maffis's personnel file is any indication of his capabilities. But enough about them. I have no doubt that they're doing just fine. How are *you* doing, Nyla? Can we get you anything?"

"I'm fine," Nyla whispered. "I just…could I have some time alone please?"

Nyla opened her eyes in time to see Ingrid share a look with Shamira. "Let me examine you first, and then we'll see about it, okay?"

Nyla nodded, forcing herself up onto an elbow, and pulled herself farther up the bed. Merry quickly jumped to her side and helped rearrange the pillows so she could sit comfortably against the headboard. Nyla took a few deep breaths to stave off the dizziness the movement had inflicted upon her consciousness. By the time it faded, Shamira had come to her bedside.

Are you upset because Xander isn't here? she asked.

Nyla gave her a weak smile. "A little, but it's fine. How long can you watch someone sleep for?"

"Three days, apparently," Merry said. "Xander stayed for two whole days before Ingrid and Grandfather—"

"I think that's enough, Merry. Why don't you tell Nyla about the celebration your grandfather is planning instead?" Ingrid said, holding her glowing hands over Nyla. As the Royal Mage moved her hands down towards Nyla's feet, she studied her fiercely. Nyla watched Ingrid's examination of her curiously. What was Ingrid doing?

Healing magic can be used in a variety of ways, Shamira said, as if sensing her confusion. Knowing Shamira, she probably could. *By invoking that skill, a Healer can use their powers to help identify pain in the body or sources of magical afflictions.*

"And physically, you're fine," Ingrid continued, "though I imagine you're sore and probably exhausted still."

Your aura is unsettled, though I wouldn't have expected anything different. It will heal as you do, Shamira added. *I think some rest will do you some good. Perhaps, when you're up for it, a change of scenery as well.*

The pumpkies and I have settled in the gardens should you wish for some company and a bit of sunshine.

"But for now, I recommend you stay put just a while longer, and if you can," Ingrid said in a way that sounded like an order as she slid one of the various potion bottles on the bedside table closer to her, "drink this. It's a healing potion Gerri left for you. It should give you some energy and help manage your pain a bit better so that you might rest a little easier now that you're fully awake."

Nyla didn't look at her, or the potion. Instead, her gaze was fixed on the portrait and the bronze frame etched with forget-me-nots and an old Eurish phrase she couldn't read. But she didn't need to because Xander had told her what it said, and her mother had said it just before she'd returned to the realm beyond.

'Love is for forever.'

We'll come and check on you later tonight. Shamira's voice broke her study of her family's smiling faces and the flaky edges of the portrait that had survived the same fire Nyla had, the one that had led her to this path.

"And I should probably see how Sir Maffis and Xander are faring," Ingrid said.

"I'll definitely be back with something to eat," Merry beamed, "that is, if you're up for company and a little snack by then."

Nyla swallowed thickly, willing herself to tear her eyes from the frame. "Thank you, Merry. That sounds fine."

Get some rest, Nyla. Shamira pinned her in place with a serious gleam in her eyes. *And don't hesitate to call for someone if you need anything.*

Nyla bobbed her head, too numb to answer. She watched with a hollow chest as they silently filed out of the room. Ingrid offered her a small smile as she shut the door behind them. Just as the door had shut for good, she saw Shamira join her, her tail flicking urgently. Nyla assumed she was the subject of their conversation, but couldn't find it in herself to care as the emotional turmoil she'd expected finally crashed over her.

Even though Dinora had been defeated and declared dead, Nyla knew she wouldn't know peace for a long time, if ever.

But she'd done it. She'd freed the spirits of the Shadow Forest wronged by the evil sorceress immortalized in the legends of the haunted forest. She'd avenged her family, though they'd never expected her to.

Flashes of the battle and her time spent alone on the sandy plain burst through her mind. The image of Sir Ian's glassy eyes lay over all of them like a reflection in a pond. Chills raked down her spine as hot tears collected in her eyes, trailing thickly down her cheeks.

How many?

How many had they lost? How many would they have to mourn without a body to lay to rest? What were they going to tell their families? How were they going to explain the great evil that had posed a grave threat to not just the country but to all of magic—how it had been averted but not without casualties?

Nyla took a shuddering breath.

She said she would fight Dinora, that she would defeat Dinora, and she had.

But why did it feel like there was still more for her to do? Like Dinora's death hadn't been the end of it all, but rather the beginning?

As Nyla contemplated this and what could be expected of her next, her gaze wandered to the window. Late afternoon sunlight spilled through the imposing window. Only the sheer curtains had been drawn, shimmering in the sunlight like fairies' lace. At the sight of it, Nyla wondered if the world was any different now that Dinora was gone. She wondered if all the magic Dinora had stolen and that she had returned to whence it came would've transformed the landscape, or if Huntington was far enough away to not have been affected.

Slowly, she willed herself to stand on uncertain limbs and made her way to the window. Not bothering to move the sheer curtain to the side, Nyla peered out at the world, studying the gardens below and sky above and the land beyond Pemberly Hall's estate as she braced herself against the wall beside the window.

The sapphire leaves of the distant trees rustled in a gentle breeze. The garden pathways below had some debris scattered throughout, though otherwise, they remained as prim and proper as she'd seen them previously. Everything seemed normal. From the pale blue of the sky to the glow of the sun's rays dancing on the courtyard pavers to the people and pumpkies milling about here and there.

Nyla's heart swelled at the sight.

Everything was as it should be. She could rest easy now and heal.

But her mind wouldn't let her. All it seemed capable of doing was replaying scenes she'd rather forget. Scenes of glassy eyes, of shimmering bonds, and of a wavering mist that craved blood, that craved vengeance just as she had.

Sighing, Nyla turned away from the window. Taking in the rest of the Lavender Room, Nyla noticed the hardwood chair with sparse cushioning pulled up beside her bed. For a young lord, Xander really didn't have an eye for luxury when he was worried. She supposed it was Merry or Ingrid who'd pulled a plush chair onto the platform. She hoped Xander had made use of it too, knowing he probably hadn't left her side since he'd come to the battlefield and somehow brought her back here—that was until Ingrid had whisked him away to serve the consequences for allowing Cedric to escape. Nyla tentatively shook her head, wary of the dizziness it might bring on, at the thought. She wished Xander was here now, even though she was glad to be alone for a moment. There was too much for her own heart to sort through before she could feel ready to face anyone, most of all Xander.

Breathing out a slow exhale as though it could cleanse her soul, Nyla hoped her family was at peace now, that Astrid and all the other souls had found peace. They deserved it, and then some. A second chance, she thought. Those souls deserved a chance at life again for the torture they'd been put through for the last 647 years.

With any luck, she prayed, this world would know peace too now that Dinora was dead.

Nyla doubted she'd know of that peace if word ever spread throughout the country of who she was and what part she'd had in defeating Dinora. Her mind held tightly to the hope that the royals, the Heirs of Tenebris, and the representatives from the Chamber of Commons that had wanted to keep Dinora's threat concealed from public knowledge would extend to the present now that her threat had been extinguished.

Indeed, there was a lot for Nyla to consider now, and little desire to want to sort through it all now—or ever. She wanted something to eat first and to get cleaned up and, of course, to rest.

After all three of those needs had been met, Nyla decided, then and only then would she contemplate what came next for her in any scenario Fate might have her face.

20. SILVER LININGS

Xander fingered the scabbed-over cut marring his palm. He wondered just what Ingrid would find once she started investigating it and the blood oath Shamira claimed had been made to him. He hoped it didn't lead to more trouble. "Do you really think they'll find an answer about the blood oath?"

Edwin turned and glanced down at him. "I wouldn't doubt it. Ingrid is very thorough, and Shamira is a very instinctual magic user. For now, I think we should really focus on the task at hand."

"How am I supposed to do that when there's a bunch of glowing symbols I can't read and I'm too busy worrying about Nyla and what Cedric might've done to us?" Xander scoffed, vaguely gesturing to the archaic symbols Casters used in their intricate spells. The only consolation in any of this was the fact that his grandfather had furnished the dank dungeon cell with a pair of cushioned footstools, one of which he sat on and the other wholly abandoned beside him as Edwin observed the glowing sigils.

"Hm," Edwin hummed, turning his back to him to resume his study of the symbols. "Then I suppose I'd better hurry up. This is an interesting bit of spellwork. It's actually kind of impressive because if you look closely, you can see…"

Xander nearly groaned as Edwin went on like a professor examining some new finding. He only hoped his friend's lecturing about the cadence of the symbols adhering to modern theory but the spell itself invoking old magical theory would lead to a solution.

Never in his life had Xander known such a delicate color as Ingrid's magic to be so menacing. An eternity had passed since they'd been paraded down into the dungeon by his grandfather, Ingrid, Abraham, and Luce, and Edwin's immediate summoning of the wards. His friend had hoped that making them visible would make it easier to find the weakness in their integrity, but Xander was beginning to think there wasn't one.

Every inch of the cell walls was covered in the careful script of Ingrid's spellwork. He'd never seen anything like it, and at this rate, he didn't have the heart to ask if Edwin had. After all, it was his friend who had studied at the University of Magic. It was Edwin who had to understand these things, the ancient symbols, the fundamentals of magic. All Xander had to do was sit here and worry. He supposed that was his punishment. Edwin's was to be trapped here until he could prove himself to be a worthy Caster and break Ingrid's wards. Xander's punishment was ultimately to be stuck here, away from Nyla and worrying about whether or not she was actually all right or if she'd regained consciousness yet. He didn't know what to expect when she did, though, or how he could help her when she did finally wake. All he knew for certain was that he would do his best to help her because Nyla deserved the world and all its stars.

Nyla had a good heart.

Nyla was the sort of person who wished vengeful souls found peace. She was the sort of person who freed those trapped souls from haunted forests, even at her own expense. Nyla had held his hand and offered to run away from the potential help offered to her, help they had hoped could save her from an impossible situation.

And while it infuriated him in this moment, Xander realized there wasn't much he could do, even if he was right beside her still. All he could do was wait and listen, to exercise a patience he wasn't wholly capable of anymore thanks to the quivering of his heart. Putting his head in his hands and resting his elbows on his knees, Xander watched Edwin study each and every symbol in the hopes of cracking Ingrid's wards.

***

Xander watched as Edwin paced the length of the cell. The glowing symbols continued to taunt them both. He hadn't the faintest clue what they meant, or if they even meant anything at all on their own. All he saw was a bunch of symbols in a seemingly random sequence, but they had to mean something. He just couldn't read them. And if the eternity that had passed since Ingrid had locked the cell door behind them was any indication, Xander was beginning to think Edwin didn't know either.

Maybe there was a pattern. Maybe, instead of looking at each symbol or each line, but rather the whole of Ingrid's wards, they could find a pattern.

Or maybe Edwin had already considered that eons ago and failed to find one.

Xander shook his head. It was no use. Slipping from the footstool he sat on, Xander moved to the center of the cell. Wordlessly, he lay down on the floor and stared at the ceiling.

Maybe those cold blocks could tell him something the walls couldn't.

As his eyes skimmed over the cracks in the ceiling, Xander jolted. He bolted up into a sitting position.

"Edwin!" he exclaimed.

His friend made a startled noise, nearly hissing at him, "What?"

"Come look at this!" Xander pointed up at the ceiling.

Furrowing his brows, Edwin tilted his head back and glanced up at the ceiling and then back at him. "There's nothing there."

"Exactly!" Xander said. "There are symbols *everywhere* except for the floor and ceiling, but knowing Ingrid, she wouldn't leave them vulnerable, right?"

"How does that help us?" Edwin asked, his voice strained with irritation.

"Because what if whatever Ingrid did to the floor and ceiling are the missing pieces we need to get out of here?"

Edwin opened his mouth, but promptly closed it. Glancing around the cell as if he were only just now seeing it for the first time, Xander watched as Edwin seemed to consider the possibility of what he'd just said.

"I'll try," he said at last.

Xander got to his feet, anxiously watching as his friend closed his eyes and a silver energy began to pulse around him. Edwin's magic pulsated like a heartbeat. Xander's eyes kept flicking to the ceiling and the rough stone floor beneath his feet, hoping to see some sort of progress for Edwin's efforts.

Just as before, the reveal of Ingrid's magical signature was slow. Weakly, the first few symbols began to expose themselves. As they grew more distinct, others began to crop up until the entire floor and ceiling were covered in the blush-colored sigils.

Xander's eyes roved over them quickly, looking for any similarities between the walls, the floor, the ceiling, and what he knew of Ingrid.

Disheartened, Xander couldn't discern any pattern or similarity. By all means, the symbols were completely random.

Eyeing Edwin, Xander waited for any sort of reaction from his friend. None came. His friend just stood there, in the middle of the cell, staring at the ceiling.

Could he see something Xander couldn't? Did he understand the symbols any better now that they were all exposed?

Just as he was about to ask, Edwin began laughing.

"What is it?" Xander asked hesitantly. Uncertainty twisted in his gut. What about their current situation was funny?

Edwin took a breath, composing himself. "When I was in university, I ended up being cursed by a clumsy classmate. This sequence here," he pointed, "is a fragment of that spell, but in the ancient tongue. It roughly means 'the bones wither,' but because the symbol for 'wither' had a different meaning to the Frambawi, this could be 'the bones *weather*,' which when combined with this phrase here," Edwin said, moving toward one of the walls and gesturing to another group of symbols, "'the dark,' ultimately leads me to believe this is more of a test than a punishment, but the question is—to what end?"

Xander shook his head, trying to follow Edwin's rambling. "Okay so 'the bones weather the dark' means…I'm sorry, but did you say you were cursed in university by a classmate, and now that phrase is here, in Ingrid's warding?"

Edwin waved his hand dismissively. "It wasn't as bad as it sounds. It can mean a lot of things, and in my case, it just meant that my bones started to decay. I experienced a lot of weakness, and it was rather inconvenient, but I eventually managed to reverse it before it became too serious. I was pretty miserable, though. I missed the *Cresmuun Oltivatae* because I was confined to bed for fear of breaking a hip or something.

"But if the bones *weather* the storm over *wither*, then…" Edwin muttered, "these symbols won't help us. They aren't the root of the spell, but a message."

"You think Ingrid left us a hint?" Xander asked in bewilderment.

"No," Edwin said, shaking his head. "She left us a challenge. These symbols are a meaningless distraction. First, only the walls appeared because the floor and ceiling were masked with a different bit of spell-work, so that even if we managed to expose one over the other, the whole message would be lost. And because there was such an abundance of magic, I didn't think to press any harder, believing that the walls were the only signature of an already strong essence of magic.

"But when you said there wasn't anything on the floor or ceiling, it made me wonder—why wouldn't there be? Would Ingrid really leave them vulnerable, as most wards fully encase the area to be protected? And now I see. This isn't one specific spell, but multiple spells. The first layer, which was the walls. Then the ceiling, but behind that…" Edwin trailed off. His hand glowed with his magic. "It's believed that Cedric didn't even expose the signatures, and if the bones weather the dark, then that's what we must do."

Xander's mouth dropped open. The symbols disappeared as if blown away by a harsh wind. The cell was plunged into darkness. Any light had been squandered by Edwin's theory, and Xander found himself blinking in the vain hope that he could regain his sight.

"Don't you think this is a little ridiculous, Edwin?" he asked into the dark.

"Not at all," the man in question said, "Cedric's magic was supposed to be bound, and yet he escaped. It wasn't necessarily the strength of the wards, but how they were created. I used a modern technique to ward the cell, one that involved symbols and actual spellwork. But that's not what Ingrid did. Ingrid wrote some wards, but she didn't invoke them, which means they're a mask for the true ward, which looks like…" Edwin trailed off for a second, leaving Xander to wonder just what he was talking about. There wasn't anything here at all but the complete darkness of the cell. Seconds passed, or perhaps it was a minute—Xander didn't know—before Edwin finally said, "*This.*"

Silver magic washed over the cell, scrubbing over the walls, the floor, the ceiling. As Edwin's magic brushed over the cell, a solid blush color emanated from every surface.

"Ingrid used the old way, the sort of magic Astrid used to create the bond between herself and the Woodlane Manor. It's brilliant, actually, because the strength of the wards is wholly dependent on the strength of her intent."

"So what does that mean for us getting out of here?" Xander asked, fearing the worst despite the excitement shining in Edwin's eyes. Was he excited because he was learning something new or because he had a solution? Xander couldn't tell, knowing the possibility was both. Edwin had always been an eager student, and he had no doubt that this exercise didn't even register as a punishment in his mind anymore, but for Xander, the longer they were stuck in here, the more doomed he felt.

Edwin cracked his knuckles. Xander arched his brow, realizing his friend was about to face their situation with no regard to mercy. "It means my will has to be stronger than Ingrid's to break these wards."

A menacing shadow darkened Edwin's face as his eyes became focused. Xander found himself taking a step backwards, uncertain of what was about to happen. Was Edwin about to unleash a wave of magic against the cell? Would he directly attack Ingrid's wards?

What, exactly, did he mean by the fact that his will needed to be stronger than Ingrid's? Was such a feat even possible?

"This might take a moment," Edwin said, "but I have no doubt that we'll be out of here shortly."

"Okay..." Xander said. "I'm safe where I am, right?"

Edwin hummed, "Perfectly."

Xander nodded, though he knew Edwin couldn't see. He'd closed his eyes and had taken on the appearance of a statue. An expression of smug calmness had taken over his friend's features, and while Xander knew that should instill some confidence in him, he still didn't know what exactly Edwin's plan was. It sounded to Xander as if he had to directly break down the strength of Ingrid's wards, but how could he possibly do that? Ingrid was the Royal Mage and Mage General for a reason. Those two positions weren't entrusted to anyone lightly—let alone a singular person very often anymore.

And if Edwin *did* manage to break down her wards, as was the intention behind this punishment, then what exactly did that mean for Ingrid's reputation—and Edwin's?

A flicker of light caught Xander's attention. Silver magic flared in the corner of the cell. Sparks of blush-colored magic burst from the spot where Edwin's magic seemed to erode Ingrid's. Xander stared hard at the corner, willing Edwin's power to overcome Ingrid's. Nothing happened, but still Xander pleaded with whatever forces—Balmae, Corruptio, Fate, some other cosmic power he was ignorant of—were at play to give them some leniency.

The two energies began to fizz. The noise grew louder, becoming a steady *buzz* that filled Xander's ears as the magics sparked and *hissed*. Neither magic moved an inch, but they grew brighter. Brighter and brighter until Xander was forced to look away.

Even still, the light was too harsh, and Xander had to cover his closed eyes with his hands.

Minutes passed, though they felt like hours. As the fizzing grew louder, the more concerned Xander became. But still, he didn't look, knowing he'd be risking his eyesight if he did. He only hoped Edwin was all right. This all seemed like a great deal of magic, though he still hadn't the slightest idea of what Edwin was actually doing.

All Xander knew was that *something* must've been happening, as the buzz became sharper and higher in pitch until Xander swore his eardrums would burst.

But it only lasted for a moment.

As quickly as the high-pitched buzz reached its crescendo, so it faded until only a faint whisper of static filled Xander's ears. Cautiously, Xander cracked his eye open and lowered his hands. The light had dimmed considerably, though it still stunned his vision. Blinking, Xander looked over the cell. The silver of Edwin's magic had mostly consumed Ingrid's. The place where the two energies met no longer hissed or spat sparks of magic, but rather seemed to ebb and flow. He wondered if that meant Edwin was still facing some resistance from Ingrid's essence, but it didn't seem to matter as the silver gained inch by inch of what was left of the blush-colored magic.

Awed, Xander turned to face Edwin.

At some point, Edwin had collapsed to his knees. His body visibly trembled. Xander took a step forward, but thought better of it, fearing what would happen if he broke Edwin's concentration. If the silver hugging most of the cell's surface was any indication, Edwin was almost done. He'd almost broken through Ingrid's wards.

Renewed hope surged in Xander's heart. Edwin had meant it. They'd be free soon enough, just so long as Edwin could maintain the strength to defeat Ingrid's magic.

He hoped it would be over soon, worried that Edwin didn't have enough energy left to fight much longer.

If only there was some way he could help Edwin other than watch, but without any magic of his own, Xander knew he couldn't be of any help at all.

***

"He's done it," Ingrid muttered. Shamira turned to look at her, her tail tapping the ground as she sat up a little straighter. "He's broken my wards."

Does that mean they've completed their punishment? she asked.

"There's still the matter of breaking open the cell door, but I can't imagine Edwin is in any shape to do so."

Shamira nodded. No, Edwin most certainly wasn't. His signature was hardly pulsing. He'd expelled so much magic, Shamira wasn't altogether certain that he would even be conscious now.

"So what would you like us to do, Mage General?" the Caster with ginger hair asked. Luce, she was called, Shamira remembered. She wondered if the name was a shortened variation of something else, but no one had addressed her otherwise in the time that they'd spent waiting for Edwin and Xander after fulfilling Nyla's request to be alone.

Ingrid's brows furrowed. Her eyes turned contemplative. "I had wanted to see if they could fully replicate Cedric's escape, but...it's better to see how Sir Maffis is faring. The amount of magic I imagine

235

was required to break my wards could have serious implications on his health if we don't take care."

"So you wish to let them out then?"

Shamira's whiskers twitched. A fizzle of energy made the fur on the back of her neck prickle.

Hold on just a moment, she said. *I think—*

She didn't get to finish her statement, as the mechanisms for the cell's multiple locks began to move. A weak silver energy encapsulated the sliding bolts and padlocks, sliding them back or forcing them open slowly but surely.

The door creaked open.

Beside her, Ingrid straightened. A strange sort of energy rippled off of her, one that bit like anticipation, but there was a hesitation there that Shamira couldn't quite explain. She supposed it didn't matter as the open door revealed Xander supporting a barely conscious Edwin on the other side of the threshold.

Edwin's arm dropped limply to his side. Shamira sniffed, noting the tang of copper in the air and the utter staleness of exhaustion radiating off of Edwin.

"Sir Maffis?" Ingrid asked, stepping closer.

Edwin only groaned.

Shamira's brows arched in surprise. Edwin was still conscious? And after the massive amount of magic he'd used?

Ingrid stepped closer to them and reached out a hand. Tilting Edwin's face up from where it lolled against his chest, she studied his face. A trickle of blood fell from his nose. Edwin's eyes weren't even open.

"Luce, Abraham," Ingrid ordered, stepping back, "please see that Sir Maffis receives treatment for excessive magical drain."

"Of course," Luce said. To Xander, she added, "Abraham will take him from here."

Xander nodded, lifting Edwin's arm from around his shoulders and shifting him into Abraham and Luce's care.

As the pair of guards led Edwin away to receive medical attention, Shamira glanced between Xander and Ingrid. Neither had said a word to each other. Ingrid didn't seem to even look at him as she shifted from foot to foot.

Edwin will be all right once he rests, Shamira said. *How are you, Xander?*

"I'm fine," he said. "How's Nyla?"

She's awake, though has asked to be alone for the time being. I'm hoping she's continuing to rest.

Shamira nearly laughed at the flood of sweet relief that overcame Xander at her answer. His eyes flitted to the end of the hallway. She suspected he would've run all the way to Nyla's room to check on her if it hadn't been for Ingrid's question.

"How did he manage it?" Ingrid asked.

Xander shook his head and blinked hard before his eyes refocused on them. "Edwin said something about having a stronger will than you in order to break the wards once he realized that the symbols held the phrase, 'the bones weather the dark,' and that the runes were merely a mask for the actual wards. He said something about magic and intent, but he didn't go into details before he set to breaking the wards."

"He does indeed have a strong will," Ingrid said, her eyes gleaming with what Shamira could only call pride. Nodding, she said, "You should probably go and check on Nyla. It's almost dinner time."

Xander hesitated, half stepping away before he paused. Fixing his gaze on Ingrid, Shamira watched curiously as he drew himself up to his full height, claiming an air of authority. "This was a test, wasn't it? For Edwin?"

Ingrid offered him a small mischievous smile that had Shamira narrowing her eyes in suspicion. "There is always a test. But I am a woman of my word, and I think this satisfies the need for punishment. Now all that's left to do is find Cedric, and the whole matter is resolved."

Mostly, Shamira said. *There is still the matter of why he fought alongside us at the battle.*

Xander licked his lips. "I suspect we'll never know the answer to that, not the whole honest answer anyway. I'll bet Cedric wanted to clear his guilty conscience, nothing more, nothing less. There was no nobility about his actions."

Ingrid nodded her head thoughtfully. "You may be right. But still, when I find him, I will seek answers, for everything."

Shamira eyed the Royal Mage and then Xander, noticing him tracing the cut on his palm that she'd suspected was a blood oath. *Cedric will answer for all that he's done. We'll make sure of it.*

21. THE COUNCIL MEETS ONCE MORE

Nyla watched the wisp of water floating between the fingers of her raised hand tremble. It fell with a *plop* just as all the others had. For each attempt she'd made at commanding the small bubble of water, she failed at maintaining it. As it was, she could feel her magic sputtering like a candle flame. She'd failed at something she'd easily mastered after first learning about her magic, and all she had to show for her efforts was a pounding headache in her temples.

Setting her head back against the towel she'd bundled up along the rim of the tub, Nyla let her eyes fall shut. It was highly possible her headache was from dehydration and hunger too. Maybe even exhaustion, she realized, noticing the hollow weariness of her bones.

But her bones weren't the only things that felt hollow in some sense. In her waking moments, Nyla had felt nothing. She wasn't quite numb, she had no physical ailments, and by all means, she had no physical reminder of the battle at all.

There was nothing. Nothing, but the emptiness sinking into her blood, her mind, her heart.

Nyla didn't know what to make of it. She thought she should feel *something*, that something should happen to let her know that Dinora was gone and that all the world was at peace, but there was nothing. Not a scar, not a bruise, nothing. Ingrid had healed her body a little too well, and while Nyla knew she should be grateful for it, she couldn't help but wish Ingrid had left her some reminder so that when her mind replayed those injuries, she would know they were real.

She would know the magic that struck her side and burned her skin had been real. The claws of a twisted soul turned stone creature that had raked across her calf had been real. That the nightmares she was bound to have were the result of something real.

Absently, Nyla picked her heavy head up from the makeshift pillow and trailed her fingers along the faded scar of her collarbone and shoulder. At least she had that still. It was the only proof she had of her own sanity, and of the unwilling astral travels she'd had only weeks ago.

In so short a time, Nyla realized, her life had been turned upside down. She hadn't thought it possible to experience more heartache, more trials, than she already had after the fire had taken her family, and yet this past season had proven her wrong.

But it hadn't all been bad. Nyla's eyes roved over the private ensuite. She had a roof over her head, and a comfortable bed. She had food and a place to hide herself away from the shadows she couldn't outrun.

Most of all, she smiled weakly, she was surrounded by people. Friends, strangers, people she'd come to consider family. She had everything she'd longed for over these past two years, and then some.

So why, why did she feel empty?

Was it because her magic was weak? Was she afraid that she'd returned more than just the magic Dinora had stolen back to the land? Had she given too much of herself and of her own magic to the land? Or was it because of what she'd done to preserve all these wonderful things—these wonderful *relationships*—that she'd come to be blessed with?

Pulling her hand out of the cooling water, Nyla found herself trying her test once again. A single droplet of water rose into the air beneath her hand as if she'd plucked it like a flower. She urged another ounce of water to join it. The second droplet rose into the air. Nyla's brows furrowed in concentration.

The droplets wavered. Nyla's lips twisted. Holding her breath, Nyla tried to regain control of the droplets.

Plop. The water fell and, with it, Nyla's spirit. She let her head fall back against the towel and shut her eyes again. She waited until her heartbeat evened out and her breaths were normal again before she peeled her eyes open and pushed herself to sit up.

Nyla groaned, forcing herself to climb out of the tub, shivering. The water had long since grown cold, but Nyla hadn't cared much until her teeth began to chatter. Quickly wrapping a large fluffy towel around herself, Nyla padded quietly across the few steps of the washroom suite to the full-length standing mirror in the corner.

Her damp hair limply framed her round face. Dark lines marred her face, the result of a stress and exhaustion someone her age shouldn't know yet. Slowly, she reached a hand up and pinched a cluster of hair between her fingers. Carefully pulling it away from her, she leaned closer to the mirror.

Streaks of auburn mingled with the silver strands.

Gasping quietly, Nyla dropped the section of hair and began to run her fingers through the tangles.

More and more, she caught flashes of auburn intermingled with the silver strands.

A mystified giggle bubbled up in her chest. Tears of joy blurred her eyes as she stilled, clutching her arms to her chest and fisting the towel in her hands.

She was beginning to look like herself again. She didn't know why her hair was turning now, or when she'd fully look like herself again, but Nyla found that a happiness had begun to creep its way into her heart—a feat she doubted would find her so soon after the battle.

***

241

Shamira's spine stiffened. Ingrid's voice skirted over her mind, causing her ears to twitch instinctually. *The council is gathering if you are interested in joining us, Shamira.*

Is something the matter? Hecates asked her.

No, Shamira assured him. *Everything is quite all right. Ingrid has asked for me to join their meeting, and I should like to represent the clans. Would you like to join us?*

Hecates yawned, stretching out his limbs. *I think I should like to stay here and rest for a moment before I am forced to reconvene with the Elders and discuss the legion's return home.*

Shamira's whiskers twitched. *So soon?* Her stomach clenched, though she quickly tamped down her apprehension at the mention of their mountaintop home—and their return. *Then I shall leave you to it.*

Hecates merely hummed in response, settling more comfortably where he sat for his nap.

Shamira forced herself to her paws even as she longed for nothing more than to rest herself or find her brother to make certain that he was all right. But the fact was there was still a sense of duty bearing down on Shamira.

She was still a representative of her kin. Even though Dinora was decidedly defeated, she was certain that there was still much to do. If what Xander had told her about Cedric was true, and he'd passed a bequeathment potion onto Nyla, they would have to investigate that immediately, and then there was still the fact that there were sixty-three—no, *forty-one,* she corrected herself—pumpkies sharing quarters with the humans. Hecates was right; they would have to return to the mountains soon. If not because they were unwelcome here amongst the humans, then because they needed more space, and they needed to return to their duties, to their kin.

At the thought, Shamira's mind turned toward her recent homecoming. The High Seer and her dearest friend had named her as his successor. Kasand wanted to train her to take his place, but the Elder Council had offered her the choice to take her freedom after she'd served in the effort to defeat Dinora as punishment for exposing the Council's prior failures to heed her and Kasand's warnings.

She'd survived the war marginally unscathed, but Shamira knew troubled times lay ahead for her heart.

The time it took her to stalk through the halls of Xander's ancestral home didn't provide her with the necessary means to sort through her feelings. In no time at all, Shamira found herself staring at the slightly parted door to the study and was forced to join the assembled crowd within.

Her own plight would have to wait until later. For now, she would do well to focus on the matters at hand and seeing to the end of this battle.

She surveyed the varied group and found that she knew only Ingrid. The others were strangers to her, though their essences were quite familiar. They were all guarded to some extent, using a means of concealment that wasn't strong enough to shield their essences from her. Politicians and Casters, a few soldiers, but none that she had known or cared to meet at the moment as her eyes settled on Ingrid's grim features.

"Ah, Shamira," Ingrid said by way of greeting, drifting over to her on light feet, "I'm so glad that you could join us."

Thank you for inviting me, she replied. *I hope that this will be the beginning of a new alliance between our kind.*

"I cannot say, though I hope that may be the case." Ingrid's eyes slid to a couple sitting beside each other at the table. Shamira followed her gaze and studied the regal pair, vaguely recognizing the fine tendrils of silver and the warmest amber in the man's essence as that of the Caradel family. "I am sure the king and queen would be happy to see the relationship between Tenebris and their oldest allies renewed, but unfortunately, it would be up to the Chamber of Commons to see to that. The Caradels only hold so much influence anymore."

I see. Shamira studied the rest of the room's inhabitants. *I have yet to meet your second-in-command. I understand he had been tasked with training Nyla for a brief period.*

Ingrid's aura soured. "I have released Frederick of his duties. He acted in a manner unbefitting of his status, as well as his position within the Corps, let alone my Circle. I haven't named his successor yet, though I have my eye on someone who I think will be quite delighted to receive the news."

Shamira's eyes flicked to her once more, studying her with a deep suspicion.

Laughing delicately at her glower, Ingrid waved her hand dismissively. "I do not mean to say that I am considering Nyla for the position, though she would be a wonderful candidate. I believe Nyla has done more than enough for this country. She should spend the rest of her life living for her own happiness and pleasure."

I couldn't agree more. Shamira smiled. Tilting her head, she asked, *So who would you name as your second?*

Glancing around conspiratorially, Ingrid drew closer to her. *I was thinking of offering the position to Sir Maffis. But an example had to be made of him first for his misguided judgement that led to Cedric's escape. I'm not much concerned about it, though, because his record is otherwise exemplary, and had he been a bit older, I probably would've considered him for the position sooner, but unfortunately, Frederick had come recommended to me through connections I couldn't slight. But now...* Her lips curled into a satisfied smirk that bordered on devious. *I can do as I wish. And I wish to offer the position to someone worthy of it.*

Shamira's tail flicked in surprise. *Edwin?*

Yes. Ingrid's eyes sparkled mischievously. *He may be younger, but he is poised and patient. He understands the game of politics, but does not play for his own gain. I am well aware that he has been balancing the will of his benefactors, as well as the Corps', but he has done so honorably. He has a lot of promise I fear I would've overlooked had Nyla not pushed Frederick into embarrassing himself.*

Shamira chittered, the equivalent of a human laugh. *No, I agree. Edwin is a fine choice. I believe he may even be able to bridge the gap between our two ways of harnessing and wielding magic.*

"So could you," she said aloud. "I was hoping you would be willing to teach me your methods."

Shamira blinked, taken aback. *I would be honored to.*

Someone cleared their throat, bringing the attention of the room to the table. A man with a long, deep scar marring his face called the room to order.

"I believe we're all gathered now," he said. "Let us begin."

Ingrid's lips pressed together. The assembled crowd gravitated toward their seats at the large table in the center of the room. Before Shamira could follow, Ingrid stopped her.

"Shamira?" Ingrid asked quietly, using the general shuffle of movement as the room's other inhabitants took their places at the table to mask her words. "I could use your assistance for something if you're available?"

I would be happy to assist you, Shamira said. *What is this matter?*

"I'll tell you on the way, after the meeting."

Shamira hummed. It must truly be important if Ingrid was being so secretive about it. But she hadn't the time to consider it now, as the council meeting was beginning, and Ingrid approached the table.

"Thank you, Sir Hubert," a man Shamira assumed to be Xander's grandfather said, taking his seat at the head of the table. "Though I am sorry to say that I haven't the slightest idea where to begin today. War is a complicated thing, but declaring its end seems a fair deal more complicated."

"I would disagree," Ingrid smirked, sliding into her seat. "Dinora is dead. The war is over, if you can even consider this a war."

Shamira's whiskers twitched. Ingrid was quite a blunt woman. She admired that. Gently climbing into the seat beside Ingrid, Shamira sat proudly and listened as the humans sputtered, begging for proof of Ingrid's claim.

"Where is Dinora's body?" someone asked. "How can we believe her threat is ended when you have yet to produce her body?"

The sharp, nearly metallic scent of irritation drifted through the room, though the majority of it stemmed from Ingrid.

"I'll have you know that Dinora's body is being meticulously preserved in Lord Huntington's dungeons," she said with an edge that could kill. "Because of her age and the magic used to prolong her life, her body had begun to rapidly decay after Nyla destroyed her aura. I would be more than happy to show you all as soon as the corpse is stable enough to withstand transport. For now," she said waving a glowing hand, "you may observe Commander Howards and her team's progress to preserve Dinora through that crystal ball if it so pleases you."

The woman who'd questioned Ingrid paled. "How…considerate of you."

Shamira watched as the man with the scar pressed his lips together to keep from snickering, glancing away as if averting his gaze would save him from his own amusement at the situation.

Ingrid bowed her head, though her posture was anything but submissive. Shamira would say she was mocking the woman. "My apologies, Representative Wesson. I've forgotten that not all present are disposed to a strong will."

At her words, the image playing within the crystal ball faded.

"Well, with that settled," the king began, "there is actually a matter I would like to bring forth. It pertains to Miss Delhart."

Shamira's heart pounded against her chest. It took all of her limited restraint not to growl at him, and even more self-restraint to not lunge at the person who spoke next.

"Yes, I wanted to say something about Miss Delhart too." Shamira's eyes landed on the fair-haired woman, hardening into a glare that the woman either ignored or did not see at all. "I think there needs to be some discussion about how Miss Delhart defeated Dinora. It's an unspoken law, but a law all the same. Does she understand—"

"I don't think you're in much of a position to speak about the method in which Nyla killed Dinora," Ingrid said. Shamira's ears perked at the edge in her voice. Stealing a glance at the Royal Mage, Shamira found her to be oddly calm despite the intent in her words. "Last I heard, *Ms.* Addams, you remained safe behind these walls as a delegate of the Chamber of Commons. You did not face the threats many of us did on that battlefield, and you most certainly don't understand the danger Dinora posed to Tenebris, let alone to the balance of magic. So, before you speak so ignorantly, I suggest you reflect on your words and all that you do not know before casting judgement on the person who saved us all from certain ruin."

Silence descended upon the table. Shamira watched the wary gaze Ms. Addams cast about the table, but she found no ally, even if there were those who shared her sentiment about how Nyla had defeated Dinora and the divisiveness that clouded her method of ending the sorceress's threat.

"I…" the king began again, hesitantly drawing the table's attention. "I had actually meant to say that Clarice and I wished to discuss matters regarding Nyla's future, in thanks for the great service she so bravely performed for this country."

"What," Lord Huntington asked through gritted teeth, "pray tell, do you wish to discuss regarding my charge?"

"I didn't realize you'd taken charge of Nyla," Ingrid nearly hissed. Shamira frowned, glancing between the two and the distinct taste of static—of tension—that crackled between them. "When was that decision made?"

I don't believe it was, Shamira said. She tried to ease the ruffle of her fur, knowing full well that the scruff on the back of her neck stood on end. *Nyla has always been quite an independent woman. I believe she should be given the courtesy of being involved in decisions that impact her.*

Ingrid nodded vigorously, likely opening her mouth to agree in earnest, but Xander's grandfather spoke before the woman had a chance.

"I only meant to say that Nyla is a guest under my household and a close friend to my family," Lord Huntington explained calmly, glaring back at the table. "As such, and given her circumstances, I feel inclined to act on her behalf until she is present."

The king glanced between the three of them, sharing a brief glance with his wife before addressing them once more. "My apologies. I only meant to inform you all that Clarice and I have remembered that the Delhart family is a distant relation of the Thornraven and Hart families. Miss Delhart is eligible to both titles, though the Delhart family forfeited their lands a little more than two centuries ago, and the state of the Thornraven estate is…uncertain."

Uncertain how? Shamira asked.

The king met her gaze. "The last of the Thornraven family was believed to have died many centuries ago. Astrid Genevieve Thornraven had no children of her own when she passed, and through the centuries, her siblings' children and their descendants have all died and at some point bore no heirs. Their estate lived in a state of suspense, especially as the Hart family became the Delhart family and forfeited their claim, moving to Eurland. There may be nothing left of that estate and the Thornravens' holdings for Miss Delhart but a ceremonial title, but it could be hers if she so wanted it."

Queen Clarice placed a gentle hand on the king's arm. "Albert and I have discussed it thoroughly over these last few days. We would like to fund a trust for Miss Delhart, as the Thornraven and Hart families had always been close allies of the Caradels, and they helped to found this country." Smiling to herself, Queen Clarice's eyes dropped to the table. "It goes without saying that both families have sacrificed a great deal for this country as well, and Miss Delhart is no different from her ancestors, however she may not know it."

Shamira shifted in her seat, kneading the cushion with her paws as the royals' words sank into her mind. Nyla would need money to support herself, but she doubted very much that Nyla would be willing to accept their generosity. From what she was able to glean, it seemed to her that Nyla wanted nothing more than to fade into obscurity.

"I will discuss it with Nyla when she is recovered," Lord Huntington said solemnly.

"From what Gerri has told me," another man started. Shamira studied the man, hanging onto his mention of Gerri and wondering if he was speaking of Nan. Could this be the George Nyla and Xander had spoken so fondly of? "Nyla needs some time to adjust, and we must respect that, however long she needs."

A stiff silence descended upon the table at his words.

"It is an awful lot, for a woman as young as she is, isn't it?" a Caster with blonde hair murmured.

"We were all that young once," the man with the scar lamented. "But we never faced a decision like that. Some go their whole lives without something so grave. Miss Delhart has witnessed far too much tragedy for someone so young."

I should like to believe, Shamira began calmly. All eyes turned to her. The cloudiness of their somber expressions cleared at the sound of her voice. Looking them each in the eye, she continued evenly, *That with time, those tragedies will lose their grip on Nyla's mind and heart.*

"I pray you may be right, Shamira," Lord Huntington said quietly. "For some scars never quite heal."

Static bit at Shamira's tongue as the weight of Lord Huntington's sentiment settled on the table.

She too knew scars that never healed. Her entire kin knew those scars all too well.

22. NO MATTER HOW RIDICULOUS

Carefully balancing the heavy tray Moretta had piled high with ponanchkas and a cake for Nyla in one hand, Xander raised his hand to knock on the Lavender Room's solid door. His hand hovered over the firm wood for a second. With any luck, he wouldn't be imposing on Nyla. After all, there hadn't been any sign from her at all that she wanted company the last time anyone had seen her. But maybe… maybe she was just resting and had forgotten all about checking in with anyone.

With that fragile hope, Xander finally knocked.

Nothing.

Silence met his knock. Xander's fingers twitched against the tray in his hands. He considered trying again, but wasn't sure if doing so would garner any response. He could always call through the door and tell Nyla that he was leaving her some food, but then what? It wouldn't exactly satisfy his concern if he just left without some form of response from her.

Just as he was about to knock again, the door cracked open. Nyla's lilac-colored eyes peeked out at him from around the edge of the door. Relief flooded her eyes as she saw that it was only him.

"Hi," she said quietly, opening the door a little wider. Her eyes landed on the tray, sparking slightly at the sight of the ponanchkas and the mini cake Moretta had excitedly whipped up when Xander had told her who he was foraging for outside of mealtime, and so soon before dinner too.

Xander held the tray up in offering. "I wasn't sure if you were hungry, so…"

"Did you make those?" she asked, a small but excited smile on her face.

"Well…no, Moretta did," Xander replied, shifting on his feet, "but I asked if she could?"

Nyla nodded, reaching to take the tray from him. Turning away, she said, "They smell amazing."

Xander watched her walk away, standing awkwardly out in the hallway. Unsure of what to do, he said, "I have no doubt Moretta—"

"Have you eaten yet?" Nyla asked, setting the tray down on the coffee table and looking at him curiously. "I don't think I can eat all of this myself."

"Uh," Xander started. His mind had gone blank. He hadn't expected Nyla to want company. Hesitating, Xander hovered in the doorway, uncertain of whether he'd interpreted Nyla's words correctly.

She closed her eyes, sighing softly. "Please don't make me tell you how much I really don't want to be alone but at the same time can't stand to be around anyone right now."

"Sounds like quite the contradiction," he said, stepping over the threshold. "What if I just sit quietly and stare at the ceiling? You won't be alone, but you wouldn't have to talk to me either. We could just… be alone together."

Nyla smiled. "I'd like that."

Nodding slightly, Xander returned her smile. Stepping farther into the Lavender Room, he pulled the door shut behind him. Nyla's attention had turned to the tray of ponanchkas before he'd even crossed the room and plopped down on the couch across from her. Crossing his legs at the ankle, Xander put his hands behind his head and stared at the ceiling, just as he'd said he would do if Nyla had accepted his company.

The scrape of her utensils joined the gentle crackle of the wood-burning fire working in vain to warm the room. Every so often, Nyla hummed in what he hoped was contentment. Moretta had been filled with a nervousness he'd never seen before as she'd handed him the plate of ponanchkas to put on the tray beside the individual cake. She'd said that she hadn't made ponanchkas since his grandmother had become ill and couldn't manage the walk down to the kitchens to make them herself.

Xander wondered if Moretta was capable of preparing them like his grandmother had, though he couldn't remember what hers were like now that all this time had passed. The only ponanchkas that resided in his memory were the ones Nyla had made back in Covington—and the one he'd snuck while Moretta was fretting over the batch.

A long sigh caught his ear. Turning his head, he saw Nyla pushing the tray back on the coffee table. Lying down on her couch, she clasped her hands over her stomach. She didn't look at him, so he returned to his absent study of the ceiling.

His mind wandered back to the first time they'd met. He hadn't thought anything could be as awkward as the silence between them in the cave, but this? This silence?

It wasn't merely awkward; it was stiff and burdensome. There was a tension crackling like lightning under the surface of this silence. Xander feared how loud the thunder would crash when the tension finally broke—whenever Nyla would be ready to talk.

He feared what would happen more if she didn't than how loud the thunder could be if she spoke her mind.

"You're worried," Nyla said to the ceiling.

Xander huffed a dry chuckle. "What gave it away?"

"Nothing really," she answered. Though her voice was even, Xander noticed it didn't quite hold the tone he'd come to associate with her. Nyla's voice hadn't any warmth or life to it. Like her eyes, her voice had gone dull in the aftermath of killing Dinora and facing her stone creatures. "I just know you."

"If you know me," he said, licking his lips, "then it's fair of me to say I know you, right?"

His eyes flicked to her, watching as his words settled on her. As she processed them, Nyla's lips twisted in confusion.

"Yes?"

"I know you're not okay," Xander said, watching her closely now. "No one expects you to be, but we're all desperate to be there for you. We want to help you, however you'll let us."

"I know," she whispered. "I just don't know what I'm asking for."

Xander's heart wavered empathetically. He ought to change the subject, but to what? Would it help, or would it only delay the inevitable?

"Your hair," he started carefully, "it's mostly auburn now. Do you like it?"

Nyla turned her head to look at him. Her brows crinkled. Silence pounded between his ears.

"I don't know," she said at last. Her lips twitched into what could've been a smile. A small spark ignited in her lilac-colored eyes, a fraction of their former light. "I'd gotten used to the silver, but it's nice to look in the mirror and see my own face again, not Astrid's."

"Do you think your eyes will change back too?"

"I don't know. I suppose I should ask Shamira." Twisting onto her side and tucking her hands beneath her head, she added, "Or Edwin. Or Ingrid…do you think Ingrid's upset with me? About…my decisions?"

Xander considered this for a moment, replaying everything that'd happened during the battle and in the face of its aftermath. Ingrid had never been angry at Nyla. Worried, slightly irritated, helpless, they all applied. But upset?

He didn't think there was a person who'd witnessed Nyla's decisions and what she'd done to save this country from Dinora's wrath that could claim to be upset with her over her decisions.

Offering her a reassuring look, he said, "No. I wouldn't be worried about if Ingrid, or anyone for that matter, is upset with you about your choices. The only thing you could worry about is the fact that nearly everyone here feels guilty for not helping you."

"They did, though," Nyla insisted. "If it wasn't for their magic, I would've never…"

"You relinquished the cooperative bond," Xander reminded her. "You did…*that*, all on your own, and that's what has people upset. They're not angry with you. They're angry at themselves for not being there, for not being at your side."

"Are you angry?" she whispered. "At yourself, 'for not being there?'"

Xander hesitated. He sat up and swung his legs so his feet were planted on the floor, curling his fingers against his knees. A slight shudder ran through his body as he braced himself for the truth he was about to speak. "Yes. More than anything, I wish this burden wasn't yours, that I had at least been there for you, or could share some of it with you."

Nyla stared at him, unblinking. Breathing hard, Xander didn't know what to do, or what came next. But he certainly hadn't expected what Nyla said next.

"I wasn't alone," Nyla said slowly. "They were there. My family, Astrid, every single person Dinora had wronged."

They'd all seen it, the moment between Nyla and her family, how the spirits Dinora had murdered, had trapped inside the Shadow Forest in her quest for power, had rallied around Nyla as she'd whittled Dinora's aura down to nothing. But Xander hadn't expected Nyla to talk about those precious moments when her family had stood by her during and after the battle.

Sitting up, Nyla's eyes turned vacant as she recounted those final moments, staring at Xander, but seeing right through him as if he didn't exist. "I didn't realize it until Astrid's hand landed on my shoulder, but I saw the smoke—the spirits. I felt them. Their anger, their thirst for vengeance, for justice. I was just as 'eager' as they were to—to…"

She broke off with a sob. Xander rushed to close the gap between them as if it hadn't existed in the first place. As he went to rest his hands on her shoulders, Nyla leaned into him. So instead, Xander wrapped his arms around her, letting her hide away in his gentle embrace. Her fingers curled against his sides, pulling at his shirt. Twisting his lips to stop from frowning, Xander started to rub her back.

They stayed like that for a long time. Nyla's choked sobs died after a minute or two, replaced by quiet sniffling and heaving breaths. And Xander let her, not knowing what else to do or what he should say.

Was there anything he *could* say to her?

Xander didn't know. All he did know was that he hadn't seen what Nyla had firsthand. He hadn't killed Dinora.

"I'm sorry," Nyla rasped, tilting her head back to look at him with puffy eyes. "I just…and now there're tears and snot all over your shirt…"

"That's the least of my worries right now, Nyla," he said sincerely, kneeling so he was mostly level with her. "What can I do for you? I don't care how ridiculous you think it sounds. Just ask and I'll do it."

She sucked in a breath, staring at him with wide, conflicted eyes. "Stay with me?"

"Yeah." He nodded. "Let me grab some pillows and blankets, and we'll stay right here, just like we did before your duel."

Nyla sighed, pulling away and brushing her hair back from her face. "I wish things were still that simple."

Xander tilted his head, gathering up the blankets from her bed and two pillows. "I think we should go back further and go back to the days when things were really simple. Like when we visited Nan and George, or the day at the beach, or…was there anything simpler before that?"

"No," Nyla sighed. "If I could travel through time, I'd choose that day in Caselle. The beach was nice, but…"

"It's the banana cake, isn't it?" Xander teased, handing her a pillow before joining her on the couch and spreading the blankets over them.

Nyla stretched her legs out. Propping herself against the arm of the couch, she wrapped her arms around her middle. "Maybe…"

Laughing, Xander made himself comfortable, stretching his legs out alongside hers. "I'm sure if you asked, Nan would be more than happy to make you another cake."

"I don't think cake is going to bring anything more than a momentary comfort," she said, turning serious again. "If I could go back…" She paused, nibbling her lip. "If it were possible, I'd try to convince myself to walk away, to let someone else defeat Dinora."

Xander's hand drifted to the ring hidden beneath his shirt. Blowing out a tense breath, he debated what he was about to tell her, knowing that someone would eventually tell her and that it should be him. "Edwin and I…" he started slowly, pinching the ring between his fingers through his shirt. "When Edwin and I went to see Cedric during the battle—you know, *before*, he escaped…he told us some things while we were questioning him. But before that, he offered us a confession of sorts."

"What?" Nyla asked. Her question was hardly audible in the quiet room, but her disbelief was like a blow to Xander's head. "*That's* what Ingrid meant when she said you and Edwin were serving a punishment because Cedric had gotten free? You really went to talk to him, for answers?"

"I thought—" he said, licking his lips. "I'd *hoped*—to get some kind of miraculous truth out of him that could end the battle sooner and save you from what you had to do. He didn't, but…he did say other things that I think you should know."

Nyla stared at him with wide eyes. "If you were me, are these things you would want to know, given everything that's happened? Or can they wait until later on in life when…when it's not so fresh in my mind?"

Her question stunned him. "I don't know. I can only tell you that as me, and who I am, I'd want to know."

Taking a shaky breath, Nyla pulled her knees to her chest and folded her arms on top. Tucking her chin in the crook of her arms, she closed her eyes. "Okay. Tell me."

So Xander did.

He told her about how Cedric had wanted to take a blood oath so they could set him free to kill Dinora—and that it was possible Cedric *had* made a blood oath to him. He told her how Cedric had claimed to want to kill Dinora, to do the right thing for once in his life, and not force that decision onto someone else. Considering it for only a heartbeat, he finally told Nyla how Cedric had claimed to perform a *Mortis tradsmagique*, and that that was the potion he'd transferred to her during the fight at the Woodlane Manor.

"Dinora set herself free, according to him," he finished. "But I don't know how much of that to believe, if any of it."

Nyla didn't say anything for a long time. She stared into the flames of the fireplace with a haunted look in her eyes. "They haven't found him yet?"

"No," Xander answered weakly. "Last my grandfather mentioned, Ingrid and the pumpkies haven't been able to find his trace. And in the meantime, the 'council' is debating what to do about him, though they're still undecided. They were going to meet again tomorrow to discuss it further."

"Oh."

Xander rubbed at the ring, causing a friction between his fingers and the fabric of his shirt. He didn't know what to make of Nyla's reaction or lack thereof.

"We should probably get some sleep," she murmured.

He couldn't stop the words that tumbled from his lips. "You're not going to…" He shook his head. "Sorry, I just didn't know how you would react to any of that."

Letting out a long breath, Nyla slumped against the pillow at her back and leaned her side against the back of the couch, curling against it just as she had the night of the duel. "I don't know what to say, or how to feel about it. All I know is that no matter what Cedric wanted or expected to do, it's all over now, and nothing he's done or hasn't done matters anymore, even if he did…" Nyla bit her lip, leaving Xander to wonder what she'd meant to say. He watched as she shook her head, apparently decided on what she was to say next. "Dinora's dead, and Cedric's probably walking the line between life and death now anyway. I got my revenge, and so did the spirits."

"That's true." Xander sagged with relief. Dropping the ring still pinched between his fingers, Xander glanced toward the door and then back at Nyla as she finished making herself comfortable. "Do you still want me to stay?"

Nyla froze, halfway pulling the blanket up around her shoulders. Biting her lip, she studied the couch cushion. "You really meant it, when you said 'no matter how ridiculous' I think it is?"

"Yes."

"Then stay," she said pleadingly, her eyes flashing between the blankets and anywhere that wasn't directly at him. "Please."

"Whatever you want," he assured her, "all you have to do is tell me."

"Okay."

Getting comfortable, Xander's mind replayed the night in Caselle after Nyla had scared him awake. She'd only just woken up from her astral travels, and neither one of them had known what had happened to her, but all she cared about was getting a glass of water.

But when he'd come back after going to find her something to eat while she'd washed up and changed into something he hadn't had to cut the neckline from thanks to the knife wound she'd sustained to her collarbone and shoulder, only then had he realized how fragile Nyla was beneath the certainty and inner strength that had guided her through the Shadow Forest.

He didn't know why that particular moment came to him then, but he supposed they were rather similar. She'd tried to hide behind a smile then, but he'd known. He saw it in her eyes, the uneasiness and the confusion, the haunted, troubled shadows lurking in her distracted gaze.

But tonight, there was none of that. Nyla hadn't tried to hide behind a forced smile or the appearance of merely being exhausted. While he hated seeing her curled in on herself and withdrawn, he was at least glad that she'd chosen to share it with him. Maybe in doing so, it could ease her burden just the tiniest bit. And maybe, just knowing that there was someone willing to be there with her even when she couldn't figure out what it was she wanted or needed, Nyla wouldn't have to feel so lost anymore.

In his last waking moments before a fitful sleep took him, Xander decided that that's what Nyla was: lost.

But weren't they all? Wasn't feeling lost what happened after such an empty triumph in the face of tragedy?

23. TRUSTS AND FUNDS

Nyla's eyes fluttered open. A hum pressed itself from her chest as she took note of the darkened fireplace before she turned over and let her eyes fall shut again. Pulling the blanket back up to her chin, Nyla curled in on herself.

"Not again," a sleepy voice mumbled.

The blanket receded to her shoulders. Nyla opened her eyes, frowning. Forcing her head up, she looked down the length of the couch and found Xander staring back at her.

"Did you know you steal the blankets in your sleep?" he asked almost accusingly.

"No," she said. "How would I know that?"

Xander opened and closed his mouth. "I guess that's fair. Your sister never told you?"

Nyla shut her eyes and made a show of going back to sleep. "Lydia and I had separate beds."

"Probably because you steal the blankets."

Nyla nudged her foot halfheartedly against his hip. "You're the one who picked this blanket. It's your fault for picking the shorter one."

Xander chuckled.

"What time is it, anyway?" she asked before he could say another word. She burrowed farther down into the warmth of the blanket, pulling it up to her chin again just to annoy him.

"A little before we have to get up and head down to breakfast…" Xander said. "Unless you'd rather eat here?"

Nyla opened her eyes and propped herself up on her elbows. "Do you think anyone would—"

"No one would mind," Xander said sincerely. "I'll go and get dressed and have something brought up. Is there anything specific you want?"

Nyla shook her head.

Xander nodded and slipped from the couch. Tousling his hair, he strode over to the fireplace. Nyla watched in silence as he arranged some more logs and lit the fire again. She dropped her eyes before he could turn around and see that she'd been watching him, worrying at her lip as she sat up fully.

"I'll be right back."

Nyla didn't immediately say anything. Xander's quiet footsteps drew farther away with each beat of her heart. The words she'd wanted to say on the balcony flitted through her mind. At the memory of how they'd stuck in her throat, heat bloomed along the shell of her ears. She didn't know how to express how she felt then, and she still didn't quite know or understand it. All she knew was that she didn't want to let another moment pass without saying *something*. Finally, as though she couldn't take the burning of her ears anymore, Nyla called out, "Xander?"

"Yeah?" he asked, looking back at her as he hovered by the door, his hand half extended to reach for the handle.

"Thank you for staying with me last night."

Xander blinked. A slow smile spread across his face as he glanced away. When his eyes next met hers, Nyla's breath hitched. "Anything you want, Nyla, and it's yours. All you have to do is ask, you know that, right?"

"I think I'm beginning to realize that," she said despite the dryness of her throat. Her heart beat like a drum between her ears as Xander offered her a broad grin before he slipped through the door.

Of all the places she'd been, and of the people she'd met along the way, Nyla was becoming ever more grateful for the storm that had forced them both to take shelter in that cave in the Shadow Forest. Moreover, she realized, she was glad her heart was still capable of loving, for that was what she must feel toward Xander. It could only be love, Nyla realized, finding comfort in the word that encompassed how much she wanted him to be a part of her future, and in her life.

Shaking her head, Nyla smiled to herself as she pushed the blanket away. Getting to her feet, Nyla grasped for the weightlessness she was beginning to feel and relished the blooming clarity of her mind.

No matter how nervous she was about what the day would bring, or what might lie ahead for her in her future, Nyla was certain of one thing: Xander would always be there. And so would the woman she'd become.

The woman who'd overcome her fears. The woman who'd stopped running from the shadows, from the past. The woman who'd defeated the evil sorceress that had stolen magic from the land and damned the souls of those who'd supported and opposed her to an almost eternity in the Shadow Forest.

All Nyla had to do was remember who she was and what it was she wanted. If she could do that, Nyla knew she would be unstoppable.

***

Nyla took a deep breath through her nose. Staring at the closed door of Alexander's study, she shifted nervously on her feet. She knew Xander and all the others were already inside, though that's what terrified her so.

She'd only seen her friends, Ingrid, Nan, and Alexander since waking up. And she knew they'd been shielding her from the others, a blessing and a curse as Nyla realized now that she was about to face the brunt of everyone's concern for her all at once.

On her way here from the Lavender Room, some of Pemberly's staff and the few Casters or soldiers she'd encountered had stopped her, asking after her health and offering their help if she ever needed it.

She'd only smiled politely and thanked them. What was she supposed to say? She couldn't lie to them and say she was fine, when it was obvious to everyone that she wasn't. She just didn't have the heart to do that at the moment. Instead, she'd swallowed the truth and offered them some semblance of surety. Somewhere deep inside of her, Nyla hoped that this false assurance would eventually consume her until it became true.

She wasn't very hopeful it would work, though.

Steeling herself, Nyla reached for the handle of the door. Without even knocking, she opened the door and slipped inside.

As the door creaked open, the low rumble of conversation stopped mid-syllable. Alexander's eyes flashed, before he saw that it was only her. George offered her a small smile and a wave that she half-heartedly returned. Nearly two dozen sets of eyes fixed on her. Casters, soldiers, King Albert and Queen Clarice, people she considered friends, and total strangers alike all came to stare at her thanks to the creak of the hinges.

Nyla's breath stuttered in her chest, nearly flinching at the sound of a chair scraping against the hardwood. Xander stood and crossed the room. He offered her his hand, and Nyla took it without hesitation. She let him lead her to the chair set beside his. She didn't realize how much the simple gesture could ground her, forever grateful for the soft hand that always seemed to be there for her—and the man who seemed to always know when she needed just a little help.

"Please, join us," Alexander said as Xander settled in the seat he'd taken beside her. "I'm glad to see you, Nyla. I don't think any of us had expected to see you today. It's a very…complicated topic of discussion today."

"I'm aware," Nyla said, forcing a smile to her face and withdrawing her hand from Xander's after giving his hand a little squeeze as way of thanking him. "But I wanted to see everyone. I heard there's been questions about my health, so I'm here to say that I'm fine, thanks to Nan and Ingrid."

Gerri bowed her head. "I did very little compared to the Mage General, but I'm glad to hear the rest did you some good."

"I can't imagine the drain—" a blonde Caster started, only to stop midsentence with a wince. She thought it was Alistair, but with how briefly she'd met him, she couldn't be certain as soon all the people she'd been introduced to before the battle had gotten mixed up in her mind. Glaring at the person beside him, Nyla wondered if he'd been kicked in the shin. "Excuse me. I only meant to say I'm glad to see you recovered."

"Thank you," Nyla said. "Now I believe I interrupted Sir Hubert?"

Sir Hubert nodded curtly at her. His eyes flashed in question as she met his gaze. Nyla's lips turned up in a way she wouldn't quite call a smile, but in its own way, it granted Sir Hubert the assurance he needed to continue. "Thank you, Miss Delhart. Now, as I was saying, even if we do find him, Cedric Kashar is a centuries-old entity. By law, he's considered dead. Judge Chauntily has provided a record from about 575 years ago declaring Cedric and Dinora both dead as a result of the war. Now obviously, Cedric Kashar is alive, but legally speaking, unless we file a motion to overturn the declaration, in the eyes of the law, he's been dead for hundreds of years, and, to be blunt, we cannot prosecute a dead man.

"As for his crimes, to our knowledge, any crimes he's committed have been illegal throughout the last 647 years. Chief among the list of possible charges include treason, murder, attempted murder, destruction of magical property..." he hesitated, glancing up from the roll of parchment he held open in his hands, "and...arson."

Nyla's cheeks warmed at the sidelong glances people snuck at her.

Queen Clarice saved her from their scrutiny, calling the attention of the table to her. "So if the majority of his charges have been illegal throughout the country's history," she began, "it *is* possible to hold him accountable for his actions, and not just those of recent years?"

"Well," a man seated near the center of the table began. Nyla furrowed her brows. She hadn't seen him before, not at the initial gathering nor at the war council of just the other day. "As Sir Hubert mentioned, Cedric Kashar is considered to be dead. You can't prosecute a dead man, regardless of whether or not he subverted natural law to extend his life using magic. Filing a motion to overturn the declaration of his death would make this a very public affair, a fact I'm sure you had all hoped to avoid. So the question becomes—how do we try a man that the law has considered dead for centuries on account that using magic to extend one's natural life wasn't even a thought until now? And, moreover, for what crimes could he be indicted? Even without considering the statutes of limitations set forth by Tenebrese law, what evidence can these indictments and even a trial be based on, proven, or supported by?" The man paused, shaking his head as his grim eyes turned toward the table. "I am sorry to say that as much as we would want to bring Cedric before the mercy of justice, I do not think it can be done through conventional means. There are too many uncertainties and legal procedures or precedents to reconcile in this particular matter."

Xander leaned closer to her. "That's Judge Vermón Chauntily from the High Court."

Nyla nodded, even as her mouth went dry at his words. The High Court of Tenebris? *That* High Court? Her head spun as she tried to understand Judge Chauntily's words.

A Representative from the Chamber of Commons spoke next, though she couldn't put a name to his face. "I think we need to face the facts here. There is no precedent for something like this, legal or practical. No one has ever done what the Kashars have done, and that's not even to mention the act of magically prolonging their lives. Perhaps this is the one time we cannot look to our past to decide the course of the future. There is only the present, and in the present, Cedric has not only aided an extreme renegade, but he's stolen magic from the land, causing grave damage to local ecosystems and the balance of magic."

Ingrid clicked her tongue, crossing her arms over her chest. A dark scowl painted her face. "Even so, no trial could be held without the past marring our judgement. We've already kept so much from the public. What's one more thing?"

Alexander shifted in his chair, the only sign Nyla had ever seen him give of his discomfort. "The press is already spreading conspiracies about the earthquake. Amateur magicologists as well as respected scholars have come forth to discuss the rapid and unprecedented fluctuations in magic of four days ago. The public is already aware of what's happened in their own capacity. Someone is going to have to report the truth, or as much of it as we can divulge to save reputation and ease public panic."

"So what do you suggest? Parade Cedric Kashar before a jury and hold a conventional trial?"

The room fell silent. Nyla stole a glance at the king and queen, then at Alexander and the other members of Astrid's secret society. The Heirs of Tenebris and their descendants had operated in secret for 647 years. Would it really hurt to have one more secret upon the heap of them?

Nyla wracked her brain for a possible solution, but none presented itself. Her mind refused to work any harder than was necessary, still bogged down by the weight of her soul's quandary.

"I don't think that would be necessary." Ingrid said. Her eyes flitted with her thoughts as she leaned forward in her seat. "What if…what if we were to create a council much like this in order to prosecute Cedric for his crimes? It would be a private trial held in conjunction with the High Court. I agree with Alexander. A statement must be made to clarify what's happened and calm the public. The longer we try to hide things, the more discontent will be sown until there's only unrest. The people deserve to know."

"And where would this statement be coming from?" Representative Wesson asked hotly. "Until recently, neither the Chamber of Commons nor the Chamber of Justice was aware of such threats, or the measures in place to combat it. But as we're all aware," she paused, inclining her head toward King Albert and Queen Clarice like a mock show of respect, "their majesties have no authority, and the Heirs of Tenebris are not a recognized…well, they're nothing more than an unofficial guild of sorts."

Across the table, Alexander huffed, shaking his head. "I trust it was explained to you how this organization began?"

"I believe what Lord Huntington meant to say," George started, holding a hand up as if he could block Alexander's words from reaching the representative sitting beside Judge Chauntily, "was, upon her death, the first Mage General had left specific instructions to her closest allies. Our families have honored those instructions these past six centuries, and while the deception was unintended, it was necessary. As the world forgot the truth immortalized in the legends, so did we. We assumed there was no threat to safeguard against, and so each generation moved away from the fears of our predecessors."

Sir Hubert's voice carried over the mutterings and disorderly outbursts at George's statement. "So where does this leave us? Who will sit on this tribunal council, and who will make this statement?"

Everyone seemed to look at each other, casting glances around the table. Nyla fixed her gaze on the edge of the table, not wanting any part in this process. She wondered if it were too late to get up and leave.

"What about a joint statement?" Xander asked. "After all, you're all involved, and if the history has to be explained anyway, it only makes sense for all these different factions to be represented in the statement."

Nyla turned to look at him, her brow arched.

"The young lord raises an excellent point," King Albert said. "As Representative Wesson reminded us, Clarice and I have no authoritative power. We're merely ceremonial figures of a bygone era, and the Heirs of Tenebris are an unrecognized group with no affiliation whatsoever. But the Chambers cannot present the facts on their own. We may want to make a joint statement to dispel the public's rising concerns and assure them that there is no threat."

"I agree," Queen Clarice added, leaving absolutely no room between the king's statement and her concurrence for anyone to argue. "A joint statement would acknowledge all involved parties and explain their necessity, as well as pacify the public's concerns. Does this suit you, Representative Wesson?"

"I cannot speak on behalf of the Chamber, only the Security Council," she said almost dejectedly. "However, both the idea of a joint and unified statement, as well as a private tribunal to prosecute Cedric Kashar, is agreeable to me. I should have to discuss this further with my colleagues before moving forward."

"As an ambassador for the Courts," Judge Chauntily started, "I can find no reason that these proposals would violate Tenebrese laws or usurp the power structure in place. The only concern I have, from a legal point of view, is the exclusion of representatives from the provincial and municipal offices. But I suppose given the circumstances, the prosecution of Dinora and Cedric Kashar would normally be under the oversight of the federal Chambers anyway, so I can't see much of an issue from that standpoint either."

Grumbles of agreement sounded all around the table.

"Then it's decided," Alexander started, standing from his chair. "We will draft an official statement and invite members of the press for a briefing upon its publication."

"And the tribunal council? What of that?" Representative Wesson asked.

Leaning upon his fists, a streak of mischief flashed in Alexander's eyes. "I do believe we're already gathered. Wouldn't you say so, Representative?"

Nyla watched as the woman narrowed her eyes and folded her arms over her chest, tapping her fingers against her arm. Pursing her lips, Representative Wesson surveyed the table. Her gaze landed on Nyla and Xander. Nyla gulped.

"Will you two be joining us?" she asked.

Xander began, "Of cou—"

"I won't be," Nyla said, leveling her eyes with the representative's. The weight of Xander's shock burned into her profile, but Nyla ignored his stare as she explained herself. "Cedric has wronged me personally, and I don't believe I would be able to look past that."

"Mm." Representative Wesson considered her for a moment before speaking again. "That's very admirable, Miss Delhart. What of you, Lord Huntington?"

Xander shook himself, turning to address Representative Wesson. "Gladly."

"Very well then," she said.

"Wait," Nyla said before she could stop herself. Ingrid froze, staring at her curiously. The others all turned to glance at her too. Some turned irritated gazes on her, but most seemed just as surprised as Xander. "There is one thing I'd like to ask of all of you."

"What is it?" Ingrid nodded encouragingly. "I think I can speak for all of us here when I say that this country owes you a debt it may never pay, though it's no less deserved."

Nyla took a breath, wishing her chair would swallow her whole. "About the tribunal…all I ask is that you judge Cedric fairly and grant him a merciful punishment. That's all."

Peeking at each of the room's occupants, Nyla's heart quivered. Some people looked taken aback, as if she'd said something entirely ridiculous. Others looked furious with their furrowed brows and curled lips.

"Please," she added, "I know he's undeserving of mercy, and I'm not asking that he goes unpunished. All I'm asking is that we don't succumb to the same threshold of volatility that he and Dinora had. If it's death that you decide to sentence him to, then make it swift. If it's imprisonment, remember your humanity before subjecting him to the worst of it. That's all I want to ask of you."

King Albert and Queen Clarice shared a glance. Alexander studied her intently. A stillness had descended upon the room. Nyla wondered briefly if she were the only one capable of moving at the moment.

"You would recommend clemency?" Judge Chauntily started, his wide eyes fixed on her. "For a criminal—no, for someone as despicable as Cedric Kashar?"

Nyla hesitated, forcing herself to hold the judge's stare. The words— the truth—stuck in her throat. A lie leapt from her tongue instead. "Yes."

Judge Chauntily studied her a moment longer before nodding. "I cannot speak for everyone here, but as a High Court Judge, I can assure you that I will uphold the highest legal and moral standards while serving as justice's representative, even for a case as challenging as this."

Nyla offered him a small smile, hoping that was it, that her part in all of this was done. She'd said her piece and had offered her opinion when she had something to say. Now, she could rest. In her heart, Nyla knew this was the last time she would ever choose to participate in these matters—or any similar matter she might face in life.

"Then all there's left to discuss are the memorials," Lord Huntington said, gathering the attention of the table and shifting it away from her.

Nyla's heart dropped. She couldn't believe they hadn't already discussed that in the few days she'd spent recuperating from the battle. Did that mean they'd lost more in the time since the battle? Had others succumbed to their injuries?

"Everything has been prepared," Ingrid said, looking years older than she was. "I have a handful of families left to notify, but otherwise, all is taken care of."

Sir Hubert sighed, scrubbing his face. "I dispatched the last of my condolences this morning. The vigil for the Royal Guard is set to take place in two weeks' time, to make sure the loved ones have time to mourn in private before the observance at the fort."

Representative Wesson nodded. "I'll make certain a fund is established for those families, from all the forces present at the battle."

"The Heirs have a small collection we would like to donate to that fund," Alexander said. "It isn't much, but it is something to help the families get by."

"I'm sure it will be welcomed," Representative Wesson assured him. "Well, if that is all," she said, glancing around the table, "I should take my leave so I might make my report to my colleagues. I'll send word as soon as we have made our decision about the tribunal."

"Splendid," Queen Clarice said, though Nyla noticed her gaze was fixed solely on Ingrid. "I'm sure Ingrid will inform you as soon as her Circle finds Cedric."

"Of course," Ingrid said, folding her arms over her chest. "Where would we be if not for our mutual cooperation and communication?"

Sir Hubert let out a cough that sounded distinctly like a stifled laugh. Nyla wondered about the meaning behind Ingrid's words, or the icy attitude she'd noticed between her and Representative Wesson. She'd have to ask Xander about it later.

"It's settled then," Alexander said, drawing the table's attention away from the tension crackling between the three women. "I cannot think of any other matter that remains to be finalized. Sir Hubert?"

The man in question shook his head. "The matter of Cedric Kashar was the only thing on my agenda."

"Then let us adjourn," Ingrid said. "I still have a rogue Caster to find and bring before this tribunal."

The general shuffle of people shifting and chairs being pushed back against the hardwood assaulted Nyla's ears. Nyla narrowed her eyes, watching as Ingrid maneuvered around those who might've approached her and slipped through the door.

Did her quick exit have to do with what Xander told her last night? Was Ingrid really trying to find Cedric to bring before the tribunal, or was she looking to find answers about the claims he'd made before he'd broken free?

"Miss Delhart?"

Nyla hummed distractedly, turning her head to meet the person who sought her attention. Her eyebrows raised, finding both the king and queen standing beside her.

"When it suits you, might we have a word?" Queen Clarice continued.

Nyla opened and closed her mouth. Overcoming her surprise, she managed to say, "We can speak now, if you'd like."

Her gaze flicked to Alexander. He simply raised a pacifying hand and resumed his seat at the table.

Nyla forced her hands to still in her lap, clasping them together as the king and queen of Tenebris sat in the seats directly across from her. Her eyes shifted to Xander, to see if he was just as clueless as she was or if she was the only one in this situation caught unawares. Letting a slow breath out through her nose, Nyla was glad to have seen the confused twist of Xander's lip and his slightly arched brow before she was forced to turn her attention back to the ceremonial regents of Tenebris.

"As I'm sure you well know by now," King Albert started almost nervously, "your family and the history of Tenebris have always been greatly intertwined. How much of your ancestors' history do you know?"

Nyla glanced between the pair, wondering just what they expected her to say. "My mother was Eurish, so most of my family is still there, and my father was born here in the Godberd Woods. His family were mariners by trade, and that's actually how he met my mother. He worked for a trading…" Nyla stopped, realizing the company she was in. For the first time since she'd met Xander, she wondered if it was *his* family's business that her father had worked for. Shaking her head, she resolved to investigate that a little later and forced herself to continue. "My mother's family are blacksmiths, and she used to run their stall by the port. But that's really all I know. For as long as anyone can remember, that's my family's history."

The king and queen shared a look. A secret conversation seemed to pass between them before Queen Clarice looked expectantly over at Alexander.

Following her gaze, Nyla sought out an explanation from anyone willing to give it. As Alexander seemed to accept his cue, his eyes met hers.

"Nyla," he started, "as the descendant of Astrid Genevieve Thornraven, you come from two lines of Tenebris's founders, or rather two of the founding families."

Nyla's lips parted. Her brows raised in surprise. What was he saying?

"Because of your heritage, it's possible that you could be inducted into the nobility and be entitled to whatever holdings or accounts may still be held by the Harts and Thornravens, if any of their estates have survived."

"What?" Nyla asked in disbelief. "You mean I..." She shook her head. "No, I can't be. You must be mistaken. My family name is Delhart, and my father's was Storen. We're not..."

But couldn't they be? Couldn't her family be descended from two of Tenebris's founding families? There had to be some truth in it, as she was clearly Astrid's descendant, so maybe what Alexander and the royals were telling her was yet another of Fate's gifts.

"As Heirs of Tenebris," Queen Clarice said softly, "it was my and Albert's duty to preserve the records of the founding families, as well as securing funds and retaining some semblance of political relevancy. The Caradel family has done so for generations, as a way to honor the wishes of your ancestor. In doing so, we're well acquainted with the histories of the noble families of Tenebris, yours included."

The queen's eyes were piercing as she stared back at Nyla, holding her gaze as though they were the only two in the room. "The Hart family emigrated to Eurland after forfeiting their titles some centuries ago. They retained their estate, though, and our records indicate that a name change occurred shortly after their establishment in Eurland. The Hart family became the Delhart family."

The monarch's words had hardly settled on Nyla's shoulders before King Albert was adding, "With a little bit of research, Clarice and I believe there might be a little something of their estate left for you, but their title is yours if you want it, just as is the Thornravens', though their estate is a little more complicated." He paused for a moment and explained, "It was widely believed that the Thornraven family was no longer extant, until we met you. With no direct descendants, their lineage was difficult to trace, and so their assets and estate were liquidated hardly even a century ago."

Nyla didn't know what to make of their presentation. Surely, they didn't mean what she thought they did. Slowly, she picked her gaze up from where it had wandered to study the table and met the cautious gazes of King Albert and Queen Clarice.

"Are you saying that…" Nyla started hesitantly, "that my family has roots that extend as far back as the country's founding? And that I'm *technically* a noble?"

"Yes," the king said, "but only if you wish to accept these titles. You don't have to, if you don't want to, Nyla."

"We only want to make certain your sacrifices and great service to this country aren't forgotten." The queen smiled softly at her. "Albert and I have discussed it thoroughly, and we would like to establish a trust for you, regardless of whether or not you accept your family's titles and whatever remains of their estates. So please," she urged, "take your time to think over your decision. We owe you our eternal gratitude, Nyla."

"Thank you," Nyla said, her mind spinning from everything they'd explained to her. "I'll…consider what you've told me."

With one final bid to take her time, the monarchs stood. As they left, Nyla watched them conversing quietly with each other, arm in arm, their heads bent together.

Letting out a breath she didn't know she'd been holding, Nyla slumped back in her chair. Before she could say a word, Xander nudged her gently with his elbow, offering her a lopsided smile. "Come on. Let's go and do something fun for a change."

"What did you have in mind?" she asked.

"Anything you want." He shrugged. "There's lots to do here, even with the repairs still being done."

Nyla tilted her head, biting her lip. After a moment, she smiled. "What's your favorite thing to do here?"

Chuckling, Xander pushed back his chair. Offering her his hand, he said, "Let me show you."

"Just be sure to be back on time for dinner," Alexander said as he stood from his place at the head of the table.

"We will be," Xander assured him as he led her toward the door. Xander's hand was soft against hers, just as gentle a hold as when he'd found her in the Woodlane Manor's study. Her hand could easily slip from his grasp if she let it, but instead, Nyla only held his hand tighter, letting Xander guide her through the corridors of Pemberly Hall.

24. A Desperate Investigation

I don't understand, Shamira said. *If Cedric had wanted Dinora dead all this time, why continue to draw magic to postpone their deaths? Why do any of it?*

"That's the question we'd all pay to have answered," Edwin grumbled, glowering at the books set before him. As it happened, Ingrid and Shamira had found him in the study-converted-workshop Lord Huntington had allowed him to keep at Pemberly Hall, already researching for ways to investigate Cedric's claims while Ingrid's Circle worked on locating him. "But I doubt Cedric would give us an honest answer."

Ingrid pursed her lips, turning a book to face her as she stood opposite Edwin. "What have you found so far?"

"Not much," Edwin breathed. "Unless we can find some of that potion, or involve Nyla, our options are limited."

The magicitric light cast a long shadow on Edwin's face, making him look far older than he was. For as brightly lit as the room was, Shamira couldn't help but feel a darkness in the wood-paneled room. It was like the deep brown tone of the wood absorbed every ounce of light in the room or that which streamed in from the open window.

Shamira flicked her tail. *Is Nyla aware we're doing this at all?*

"It was mentioned," Ingrid said tensely, "though I'm not certain she knows we're acting on it at this very moment." Shamira watched her carefully, noticing how the woman's lips twisted slightly as she fingered the corner of the page she was studying, pausing before she turned it to the next. "I struggle with telling her things anymore. I worry it would only bring her back to that battlefield, or destroy what healing she's done since. I don't want to worry her any more than necessary, and I most certainly don't want her to think that it's…her 'duty' to walk this path. She has been through enough, and I will not add to it. It is my understanding that Xander had spoken with her about this, so I would prefer not to trouble her further until we know more."

I see, Shamira replied. *Then I suppose we'd better work quickly so that we may present our findings to Nyla in full.*

"I couldn't agree more," Ingrid said. Her voice held a tension that hinted at how overwhelmed the woman truly felt. "The only question is, where do we even begin?"

At the source, Shamira replied. *If we can find the source of Cedric's claims, we can begin to investigate them.*

Edwin sent her a sour look, as if she'd said something impossible. Ingrid arched a delicate brow.

"It could take forever to find the source," Edwin countered. "We should find an alternate method."

That won't be necessary. Shamira bared her teeth in a sly smirk. *We can trace his signature back to where he cast or developed it. And if we look into Nyla's, we may find the link we need to discover what the potion actually was.*

Ingrid tilted her head. Her hand slipped from the book she was holding open. A few of the pages turned of their own accord, settling as they pleased. Turning to her, Ingrid's eyes traveled with her thoughts. "Yes…we could 'trace his signature?' Like scrying?"

It's more direct, but yes, like scrying. Instead of searching for one specific presence, we'd be following his signature to the instance we need.

"Edwin," Ingrid said sharply. "Do you have a map?"

Wordlessly, Edwin walked to the shelves and cubbies built in along one wall of his workshop. He plucked a scroll from one of the cubbies and rejoined them at his desk. Setting the scroll down on the wood surface, he reached inside a drawer and pulled four weights from within its depths.

Ingrid unrolled the map and held the sides open as Edwin placed a weight on each of the four corners. Shamira studied the map, marveling at just how large Tenebris was—and how far she'd followed Nyla over the last two years. Nyla had truly crossed the country when she'd fled home, and Shamira with her as she worked tirelessly to track the girl she'd known to be the source of one of the disturbances she'd sensed.

"If we can combine these two techniques, we could save a little time and find Cedric's hideaway without needing to physically follow his signature's trail, not only finding him but also the answers we seek." Ingrid paused, taking a breath as she stared at the map. "I hope we don't encounter many issues with the protective and concealment wards he's used. That's what gave us so much trouble in finding him the first time. I wish then that I had thought of using his signature to trace him…it might have helped us find him sooner."

"Or might not have," Edwin pointed out. "You didn't know what his signature was then."

"Perhaps, perhaps not."

You cannot change the past, only the future, Shamira echoed. It was a sentiment she'd held these last few weeks, thinking of all that the clans perhaps should've done, that she'd wished *she* had done when she first sensed the disturbances in magic. It was something she'd considered when her mind had mulled over Cedric and his motivations, recalling the memory she'd found in Astrid's looking glass, of the day she'd been murdered. It was the only thing that had comforted Shamira enough to quiet the regrets simmering in her heart, threatening to rage and boil over if she gave them too much thought.

"I'll trace his essence over the map," Ingrid said decisively. "Could you and Edwin find a way to isolate the potion from Nyla's signature without involving her?"

We could recall the memory of her aura the day she and I tried to sever the bond from her? Shamira offered, looking to Edwin. *All I would need is a basin of water or a glass not yet imbued with magic.*

"You're going to interact with the memory?" he asked, bending over and opening one of his desk drawers.

Shamira watched as he searched through the drawer, closing it without success as he pulled open another to continue searching for a mirror. *Yes. It would be the only way to discover which thread belongs to the potion.*

"It's dangerous magic," Edwin cautioned, glancing up at her, his hand still fumbling around the drawer. "Ah! Here we are."

Edwin held up a hand mirror. Inspecting it, he twirled it in his hand. "Will this work?"

Perfectly, Shamira said. A tendril of her sage-colored magic reached out and grasped the mirror, taking it from Edwin's hand. *This shouldn't take me long. My kind performs this sort of magic quite often, so there's nothing to fear.*

Edwin raised his brow. "You're certain?"

Absolutely.

Bringing the mirror to eye level, she stared intently into the smooth pane of glass. It misted over with her magic as Shamira settled herself more comfortably, focusing her energy intently. Keeping her breaths easy, Shamira eased the tension from her form, opening herself up to the mirror and allowing her memories to become one with it.

Images flashed before her, all memories of her past. Training with High Elder Florence as a cub, sneaking off at night with Talmec to winding unseen trails atop the mountain, meeting with Kasand as she continued to sense the emotions and essences of others beyond her youth as her peers had grown out of their empathetic gifts.

More memories played before Shamira's very eyes, swirling in the glass as her consciousness became one with the mirror. She'd never imagined using a looking glass of her own, but Nyla needed her help.

And besides, she would've needed to create one anyway if she accepted Kasand's appointment to make her his apprentice.

At least a hand mirror was easily transportable compared to the stone basins her clan's Seers had used for generations to store their memories and archive the clan's knowledge and history.

With this mirror, she could go anywhere and do as she so pleased. Could this be the solution she'd been praying for these last few days?

Shamira didn't know, but she did know she was fast approaching the memory she'd intended to peruse.

Halting the flow of memories, Shamira narrowed her eyes in concentration. In the glass, she and Nyla were back in that attic workroom at the Woodlane Manor. Shamira watched for a moment as the memory played, with her past self actively concentrating on the potion as Nyla painted the sigils required by the spell on the newly swept floor beyond.

She couldn't believe how recent this memory was, for it seemed to her like their time at the Woodlane Manor had been a lifetime ago. By all means, maybe it was. She certainly didn't consider herself to be the same pumpkie she was when she'd met Nyla and Xander, and she certainly didn't feel like the pumpkie that had returned home and barged into the meeting hall, defying even the barest respect required of her toward the Elders.

And Nyla and Xander certainly weren't the same humans she'd met back then either.

There was a contentedness and an overall lightness to their essences, but it was more than that. It was like they hadn't a care for what might be lurking behind their happiness, waiting to snatch it away. Even after all that had happened, she'd sensed a peace blooming in Nyla, simmering under the surface despite the disturbance in her aura upon her reawakening.

Moreover, Shamira hoped that Nyla and Xander had found a sort of blissful ignorance in their hearts once more. She hoped they'd never lose it, or face something ever again that would threaten to burst it.

Let them be young, she prayed. *Let them be happy.*

She would've asked the same for herself, but she knew that wouldn't be possible for a long time, and quite possibly not even then.

Shamira hadn't made a decision yet. She'd discussed it only with Talmec, about Kasand's offer to train her as his successor and the Elders' permission to do as she pleased now that she had completed her most sacred duties as a pumpkie, as a guardian of Tenebris. Hecates had confirmed for her that the Elders were pleased with how she'd commanded the host of pumpkies and was now acting as a liaison between the clans and the humans in this 'transitional period in their shared histories.' He'd assured her that they would not be rescinding their offer of her freedom.

But with that freedom came a great consequence.

Could she wander and explore, knowing she might never return to her home? Would choosing freedom also mean choosing to exile herself from her clan and kin?

She didn't know, and if she were being honest, Shamira was too afraid to ask what the terms of her freedom would be.

But she knew exactly what accepting the High Seer's apprenticeship would mean.

It would mean never being able to leave the clan again. It would mean being bound to their ancestral lands and the mountaintop home she'd missed so dearly over the last two years. Shamira didn't know if that was a commitment she wanted to undertake, not with the curiosity swelling in her heart.

She wanted to study the magic of Tenebris, the properties of the land. She wanted to establish and nurture ties with the humans of Tenebris, with Ingrid and those under her command.

She didn't want to forfeit the connections she'd made for the sake of the duty she knew in her heart.

Her heart wanted the ability to accept both. She wanted her freedom, but she didn't want to face the consequences that freedom might force upon her.

Shamira resigned herself to the fact that the question of what she should do would consume her long after she'd made a decision. No matter how content she seemed with her decision, there would always be that part of her that would wonder, and it would whisper to her from the far reaches of her mind until it drove her mad.

It was that realization that had kept her from making a decision thus far.

Her whiskers twitched with the possibilities flitting through her head as she watched her memories sail across her eyes. She knew she should banish the conflict from her mind so she could focus, but Shamira couldn't seem to muster the will to do so. All she wanted was to come to a conclusion, to find some way to soothe the quiet insanity stemming from her indecision.

After some struggling, Shamira managed to force the matter from her mind. She closed her eyes. The weight of her body fell from her as she allowed her soul body to split from her physical form. A sensation like water rippled over her as she entered the memory. Opening her eyes, Shamira took in the slight haze of the memoryscape.

That was the funny thing about stored memories. Everything was too crisp, too defined. They were so defined it almost hurt to look at them, their image nearly blazing the onlooker when they stepped into the memory. But they were true and unfiltered.

Viewing memories in a looking glass often led to different tales than what one recalled. They were more detailed and less prone to overwrite details upon recollection. But most of all, looking glasses were unbiased. Shamira *might* be able to remember what she'd seen of Nyla's aura, but her own memory would allow her to study it as her eyes had truly seen it. There would be no room for the error of her mind and how she recalled Nyla's aura. There would only be the fact and how it had truly appeared to her in this moment.

Sitting proudly near the staircase, all Shamira needed to do now was wait for her past self and Nyla to begin the spell. This time, she would be looking for the potion's interaction with Nyla's aura and not the bond's. This time, Shamira knew her efforts wouldn't be for naught.

She observed as Nyla drew the sigils. The girl's brow was creased with a different sort of concentration Shamira hadn't noticed in the moment. Though Nyla was careful with her movements, her mind appeared to be elsewhere, her face painted with bewilderment in the slight quirk of her lips and the subtle furrow of her brow. She wondered what the girl could possibly have been thinking about in this moment that could've been more important than the spell they were about to try, though she supposed it didn't matter now. The ritual wouldn't have worked regardless of where Nyla's mind had been while she prepared the casting circle. Its aim was to break a curse, not a bond. A bond was too complicated because there was another part involved that they hadn't known at the time. And even if they'd known Astrid's spell had been a bond, they would've been faced with a different set of obstacles—ones that they'd only avoided thanks to Nyla's willingness to meet with her ancestor on the astral plane.

Tapping her tail against the floorboard, Shamira waited even as her patience wore thin. She turned her mind toward Cedric, trying to conjure the way his essence felt to her so she would know what to look for in Nyla's aura when she finally bore it to her past self.

It was heavy, but not oppressive. Cedric's signature was often lighter than the color of air to her, like it didn't want to leave much of an impression on where he'd been or what he'd done. But its timidness wasn't enough of a match against the laws of magic.

No matter who or what you were, magic always left some form of residual presence specific to its wielder.

And that's what she was looking for in Nyla's aura.

She needed to find that nearly translucent bit of scarlet threading through her aura, and once she did, she needed to remember what it felt like so they could isolate it and use it to pinpoint where some trace of it might remain in its purest form.

That was the problem with essences—the residue left behind in the wake of wielding magic—it didn't speak toward the act itself but rather to the scale of it and the time that may have passed since.

Shamira straightened.

Finally! Her past self came to stand before Nyla in the circle. Nyla's aura began to emanate softly as she let it shine through her, growing brighter as Nyla closed her eyes. Shamira stalked forward to get a better look without her past self blocking it from view.

Nyla's aura was as she remembered it. A mix of colors, the core of it was the purest hue of purple lilacs, just like Nyla's magic. Shamira fought against herself to ignore the shadowy spots strewn throughout Nyla's aura, encroaching on its core. She was still curious about what they might indicate, but that wasn't her mission today.

Besides, after all that had happened and how Nyla had defeated Dinora, it was possible that these shadows had lessened just like the burden on Nyla's shoulders had been lifted.

Shamira narrowed her eyes. She didn't have much time before it all went wrong.

She closely examined each thread of magic and the interactions that made up Nyla's aura. Carefully walking around and around, Shamira studied it from all angles. There were a few strands of scarlet energy tangled within the web of Nyla's essence. Seldom did the strands match the signature she was looking for, with most of them buzzing with a sort of volatility she attributed to Dinora. And the couple of strands that matched her impression of Cedric's essence were pure magic. None of them bore the hint of a potion or other spellwork.

As the last thread subject to her examination failed to provide the lead she desperately needed to report good news back to Ingrid and

Edwin, Shamira's mind turned to a frenzy of half-formed hypotheses and hopes.

If only she'd gotten a look at that potion, if only she could trust Nyla's description of it. When she'd asked about it, Nyla had told her that it was a thick, dark liquid that shimmered in the light. She'd said that it'd felt like a thick sap against her skin as it slowly sank into her.

Shamira nearly mewled as the realization struck her.

Walking right up to Nyla, she hastily studied the dark spots plaguing the girl's aura.

Most of them were just black, a dark cloak against Nyla's essence that Shamira had once feared would encroach on her core.

But some of them, she smiled satisfactorily, some of them had a slight sheen to them.

A slight *scarlet* sheen.

Nyla's aura wavered.

Shamira heeded the warning and reached out to the shimmery black with her magic. Nyla's aura flared. Shamira's magic recoiled at the touch of the aura from her memory, but Shamira persisted.

Heavy, yet lighter than the color of air.

Cedric.

Nyla's scream tore through the air as the blast of her aura recoiled against her past self's efforts to sever the bond from her being.

The impact slammed into Shamira, affecting even her astral body as the body of her memory went flying through the air from the force of it.

Shamira shook her head, regretting what had become of their attempt, but at least now she had what she'd come for.

Reaching out toward the thread connecting her to her physical body, Shamira started back the way she had come. A deep shudder wracked through her body as she reconnected with her physical being.

Blinking her eyes open, Shamira found that her sage-colored eyes stared back at her. She didn't know why humans were infatuated with their own reflections and had special tools for it, but she supposed they had their use. Her whiskers twitched at the thought—and her inability to provide her curiosity with a plausible answer. Averting her gaze, she used her magic to set the mirror down softly on the edge of Edwin's desk.

"Did you find the potion's essence?" Edwin asked, watching her carefully.

Yes, Shamira said. *I'm sorry about your mirror. I hope it wasn't something precious.*

Edwin smiled genuinely. "It's only a trinket."

I see. Shamira's eyes settled on Ingrid. The map before her glowed with wavering tendrils of scarlet, marking all the paths Cedric had taken in his long life. Shamira approached slowly, analyzing the paths drawn by Ingrid's essence tracking. *It seems Cedric has traveled just as much as Nyla. Though I wonder…what's this patch here?*

She nodded her head, gesturing with her nose toward a spot on the map where the tracks seemed to avoid despite so many running alongside it or stemming from it in the Barrier Plains.

"I think it's where he lived, though I doubt he'd return there now," Ingrid said quietly, glowering at the map. "Shamira, can you overlay what you've garnered about the potion's essence so we can see where it intersects?"

Of course.

Edwin shifted, edging closer to the desk as she honed her focus on the memory of the potion's signature.

A black dot spilled over the map outside of Hart. Shamira glared at the map, concentrating harder.

No other sign of the potion appeared.

"That's it?" Ingrid muttered. Huffing, she pushed away from the desk. "Could he have been residing near the Woodlane Manor once it became clear Nyla was heading there?"

It's not likely, Shamira answered tensely, still working to bring more of the potion's essence to the map, hoping something would bleed through. *It had to have been forged in a concealed place, but not near the*

Woodlane Manor…unless…no, I would've sensed him if he were inside the manor while we were there.

Edwin cursed under his breath. "Then what do we do?"

Shamira relented, knowing that unless they worked to untangle the concealment charms cast over the place Cedric must've resided, there wasn't anything they could do. And it's not like they truly knew where he'd resided all this time. With all the places he'd been over the last six centuries, there was no way of knowing for certain where he would've concocted that potion.

Still, she found herself staring at the patch of exposed map in the Barrier Plains, nestled amongst the trails of his essence that started or broke off from that specific point.

These trails, she started, *you've circumvented the concealment charm on his person to expose them?*

Ingrid glanced at her, frowning slightly. "Yes, I—" She broke off, swearing. "He must've used a similar concealment charm to hide his workshop, or home. All we have to do is…"

Closing her eyes, Ingrid's blush-colored magic joined the wavering tendrils sprawled over the map. Her lips twitched. Deep lines creased the space between her brows.

"Edwin," she whispered. "I could use your assistance."

"Sure," he said, straightening up and squaring his shoulders.

His silvery magic glowed, blanketing over the map like a gentle wave. Shamira reignited her efforts to expose the potion's essence, watching with rapt attention as the scarlet lines quivered with their efforts to break the second concealment charm.

The utter silence of Edwin's office pounded in her ears. Shamira found herself holding her breath, eagerly waiting for something, for some sign that their efforts would prove to be successful.

The glow of Edwin's and Ingrid's magics increased, becoming a stark contrast to the faded scarlet of Cedric's essence.

Shamira's eyes widened. A thin scarlet tendril grew, extending from one of the existing lines and into the otherwise bare patch in the Barrier Plains.

Her heart thudded against her chest, watching as a shimmering black dot slowly bloomed on the map, unfurling right in the center of the growing web of Cedric's essence. The lines began to intersect and connect with one another, forming a glowing red dot that pulsed beneath the potion's essence.

Cedric's home.

They'd found it, or at least the place where he'd forged the potion.

I suppose we'll be paying a visit to the Barrier Plains? Shamira asked.

Ingrid peeked her eyes open. Arching a brow, she said, "It appears we are. Edwin?"

"Yes?" he asked hesitantly.

"Handle my affairs here," she ordered, "Shamira and I are taking a little trip, and if anyone asks, I trust you to come up with an innocuous excuse. My Circle will be coming with us in case Cedric has returned there."

I'll gather some pumpkies as well, Shamira offered, recognizing the danger of what they were about to do.

"Yes, Lady Ravencroft."

"Oh, and before this goes on any longer," Ingrid said, glancing briefly at her with mischievous eyes before she fixed her gaze back on Edwin, "my apprentice should call me by name. It seems formality didn't work with my former, so perhaps a different approach is necessary with my new apprentice."

"I'll be sure to pass that mes—" Edwin's eyes sparked, as if the woman's words were just now settling their weight on his mind. Shamira found herself smirking. Her whiskers twitched in amusement at Edwin's shock. "Wait? Your new apprentice? I didn't realize you had named a new—"

"I'm asking you, Edwin," she laughed. "I would like for you to study under me. You've quite impressed me as a student during your years at the university, and now as a graduate and serving member of the Caster Corps, you haven't shown any signs of stagnation. You seem eager to continue learning, yet you do not do so arrogantly. You have a true passion, Edwin, but most of all, you seem to have mastered the balance between your new allegiances and your former. It's quite respectable, and I for one would be honored to have you as my apprentice. It seems I have much that I could learn from you as well. So think on it, and have an answer for me by the end of the week."

Edwin sputtered, blinking in shock. "Yes, I'll have an answer by—wait, what am I saying?" Edwin took a breath and laid a hand over his heart, bowing his head. "I would be honored to accept the opportunity to be your apprentice, Lady Rave—Ingrid."

"Then it's settled." Ingrid nodded. "We'll be back soon, I expect. Not a word of this to anyone but the Huntingtons, but more specifically to Lord Huntington, the elder."

"Of course," Edwin agreed.

Shamira couldn't stop herself from snickering. She'd never seen Edwin so flustered before, but the prideful gleam in his eager eyes was almost that of a cub who'd received their first mark in High Elder Florence's training. His chest was practically puffed out in his excitement at the offer of the prestigious position.

"Right, well, with that settled," Ingrid said, looking to her now, "it's best we get going now. Shamira, are the pumpkies able to wisp there, or will they be in need of assistance?"

Elders Hecates and Myra are confident they can wisp a few others with them. Should we wisp directly to the location, or near it, in case of extra wards we hadn't anticipated? she asked.

"Perfect. Edwin and I dismantled all the wards and replaced them with our own," Ingrid explained. "But for the element of surprise, we'll wisp near it."

Then let's not waste a moment longer. Shamira bared her teeth. *The sooner we settle this matter, the better.*

Ingrid only nodded. "My Circle is ready if your kin are."

Then let us depart. My kin will meet us there.

"As will my Circle." Ingrid's blush-colored magic emanated from her in a cloudy halo, almost like she was baring her aura. At her cue, Shamira prepared herself for what was about to happen as Ingrid's magic engulfed her as well. Warmth spread from her chest outward, to the very tip of her tail. Her fur prickled. When she next blinked her eyes open, Shamira found herself staring at a rather small cottage.

This is it? Hecates asked, coming to stand beside her.

The tall grasses of the Barrier Plain tickled her, irritating her senses as she nosed at the air. *It must be. I can sense him here.*

"Then what's our plan? Barge in and arrest him?" one of Ingrid's Circle asked. Shamira's eyes cut to the woman with long brown hair.

"I think," Ingrid replied slowly, "we should set up a perimeter to secure the cottage. There's evidence here that we'll need to preserve, and I for one am curious. I want to study every inch of this place for answers."

"Understood," the woman said. "And *then* we barge in?"

"Maybe not so cavalierly, but yes, *then* we can barge in."

The assembled team of pumpkies and Casters stood and stared at the cottage a moment longer. Shamira couldn't help but wonder what they might find inside. This was where Cedric had spent a great deal of his time, if the paths of his essence diverging from this spot were any indication. For as many awful things as he had done, for as wicked as she'd wanted to believe his soul was, *this* plain and unassuming cottage was where he'd chosen to conduct himself, to maybe even call home?

Of all the places in Tenebris, he'd chosen the Barrier Plains. Shamira herself had been gifted with the opportunity of seeing the region's picturesque sunsets, of traversing its peaceful grasslands and tranquil prairies. She remembered the longing in her heart as she stared out across the plain from beneath the shade of a tree with long spindly vines flowing from its thin boughs. It was the first time she'd ever missed home, but still, she'd pressed on, following the trail that had eventually led her to Nyla and now to this moment.

Beside her, Ingrid huffed. "If only we'd known about this place sooner."

It might not have changed anything, Shamira reminded her.

"But it could've," the woman muttered. "We should get on with this before we lose daylight. Howards, Leviston, set up the perimeter."

Wordlessly, the two Casters peeled away from the group.

We'll go with them, just in case the raverins are still around, Hecates offered, breaking off with Myra to join the pair of humans.

And the rest of us will see to the cottage, Shamira replied. *Talmec, could you go around and see if there are any other entrances?*

Of course, he said, *I'll be back in a moment.*

"Good," Ingrid said. "Once you return, we'll be ready."

Shamira watched her brother stalk off through the tall grasses. A tense silence overcame the group as Talmec wholly disappeared but for the slight rustle of the grass with his movements. Shamira tracked his progress as best as she could until he moved around the side of the cottage and she lost sight of even the sway of the brittle grasses surrounding the cottage on all sides but for a few feet nearest it. She supposed it was Cedric's way of maintaining the structure. In the pumpkie villages, they often cut back bramble and underbrush to help prevent the spread of fires, though that force in and of itself was rare. But they did so, and Shamira supposed it was because the lack of roots and brush made it easier to travel through the village and into their homes. A small comfort, but still a bit of luxury. Perhaps that's why Cedric kept the grass away from the structure, to give himself some semblance of an easy life.

Shamira perked up. The grasses in front of their group swayed with the gentle rustle of Talmec's return.

Coming into view, he announced, *There's only a window and then the chimney. There are no other exits.*

"All that's left is to wait for Howards and Leviston to finish the perimeter," Ingrid said, "and then we can breach the cottage."

Shamira bobbed her head. This was it then. They'd found Cedric, and his cottage, and with any hope, they'd find what they needed to help Nyla inside that cottage too.

25. WINDS OF FREEDOM

Nyla bit her lip, staring anxiously at the stomping and snorting sagittarii. The great beast shook its head, its wild mane flowing with the wind like the licking tongues of a flame as Xander held the reins. Nyla squinted against the almost setting sun beating down on the field where Pemberly's stables resided. It was odd, seeing the grass in its different shades of teal and mossy green. She was so used to the amber dirt of the Shadow Forest and the thick canopy of sapphire leaves that she'd all but forgotten what grass looked like. Even in the glimpses she'd had of her home—of Hart and the Godberd Woods— when they'd passed through, Nyla had seldom seen grass. And when she had, it certainly wasn't so short.

"Well?" Xander asked with a grin. "Do you want to go for a ride?"

"Uhh…" Nyla hesitated. "I don't know how to ride a sagittarii. Remember? My family's archette wasn't too keen on carrying people on his back."

"Where's your sense of adventure?" he teased, holding out his free hand to her. "Fi is one of the gentlest sagittarii I have ever met, I promise. He can just sense your nerves."

Nyla looked from Xander to Fi and back again skeptically. "I think I've had quite enough adventure to last me through even my next life."

"If it's any consolation," Xander offered, "you won't be alone. I'll be right here with you this time. Or we could walk to my surprise instead."

"That's an option?"

Xander nodded, giving her a light hum of affirmation. "There's always more than one option."

"But?" Nyla prompted.

"But… I promised we'd be back for dinner, so my actual favorite thing to do might have to wait until tomorrow," Xander explained, rubbing the back of his neck. "We could always—"

"No," Nyla said decisively, "I'm too curious now."

"Nyla, we really don't have to—"

"I know," Nyla said, playing with her fingers and twisting her hands, "but…I just want to forget…for a little while. And you're good at…I don't know how to put it, but your schemes always bring me a bit of peace."

Xander chuckled, "Then maybe one day, I'll think of a scheme that brings you more than just a temporary peace."

"Unless you intend to build a house on that lake and let me visit you indefinitely," Nyla started, slowly walking up to Fi and placing her foot in the stirrup, "then I'm not sure eternal peace is something I could ever achieve."

Helping her into the saddle, Xander said, "What if I just let you live in that house by the lake?"

Nyla sighed, situating herself atop Fi and getting used to the feeling of being up so high. Glancing down at Xander, she smiled. "Are you offering me a house by the lake?"

Xander hauled himself up behind her. "Only if I can come and visit you."

"What a pity." Nyla bit back her smile, glancing over her shoulder at him. "I was hoping you would cook."

Laughing, Xander took Fi's reins in both hands, framing her in between his arms. With a click of his tongue, Fi began to walk a slow and steady rhythm. Nyla jolted a little, not expecting the movement, but she quickly steadied herself as Fi started toward the end of the field and toward a path only Xander could see through the ashen trees beyond.

"Oh I see, so I'm supposed to build the house by the lake and work as the cook? What are you doing in this scenario?"

Nyla considered the question for a moment, slowly getting used to the rhythm of the sagittarii's gentle walk. Breathing in the fresh air and savoring the hints of Harvum's spicy scent, Nyla took in the wooded path Xander was guiding them down. "I'd stare out the window on rainy days, and when it's warm and sunny out, we'd picnic by the lake. I'd, of course, clean and tend to the garden, but I could help with the hunting and setting traps too. I only need you to cook." Nyla paused, smiling to herself knowingly. In the lapse, Xander scoffed in mock offense. Nyla laughed, finally adding, "And because I like your company, of course."

"Ah, so you finally admit it," Xander teased. "You like me."

"Would I be sitting on a sagittarii with no idea where you're taking me if I didn't?" she laughed.

"I was starting to worry you'd consider this a kidnapping."

"At the rate we're traveling," Nyla laughed, "I could jump off and run back to Pemberly."

She felt Xander's grin against her ear. A trickle of fear curled its way into her bloodstream. Regret immediately flooded her, but it was too late. Xander flicked the reins, wrapping an arm around her as Fi reared his head and began to run faster.

Squealing, Nyla curled her hand tighter around the pommel and grabbed for Xander's arm. Her hair whipped against her face, trailing behind her as Fi went from a trot to a steady gallop. Squeezing her legs tighter around the sagittarii's torso, Nyla didn't know if it felt more like she was going to fall off or if she was flying.

"Just let me know if you want to stop," Xander said in her ear. She barely heard him over the beating of her heart and Fi's heavy hoof falls.

Nyla giggled, "Not a chance!"

The trees and changing leaves were a blur as she and Xander sped by. With practiced ease, Xander guided Fi down the amber dirt path of the Shadow Forest surrounding his family's estate. Nyla's eyes teared up from the cool wind blowing through the trees. Veering off to the right, Xander led them up a gentle incline, slowing Fi back to a trot and finally a walk for the ascent.

Nyla watched in wonder as the trees began to thin. Teal and mossy green leaves littered the forest floor, crunching under Fi's hooves. Xander's arm shifted against her. Pulling away from her, he returned his hand to the reins as Fi crested the hill.

Nyla's breath hitched in her throat.

Her eyes settled over the view from the hilltop, watching as the setting sun bathed Pemberly Hall and its gardens in golden sunlight. She'd seen plenty of beautiful sights in her life and had found none so wonderful as the way the Godberd Woods' plum-colored leaves danced in the sunlight, but this...

"This is beautiful," Nyla whispered, slumping back against Xander.

The sight before her seemed to rival even the memory of her home, though Nyla wasn't sure which would ultimately win her heart. Her mind flooded with memories of Hart and the idea of what could be as she stared in wonder at the valley glowing in the golden sunlight. It was like all the gods and Fate were trying to show her that everything she'd ever longed for could be found in those golden rays. But even so, Nyla was too awestruck by the beauty of the tranquil image before them to truly realize what was within her reach, too content to simply be at peace for as long as the light glowed.

***

Xander hummed, watching Nyla as her eyes widened at the sight below them, eagerly drinking in the serenity he remembered so fondly. "Yeah, it really is."

Dropping the reins, he braced one foot on the stirrup and stood, slipping from the saddle with a practiced ease. Nyla glanced down at him with slight hesitation written on her face.

"Here," he said, offering her his hand, "just swing your other leg over to this side and slide off. I'll help you."

Fi snorted, clopping his front hooves as if in agreement.

Slowly, Nyla took his hand to help steady herself and brought her other leg to this side of the saddle. As she began to slide off, Xander grabbed her waist. Giggling, Nyla braced her hands on his shoulders.

"Sorry!" she laughed as he set her down. Xander's brows furrowed as she quickly stepped away from him. "I'm ticklish there."

"Oh," he said, starting to laugh himself. "I thought…I thought you might've been hurt still."

Nyla shook her head. "I really am okay now. It's just…a lot to process, and my mind doesn't seem to want to."

"I understand," Xander said solemnly, grasping Fi's reins. "And I'll be here when you want me to be, to listen, to help. Whatever you need."

"I know," Nyla said, staring back at him with a small smile on her face. "You keep reminding me."

Xander chuckled. He led Fi over to a nearby tree and looped the reins around a low-hanging branch. "I just want to make sure you won't forget."

"How could I?" Xander glanced at her over his shoulder, making certain that Fi was comfortable where he stood. Nyla had moved to a sunny patch of grass on the hilltop with her back to him, staring across the world with her arms wrapped loosely around herself. "You're nearly always with me anymore."

"Is that a bad thing?" Xander's shoulders tensed, and in the shock of panic that struck his veins like lightning, Xander found that he couldn't move no matter how much he'd wanted to join Nyla at the edge of the hilltop.

"Not at all," she said, almost matter-of-factly. "In fact, it's the exact opposite of a bad thing."

Sighing in relief, Xander patted Fi's neck. Fi nudged his shoulder before ignoring him completely, and Xander took that as his cue to join Nyla. As he sat, he said, "Well, that's certainly a relief."

Nyla laughed, joining him on the grass and laying her head on his shoulder. He wrapped an arm around her, wishing he'd thought of bringing a blanket or two, or that they'd prepared a picnic.

"I'm glad places like this exist, even in a city as old as Huntington," she murmured.

"Me too."

Growing up, Xander would come here every so often and watch the sun set on Pemberly Hall. Bathed in a golden light, the gardens and house itself seemed magical. It was a place to sit and think or clear his head on days when too much had obscured him from that light.

But here today?

It seemed more like paradise than a place to catch his breath.

Maybe he'd been gone for so long that the impact of those unfavorable memories had faded and lost their hold on his mind. Or maybe it was the way that Nyla looked with the sunlight glowing in her eyes and crowning her changing hair with its rays.

Maybe it was just the relief that they were safe and that Nyla had won and this was the end of all their—of all *her*—troubles.

"What are you thinking about?" Nyla asked softly.

Xander blinked, startled to find her staring at him. "Nothing in particular, just life."

"That's an awful lot to be thinking about right now," she said, turning her face away to stare out over the land once more.

"What are you thinking about then?"

"For the first time in a long time," she replied slowly, the hint of a smile on her face, "nothing."

Xander chuckled, but didn't reply.

Watching as the sun dipped lower until it sank beneath the distant trees of the Shadow Forest, neither he nor Nyla shared another word. The sweet chirps and low hums of the niphonies and chirpets created a subtle symphony that filled the hilltop with a quiet song.

Peace settled itself in Xander's bones for the first time in days. It seemed quite content to remain too, a fact that offered him a great comfort.

For so long, longer than even he dared to recall, peace had evaded him. He wondered if Nyla felt the same, or if there was still a sense of urgency simmering in her bloodstream. He hoped there wasn't, that she was truly content even if it only lasted for this single moment.

Who knew how long they had before either of them would be forced to make a decision about their future? Xander dreaded the day they would have to, wishing for all the world that he could freeze time just to delay the inevitable a moment longer. And what better moment to freeze time on than a moment like this?

He couldn't think of any better time…except maybe the day they'd spent at the beach.

With each inch the sun sank, Xander knew they would have to head back to the estate soon, but he would be lying if he said the thought hadn't crossed his mind to stay here until the sun rose again in the morning.

"Do you think we'll be missed at dinner?" Nyla asked, apparently thinking the same thing.

"More than likely, yes."

"Even if we told them we weren't coming?"

"Unfortunately," Xander murmured.

Nyla sighed heavily, picking her head up from his shoulder. "Then I guess we should start heading back before I lose the will to. I could stay here forever."

"Me too."

26. A COWARD'S TRUTH

Shamira watched the cottage door burst open in a flurry of Ingrid's magic. Talmec expanded his magical shield, stalking inside with both herself and Ingrid close on his tail. Dust choked the air, and a mustiness invaded Shamira's nostrils. Pale sunlight filtered through the thin curtains of the ill-kept cottage.

A harsh coughing assaulted Shamira's ears joined by a raspy *squawk*. Her ears swiveled in its direction, followed immediately by her eyes. A raverin flapped its wings. Its eyes gleamed ferociously as it dove for them.

"D—" Cedric coughed, "Dia!"

The raverin darting toward them pulled back with a great flap of its wings. Turning its head, Shamira watched as the creature blinked, letting out a confused-sounding *caw*.

"Had I," Cedric began weakly, coughing once more, "known to expect company, I would've tidied up."

Shamira's gaze landed on him, lying in the bed. Shamira's eyes widened at the sight of him—or rather the scars across his face from claws and magic alike. Narrowing her eyes as she recovered from her shock, Shamira took in the weak pulse of Cedric's aura. Cedric was dying. As the raverin settled back on its perch by the mantel, Talmec let his amber-colored shield drop.

There wouldn't be a battle today. The fight was truly over. Dinora's legacy had been destroyed along with her death.

As if she sensed his impending doom too, Ingrid glanced at her, a question flaring in her eyes.

What now? Shamira asked. *We can't exactly bring him back to Pemberly to stand trial in this state. He'll be dead before the week has drawn to a close.*

I know, Ingrid said, her eyes flitting back to Cedric. *But I have my duties to consider as well.*

Straightening, Ingrid put her shoulders back and let her magic drop. "Cedric Kashar, you are hereby—"

"Save your breath," he said, voice crackling. "I submit."

Ingrid raised an eyebrow. "Well then, I suppose formalities can be skipped due to the current circumstances. You don't look so well, Cedric."

Cedric scoffed, no more than a puff of air. "Did Nyla succeed? Did she kill Dinora?"

Yes, Shamira answered. *Dinora is dead.*

"And Nyla?" he asked, letting his eyes fall shut. His head went limp against the pillows of his bed as if he hadn't any strength left in his body now that the initial shock of their arrival had worn off.

"Perfectly fine," Ingrid nearly growled. "Though I have to wonder for how much longer she will be. What sort of potion did you use on her?"

Cedric's eyes blinked open to look at her before they fell shut once more. "Like I told the boy. It was a bequeathment potion." His face scrunched up in pain for a moment, making Shamira wonder just what it was that ailed him beneath the surface, of the injuries she couldn't see. A few seconds passed before Cedric let out a long breath. Mumbling, he said, "Needed to be sure…she could do it."

And what of the blood oath you made to Xander? she found herself asking. *What was it?*

Cedric frowned, not bothering to open his eyes. "Just wanted to grant him some assurance."

Assurance for what? Shamira pressed.

"That I was being truthful, that I—" Cedric broke off in a coughing fit. Shamira waited patiently for it to pass, hoping he would continue in his explanation, but he never did. He only went limp against the bed, his head lolling to the side.

Ingrid pursed her lips. She studied Cedric for a moment longer, though Shamira highly doubted there was anything left for them to ask him or for him to answer for.

We should begin our search, Shamira said. *Talmec, can you ask Hecates and Myra if they could muster some volunteers to guard the cottage for a while? Until our investigation is done?*

Sure, he replied.

As he left, Shamira found that Ingrid didn't seem inclined to move. She watched Cedric closely, as if staring at him would provide her with answers to the questions she'd left unasked.

Is there something wrong, Ingrid?

No, the Mage General said, *I just don't know what to do with him now. The council had wanted…I suppose it doesn't matter. We came here for Nyla. I'll have Edwin report this, and they can debate it amongst themselves. For now, we should set up a guard watch. I doubt he has the strength to move or wisp, but just in case…I'll instruct my Circle to remain here and watch over him alongside whichever pumpkies would aid us.*

It's decided then. Now all that's left for us to do is find what we're looking for, and then we can settle our investigation. Shamira nodded, turning away to take in the rest of the cottage now that the obvious danger had proven to be anything but. A cold fireplace sat empty on the wall across from the bed, accompanied by a lonely armchair with tattered cushions and a dull fabric, the only signs of its age.

Taking in her surroundings, Shamira couldn't help but feel underwhelmed. A threadbare carpet lay under Cedric's bed. A shabby nightstand was bare except for a single candlestick in the center. A crammed kitchen sat in the corner, though there wasn't much of anything there but a few pots and pans sitting on the counter. Along the far wall was an encumbered workbench and various magical items. Shamira gestured toward it with her nose. *That must be where Cedric made the potion.*

Ingrid hummed, shifting toward it. *All this time, and he was right here. I still can't believe any of it, or keep myself from wondering what would've happened had we discovered either of them sooner.*

Or perhaps the same thing would've happened. If Fate wanted this to happen, it would've happened with or without Nyla.

Very true, Ingrid relented. *I guess it's best if I stop examining the will of Fate to circumvent my own regrets and disappointments.*

It seems as though we're all in need of that reminder.

Shamira's eyes roved over the workbench. Dusty scrolls, brittle with age, lay scattered across the workbench, heaped among various scales and large tomes. Ingredient bottles sat throughout the mess, their labels faded and their contents either missing or so dry they had begun to flake and wither.

She focused her gaze, searching for any sign of the potion. Ingrid began to sift through the mess, disturbing the dust as she went and causing the particles to float in the air and tickle Shamira's nose.

A faint trace of the potion presented itself to her, but none that would result in them discovering enough of it to examine properly. A tendril of the potion's essence floated by her, leading away from the table and farther into the cottage. Shamira turned her head, finding Cedric's gaze on her.

"What are you looking for?" he asked. "Perhaps I could help?"

Shamira's whiskers twitched. *Intentions aside, I highly doubt you're in any condition to offer your help.*

Cedric didn't respond. She waited for him to close his eyes again before following the trail with her gaze across the room and toward the side closest to the only door serving the cottage.

Her eyes widened slightly. The tendril grew stronger, sinking into the basin affixed to the cramped countertop and adjacent cupboards.

Ingrid, she said, drawing the woman's attention.

Yes? She turned, following Shamira's gaze toward the kitchen. *What is it?*

I think there might be some residue of the potion over there.

Ingrid frowned, closing the book she'd been studying. *It makes sense that there might be something in the basin if we can't find any here. Perhaps it's the cauldron he used? He may not have had time to clean it properly if he bottled the potion and set off to ambush you three at the Woodlane Manor immediately after it was brewed.*

Shamira watched as she set off for the basin, hesitant to follow after her. She didn't know what they would do if they couldn't find a drop of the potion to examine. The only way they'd be able to prove one way or another what Cedric had done would be to examine both his and Nyla's auras, to see how the link he claimed to have established by casting a bequeathment ritual on Nyla interacted with their auras.

If the link wasn't there, then they would know he was lying. But if that was the case, they wouldn't be any closer to determining just what he had done to her with that potion.

And if there *was* a link, and they were able to determine that it was the *Mortis tradsmagique* like he claimed, then there was nothing they could do unless Cedric himself reversed the bond.

Shamira! Ingrid gasped, *It's here!*

She was across the room in a blink, her heart pounding against her chest. Staring into the basin, Shamira was greeted by the sight of a squat cauldron, crusted over with a black substance that bore the slightest sheen of red to it.

The potion—or rather, its residue.

What do we do now? she asked.

Ingrid smiled, lifting the cauldron gently from the dry basin. *Now, we bring it to the best potions master we can trust. Edwin and I will be able to examine it and determine, for better or worse, whether Cedric's claims are lies or some version of the truth.*

***

Shamira lounged by the fireplace in Edwin's wood-paneled office as he and Ingrid dissected the potion residue. She was in part fascinated by their human methods and utterly exhausted by the sleep that had escaped her in the days since the battle.

Edwin's large desk was crowded by beakers and winding tubes of glass. There were things called Bunsen burners that created a little flame wherever Edwin or Ingrid wanted to heat one of the beakers as they needed to without the use of magic. She watched the little flames bobbing and flickering where they sat, soothed by their steady presence.

Working in silence, the pair focused intently on their task, seeming to work instinctually together without exchanging a word. Shamira observed as the liquid they'd created from the potion scrapings traveled through the labyrinth of glass beakers and coils, changing from the shimmering black potion into a grayish purple and then finally a scarlet that matched Cedric's essence.

As it moved through the tubes, Shamira noticed its signature changing as well. It seemed that each stage broke it down a little by little, changing from the writhing dark concoction of the whole potion into its individual components. Her whiskers twitched as she noticed the colors of the land's magic and then Nyla's vibrant energy. Through it all, she saw a thread of Cedric's essence, which made sense to her when nothing else about the potion did. Why incorporate the land's magic in a bequeathment potion?

Edwin and Ingrid had already explained to her that a proper bequeathment ritual included a piece of the benefactor and the beneficiary, so as to establish a connection between them. And as in most cases, the beneficiary often wasn't aware of their coming inheritance.

But that still didn't explain why the presence of the land's magic was entwined with Cedric's version of a bequeathment potion. It made her wonder just what conclusion they might draw from this experiment, and what it would mean for Nyla.

When the potion had reached the end, Edwin allowed the substance to drip into yet another breaker and shut the valve once more.

Shamira picked her head up, sniffing. Edwin held the beaker up to the light, observing it with narrowed eyes and a slightly tilted head. Ingrid walked around the desk to stand beside him, staring up at the scarlet residue shining in the light with pursed lips.

"We should probably examine it under a microscope," she muttered, "just to be absolutely certain."

"I'll prepare the slide," Edwin replied, turning away and taking the beaker with him.

Shamira watched curiously as he strode to the far corner of the room where a small desk and matching chair sat with an odd metal instrument atop its surface.

Ingrid closed her eyes for a moment, taking a long breath as if to compose herself before she crossed the room and sat heavily upon the floor beside her.

"It looks as though Cedric was telling the truth." She draped her arms over her knees and clasped her hands together, watching as Edwin performed his task across the room from them. "I've asked Edwin to observe it through a microscope just to be certain that the molecules match those associated with a bequeathment potion, but...I don't see how this potion could mimic the reaction of a *Mortis tradsmagique* unless he used illusion magic to mask the true behavior and presentation of the potion. But he can't change its molecules, which is essentially the core—"

Essence of the potion, its energy, Shamira finished, finally understanding their process. *So all these beakers and tests, they're meant to break down the essence to expose its purest form?*

"Precisely," Ingrid said. "Did you notice anything about it as you were observing us?"

Nothing that counters your conclusion, Shamira admitted. *Both Cedric's and Nyla's essences were present in the potion as it broke down, but...I noticed the land's magic too, in its energy.*

Ingrid's brows drew back in quiet surprise. "Why would the land's magic be there?"

I suppose that's a question we'd have to ask Cedric, Shamira said grimly.

Ingrid sighed heavily, but didn't reply. It seemed neither of them wanted to accept that task, knowing how difficult the man could be when it came to providing answers.

Or acknowledgement of any kind.

If Shamira was able to say with any degree of certainty, she would say that Cedric had given up. But on what—life, himself, or something unknown to them—she couldn't say.

All she knew for certain was that there were never enough answers to satisfy her questions.

27. A TALE OF TWO TREES

"Nyla," Ingrid called after her. Nyla gave Merry an apologetic look before she turned to address Ingrid.

"Might we have a word with you?"

"Uh…sure," she said, noticing the small group remaining at the table behind her. If Shamira and Edwin were amongst them, as well as Alexander, Nyla knew it was a serious matter they needed to speak with her about, and not something as trivial as the story Merry had been telling her about the dream she'd had the night before as she led Nyla from the dining room arm in arm. Turning to Merry with a frown, Nyla apologized, "I'm sorry, Merry, but it seems you'll have to tell me the rest later."

"That's okay," Merry assured her, patting her hand before she slipped her arm from hers. "We'll set a whole day aside for just the two of us when there aren't so many people around or things that need your attention."

"Maybe tomorrow," Nyla offered. "Or the day after? I've decided to take a vacation from responsibility for a while."

Merry grinned. "Tomorrow, then!"

Nyla shook her head, watching as Xander's younger cousin practically bounced away down the hall. How her heart longed to be that carefree.

Beside her, Ingrid said, "I heard Merry spent most of the battle in the infirmary, running supplies as needed when she wasn't in the kitchen with Moretta. Apparently, keeping her confined to the kitchen where they were making potions and tonics was a difficult task, as Merry noticed how thinly spread the messengers and pages were."

Nyla's head whipped in her direction. "I didn't know that."

"Hardly anyone does, except those who saw her."

Nyla swallowed hard. So Merry hadn't completely escaped the horrors of the battle. It made her wonder whether anyone truly had, not if the public knew of the earthquake and had begun to investigate its cause for themselves.

Nyla realized the travesty she'd known, that this estate had known, would travel as news of the joint statement from the council spread. That, and also the notifications of the memorials for those they'd lost.

"I didn't mean to upset you by telling you about Merry," Ingrid said, mercifully preventing her from falling farther into her dark thoughts. "I only wanted to commend her for her determination and grace."

Nyla nodded absently, staring after the way Merry had gone. Shaking her head, and with it the rest of her thoughts away, Nyla asked, "What was it you wanted to talk to me about?"

"You know about what Cedric had told Xander and Edwin during their, uh, *visit*? About the *Mortis tradsmagique*?"

"Yeah…" Nyla replied cautiously.

"We have news," Ingrid said, gesturing for Nyla to take a seat.

Gulping, Nyla resumed her dinner seat beside Xander as Ingrid called the table's attention to her as she stood where Merry had once sat at the head of the table opposite Alexander.

"I figured it didn't make sense for us all to gather again, or for me to report the findings of our investigation multiple times. As the council has already been made aware, Edwin, Shamira, and I have found Cedric. He's under guard and will not be transported to stand trial at the tribunal like we'd planned, for his condition is too unstable for me to recommend doing so.

"But more importantly, the three of us have news about his claim to have bequeathed his magic to Nyla."

Ingrid's words twisted the worry flooding Nyla's gut. Thankfully, the woman didn't hold them in suspense, barely letting a breath span before she was supplying them with the answer to the question that had been brought to her mind. Just what had Cedric done to her?

"After some investigating, we've come to the conclusion that Cedric is telling the truth. The potion he got on Nyla at the Woodlane Manor *was*, in fact, a *Mortis tradsmagique*." Turning to her, she said, "As far as the potion and his enchantment of it goes, you're perfectly safe, Nyla, though Edwin, Shamira, and I are more than willing to do some further testing if you'd like to participate in them. We've done everything we can without studying you as a part of our investigation. Though we still have some questions about the makeup of the potion, as it's not one I've ever encountered before…"

As Ingrid trailed off, her eyes glanced to Shamira. Thankfully, the pumpkie picked up where the Royal Mage left off. *I noticed a thread of the land's magic mixed in with the concoction. It's a rather unusual mixture, and I suspect not often mixed with a bequeathment potion, but without speaking with Cedric about the process of the brew and its design or his intention behind it, I'm afraid we're at a loss as to why it was included.*

Nyla didn't know what to say. Her mind raced with questions as she tried to understand what Ingrid had said. Cedric had really bequeathed his magic to her, but why? Had it been a mistake? Had he meant to bequeath it to Dinora, but somehow, in the confusion of the fight and his own injuries, had mistaken her for his mother?

But the question begging for an answer was something far simpler than any of the others, especially those regarding Cedric's motivations.

"Will—" Nyla started, closing her eyes for a moment to gather her courage to ask it. "Will I assume his hair and eye color, like I did with Astrid?"

Ingrid blinked. After a second, she smiled, her eyes twinkling with unshed laughter. "No, I don't believe so, but we could certainly look into it more to be absolutely certain."

"Okay," Nyla said. "I'm sorry. I know that's probably ridiculous—"

I don't think it is, Shamira said. *Not given your history with your inheritance of Astrid's magic.*

"Yeah," Edwin agreed. "Most bequeathment rituals don't have that result, so I'm not sure why Astrid's had, but then again," he smiled crookedly, "does anything that's happened throughout the course of this prolonged war make any sense?"

Beside her, Xander chuckled quietly. "Not really, no. And it all started with that wisp of smoke that led us to Fortune Falls."

Ingrid's eyes widened in shock. "You've been to Fortune Falls?"

"Yeah, and it was more trouble than it was worth," Nyla replied at the same time as Xander said, "I wouldn't have made it without Nyla."

As if he registered what she'd said, Xander turned to her with raised brows. Nyla gently set her hand on top of his. "I meant because of what drinking from the Falls showed me and inspired me to do. The next time I decide we should follow an anthropomorphic trail of smoke, stop me."

Xander laughed, flipping his hand so their fingers were laced together instead. "If I remember correctly, I *did* try to stop you, but you insisted and left me with the choice of staying where I stood or following after you."

Nyla shrugged. "I guess that part worked out all right. But I definitely don't recommend seeking Fortune Falls unless you're prepared to get what you *need* and not necessarily what you *want*, though I guess the Falls gave me both."

Silence descended upon the table as Nyla contemplated the difference. She'd gone to Fortune Falls seeking answers about the fire that had taken her family from her, and they'd shown her three visions that had ultimately led her down this path.

Well, that, and her astral travels in Caselle had been difficult to ignore.

But would she have done anything differently? After all, hadn't she gotten what she wanted in the end? Hadn't she gotten what she needed?

She'd gotten answers to satisfy her anxious mind. She'd gotten closure for the deaths of her family and discovered why her hair and eyes had changed color after the fire.

She'd even found a home, or rather a sense of it in herself. Wasn't that all she'd longed for on the dark nights during the two long years she'd spent wandering all alone?

Nyla nibbled on her lip, turning over the question in her mind. The memory of King Albert and Queen Clarice's conversation about the trust they wanted to establish for her came to mind, and with it the two titles her family had once held. She had yet to truly consider the royals' offer or the fact that her family tree extended to two founding families of Tenebris. It wasn't a decision Nyla could make lightly, no matter her initial aversion to accepting the titles or the trust. After all, she had her future to think of. Even after all that she and Xander had been through together, she still had to look after herself, no matter how many people she'd come to be surrounded by.

Fate had given her one final decision to make, and Nyla didn't know how it fit into the future she'd begun to see for herself.

***

Shamira watched quietly as Nyla mingled with her kin, speaking quietly with Myra now. A few other Casters had paired off with some pumpkies to practice magic together, and if Shamira wasn't mistaken, Edwin had been among them, if his near presence was any indication.

As if sensing her eyes on her, Nyla glanced up and smiled at her. Shamira nodded her head in acknowledgement, too bogged down by other thoughts to wholly notice the flicker of confusion licking at Nyla's eyes.

Now that Dinora had been defeated and her own duties fulfilled, the Clan Elders had reminded Shamira of their promise. She was free to do as she pleased, to return or to wander. But Kasand had reasserted his decision to train her as his successor should she accept the position of becoming the Brewardt Clan's High Seer upon his passing.

A part of her postured to accept Kasand's offer. It was the part of her that had always abided by her duties and her commitment to her clan. But another part of her, the part that stemmed from her previously suppressed curiosity, wanted to see more of the world. Her heart yearned to hold tight to the sense of wonder she'd been instilled with, for the sense of belonging she had amongst the friends she'd made in the human realm…but it also missed the friends she'd had and the kin she'd known since she was a cub.

Could she really forsake them?

Could Shamira earnestly forsake a world she hardly knew, but had grown to love just as fervently?

"You seem troubled." Nyla's voice sounded much closer than Shamira remembered her being.

Blinking rapidly to clear the haze from her mind, Shamira turned toward the sound of Nyla's concerned voice. In the time since Shamira had succumbed to her inner thoughts and when she'd last seen Nyla, the girl had come to sit beside her.

I suppose I am a little troubled, she admitted, shifting on her paws. Sighing, she closed her eyes for a second and explained, *It seems I have a lot on my mind to consider.*

"Me too," Nyla said, sounding exhausted at the idea. "Did you know my family was once a part of the nobility?"

I had heard, Shamira said. *Are you going to accept the title?*

Nyla shook her head. "I don't know. What about you? Are you going to accept being the High Seer's successor?"

Who told you? Shamira narrowed her eyes.

"Talmec."

Shamira's eyes darted to her brother, finding him in the thick of the unofficial training grounds with the other pumpkies and the Casters. She rolled her eyes. Of course he would be leading the coalition despite Gerri's insistence that he rest a while longer before participating in any vigorous activities.

I hadn't wanted to add to your troubles, she said by way of explanation. *I know you have much to consider without being burdened by what troubles me.*

Nyla shrugged, settling a little more comfortably on the blanket she'd laid on the ground. "Maybe if we shared our troubles, we could help each other. That's what friends are supposed to do. They help and support each other as much as they can."

Shamira allowed Nyla's words to sink into her consciousness. She knew exactly how friends were supposed to act, especially from a human point of view as she'd witnessed countless interactions between Nyla and Xander.

Slowly, Shamira surveyed the assembled crowd. Pumpkies lounged throughout the spacious garden enclave Lord Huntington had generously allowed them to use for their time here before they'd eventually have to return to their mountaintop home.

Shall we go for a walk? she asked over the unease simmering in her gut. While Shamira doubted anyone was eavesdropping on their conversation, she was hesitant to hold such a discussion in the presence of others.

"Sure," Nyla said brightly. Gathering her blanket and wrapping it around her shoulders like a shawl, she added, "I'll follow you. I still get a little lost on the garden paths."

Shamira snickered. *Why not use your magic to find your way?*

Her ears pricked at Nyla's sharp breath. Shamira looked at her as they stepped onto the garden path beyond the enclave in time to see a dark shadow pass over Nyla's features.

"I…" she started hesitantly. "I haven't been using my magic since…"

Is it because of the burnout? Shamira asked when she realized Nyla didn't mean to continue. She watched Nyla from the corner of her eye as they ambled down the hedge-lined path. *Or do you think there's something more going on?*

"I'm not sure. It's probably just the magical drain, but…" Nyla expelled a shuddering sigh. A tense air roiled around her as she said, "I tried conjuring it after I woke up, and a few times since, but all I feel is a quiver in my blood. I know I still have my magic, but it's like it isn't mine anymore. It's unstable, or weak, or—I don't know—it's like I'm just learning how to use it all over again. Does that make sense?"

Shamira's tail flicked back and forth as she considered Nyla's words. *It does, actually. When you woke up, I said your aura was unsettled, and I too thought that it had to do with the magical drain, but looking at you now…It's different. I can't see all of it without you baring it to me, but from what I can see of your aura, your essence has changed. There's not as much lilac as there was, but yet it's still familiar to me. Your aura is still yours. I can't quite explain it or the change I see, but something is missing from your signature, though it doesn't seem to have had an adverse effect on you.*

"My aura has changed?" Nyla asked, turning concerned eyes matched with a frown on her. "I suppose that makes sense. When I tried to conjure my magic, it…it was different too." Nyla's words stopped with a slight choke, as if she couldn't bring herself to say what she'd intended to. Shaking her head, she added, "You're right, though. It's like there's something missing, but I don't feel like there is. Aside from my magic, I feel whole…but when I've tried to use my magic, I did notice it felt hollow or weak, and I just thought it was my exhaustion."

Perhaps you just need to give yourself some time, Shamira said patiently, mulling over Nyla's explanation. *Magic is like a muscle. It will always be there, and it will always be worked to some extent, and like your body, it can become injured if you use it too much, and it can grow weaker the longer it goes without stimulation, just as it grows stronger the more you use it properly. I have no doubt that in time, your magic will return to you in full—that is, if you wish to continue wielding it as you have been. It's okay if you don't want to hone your abilities, or grow stronger. The choice is yours, Nyla, and yours alone.*

Shamira added almost as an afterthought, *Perhaps when you're feeling up to it, we can look into it and your aura to see if we can't find an answer. There has to be a reasonable explanation, and I have a sneaking suspicion the two are related.*

"Thanks, Shamira." Nyla smiled softly, folding her arms against her chest. "I should probably be more concerned about it, but as it stands, I think my magic can wait. It just needs time, and I'm pretty confident in the fact that I have that now. It seems we both just have to listen to our hearts. What's holding us back from doing what we want?"

Shamira hummed. *For me, it's the pull of duty and expectation versus what I thought my heart had known to be true. I find myself wishing there was a way to balance both desires so I don't have to choose between the two, as they're both important to me—my clan and you and Xander and all who I've met here are important to me. It's become that I refuse to think about it in the hopes that I won't have to choose between the yearnings of my heart.*

"And for me, it's always been my own fear despite the courage and surety of my heart." Nyla turned her face toward the other side of the courtyard. Shamira followed her gaze, straining her neck to see over the tall hedges.

The sun glinted off of the delicate lilac-colored leaves belonging to trees whose bark was the purest of silvers Shamira had ever seen. Her eyes slid back to Nyla, eyeing how her hair had become a mix of auburn and silver, with the auburn quickly overtaking the silver strands.

It seems as though we both know what it is we want, but are too afraid to reach out and grasp it, she observed, studying Nyla intently.

"So it seems," Nyla said sadly. "Do you think my ancestors will be offended if I relinquished the titles? Specifically, the Thornravens?"

Your family once relinquished their title and holdings, so I do not think they would be offended if you were to uphold that decision, Shamira replied, keeping pace with Nyla as she aimlessly continued down the path. *And as for the Thornravens…from what I understand, they had done a great deal for this country. I don't think they could be any prouder of how you've upheld their legacy.*

"Alexander said something over dinner tonight, more to Merry and Xander while we were discussing the matter of what it means to be a part of the nobility and how I was undecided about the titles still, but I think he'd meant it for me too," Nyla said slowly. "He said that our actions make our names, not our rank. I've been turning it over in my head all night, in the background of everything else consuming my mind. I didn't realize how helpful that sentiment would be until now."

Lord Huntington is a wise man, Shamira agreed. *Thank you for sharing his wisdom with me. I think it has helped me a great deal.*

Nyla laughed lightly as the tension dissipated from her being. "I'm glad you found it as helpful as I had. Does that mean you've made a decision?"

Have you? Shamira countered knowingly.

"I think so."

Me too.

***

Nyla wandered through the corridors of Pemberly Hall, clutching the blanket she'd brought with her around her shoulders. She wasn't sure where she was going, but that was fine with her for now. At some point, probably sooner rather than later, she would have to find Alexander and tell him her decision.

Or worse, she'd find herself standing before the entire council again and have to divulge her decision to everyone all at once.

Maybe she shouldn't delay the inevitable. Nodding to herself, Nyla decided to see if Alexander was in his study. Biting her lip, she wondered what she would do if he wasn't there. She'd never known him to be anywhere but his study, so where else would she be able to find him now that she needed to speak with him?

Turning down another cream-colored hallway, Nyla wondered if she should call upon her magic to find him. Glancing down at her hands, Nyla took a deep breath and made to rally her magic.

A shrill shriek pierced through her memory. The glow of magical bonds and a voice that wasn't wholly her own followed on the nightmare's heels.

She swallowed hard against the memory. Forcing it from her mind, Nyla refused to acknowledge the last time she'd truly used her magic. She repeated the mantra she'd said to herself a thousand times over since she'd woken up and tried to rub the roving goosebumps from her arms.

Dinora's death was just. Even if Nyla hadn't shredded her aura, if she'd killed Dinora by a different means, her conscience would still be haunted by that moment. The only difference was she'd saved herself from the memory of Dinora's face, of her blood staining her hands.

Heat and chills crept along Nyla's skin at the mention of blood in her own mind.

It might not have been Dinora's blood that haunted her, but the wide glassy eyes of Sir Ian certainly did.

Nyla took a long, shuddering breath. Steeling her mind against the worst of the battle, she gripped the blanket tighter around herself.

She would not let this consume her.

She would not let it haunt her.

She would not let this eat away at her conscience.

She would live, as she'd promised her family, as she'd promised Xander, as she'd promised herself.

It was only a matter of time before the memories lost their hold on her mind, on her heart. Until then, Nyla promised to work to banish them from her mind. It didn't matter to her if the method would work in her favor or not; she only knew that it was that fight that had gotten her through yesterday and today.

Well that, and the steadfast support and patience she'd received from everyone—but especially Xander.

It amazed her when she thought about how much they'd been through together in such a short period in their lives. They'd hardly known each other, and now it was truly like they'd known each other all their lives.

Heat trickled along her cheekbones. Smiling, Nyla was glad to be alone so no one would see the absurdity of her grin or the twinkle she could feel in her eyes.

She'd never been in love before, had never had the time for it, and—if she were being completely honest—she was too young to have experienced love before.

But, if she had to guess, she would call the feelings she had toward Xander love—or some form of it.

It seemed crazy, to think about how much she relied on his presence in her life now, given how briefly they'd known each other, but maybe it wasn't. Maybe it was Fate's gift to her for the trials It had put her through. Nyla wasn't certain if that made less sense or more, but she did know one thing: Xander had most definitely kissed the top of her head that night in the study, just as she'd fallen asleep.

They might've kissed that day in the season room, if only they'd had a second longer before Shamira had come bursting in.

Most of all, Nyla knew she never wanted to lose Xander, or the gift of his company and companionship in her life.

So maybe it wasn't love that she felt for him, but fondness. Maybe there wasn't a difference between the two, but Nyla was glad to have the rest of her life to spend figuring out just what the two meant to her, and what she might mean to Xander.

Chuckling softly to herself, Nyla's footsteps felt lighter for the first time since she'd opened her eyes upon regaining her consciousness. She wasn't certain if it was the memories flitting through her head of all the good that had happened in her life, from Harvum Feasts to the day at the beach with Xander and everything in between, or if it was the idea of how *long* she had ahead of herself to make new memories like the ones she already held dear.

It was strange what a difference a day or two had made on her mood. It was strange that an hour or two had made such an impact on her mood for the better. She hoped Shamira felt the same way, that she'd also decided to seek her own happiness in this life. No matter how long pumpkies lived or how short of a lifespan humans had in comparison, Nyla knew that they each deserved eternal happiness and peace. They'd been through enough, a fact she was certain even Corruptio might agree with.

Lighthearted, Nyla hurried down the hallway and tried to figure out just where she was now. Pemberly's hallways all looked the same to her, what with the cream paint on the walls and family portraits or tapestries. She hadn't paid enough attention to them to know where they hung in relation to the different rooms she might need to find on her own, but she thought she'd seen that vase before. She only remembered it because it rattled anytime someone walked by it. Visibly lopsided on its unsteady base, Nyla carefully tiptoed past it, hoping that she wouldn't be the one to accidentally tip it over.

No matter how much kindness Alexander had shown her, she was still a guest in his home, and she'd be mortified if she broke what she could only assume was a priceless family heirloom.

But at least now she knew where she was. She was actually closer to her room than she was to Alexander's office, and perhaps that wasn't such a bad thing. Nyla didn't know if he would even be there given how late it had gotten since she'd started wandering the halls after her visit with the pumpkies. And in truth, she didn't want to crack the shield of comfort her musings had brought her.

Turning down the hallway she knew to be where the Lavender Room resided, Nyla watched the carpet beneath her feet, counting the flowers she passed in the repeating pattern.

A slight rustle and a small crack like a joint popping caught her ear. She glanced up, watching as Xander got to his feet.

"Have you been waiting outside my door this entire time?" she asked, laughing a little at the absurdity.

"Not the *whole* time." He smiled sheepishly. "Just part of the time. I just wanted to make sure you were okay…and to say goodnight."

Nyla bit her lip. "That's really sweet of you."

"I don't know," Xander admitted, rubbing the back of his neck. "I may or may not have been talking to the empty room, thinking you'd maybe shut yourself in."

Nyla couldn't help the laugh that escaped her. "You're really worried about me, aren't you?"

"Only a little," he said, shrugging insecurely.

"I think…I think I'm going to be just fine," Nyla said, wiggling her toes against the carpet and shifting her fingers against the boots she held in her hand. "I mean, there might still be days when I'm not, but…I think I'm coming back to myself a little."

"I'm glad." Xander smiled softly, his eyes twinkling just the slightest bit. "Goodnight then, Nyla."

"Goodnight, Xander." Nyla watched as he turned slowly, watching her for just a second longer, before he finally made his way to his own room.

Shaking her head a little as she reached for the delicately made metal vines and leaves decorating the Lavender Room's door handle, Nyla couldn't stop the smile pulling at her lips.

Tomorrow would be a brighter day; she just knew it.

28. THE HEART OF HART

"You're certain?" Alexander asked, watching her closely. "You don't want to at least explore the possibility of what may be before relinquishing your family titles?"

Nyla nodded her head. "I'm certain. I've gone all my life without a title, and if my ancestors had relinquished their title, they probably had a good reason for it. I want to respect their decision, but more importantly...I don't want the attention of being a newly coronated noble. I've done enough to put the country's eye on me. I don't want to be made a spectacle of too."

"You wouldn't be a spectacle," he said, nearly chuckling as he reclined back in the plush armchair he'd chosen by the sitting room's fireplace. It was the first time Nyla had been in the Huntington family's private sitting room. Nestled away from the guest suites of Pemberly Hall, the wallpaper was a dark maroon with a thick, deep brown molding and an imposing fireplace of the same brown wood, making the room cozy. "And as far as being in the public's awareness, all mention of you and your part has been avoided in the statement. No one will know who you are except for those of us present here."

Nyla sighed with relief, sinking farther into the couch cushions as she eyed the breakfast tray on the coffee table set between the couch she'd claimed and the pair of armchairs across from her, the one being occupied by Alexander with a renewed interest. "Good."

"Ingrid and I had thought you'd want it that way," he explained, offering her a wry smile.

"You're both correct in thinking that," Nyla agreed, taking a sip from her steaming mug and dunking a butter chip cookie in it. "I couldn't imagine dealing with that sort of attention and publicity."

Alexander shrugged, waving his hand to dispel her worry. "You grow accustomed to it, and learn how to gently redirect it to your will."

"Is that what you call it?" Xander's voice carried through the room, causing Nyla to glance over her shoulder and watch as he strode in. "I think Grandmother used to say you and George were like puppet masters when it came to the press."

Taking the seat beside her, Xander chose a cookie from the breakfast tray and offered her a small smile by way of greeting. She returned it warmly before turning her attention back to the man across from them.

Alexander chortled. "Is that what she used to say? Well, she never said as much to me, though Gerri certainly has."

"The art of redirection," Xander mused, pouring himself a cup of cocholee. "It's a rather important skill, though it's a pretty difficult art to master. Probably one of the hardest ones to perform and appear genuine while doing it."

"It must run in the family," Nyla said pointedly.

Xander raised his brows, glancing over at her in confusion.

"Don't act like you don't know what I'm talking about, Mr. 'it's a surprise' or 'absolutely essential to our overall journey.'"

"I thought we were past that now?" he teased.

"I suppose we are." Nyla grabbed a pastry and a small plate from the platter set on the low coffee table. Pausing briefly, Nyla realized someone was missing. "Where's Merry?"

"I haven't seen her yet this morning," Alexander said. "I would assume she's sleeping in, decided to take her breakfast in the garden, or visiting with Shamira and the pumpkies. She's been very eager to learn more about them."

Nyla nodded. "Shamira says that Ingrid and a handful of Casters are working with them to learn different magic techniques. She hopes that we can form a new alliance with each other, just as it once was."

"Hopefully we won't ever have need of the role they've planned in our alliance again," Alexander said, "though the diplomacy would be a great improvement to our country. It would be comforting to know that alliance remains open, as the pumpkies know things we could only ever dream of knowing."

Nyla nibbled on her pastry, glad to have found her appetite once more. She hadn't eaten much the first day after she'd woken up. Too consumed by exhaustion, the effort to fuel her body had been like an insurmountable obstacle in her path, but in the days that had followed, it was like she couldn't get enough food. She was finally starting to feel like her stomach was content again, having dined heartily yesterday and intending to do the same today if she was able to.

But there was something she needed to do, something no one was going to like.

Taking a breath, Nyla said the one thing she knew would bring outrage to the peaceful sitting room. "I think I'd like to see Cedric."

Alexander's teacup clattered against his saucer. Beside her, Xander tensed, freezing as he reached for the breakfast platter.

Sitting back, Xander looked at her with concerned eyes. "Do you think that's a good idea?"

"Maybe not," Nyla said, setting her breakfast plate beside her cup and saucer on the warm-toned end table next to the couch. "But there're a few things I'd like to ask him, given everything you told me."

"Will it bring you peace, what you hope to ask?" Alexander asked, his lips drawn into a grim line.

"I think so," she considered, "maybe not today, but one day at least."

"Then I won't stop you from seeing him." Alexander set his cup on the coffee table and straightened in his chair, looking quite like the lord and shrewd businessman she'd imagined he'd be when Xander had first told her about him. "But I would ask that you bring Ingrid with you."

"And I'm coming too," Xander said.

"That's fine," Nyla agreed. "We'll go after breakfast."

"And then what?" Xander grumbled, "We'll travel through the heart of the Shadow Forest again?"

Nyla hummed, tilting her head from side to side as she chewed. Finally swallowing, she replied, "No, I haven't thought that far ahead yet, though I can say with absolutely certainty that I will be glad to never see the heart of the Shadow Forest again."

Alexander shook his head, chuckling. "Well, it sounds like you two have quite the day ahead of you, as do I. Perhaps I'll inform Albert and Clarice of your intentions to relinquish your title. Have you thought about the trust they'd like to establish for you?"

"Wait," Xander started, seeming to shake himself from his disgruntled mood at the prospect of their visit with Cedric after breakfast, "you're abdicating your titles?"

Nyla shrugged. "They don't feel like mine, especially since my family had already given them up, and I didn't grow up knowing about them. It just seems like a lot of trouble for something that I never really knew about, or wanted."

Xander considered her for a second, his lips quirked in a small smile. "That's fair. I guess I shouldn't be so surprised then."

A clock chimed the hour, stopping Nyla from speaking the quip that had formed on her tongue.

Alexander looked toward the clock ticking away beside the fireplace and slowly rose to his feet. "I suppose," he started, "now is as good a time as any to begin my day. Try to stay out of trouble, you two. And if you see Merry, be sure to keep her from making trouble too."

"When have I ever…you don't get to look at me like that, Miss 'I'll challenge the Royal Mage's apprentice to a duel in front of the entire banquet.'" Xander glared.

"It wasn't a banquet," Alexander corrected. "It was a gathering, though otherwise I do believe you may have a valid argument, grandson who once snuck out of the estate disguised as a member of the traveling theater group."

Nyla looked to Xander with wide eyes. Without another word, Alexander left them, leaving a cloud of shock and exasperation in his midst.

"Let's not talk about it," Xander groaned. "I hardly got past the driveway before the theater troupe realized they had an extra person."

"But you're going to tell me the whole story one day," Nyla begged, "right?"

Xander made a show of considering her plea. "Maybe. If you tell me a story of yours in exchange."

"I think we've just figured out how we're going to spend the rest of our day."

"Or we could start our day with that instead," Xander said hopefully.

Nyla shook her head. "I have to do this."

Xander sighed heavily. "I may not want to, and I definitely do not want you to, but I guess," he huffed, "if you absolutely must, then I'll support that decision."

"That's all I ask," Nyla said, "because you did say you'd be there for me, 'no matter how ridiculous' it seemed."

"I did say that, didn't I?"

"Yes, yes you did."

"I suppose we should get this over with, that is, if you're ready?" Xander said, standing from the couch and offering her his hand. She gladly accepted, letting him pull her from the couch.

Tensely, Nyla replied, "As I'll ever be."

29. THE LAST OF CEDRIC

Nyla took a steadying breath. Eyeing the sigils etched into the wooden door of Cedric's quiet cottage, she reached out to them with her magic. The feeling of her magic coursing through her veins was oddly foreign to her, as she and Shamira hadn't yet tried to figure out the change in her aura and how it impacted her magic. Nyla still held onto the hope that it was only the magical drain she'd experienced and that, in time, everything would settle within her for the better. She hadn't wanted any company as she did this, though her friends still waited a little ways behind her, chatting with the guards Ingrid and Shamira had placed here to help secure the cottage.

There wasn't any particular reason why she wanted to do this alone, only that it was her preference, like she was testing herself one final time. She had to do this; she had to see him and ask the questions that had plagued her for two long years. With a fragile hope, Nyla considered that maybe her chances of receiving answers from him were better if she was alone. Or maybe they were the same regardless. There was still the possibility that Cedric wouldn't even speak to her.

Nyla pressed her lips into a grim line.

The sigils flashed, glowing for only a moment before they returned to their natural state of worn wood. Approaching the weathered door, Nyla reached for the handle. Each inch brought her one second closer to seeing Cedric. She hoped this would be the last time she'd ever see him. And as the one blessed with freedom, Nyla supposed that was nearly a guarantee.

But Xander's words stalked the outskirts of her mind. He'd said that Cedric had claimed that their wards were weak before he'd escaped from Pemberly Hall's dungeons. The implied threat sat like ash on her tongue as she opened the door and stepped inside the cottage, shutting the door behind her.

If she could face Dinora and win, she could face Cedric and his dejectedness with ease.

"What do you want?" he rasped. Limp against his bed, Cedric didn't look at her. The closer she got to him, the more pronounced his scars from the battle were. She realized his eyes were closed, as if he couldn't even open them if he tried. His chest rose and fell with each laborious breath he took. Each breath, accompanied by a gurgle, made a shudder wrack down her own spine like a claw grazing her bones.

Nyla didn't answer him as she stopped to stand at the foot of his bed. Instead, she studied him through narrowed eyes. His hair was unruly, his skin ashen just as it was when she'd visited him with Ingrid to obtain some information on how to defeat Dinora, only this time his pallor was made worse by the long jagged scars that hadn't quite healed since the battle. This time, Nyla realized it would truly be the end for the red-eyed man.

Scoffing at the silence, Cedric slowly peeled his eyes open. His eyes widened slightly as he forced his head up to get a glimpse of just who had come to bother him in his wait for death's embrace. Nyla stared back, unflinching and unafraid.

"Why?" she demanded, crossing her arms over her chest. "Xander told me everything, about the potion and how Dinora transferred the bond to me and about the blood oath you'd made to him after you attacked him and Edwin to escape the dungeons. Why did you do any of it?"

Cedric considered her, his chest heaving with shallow, rattling breaths.

He shrugged, letting himself sink back into the pillows and cushion of his bed, letting his heavy-lidded eyes fall shut once more.

"You don't get to ignore me, not after everything I've been through," she said through gritted teeth. "If you won't answer that, then at least tell me why you were there that day, watching as…as that fire took everything from me."

"Why are you here, Nyla?" Cedric whispered. "For answers that won't bring you peace? Or to tout your victory?"

Nyla glared at him. "I don't believe you. You claim to have made a bequeathment potion, but yet you still worked with Dinora all these centuries, following her orders. Why not kill her yourself and be done with it? Why offer to kill her and end that battle if you couldn't even do so before?"

Cedric didn't respond.

Nyla sighed. Glancing around the cottage, she decided to drag the lonely chair from the fireplace over to his bedside and make herself comfortable. If she wanted answers, Nyla realized she would be here for a while at the rate their conversation was going. As she settled, Cedric turned his head toward her chair, watching her with those dull, scarlet-colored eyes.

"If you want peace, you should answer my questions because I'm not leaving until you do."

Silence ticked by with the few seconds that passed before Cedric turned away again. His eyes remained open despite the dark circles Nyla noticed plagued him. Up close, he looked even worse than she'd ever thought possible—worse even compared to the day Ingrid and her Circle had dragged him into Pemberly Hall's ballroom.

"No wonder her magic took to you," he muttered, calling her attention away from the hollows of his gaunt face. "You two are so much alike."

"It's nice to have my hair back, though," Nyla replied. "Or do you still see me as Astrid?"

Cedric shook his head. "No." He paused, reconsidering. "Yes."

"You loved her," she said. The words sounded like an accusation, spun by bitterness and Nyla's own hatred for the man lying mere feet away from her.

"I do."

Nyla scowled, biting her tongue to keep from interrupting him with the scalding accusation that wanted to drop from her lips like acid. If he really loved her, and still considered himself to be in love with Astrid, then why? Why had he acted as he had? She wondered it so many times over the last few weeks that receiving an answer to satisfy her curiosity had become almost just as important as getting answers for all the rest. It was a question her mind had turned over during the long days of her confinement to the Woodlane Manor thanks to the bond Dinora had transferred to her or on the journey to Huntington when all was otherwise silent. She'd pondered over that detail almost as much as she'd explored her questions surrounding the fire that had taken her family from her.

"I have lived my life with regret," Cedric said slowly, his ragged breaths filling the gaps between his words. Nyla's attention shifted to him. For the first time since she'd almost killed him at the Woodlane Manor when he and Dinora had ambushed her, Cedric's eyes were clear and focused. With his gaze pinned on her, he said, "I had everything that's supposed to matter in life, and I shunned it all for something I could never hope to gain. Dinora has—*had*—a way of ruining things from the inside out. She was rot, and I have lived these last six centuries still consumed by that rot, too afraid to turn back and fix what had already been done."

Nyla watched him. Her fingers absently traced the smooth wooden arm of the worn chair as she considered his response. She licked her lips. "All this time, you've been afraid to do what's right because of what you'd already done wrong? What was there to be afraid of in doing what was right?"

Cedric scoffed, shaking his head in amusement. "No matter how much you repent, there will always be those unwilling to forgive and accept your reform. And they're right to do so. Have you forgiven me? Accepted the wrongs I've done, or the steps I've taken to right them?"

"No," Nyla said without hesitation, "but there's more than one way to earn forgiveness. Have you forgiven yourself?"

Cedric stared at her as though she'd struck him.

"Did no one ever teach you that you cannot wholly rely on the forgiveness of others to absolve you?" she asked, arching her brow. She didn't wait for a response, knowing the answer in her heart. "Of course not, though now I wonder what would've happened if you'd known that all along. Would you have found the courage to do what you knew was right and just?"

"You think me a coward?" he asked quietly, staring at her intently, though the great effort marred his features. As if he thought better of it, Cedric shook his head and turned his face away once more. Nyla wondered if it was so he wouldn't have to face her reply, because deep down in what was left of his heart, he knew the answer already. If not hers, but most certainly his own.

"I do, but not because you couldn't kill your own mother." Nyla licked her lips, considering her words and what she thought of the pitiful man before her. "You're a coward in my mind because you never tried to reverse your mistakes, regardless of the consequences that would befall you. You ignored your own instincts for your own comfort—"

"Plenty of people do," Cedric interrupted quietly.

Nyla nearly vibrated with indignation at the context sewn into his interruption. "Sure, but did they prolong their lives by centuries? Did they help cripple a kingdom? Or steal the land's magic? No. Only you and Dinora have done that."

Cedric shifted, pulling the blankets tighter against himself as if they could shield himself from her words. "You're enjoying this, aren't you?"

Nyla shrugged. "I came here for answers, but telling you exactly what I think of you is a different sort of catharsis I didn't realize would bring me such peace."

"I imagine Astrid would have too and will if our paths cross again."

His words made Nyla think about what Astrid had told her on the astral plane. She'd claimed to hate herself, for the part of her that still loved Cedric. Perhaps Astrid would be more conflicted about this situation than Cedric believed. For all of his regret thanks to his own cowardice, it seemed to Nyla as though Astrid regretted a love she'd lost but had never let go of—a love Cedric still held on to despite all he'd done that had ultimately been the reason he'd lost it.

Each of them had regrets, but Nyla had been blessed with the opportunity to chip away at her own until they faded. She'd been blessed with the opportunity to live her life and choose her path. And she would never take that for granted. Fate had blessed her with this gift, a gift to make the most of her life and ease the regrets worming their way through her conscience by seeking out what she held dear.

All she had to do now was grasp it and never let go.

"Dinora…" Cedric began. The vacant expression had returned to his eyes, causing Nyla to wonder just what he was about to tell her. "It had taken quite a lot of magic to keep us alive these past centuries. I supposed I could've stopped collecting the magic at any point in history, but…I didn't. I'd discovered how Astrid's 'curse' worked only a few years after her death, so I knew it was only a bond, and I knew what it was doing to Dinora. I knew she could sense everything, and even if I hadn't discovered what Astrid had done, Dinora never stopped complaining about the breeze or the stiffness that plagued her bones in Serenmae because of the chill outside.

"I suppose I went along with her plan and desire for near immortality just to see her suffer while I dawdled on her instructions to free her, failing time and time again." Cedric smiled ruefully. "It went on like this for years. The mechanics of Astrid's spellwork was never far from my mind, so I knew what boundaries I could test to make Dinora think my efforts to free her were honest failures. And so it became a game. How long could I make her suffer before she'd given up and was ready to fade? How long would I be able to keep this charade before it became tiresome? But as the centuries passed, it didn't. My heart still seethed, and Dinora hadn't given up. She still raged as much as I'd come to resent her.

"Sometimes, years would go by without a word from her, and I would wonder if this was finally it, if Welrelm were calling her, and by virtue me, back from whence we came. But alas, each time I'd prepared to live the rest of my natural life in peace, a raverin would tap at my window and squash those dreams."

Nyla's memory sparked, recalling the flock of raverins that had joined their battle and subsequently departed after Cedric had been injured and carried off from the battle. "A raverin?"

"Yes, a raverin," Cedric drawled, jarred from the memories of how these six centuries had passed in what seemed like near idleness to Nyla. "We used raverins to communicate with each other, as Dinora's magic was too depleted to use over long distances…until I gave her some magic to rejuvenate her life."

Nyla raised her brow in question as he let his words hang in the air, seeming as though he wasn't willing to continue. From the tone of his voice, she guessed that they'd broached a more difficult subject. "Go on."

Cedric wavered. Heaving a breath, he propped himself up on an elbow. Nyla watched as Cedric dragged himself up well enough to slump against the headboard. Panting, Cedric took a moment to regain his breath. Pursing her lips, Nyla stood and went to the kitchen crammed into a corner of the cottage. Finding a glass, she pumped some water into it and returned to Cedric's bedside, offering it to him. She forced herself not to cringe as she realized he hadn't the strength to drink from it himself and resigned herself to help him. Hardly taking a sip, Cedric crumpled back against the headboard, nodding his thanks to her. Nyla set the glass down on the floor beside her and waved her hand, urging him to carry on in his tale, in his confession.

"The last time…" His eyes flicked to her and then to his hands in his lap. Cedric shut his eyes. His face screwed up as if in physical pain, and perhaps he was, as the expression had to pull at the fresh battle wounds. "The last time I gave Dinora magic was two years ago."

Nyla's heart stopped. Her lips parted, but no sound escaped.

"I never imagined she would've noticed the shift in magic when you were born, or be able to sense the genetic link in your essence to Astrid, or else I would've worked harder to obscure the manor's pull on you.

"But I was curious and foolish. I wanted to know more about the children with Astrid's bloodline, the ones who'd returned to her ancestral home." He bowed his head. "I never should've given her that magic. Of all the things I've done or failed to do in my life, and of all the sins I've committed, I fear this one is the worst."

Nyla couldn't breathe. He didn't have to tell her what happened next, what she feared Dinora had used that magic for. If he'd made the point of telling her this had happened two years ago, then he knew they were both aware of what he was insinuating.

But Cedric continued because, after all, hadn't Nyla asked about the fire? Hadn't she wanted to know what'd happened that day?

"Dinora used the magic to spin a curse of her own," he uttered. His voice was hollow and devoid of any emotion despite the weight his words carried. "But Dinora had never been a patient woman, and so her curse hadn't worked as intended. If anything, I would say that her curse resulted in this turn of Fate. Astrid's magic hadn't bloomed in you until after the fire, though I'm sure you are more than aware of that fact now, but you asked me for answers, so I will give them.

"Dinora had wanted to destroy Astrid's bloodline, once and for all. She wanted to…well, she used some specific phrasing in the design of her curse, but what she wanted isn't of great importance, not when we know the result of her curse."

"Why?" Nyla breathed. Her eyes stung, though there weren't any tears to shed. "Why not stop her then? Why let that burden fall to me or watch as I stumbled through life terrified and alone and lost and… Why did you let this happen?"

Cedric remained silent. No matter how much she willed him to answer, Cedric refused to look at her, an obvious admission of shame if she'd ever known one. Nyla pushed herself to her feet. Her legs trembled as she took a step toward him and then stopped.

"I hope you find peace, I truly do," Nyla seethed, "but I will never forgive you, whether you bequeath your magic to me or not, whether you find forgiveness for the sins you've committed or not. Dinora may have woven the curse that set the fire, but you gambled with my family's lives. It's just as much your fault as it is Dinora's that they're dead. Everything that's happened is your fault because you couldn't forgive yourself enough to let the both of you die after a natural life. *That* would've been enough suffering, I assure you. Having been bonded to that blasted manor myself, I promise you—a single lifetime would've been more than enough punishment for Dinora." Nyla's words were like acid on her tongue. Cedric didn't look at her as she rambled on furiously. Hot tears trailed down her face, her hands clenched into fists at her side. The only indication he'd listened to every word thus far was the subtle flinch and twitch of his face each time Nyla reminded him of his blame.

"I was asked to sit on the council for your trial. It wouldn't've been public, so there would have been no jury," she said, "but I declined. I refuse to take part in this game any longer, and that's truly what it was to you before I was born, wasn't it? A game, to see how long you could make Dinora suffer?"

Cedric nodded weakly.

"Whatever your end, it will not be my decision," Nyla said, drawing herself up to her full height as she stared down at him. "And thanks to the injuries you sustained in battle, the council that would've been your jury has decided to let you die here, believing you've already punished yourself a thousand times over. You know your regrets and your grief, and seeing you now, realizing that the apathy was only a mask for a beaten soul? It's enough to bring me peace."

Nyla turned away, walking toward the cottage door with even strides. Just as she'd crossed the threshold and reached to pull the door shut, she paused. Taking a breath, she glanced over her shoulder to find Cedric watching her with a drawn expression and hollow eyes.

"Maybe you don't deserve to know this," she told him solemnly, "but Astrid continued to love you, even after you betrayed her. She may still love you, and a part of her hates herself for that, for loving you even after all you'd done to betray her and how you've hurt her."

Cedric's eyes widened. His mouth dropped open, though he didn't utter a single sound as Nyla turned and forced the door shut behind her. His scarlet-colored eyes haunted her for the last time as she called upon her magic and restored the wards. Stepping back with a satisfied sigh, Nyla studied the door, committing its etched sigils to memory but more so because she wanted to take a breath before rejoining Xander, Shamira, and Ingrid.

Shaking her head, Nyla bit back a smile. How had she found such amazing friends in all this tragedy?

As she stepped into the little camp the pumpkies and Casters tasked with guarding Cedric had made in a clearing they'd created, her eyes naturally gravitated to the small group waiting for her under the canopy. Ingrid smiled wryly at her.

"That went rather…" Ingrid began, "Did that bring you peace, Nyla?"

"Time will tell," she replied, coming to stand beside Xander. Her eyes fixed on the crystal ball they had set up to monitor Cedric. She glanced away without studying the image of the cottage's interior—of Cedric—displayed within the curvature of the glass.

"Are you sure you're the same woman who advocated for mercy?" Xander teased, letting the thin chain around his neck rest against his chest from where he'd been twisting it around his fingers. A ring flashed in the sunlight, catching Nyla's attention only briefly. "After what we just witnessed, I do have to wonder."

Nyla grinned mischievously, shrugging. "I needed to make peace with my heart. A trial is no place for that. Trials are for justice, not confrontation."

"And your request to consider mercy?" Ingrid inquired.

"Selfish, I'm afraid." Nyla cringed under the weight of their gazes. Shock flitted through Ingrid's gaze. Shamira's tail flicked in the way it did when her mind was in the midst of processing something. But Xander remained unchanged. He only grasped her hand and gave it a gentle squeeze that Nyla gratefully returned.

"After what happened…what I did…I needed to ease my own conscience. Whatever the council decides, I just want to know that they won't be unnecessarily harsh and that whatever happens next won't continue the brutality Dinora has become famous for in the myths. That isn't justice. That's vengeance, and honestly?" Nyla paused, forcing her gaze to meet Ingrid's and then Shamira's. "It didn't make me feel any better. I'm still angry and hurt and bitter. It didn't bring my family back. Things haven't changed, or not really, not for me at least. The world is still as it was before, only the threat to it and all of magic is truly gone now."

That may be true, Shamira said sincerely, *but you did free the souls imprisoned in the Shadow Forest. I would consider that the true victory in all of this.*

Nyla nodded, too choked up to reply in earnest.

"Come on," Xander said, lightly tugging on her hand. "Let's go bask in the sun for a while."

Nyla managed a small smile. "I'd like that."

***

After some deliberation upon their return to his home, Xander had led Nyla to a quiet spot on Pemberly's estate, as neither one of them felt particularly interested in much of anything. He didn't know what sort of toll visiting Cedric had had on Nyla, but he was glad that she was at least taking a moment to recuperate from it. They were sitting on a cushioned lounger in the small greenhouse his grandmother had tended to with Nyla's head in his lap and his fingers playing with her auburn hair.

Neither one had spoken a word in ages. But the silence didn't bother Xander. And it didn't seem to bother Nyla either as she watched the clouds floating overhead through the glass roof of the greenhouse. The humid air wafting off of the plants was actually pleasant given the cool weather outside. It was like a hug caressing the soul.

Eventually, Nyla's fingers found his mother's wedding band resting against his chest, dangling from the chain around his neck. He watched as she studied it, twisting it this way and that in the light.

Nyla smiled softly. "I've never seen this before."

Xander hummed. "I never really show it to anyone, so that's not much of a surprise to me."

"Sorry," she said, letting the ring slip from her fingers. "I didn't realize…"

"No," Xander laughed, "it's fine. I would've said something if I minded."

Her lilac-colored eyes met his. "Can I ask about it?"

Xander tilted his head to the side, watching the shadow he cast shift over Nyla. "What about it?"

Nyla rolled her eyes. An amused smirk pulled at her lips. "You're so difficult, my lord."

"We're back to that are we, Lady Nyla?" he laughed. Nyla's eyes narrowed into a halfhearted glare. "All right, all right," he continued, "I won't mention it again."

"I'm not really a noblewoman," Nyla muttered. "My ancestors gave up our holdings when they moved to Eurland."

"Maybe so, but the Caradels never retired or demoted their titles. They've just been…unused all this time, waiting," Xander teased. It really shouldn't have surprised him when she'd refused the titles, not after all that had happened. Being a noble by title didn't suit the life Nyla was trying to reclaim. Though he couldn't pretend to know what she was planning, or if she even had anything in mind for her future. She hadn't mentioned anything to him about what she'd hoped to do next, and he hadn't asked for the fear of instilling some kind of urgency in her that made her feel like she had to make some kind of decision.

What shocked him more, though, was the respect his grandfather had shown him by not immediately expecting Xander to make a decision about his life and his future as a member of the Huntington family. He didn't know if it was a lesson he'd learned when Xander had exiled himself from the family, or if it was something his grandfather had learned recently. But what he did know was that he was rather glad to have found that his grandfather had learned it after all. Xander supposed his grandfather could say the same of him too, though he couldn't figure out what lessons he'd learned over the time he'd been gone.

Xander clasped the ring in his hand, lost in the memories of all that had brought him here to this very moment. The weight of Nyla's gaze pressed down on him as he gathered his thoughts.

"It was my mother's," he started. "When they passed, it was decided that their wedding bands would be given to me and Issie." His words hung in the air between them. His eyes saw the memory of that fateful day, when his parents' wills had been read and the decision made to give the rings to Xander and Issie. As he lost himself to the memories that followed, the plentiful plant life and the sunbeams streaming through the greenhouse faded into the background, swept away by the winds of a harsh Serenmae day and a day even more bitter than that.

"My grandfather gave me my mother's wedding band, and Issie got our father's wedding band," he explained. Swallowing hard, he added, "My grandfather and I had a…spirited disagreement about what to do with my father's ring when Issie…when Issie passed."

"That's sweet," Nyla whispered. Xander shook the memories from his mind, looking at her in confusion. A soft smile played on her lips. "I mean, not the fighting part, but the sentiment. I think it's really sweet."

Xander returned her smile, brushing back her hair, still in awe of its natural color. Lightly, he said, "I guess it is."

"Will you come with me? To Eurland?" Nyla bit her lip, watching him carefully.

"What?"

"Come with me," she said, reaching for the hand that'd stilled in her hair and weaving her fingers with his. Clasping their joined hands against her chest, her eyes flashed pleading. "I've never been to Eurland before, but I want to find my family."

A slow smirk spread across Xander's face. "So you want me to be your escort because I've been to Eurland?"

Nyla snorted. "Well, you are a gentleman by birth, and you do know the language."

Xander laughed, shaking his head in amusement. "Are those the only reasons why you're asking me?"

"No," Nyla said, her voice turning sober. Glancing back down at her, Xander saw the contemplative worry in her eyes. "I don't want to go alone, and I…I want you there."

Smiling, Xander leaned over her, softly cupping her cheek to get her attention. "Of course I'll go with you. I'd love to."

"Really? You'll come?" she asked excitedly.

"How many times do I have to tell you? We aren't getting rid of each other anytime soon."

"Maybe just one more time." Nyla cupped his face in her hands, holding him there just as gently as her gaze. "I'm glad you're coming with me."

"I'm glad you want me to."

"I can't imagine going on an adventure without you," she admitted quietly. "I actually can't even…" Nyla trailed off, her brows furrowing. Shaking her head, Nyla shifted as her hands fell from his face. Xander sat back, allowing Nyla to sit up and twist herself around on the seat to face him. "This is so stupid—well, not stupid, but please don't think this is weird," she rambled, looking anywhere but him. "I can't imagine going on with my life, living it, and building something for myself if… if you're not there to share it all with me."

Nyla fixed her gaze on the space between them. Her words hit him like a killing blow.

Slowly, Xander reached out to her. Tilting her face up to meet his gaze, he said, "It's not weird. Not when I feel like I've known you all my life."

Nyla's shoulders slumped with her relieved huff. Grinning, she flung herself at him. Knocked back against the arm of the lounger, Xander laughed, wrapping his arms around her. Nyla's giggle echoed in his ears. Propping herself up on her hands, she stared down at him with bright eyes.

"When do we leave?" Bright sunlight crowned her hair, making it appear like spun gold as she grinned down at him.

"Whenever you want," he answered, thinking about that day at the beach again. Already, his mind turned over all that they needed to arrange before they could actually leave, but knowing Nyla, she would leave tomorrow if she could, given how excited she seemed right now. "This is your adventure, Nyla. I'm only here to share it with you."

She shook her head. "It's our adventure."

"In that case," Xander smiled, "I know a place, in Eurland, that I think you'll love."

"Oh?" she laughed. "Are you going to tell me, or am I going to have to wait and see what it is?"

Xander hummed, making a show of considering her question. Finally coming to a decision, he smiled deviously. "You'll see."

Groaning in exasperation, Nyla pulled away. "You're impossible."

He laughed, sitting up and running a hand through his hair. As he caught Nyla's eye again, he noticed the teasing quirk of her lips and the light gleaming in her lilac eyes.

He only smiled back and said, "So are you."

30. TIME MAGIC

Three quiet knocks sounded on her door. Nyla turned away from the mirror and gave entry to the only person she knew who would be knocking on her door at this very moment. As surely as the sun set in the west, Xander slipped inside her room, fiddling with his cufflink.

"I haven't had to dress formally in—"

"A week?" Nyla joked, recalling the memory of Xander waiting for her in the bedroom hallway of the Woodlane Manor in an ill-fitting suit as part of his distraction while Shamira and Edwin had examined the manor's aura for a way to break the spell that had bound her to the ancient manor home.

"That just barely counts, as it didn't fit." Xander scrunched his nose. Nyla laughed, walking over to him, and gently took his hand away from his sleeve, fixing the cufflink herself. "Thanks."

"Anytime," she said, brushing off a speck of lint from his shoulder.

"We're going to be late." Xander didn't move, though, nor did he try to pull away from where Nyla had left her hand resting on his shoulder, caught up in the fact that today was the day.

Even though she'd managed to break through the clouds hovering over her mind after the battle, and was taking every opportunity she could to smile, to laugh, to push away the memory of that day, Nyla hadn't been able to wholly overcome its shadow.

"Hey," Xander said softly. His hand was warm against her cheek as he cupped her face. Gently wrapping his other hand around the one she still had resting against his shoulder, Xander made certain he'd caught her attention before speaking again. Nyla swallowed against the tears that tightened her throat, staring back at his earnest eyes. "I'm right here. I'll always be right here. We don't have to stay for the whole service. No one will notice if we leave early, or if we only stay for a little while."

"I know," she said, biting her lip. "But I really should be there."

"As a member of the esteemed Huntington family, and newly appointed Heir of Tenebris, I really should be too, but I really don't think anyone will miss us. It's a memorial service, not a celebratory ball."

Nyla nodded. "Still, though," she breathed, "it doesn't sit well with me to not be there."

"Then I'll be right there with you. Whatever you want to do," Xander said, squeezing her hand, "I'll be with you."

Nyla gave him a watery smile. "Then we should go before I change my mind and decide to never leave this room."

Xander smiled back at her solemnly. "I'm sure everyone feels the same way, no matter how much we want to honor and acknowledge those we lost."

"You have a handkerchief, right?"

"I have two, and I think Edwin is bringing two just in case, though he didn't mention who for."

Nyla frowned. "That's odd, but Edwin seems the type to always be prepared, so…maybe it's not as odd?"

"Maybe…" Xander said, taking her arm in his as they started toward the bedroom door. Shaking his head as if dismissing a thought he hadn't voiced, Xander added, "I hope this is a lighthearted memorial."

"Is there such a thing?" Nyla asked as they started down the hallway.

"Probably not, but one can hope."

Nyla silently agreed, glad to have Xander beside her as they slowly made their way to the courtyard. In all the long days that had passed since she'd woken up, she feared today would be the longest of them all. But at least there was tomorrow to look forward to.

Alexander had announced at breakfast this morning that he was naming Xander as his successor in the Heirs of Tenebris and Merry was to be Alexander the First's apprentice for all matters related to H&R Trading until she came of age so Alexander could finally retire, with a celebratory banquet to be held tomorrow. Xander had explained that he'd declined his grandfather's offer to take his stead as president of the Huntington's half of the company, and after discussing it with him thoroughly, they'd both decided that Merry was the better candidate, as she seemed to already know everything about the company anyway and had a particular skill with people that would serve her well. In confidence, Xander had also told her that he didn't want to be saddled by the company forever. He wanted to see where their futures would take them, just as Nyla wanted her own chance at happiness too.

They'd talked about their futures a little in the greenhouse the other day, but they hadn't had much time, just the two of them, to talk about it since his grandfather's announcement earlier in the morning, as the memorial services were scheduled to begin shortly after breakfast and Nyla had yet to find something to wear. In the end, Merry had given her a dress that she'd 'borrowed' from an older cousin. Nyla adjusted the lace of her sleeve at the thought. She kept at it as the doors to the courtyard came to loom before them.

She didn't know how the staff had managed to repair the estate so quickly, or how Alexander, Ingrid, and Sir Hubert had organized the memorial just as fast.

Crossing over the threshold and out into the courtyard, Nyla's eyes roved over the assembled crowd. The scent of lilacs choked her throat, making her eyes sting. There were a few bouquets throughout the courtyard, but it was enough to fill the almost Harvum air with their scent. She also noticed displays of forget-me-nots throughout the courtyard, usually accompanied by the colors of the Caster Corps. She wondered what the flowers meant to the Corps, or if it was more so for their symbolism in general that the Corps had donated the flowers to the memorial service.

Most of all, Nyla's eyes took in the amount of people already gathered in the courtyard. She hadn't realized how many people had gathered at the Huntingtons' estate until now, nor had she realized how many people and pumpkies had taken part in the battle. She knew some of the local families who had lost someone in the battle had been invited, as Alexander had told them over breakfast yesterday, but she hadn't expected this many people. Where had they all come from? Where had they all been before the battle, when they were still just having war meetings and discussing Dinora's threat?

Had they really all come to the estate before the battle, or had they wisped there when commanded?

"Xander! Nyla!" a voice called from somewhere off to the side. Nyla glanced around Xander to see Edwin strolling toward them in his Caster Corps uniform.

Breaking away from Xander to hug Edwin, Nyla said, "Thank you for keeping them safe."

Edwin huffed a laugh, pulling away. "It was a nearly impossible task, you know."

"I realize that *now*," Nyla chuckled quietly, "but you managed."

"Barely," Edwin muttered, going to shake Xander's hand.

"I don't seem to remember you talking me out of anything," Xander said.

"If I have learned anything over all the long years of being your friend," Edwin drawled, "it's that talking you or Issie out of anything is a complete waste of time and energy."

"I think I know the feeling now," Xander replied, pointedly looking at her.

Nyla blinked, staring at both of them as innocently as she could. "I haven't done anything."

"Not today," Xander teased, "but the sun hasn't set yet."

"And the memorial hasn't started yet either," Merry said, coming to stand with them. "I hope it's not going to be too long."

"I wouldn't get your hopes up, Merry," Xander said. Nyla turned to ask how he could sound so sure, when she noticed his eyes were set on the raised dais set up at the very back of the courtyard before the hedge maze began. Following his gaze, Nyla could just make out a host of figures sitting on the chairs set up on the stage. "It looks like all the representatives from the Security Council are here today too."

Merry groaned. "That means they'll all make a speech."

"And the longer they go on, the less it will be about memorializing those we've lost," Edwin added.

"We'd better take our seats then. The sooner we get this started, the sooner it will end," Xander finished. Turning to her, he offered his arm. "It's not too late. We *could* run."

Nyla accepted and looped her arm through his. "Do you think that would work?"

"If it does," Edwin interjected, "I'm following after you both."

"Me too," Merry sighed. "I should've had a bigger breakfast."

Carefully weaving through the crowd, Xander led them to the front of the crowd, where seats had been reserved for them with the other members of the war council that weren't scheduled to speak today. Exchanging pleasantries with Nan and George as she sat, a voice from the stage called the courtyard to order.

It was Representative Wesson who spoke, asking people to please take their seats so the memorial could begin.

Nyla shifted where she sat as the representative crossed the stage and resumed her seat. Alexander took the podium next, looking rather dour in a crisp suit decorated with an emblem of his status pinned near the lapel. Like their grandfather, Xander and Merry each bore some symbol of their family's crest, though theirs were smaller. As Alexander began to speak, Nyla found her mind wandering toward the necklace she'd found at the Woodlane Manor.

By all means, it shouldn't have been there. Nyla knew with an unshakeable certainty that her necklace had been inside her home as it burned. She never wore it out in the fields while she was working, so it *had* to be inside the house as it burned, and yet she'd found it in Derek's hiding place at the manor, tarnished and somewhat scorched from the flames that had taken everything from her.

Maybe she'd have it repaired one day.

The thought almost made her smile, but she remembered herself as Alexander's steady voice finally reached her ears.

"…it is not their sacrifices that we will remember them by, but by the way they lived. Let their memory not be marred by the sadness of our grief and sorrow, but let us remember the way they laughed, the way they smiled, and the way they touched our lives with kindness, with love, with friendship.

"Words alone cannot express our gratitude for their service, and by virtue their sacrifice. Usually, announcements such as this are at a great expense of time and debate. I am honored to say that this was not the case, as my fellow businessmen and acquaintances had no question in our minds about how we wished to pay our respects to the families of those we lost in this recent battle for Tenebris's sovereignty. From this day forth, families of those we lost will receive a pension of our gratitude from a fund we intend to maintain and disperse regularly."

A small ripple of surprise went through a part of the crowd. Nyla imagined it was the expression of shock from the families present who would likely receive this pension. She didn't look for them in the crowd, afraid of knowing their faces and knowing she was in part the reason their loved one wouldn't be coming home, and found herself grateful that Alexander was wrapping up his speech.

"This fund is but a small token of our gratitude. We know it cannot heal your hearts, but we hope it can at least help ease this time of grief."

Nyla sniffled, wringing her hands together in her lap. She didn't dare listen to the rest of Alexander's speech, choosing to focus more on the way the sunlight warmed her skin or the chirp of the birds in the distance.

Before her mind had gotten too distant, a hand wrapped around one of hers. She glanced over at Xander, finding his concerned eyes already on her. With the way the sunlight hit them, the golden flecks in his dark eyes were illuminated, sparkling alongside his worry.

"Are you okay?"

She nodded. "Your grandfather is too good at making speeches."

Xander offered her a small smile and brushed his thumb over her knuckles as if to say he understood. Nyla rolled her eyes and decided to lace their fingers together, hoping that the comfort of Xander's hand in hers would help ground her—or distract her with happier memories.

He'd promised to go with her to Eurland, to help her find her extended family.

Nyla bit her lip. But would that change now that his grandfather had chosen to appoint him as his successor in the Heirs of Tenebris?

Watching as Alexander traded places with Ingrid at the podium, Nyla cast the thought from her mind. They had plenty of time to decide their future, and if she was being entirely honest with herself, she wasn't in a rush to depart from Pemberly Hall—or anywhere—just yet. She wanted to catch her breath first, and heal her wounds, as Ingrid was saying now.

"Time is a sort of magic we have tried to understand for far longer than humans have even been able to wield magic ourselves. Time is a wholly infinite sort of magic that seems endless until we find ourselves standing at a point when we cannot fathom how much has already passed us by.

"With loss comes that feeling, though it is less of a reflective course under the weight of our grief. While mourning our losses, we may wonder if time is drawing to a close, but I choose to believe that each loss is a new sort of beginning. I am not a woman of poised speeches, so I shall be brief in my explanation, as I know it may seem unconventional, but in my time as Mage General, I have lost many and have been forced to move forward time and time again. I still feel each and every loss in my heart, but I choose to look toward the future each time with a new heart and new view on life.

"Loss does not mean that life is lost. I choose to believe loss can mean life as well. Loss can bring people together and make our bonds stronger. It bids us to reflect on our values, on our lives, and on our hearts. So while we pray these souls find their peace, I pray we may also find the strength to look for the sunrise and find happiness in our hearts even though it may seem impossible today. Let us come together and share in our grief, but also, let us come together and remember that time is endless. We cannot forget those we've lost and what they were fighting for. For us, for themselves, for time. Rather than standing at the cliff's edge, we are standing on a precipice with an endless horizon of time in our future. I pray we can find the courage in our hearts to make the most of it. Even if those we had hoped to hold hands with through these new horizons are not here to do so, we can carry them with us in our hearts and in our memories. Through our grief, let us never forget to live."

Nyla wished she hadn't listened to Ingrid's speech. Accepting the handkerchief from Xander, Nyla's eyes strayed back to Ingrid only to find her eyes already on her. The woman offered her a nod, and it was only then her final words registered in Nyla's mind.

That was her vow. It was the one she and Xander had made together the night before her duel against Ingrid's former second-in-command, Frederick de Chante. It was also the single sentiment that she'd carried with her through her time alone on the battlefield.

Too overwhelmed to do much of anything, Nyla offered her a

solemn nod of acknowledgement before Ingrid swapped places with Representative Wesson. Nyla thought it odd that Sir Hubert wouldn't be speaking today, especially since he'd led the Royal Guard on the battlefield, but she supposed he would speak at the memorial held by the Caradels. For now, the head of the Chamber of Commons' Security Council would speak and offer her condolences on behalf of the Tenebrese military and the government itself.

Her speech was relatively short, and she too mentioned a fund being created in the memory of those lost on the battlefield. When she was done, Nyla was relieved to see Alexander approaching the podium again. She'd thought Merry had been right about the other representatives making a speech, but luckily, that wasn't the case. They'd probably speak at the national memorial service to be held in the capital, but today, the memorial was truly about remembering those they'd lost and not the grandstanding of who could honor their memory more earnestly than the others.

"At this time, I would like to invite you all to dine with us and share stories of those we love and have lost. Food has been set out in the main dining hall with tables and place settings throughout the banquet and ballrooms. Today, there are no table markers or divisions, as we are one host and friends sharing in our grief. Please make yourselves comfortable and eat your fill, as there is more than enough to feed an army twice this size."

At this, some of the crowd chuckled. Nyla managed a smile. She knew Moretta and the cooks had likely prepared an overabundance of food, though she couldn't imagine how they would find the energy to prepare tomorrow's feast for the Huntington family's return, or as Xander and Alexander had called it, 'the great descension upon Pemberly.'

"Shall we?" Xander's voice broke her from her thoughts.

"We shall." Looping her arm through his, Nyla drew close to him and whispered, "Do you know what Moretta made for the banquet?"

"No idea, but whatever it is, I'm excited for it."

"Me too," she laughed softly. "I'm starving!"

"I think we should visit the dessert table first before the good stuff's gone."

Nyla's eyes widened excitedly at the idea. "Good idea. Should we tell Merry and Edwin?"

Xander glanced over his shoulder, his brows arching in surprise. "They're right behind us, so I can guarantee they'll follow us. Besides, it's a tradition. Merry will tell you. More importantly, I think I know who the second handkerchief was for."

"Who?" Nyla asked, too afraid to turn around and make it obvious that they were talking about them.

Xander shook his head. "I don't know her name, but she's wearing a Caster Corps uniform and looks awfully content walking arm in arm with our dear Eddie. I think I'll make a point of asking him over dessert, you know, because we're friends and all."

Nyla smiled, shaking her head. She wondered what other Huntington family 'traditions' would expose themselves between today and tomorrow—and whenever she decided to leave for her next adventure. She supposed only time would tell, but for now, all she wanted was to cherish every moment of this new horizon, as Ingrid called it.

***

"I see your straight in the making and am still raising you a sishade." Nyla tilted her head and smiled wryly at Xander. While the four cards on the table in front of her were seemingly random, the two she held in her hand bore a promise she couldn't deny, especially with one more card left to be dealt.

Beside her, Edwin grumbled, "I'm folding."

"Me too. I'm almost out of change anyway," Merry sighed.

Nyla didn't break Xander's stare. Locked in a battle of facial expressions and deceit, she knew any twitch, any waver of her stature would be an indicator that Xander could use to his advantage.

"Fine," Xander sighed, dropping two sishades on top of the large pile of change in the center of the coffee table. "If you think those cards are going to beat a straight, I'll humor you."

Edwin shook his head. Pursing his lips, he dealt them each their last card face down. Nyla held her breath. If she didn't get her fifth star-suit card, she'd lose.

Lifting the card, Nyla squinted, forcing her lips to twist into a frown.

"It's still your bet, Xander," Edwin reminded them.

Nyla flashed her eyes to Xander. He sat back in his chair, studying her for a moment. Finally, he said, "I'll pass."

Nyla debated what she should do. She hadn't won a hand for quite a while, but if she made a bet now…

"I'll pass too."

Xander laid the three cards in his hand beside the others face up on the table. "I got the king-high straight."

Nyla blew out a breath, laying down her cards. "And I got the flush."

Merry laughed, seeing the five stars Nyla had lined up. They didn't call it gambling for no reason. With so many stars already on the table between the four of their hands, Nyla didn't think she'd manage to get another. She was glad she had, though, or she would've had to call it quits before she lost too much of her precious prize money from the duel.

"I can't believe it," Xander uttered. "You played me! You bit your lip and everything!"

Edwin failed to stifle his snickering. Nyla batted her eyes at Xander. "It's not *my* fault you fell for it." She leaned over the table and slid the pile of change closer to her reserves with a little help from Merry. "After all, deceit is an integral part of the game."

The clock on the mantel chimed the hour.

Nyla glanced at it, nearly balking at the time. "Is it really that late?"

"I think the better way to phrase that question is how can it be this early?" Edwin said, stretching his arms.

Merry gasped. "We've been up all night?"

"So it seems," Nyla yawned, finally feeling the exhaustion clinging to her bones. "We should probably get some rest before your family arrives."

"You mean the ones who haven't already descended upon the house?" Xander grumbled.

"Yeah, them."

"In any case," Edwin started, sliding his pile of change into his pouch, "Nyla's right. We have a full day of buffets, mingling, and a celebratory dinner banquet ahead of us."

"Ugh, don't remind me," Xander groaned, lying back on the carpet and pressing his arms over his eyes.

"Come on," Nyla poked him in the side, "it can't be all bad. Moretta told me after the memorial luncheon that she made your favorite for dessert again."

"Yeah," Merry said, "and Nyla is going to wear a pretty dress—"

Nyla turned to her in confusion. "I am?"

"Yes, you are! I already picked out another of cousin Iris's dresses for you to wear," Merry explained, taking her by the hand and pulling her across the room to the armoire. Flinging the door open, she said, "See?"

Nyla nearly fainted from the shock at the lacey emerald dress hanging inside. It was almost like the one Xander had found at the Woodlane Manor, but the skirt was slimmer. Unlike the other dress, this one had delicate lace sleeves with tails that trailed down nearly to the hemline.

"Are you sure Iris is all right with lending me this dress?" she asked.

"Iris won't be coming today," Merry assured her. "She's in the east for university."

"Oh," Nyla said.

"Isn't it pretty?" Merry asked excitedly, nearly bouncing on her heels.

Nyla nodded, still thinking about the dance she and Xander had shared in the Woodlane Manor's season room. "Very pretty."

Merry yawned. Frowning, she turned to Nyla and hugged her quickly. "We should really get some rest while we can. Goodnight, Nyla."

"Goodnight, Merry."

"Yeah, I should be going too," Edwin said. "Goodnight, everyone."

"See you at breakfast," Xander said in reply, reminding them all of the early hour and how long they'd been awake.

Nyla shook her head and shut the door to the armoire.

"That was a good play," Xander said, closer than he had been before.

"Hm?" Nyla turned to see him standing a few feet behind her, leaning against the back of the couch.

"The game." Xander's eyes sparkled humorously, watching her as she made her way to stand beside him.

"Oh right." Nyla sagged against the back of the couch and hugged herself, her mind already elsewhere. "Will there be dancing? At the banquet tomorrow?"

Xander hummed. "Probably. Why?"

Nyla shrugged, trying to stifle the way her heart beat between her ears like a drum. "I don't think I remember how to."

"Oh?" Xander turned to her, his brows raised even though his eyes danced. "What do you mean? We *just* shared a waltz at the Woodlane Manor."

"Yeah," Nyla admitted sheepishly as she turned to face him, "but a lot's happened since then. Maybe you could show me again?"

Xander made a show of thinking it over. Before Nyla knew it, he was gently taking her hands and looking at her softly. "If you wanted to dance, all you had to do was ask."

Letting him thread his fingers with hers as he guided her other hand to his shoulder, Nyla bit her lip. Xander pulled her an inch closer to him, wrapping his free arm around her waist. She was grateful that he apparently wasn't waiting for a response as he started to guide her through a slow waltz.

Smiling softly, Nyla pressed herself closer to Xander so she could lay her head on his shoulder and let her eyes flutter shut. A contented sigh left her. Swaying in time to a song only Xander could hear, Nyla didn't ever want this moment to end, especially as she could feel the promise of a peaceful night's sleep reaching out to her.

"You know," Xander said quietly, "you can ask me for anything, right?"

Nyla forced her eyes open and picked her head up from his shoulder. Nearly melting at the soft gaze she found staring back at her, she replied, "I know. I just didn't know how to."

Xander quirked his head.

"I just wanted to be held," she admitted at last, dropping her gaze.

At her words, Xander stopped moving. Nyla's eyes snapped to him. Her heart clenched, fearing he'd pull away, but instead, she found him wearing a lopsided grin.

"Well, you see," he started, "people typically say something like, 'can you hold me?' and then the other person usually complies."

Nyla laughed at his attempt to impersonate her. "Let me see: Xander, will you hold me?"

"I would love nothing more than to honor your request, my lady." Nyla regretfully let him slip his hand from hers as he went to hold her.

Huffing a laugh as Xander wrapped both his arms around her, Nyla tucked herself into his embrace and grumbled against his shoulder. "I'm not technically a noblewoman. I abdicated my titles, remember?"

"To me, you are."

Nyla smiled, her heart fluttering at his words. Truly content for the first time in days, Nyla found herself hoping Xander didn't mind staying like this until the sun rose. As his hands began to rub her back, she realized he had no intention of leaving, and if she were being honest, she was glad for the assurance that he was here, that he wasn't going to leave, that she wouldn't have to face the rest of the waning night alone.

All she had to do was ask. For right now, all she wanted was this. For once, she felt like this moment was all there was, and everything else was simply inconsequential as this single moment froze in time with just her and Xander, the rest of the world utterly forgotten.

31. BYGONE MAGIC

Walking through the halls of Xander's ancestral home, Nyla tried to remember the way to Ingrid's rooms. She hoped the woman was there, or else she'd never be able to find her. Grumbling to herself, Nyla tried again to open her senses to the signatures around her, but found only a phantom tingle of the energies before her awareness faded. Maybe she still just needed time, but after two weeks of recovering from the recently dubbed Battle of Heart and her magical drain, Nyla had hoped that she'd regain her magical abilities. But as far as she and Shamira could tell, her magic and her aura had remained changed.

Nyla recalled what Shamira had said when she woke from her coma. Her aura was unsettled, though neither of them had since found an explanation. Perhaps they should've asked Ingrid to join them yesterday. It certainly would've been easier to have another set of eyes on her aura as Shamira had examined it.

She supposed she should take solace in the fact that her aura had "settled" since she regained her consciousness, but Nyla still couldn't explain the hollow feeling anytime she tried to summon her magic or her ability to conjure energy magic. Thus far, all she'd managed was elemental manipulation and conjuring a spark of light before it sputtered out. At least her hair and eyes were back to how they used to be before the fire: auburn and as rich as the soil of her home.

"Oh, Luce!" Nyla called, catching a flash of the Caster's fiery hair up ahead as she turned down another hallway.

The woman stopped and turned to her. "Nyla? Wow, your hair is completely turned now! I'd heard it was turning auburn, but I couldn't quite believe it!"

Nyla shrugged, tucking her hair behind her ear. "Yeah. My eyes finally changed back too, but I was wondering—have you seen Ingrid?"

"Yeah, we just had a meeting, so she should still be in her sitting room. Shamira might still be there too," Luce offered. "Is everything okay?"

Nyla nodded absently, wondering what sort of meeting Ingrid and Shamira had had and if she'd needed to be present for it. "Fine."

Luce studied her intently, her lips pressed into a thin line. "Has someone said something to you? Because I can—"

"Like what?" Nyla interrupted. Tilting her head, Nyla quirked her brows, uncertain of what Luce was referring to or why her eyes had darkened with a dangerous glint.

"Oh, it's nothing," she said unconvincingly. "Just some talk about…" She waved her hand, making a scoffing noise. "It's really just petty talk from people who don't understand about…Dinora…and what needed to be—ah, Ingrid! Thank goodness, Nyla was just looking for you!"

Furrowing her brows at Luce's rambling, Nyla turned slightly to look at Ingrid.

"You were looking for me?" the woman asked. "Is something the matter?"

"Well, no, but maybe?" Nyla tried to focus on why she'd sought Ingrid out in the first place, but all her mind could think about was what Luce had meant by what people didn't understand about Dinora. Were people talking about what had happened during the battle? Or were they talking about how Nyla had—

She swallowed hard and shoved the memory from her mind. "I was hoping to ask you something, about my magic?"

"Of course," Ingrid said, gesturing for Nyla to follow her. "Let's go someplace more comfortable so we can chat about it."

Nyla nodded, following after the Royal Mage. Offering only a half-hearted wave to Luce before she went, Nyla still found herself turning the woman's answer over in her mind.

"Ingrid?" Nyla started hesitantly. "Are people...are they talking about the battle, and Dinora?"

Ingrid went rigid, her shoulders straightening. "It's nothing," she assured her, opening the door to the private guest suite and letting Nyla enter ahead of her. Closing the door firmly behind them, Ingrid added, "There are just a few people who don't understand the method of Dinora's defeat. It's already been taken care of, though I'm sure there are still grumbles. It's all hearsay, Nyla, and people offering their opinions when they know very little about the matter."

Taking a seat on the couch, Nyla kept her gaze to the floor. "Is it because I killed her or because...it was gruesome?"

"I don't think it should matter because they're all cowards. If there had been a different way, if *they* had *wanted* to help, they easily could have done so, but they didn't. I would not put much stock in the hollow words of those who ignorantly observe and cast only shortsighted judgement."

Nyla's eyes flicked to the woman across from her. Despite the fire in Ingrid's eyes, her face was sincere. "Trust me, Nyla, there will always be people who think they know better or that their opinion carries weight, but the truth is they only hold as much influence or legitimacy as we allow them. Don't let them hold such power over you. It'll take time, but you'll learn to ignore them."

A small smile pulled at Nyla's lips at Ingrid's advice and the support offered in them. "Thanks, Ingrid. I'll have to try that."

"Now what is it you *really* wanted to talk to me about? I imagine it wasn't something so…" she waved her hand around, plopping down in the adjacent armchair, "inconsequential."

"Well…" Nyla started, gripping her knees as she braced herself to tell Ingrid about her magic. "I think there's something wrong with my magic. It's been different since…since the battle, but I don't know how to explain it."

Ingrid's features hardened as she gave Nyla her undivided attention. Nyla tried her hardest to pinpoint exactly what she was feeling and what was happening to her, but the more she spoke, the more certain she was none of it made any sense. She even summoned what she could of her magic, showing Ingrid a wavering wisp of light that sputtered and extinguished like a flame seconds after she'd called upon it. Tamping down her disappointment at the display, Nyla continued on in her explanation, stressing her dismay that this was all she could dredge up: a spark of amber and nothing more. Not even a ball of light like she had that day outside of Deering.

When Nyla finally finished, Ingrid tapped her fingers against her arm. Nyla squirmed in the silence that ensued as a result of her explanation. The Royal Mage studied Nyla with a piercing gaze as she sat with her arms folded against her chest. Nyla held her breath, waiting for the woman to say something, *anything* about what she'd just divulged to her.

Ingrid hummed, pursing her lips. Her dark eyes flicked with her moving thoughts. "Well…it's possible that the two bequeathment rituals acting on your aura are in conflict with each other or…perhaps something else, something that we'll just have to sort out for ourselves."

Nyla took a breath. "I was hoping that after a couple weeks of rest and limiting my use of magic, everything would kind of settle, but it hasn't. I still have this empty feeling when I try to call upon my magic."

Ingrid nodded thoughtfully. "Have you asked Shamira about what she'd meant by your aura being 'unsettled?'"

"I have. Shamira and I actually spent some time together yesterday so she could study my aura. She said it seemed fine now, but that it was different. The shadowy spots of Cedric's bequeathment are still there, though the lilac seems to have dulled or gone away for some reason. Shamira isn't sure, though. She said she would consult with her clan's High Seer for any information he might have."

"Do you mind showing me your aura?"

"Not at all," Nyla said, getting to her feet. Ingrid followed suit and gestured for her to stand in a clear spot of the sitting room. "I just want to figure out what's happening to me and if it's something I actually have to worry about or not."

At her words, Ingrid laughed. "I'm glad to see you're in good spirits despite this."

Nyla let out a breathy chuckle. "I've lived most of my life afraid and also not knowing I had magic. I won't live the rest of my life with that fear, and though I've come to love my magic, I think I can make my peace without it too. There's so much more to my life and what I want to do with it than worrying about whether I can manipulate water or start a campfire with a flick of my fingers."

"Oh?" Ingrid arched her brow. "And what is it you want to do next?"

"Xander and I are making plans to travel to Eurland this Agergy. I'm hoping to reconnect with my mother's family."

"That's wonderful, Nyla. I wish you luck."

"Thanks," Nyla said, suppressing a shudder. "I'm not even sure what to say to them or how to explain all that's happened these last two years. I don't even really know them, so it might just be another adventure to add to our memories."

"I'm sure it'll be fine," Ingrid replied almost knowingly. "The worst has come to pass. Nothing could ever surpass that."

"I hope you're right," Nyla grumbled, closing her eyes. Magic fizzled in her bloodstream, only a faint tingle now compared to the torrential buzz it used to be, displaying her aura to Ingrid. "I just want to make sure there's nothing wrong with my magic before Xander and I go gallivanting off to another country, you know, *just* in case we need it."

Ingrid snorted. "I highly doubt Lord Huntington would allow you and his grandson to travel to Eurland without the proper protections and precautions in place."

"Still, though," Nyla insisted, "we haven't had the best luck on our adventures. On our way to Fortune Falls, an ogre invaded our campsite."

"And?"

Nyla blew out a tense breath. "I obliterated it, apparently, and then passed out."

Ingrid laughed, "Now I see. You really have embraced the scope of your magic. But I'm afraid I can't see anything in your aura either. Granted, I don't know what it looked like before, but there isn't anything here that is giving me cause to worry."

Nyla opened her eyes. The trickle of magic in her veins receded. Crestfallen, Nyla nodded. "I feared you'd say as much. Do you have any idea what might be happening to me?"

Ingrid met her gaze hesitantly. Her eyes shone with caution. "Well…I have an idea or two. Your magic, it always presented itself as a lilac hue, correct?"

Nyla nodded, eyeing Ingrid uncertainly.

"What color was Astrid's?"

"Lilac." Nyla blinked, her voice tilting with an unasked question.

"And now you've only managed to conjure light, something like the amber you just showed me?" Nyla nodded, trying to wrap her mind around what Ingrid was saying. "It's possible your magic is weaker than you're used to despite weeks of rest and trying to push its boundaries. Does it feel like you're beginning all over again?"

"Yeah…" Nyla took a subconscious step back. "What are you suggesting, Ingrid?"

Ingrid's lips twitched. Nyla's heart fluttered in her throat.

"I think this is *your* magic, Nyla, not Astrid's."

Nyla's breath hitched. "You mean…you think Astrid's magic…what do you mean that this is *my* magic and not Astrid's? Wouldn't they be the same if she bequeathed her magic to me?"

Ingrid bobbed her head, considering the question. "Normally, yes, but if I have learned anything these last few weeks, it's that nothing about any of this is 'normal.' And that includes whatever bequeathment ritual Astrid used. Without knowing the specifics, I don't feel confident in saying Astrid's magic has faded, leaving you with only your own magic—that is, the magic you were born with and have apparently cultivated alongside Astrid's—but that does make the most logical sense to me."

Nyla forced the tension from her throat, asking, "How do we find out for certain?"

"I'll look into it some more. Perhaps Shamira can join me." Ingrid began to pace. "Do you know where we might find some of Astrid's things?"

Nyla opened and closed her mouth. Her mind went numb as the singular impression of an ivy-covered estate flooded her consciousness. "I can think of only one place: the Woodlane Manor."

"Then that's where I'll begin my search." Ingrid ceased her pacing and turned to face her. "Don't worry, Nyla. Between myself, Edwin, and Shamira, we'll figure this out long before you and Xander depart for Eurland."

"Thank you, Ingrid." Nyla closed the distance between them and offered the woman a hug that she didn't hesitate to accept. "Just be safe. I don't like that manor much anymore. I wouldn't be surprised if it was actually haunted now."

Ingrid laughed, pulling away. "Ghosts are the least of my concerns. I think it's more pressing to collect Astrid's work so we might learn what we've forgotten over all these centuries."

Even as agreement settled over her mind, Nyla couldn't stop the question Ingrid's statement had brought to mind. "Have you learned anything from what you brought back from Cedric's cottage?"

Ingrid pressed her lips together. "A great deal, actually. I found several rough and revised drafts of magicology papers I know to be published and widely referenced. I also found some personal things he must not have had the heart to throw out for some reason or another, but so far, nothing of much consequence. A few books that might be helpful, but nothing unknown to me."

Nyla's brows furrowed. "What sort of personal things?"

Ingrid shrugged. "Sketches, mostly." Turning on her heel, Ingrid moved toward the writing desk against the wall and pulled open a drawer. "Would you like to see them?"

Nyla bit her lip. "Maybe another time, unless they concern me?"

"Definitely not," Ingrid laughed, scoffing. "I did find a few of Astrid, but they're mostly scenes from the Plains or of a raverin."

"He seemed fond of them, didn't he?"

"The raverins, or Astrid?"

The corners of Nyla's lips quirked upwards. "I meant the raverins, but I suppose both."

"I think there's a lot to Cedric we may never discover."

Nyla nodded slowly. "Let's hope all that's left bears no relevancy to today or tomorrow or the future at large."

"Yes. Let's hope the rest brings only peace."

32. THE WOMAN WITH ORANGE-COLORED MAGIC

I *still think a more immersive training technique would lead to the faster improvement Nyla is looking for,* Shamira said.

Xander tore his eyes from Nyla and the flaming target she was trying to put out. "I'm not sure that's a good idea, all things considered. Besides, I think she's happy with her progress."

His eyes returned to Nyla and Edwin just in time to see Edwin conjure water seemingly from thin air in order to put the target out before the flames could leap to the surrounding shrubbery.

"Or maybe you're absolutely right, and this is too slow-going," Xander sighed. "I wish I could help, but Ingrid won't let anyone near Astrid's things, and honestly, I'm too afraid to ask."

I'm sure Ingrid wouldn't mind you asking. She's just being cautious, given that Astrid presumably knew things most Casters could only ever dream of knowing, and that could be dangerous, depending how they choose to wield that knowledge. Shamira paused, shifting beside him. *Is Nyla still experiencing nightmares?*

Xander stared across the pavers between their seats on the back steps of Pemberly Hall and where Nyla and Edwin had set up their training grounds. "She doesn't really say either way, but I can tell sometimes.

She gets a shadow in her eyes when something's bothering her, and then if it's about the battle, she'll get that withdrawn look, and that's when I know."

Shamira hummed. *Then perhaps it's best not to immerse her in an active training environment just yet. I wouldn't want to feed these nightmares or draw them to her conscious mind.*

Xander didn't respond, too consumed by the darkening of his thoughts. They'd all watched as Nyla had killed Dinora. He'd thought the raw magic she and Edwin had used to kill the creatures that had attacked their carriage was brutal, but the way Nyla had ultimately defeated Dinora?

He couldn't pretend to know the burden it weighed on Nyla's mind. And though it offered her little comfort, he knew that no one could truly demonize her for killing Dinora.

Even so, it hadn't stopped the air of wariness that'd rippled through the estate the more the story spread. From what he understood, shredding someone's aura was a cruel death, and one of the few unspoken laws of magic. It was considered a banned practice, one unbecoming of a modern Caster.

Ingrid had made certain to dispel any talk amongst the Casters that dared to think differently than the circumstances Nyla had been up against, reminding them precisely of the sort of threat Dinora posed. She'd reminded them that Nyla was young and untrained. She'd reminded them that Nyla wasn't a soldier, that she was a teenager and barely an adult by any definition, regardless of the maturity and courage she'd shown.

And what about you, Xander? Shamira's voice stole him from his thoughts.

"What about me?" he asked, still half-distracted by the memories plaguing his mind, memories of grief and death and barely escaped fates.

How are you doing?

Xander opened his mouth to respond, but caught himself. How

many times had he wondered whether Nyla was lying when she said she was fine? If anyone would realize the truth behind the thin assurance offered by "fine," it was Shamira. "I…I've been worse, and I've been better, but we're alive, so I guess that's good."

Shamira huffed in a way that sounded like a laugh. *Yes, I would say being alive is good. You seem haunted, though, like Nyla.*

"Like Nyla?" he asked, his brows arching.

You've both been through much heartache. It's understandable that there would be a shadow on your mind even now. Shamira's words were gentle despite how blunt they were. *I'm here if you want to talk about it.*

"Ah, yes," Xander said, stretching his legs out in front of him and leaning his elbows back on the step behind him, "it seems fair to unburden myself on the newly appointed ambassador for pumpkie-human relations. Suppose *you* need to talk about things?"

That's why Nyla and I are friends, Shamira jested, whacking him with one of her paws. *I mean it, though. You shouldn't try to hold your emotions at bay. Talk to someone, Xander.*

"I do," he admitted quietly. "I talk to you and to Nyla and—"

That's not what I mean, she chastised.

A flare of orange burst out of the corner of Xander's eye. Both he and Shamira turned their gazes upon Nyla and Edwin's chosen training ground just in time for Xander to catch sight of Nyla's magic flitting around her. The orange bands of magic circled around her, ebbing and flowing. Her auburn hair floated around her in a breeze Xander didn't feel himself. He still couldn't help but see her as the avenging angel she'd once presented herself as at the Woodlane Manor when he'd thought for certain Dinora would kill him, though the way she appeared now was calmer, like a sunset. Perhaps it was the new color of her magic.

The amber suited her. It could be vibrant like Nyla was or soft and gentle like the way she treated other people. Most of all, Xander had come to realize, just as Nyla had, it was hers. Ingrid had been right.

Nyla's magic was orange, and that certainly explained the lack of lilac in her aura that Shamira had discovered.

As the light of Nyla's magic faded and the bands grew smaller, Nyla opened her eyes. Her hair fell still, and a smile spread across her face.

"Shouldn't be much longer now, right?" she asked, turning to Edwin.

"I couldn't say," Xander heard him say. "It all depends on your goal. How strong do you want your magic to be again?"

Nyla shrugged. "Enough."

Edwin shook his head and waved her off, saying something Xander couldn't hear as he walked off to clean up the burned targets at the far end of the courtyard.

Nyla met his gaze next, taking a step closer to where he and Shamira sat. Xander straightened as he realized Nyla and Edwin were done for the day. Nyla slowly made her way over to them. Before he could stand, she'd plopped herself down on the step beside him and leaned her head against his shoulder.

"You might have to carry me inside this time," she grumbled. "I couldn't even draw enough water from the air to put out that fire."

"You'll get there," Xander assured her, wrapping an arm around her.

"Mm, I know," Nyla said. "It's just a matter of *when*."

"And the good news is there isn't any rush to get there," he reminded her.

"None at all," Nyla agreed.

***

Xander stared into the flames, watching them leap and lick as their quiet crackle soothed his mind. Taking a deep breath, he let it go slowly. Since Ingrid had returned from the Woodlane Manor with the entirety of Astrid's workshop packed into boxes, he hadn't known any rest—or at least, his mind hadn't. He knew they would find an explanation for why Nyla's magic was different, but until then, he found himself wondering how many more mysteries they'd face together, or if this was the final piece of the large puzzle Nyla had been entangled in thanks to Dinora.

"You look troubled." His grandfather's voice broke him from his near stupor, calling his attention to the private sitting room's doorway. "Care to share your burdens?"

"They're not really burdens, per se," Xander said, "but they're bothersome all the same."

"I see," his grandfather replied inquisitively as he took a seat on the couch and propped his feet up. "It's nice to have the estate back to normal, though I do miss the solitude. Do you think it would be too much to expel the family with their own homes from Pemberly except for special occasions?"

Xander chuckled. "I doubt they'd let you. At this rate, I'm surprised they haven't sold their homes just to guarantee you'd never banish them from Pemberly, even intermittently."

"I suppose you're right." His grandfather's words settled upon them like a lamentation. "How is Nyla faring with her magic training?"

"Fine, though it's going rather slower than it had before. Shamira thinks it's because she's solely cultivating her own magical energy without the power of Astrid's magic adding to it."

His grandfather quirked his head. "But didn't Cedric bequeath his magic to her?"

"He did," Xander said, nodding, "and that's another question we all have. He's been dead for weeks now, so why hasn't Nyla felt a surge of power? They're still researching the potion and how it functions, but their theory is that Cedric may have placed an inhibitor on it so that the magical energy builds over time so as not to overwhelm Nyla, but I still find that hard to believe. Ingrid is hoping to find his research or notes about the potion amongst his things."

"Even with the confirmation of what the blood oath he made to you was?"

Xander scoffed, "By his own words, and I certainly don't believe them."

"He did save Nyla on the battlefield," his grandfather reminded him.

"That he did," Xander said begrudgingly, sinking back into his chair. "It's still hard to believe how much time he'd spent tormenting Nyla only to save her then. I have trouble believing his actions were anything but selfish."

His grandfather laughed. "Then I suppose we shall have to wait for Ingrid, Shamira, and Edwin's verdict about why Nyla hasn't inherited Cedric's magic yet or if the blood oath was satisfied. It's a good thing Ingrid is so devoted to this cause. It is comforting to know that there are more people who can help Nyla where we cannot, though I fear Ingrid often leaves me with a headache."

"But at least there's one thing you two have in common," Xander laughed. "You both care a lot about Nyla."

Eyes twinkling, his grandfather added, "And so do you."

Xander smiled. Dropping his eyes to the floor, his hand reached for the ring still hidden beneath his shirt. "So I do."

33. New Horizons

Nyla stared, watching the ashen trees and the bright Agergy leaves of the Shadow Forest fade away until the golden honey-brown trees and plum-colored leaves of the Godberd Woods had overtaken them. She clenched her hands anxiously in her lap.

When she'd asked Xander to go with her to Eurland, she was excited and eager to chase after the wind calling her attention into a new adventure, but in the quiet moments after her excitement had faded, Nyla realized she couldn't go to Eurland.

Not yet, at least.

There was something she needed to do first. Even if finding her extended family proved to be of the utmost importance to her and the possibility they presented for her future, there was someone here that Nyla needed to reconnect with just as much as her blood relatives.

She'd thought an awful lot about her home and the people she'd known then. It was for them that she'd defeated Dinora just as much as for herself and her family. Her friends and neighbors deserved to know what had become of her, especially as Xander had admitted to meeting her neighbor when he'd left her at the Woodlane Manor to send his message to Alexander.

He'd said that Mr. Loch still left lilacs on the stacked-stone marker they'd built for her beside her family's.

The thought of leaving her friends and neighbors to mourn her—especially the Lochs, who had been like grandparents to her and her siblings—had made her queasy. Nyla hadn't realized the impact her disappearance had had on their lives, or that they'd spent all these seasons wondering what happened to the girl who'd fled in the wake of that tragedy.

When she'd gone to Xander with her concerns, he'd only smiled and said that they could leave from Gossamer instead. And that's exactly what they'd decided to do. Her head was still whirling from how quickly these last few weeks had passed. Like a flurry, they'd packed and planned. Alexander had insisted they go shopping for more supplies, namely clothing, and once the word had spread that Nyla intended to leave the country for some time, King Albert and Queen Clarice had immediately offered their services.

She'd barely managed to assure them that their assistance was generous and well-appreciated, but unnecessary. In the end, though, they'd insisted on the stipend. No one—not the Caradels, not the Huntingtons, or even Shamira—had allowed her to protest the allowance they intended to set aside for her. The royals had assured her that it was the least they could do for her, after all she'd done for Tenebris and the legacy of all of their ancestors.

Nyla supposed having a bit of money to call her own wouldn't be so bad. If anything, it had made things easier for her when they'd gone shopping for travel necessities or paying for the train ticket back to Covington. She'd managed to pay for everything, despite Xander's protests that it was unnecessary for her to pay him back for the courtesy he'd shown her only two seasons earlier when they'd set off for the Woodlane Manor from Caselle.

From Covington, she and Xander had decided they'd arrange for a carriage, as Nyla still wasn't quite comfortable with riding sagittariiback yet. Besides, they hadn't sent their luggage ahead, and Merry hadn't let her leave with less than three trunks. Nyla wasn't entirely certain what was in the two trunks she hadn't packed herself, though she hoped they contained something useful. She hadn't had time to look between the festivities Alexander had planned for their going-away feasts, and she doubted she'd ever feel this overstuffed again.

The pastries Moretta had made were well worth the slight stomach upset she'd experienced by the third day of feasting. But it wasn't quite enough to stop her from looking forward to the leftovers she'd packed for their journey.

But until then, there was only one thing for Nyla to do: gather her thoughts and watch as the world outside the quickly moving train brought her closer and closer to home with each passing second.

***

Nyla woke up, startled awake by the gentle touch to her shoulder that shook her slightly. Flicking open her eyes, she blinked away the cloudiness lingering over her mind from her nap. Sitting up, she stretched before offering Xander a lazy smile.

"We're almost there," he said, pointing to the carriage window.

Nyla glanced outside, taking in the fields she'd known so well, wondering if she would ever be compelled to leave them again once they'd stopped.

"I still haven't the slightest idea what to say to them." She sat back, falling against the cushioned wall of the carriage. Her stomach rolled almost as much as the landscape of her home.

"You could start with 'hello,'" Xander replied, his eyes twinkling with amusement.

Nyla rolled her eyes, playfully shoving him away from her. "That's very helpful, thank you, Xander."

He snickered, "It's a start!"

"Should I follow it up with, 'I'm not dead,' or just wait for a response?" she teased, trying in vain to stop her own giggles from escaping.

"No, I'd just see where 'hello' gets you before jumping into the whole of what you've been doing recently," Xander answered more soberly.

"Maybe I shouldn't mention that at all." Nyla bit her lip, turning toward the window once more. "If it comes to it, I could always tell them about going to Fortune Falls and meeting you, and then just… make something up, I guess?"

"You could," Xander said thoughtfully, "though I'm not sure you'll get that far."

Nyla turned her head to face him, frowning. "What do you mean?"

Xander shrugged. "You'll see. Reunions are a very overwhelming ordeal for most people."

She didn't have time to press him any further for a straight answer, catching sight of the school building she knew was only a stone's throw away from her neighbors'. Nyla and her siblings used to cut through the patch of woods between the Lochs' and her parents' fields, taking the path the Lochs had cut for them along the perimeter of their fields.

Xander followed her gaze as the carriage ambled by.

"My mother was a teacher," Nyla offered softly, reaching for his hand. "We couldn't get away with anything in that schoolhouse."

He laced their fingers together, brushing his thumb across her knuckles. "I can only imagine."

"Yeah…" Nyla blushed. "She wasn't particularly happy when the chirpets I'd caught to show the class escaped from the jar I'd put them in. Three weeks passed before she finally stopped talking about it, but at least she hadn't been angry with me for the whole three weeks."

Xander laughed heartily. "You what? How many were there?"

"Seven? Eight, maybe?" Nyla laughed. Xander shot her a bewildered look that sent her into a fit of giggles. She tried in vain to answer the question exposed plainly on his face, but found that she couldn't stop laughing. "I—I was really…"

"How did you catch that many?" he finally managed to ask.

"I don't know! I was really good at catching them, I guess?" she said between her giggles.

Xander shook his head. "Edwin, Issie, and I only managed to catch one or two between the three of us. Did your siblings help you?"

"No!" Nyla cried, wiping at the tears pooling in her eyes from how hard she'd laughed. "They didn't have any idea I'd planned this until after." The scene replayed before her mind's eye, of her mother frantically running around the classroom as she tried to catch one of the rogue chirpets while also keeping everyone calm. She remembered she tripped a lot as she tried to help catch them again. "It caused such a ruckus that the older kids and their teacher came downstairs to see what was the matter. Then Lydia's class came in from outside, and the chirpets fled one by one through the open door as we eventually chased them out or they got scared by all the squealing and chasing."

"Is it too late to ask you to be my childhood best friend?"

"Maybe a little late," Nyla said, making a show of considering the question again before she added, "but seeing as we're stuck with each other for the rest of time, I guess you could ask me now."

Xander turned to her as the carriage began to slow. "I could, though I think we'll have to wait."

Nyla's eyes slowly gravitated toward the window as the carriage turned off of the main road and onto a long driveway. She took a deep breath through her nose and sat back in her seat. In part, she wished the soft, velvet cushion would swallow her whole, but another part—a stronger part—was comforted by the familiar sight of her neighbor's fields, however much they looked empty now that the planting season had only just begun. She wouldn't necessarily call the sparks flitting through her chest a sign of happiness, but she couldn't find any other word to describe how she felt. Bittersweet perhaps, but she was happy all the same and maybe even the tiniest bit excited.

The Lochs remembered her.

The carriage rattled to a stop. Nyla squeezed Xander's hand, biting her lip as she heard the carriage creak with Quentin's movements as he dismounted. Xander squeezed her hand back reassuringly. She took another full gulp of air as Quentin opened the door for them and Xander ultimately let her hand go so he could slide out of the carriage.

Blinking out into the dazzling afternoon sunlight, Nyla felt like a witness in her own body as she gathered her skirt in one hand and tried her best to scoot out of the carriage in the dress. Why had she let Merry convince her to bring the silly garment along? She only hoped she didn't find more of them in the two trunks Merry had packed for her. While she loved the freedom and flow of the skirt, the extra material had proved cumbersome, a harsh truth she hadn't realized after exclusively wearing pants for such a long time.

Placing one foot down onto the tiered footstool Quentin had set before the carriage, Nyla eagerly took Xander's offered hand. At least she hadn't let Merry talk her into the matching shoes. The surety of her boots was a welcomed comfort that offered her stability in both her steps and in the uncertain task before her.

"Thanks, Quentin," she said quietly.

"My pleasure, miss." He tipped his head and rejoined Huey at the front of the carriage to check on the sagittarii.

Nyla stared at the quaint home. It was simple and a little plain, but she'd be damned if she claimed the sight hadn't made her heart sing with joy. She hadn't seen something so lovely as the wooden cottage in far too long. Sure, she'd seen stately manors and historic estates in her time away, but there was something about the Lochs' cottage that tugged on her heartstrings the way only home could.

"Ready?" Xander whispered.

"More than ready," Nyla whispered back, taking a step up to the house.

Xander followed beside her, and together they mounted the two steps up onto the front porch that sprawled the width of the small cottage.

Nyla's heart pounded so hard against her chest, she'd feared it would burst. Her hands trembled, though she wondered if it was more from excitement than nerves.

All she knew was that her mind had gone blank the moment she'd knocked on the solid door. She held her breath, waiting as the seconds drew on and no answer came. A numbness settled over her bones as the sound of approaching footsteps padded toward the door from inside the cottage.

She'd just managed a breath as the door creaked open.

"Nyla?" Mr. Loch asked, his eyes going wide. She didn't have time to respond before he'd pulled her inside, wrapping her in a desperate hug. "It's you! You're all right! Dear girl, let me look at you."

Nyla smiled, her eyes swimming. They'd hardly pulled away long enough for her to get a look at his worn face before a sharp gasp had her turning around to see that Mrs. Loch had come to see what the fuss was all about.

"Nyla?" she murmured, her voice choked by tears.

She didn't even have time to utter a single syllable before Mrs. Loch had rushed forward and wrapped her in a hug even more bone-crushing than her husband's.

Nyla eagerly returned her hug. Warm tears trailed silently down her face. "Hi, Mrs. Loch."

"Please," Mr. Loch started thickly, "come in. Both of you."

Pulling away slowly, Mrs. Loch sniffled, "I'll put the kettle on. Make yourselves at home."

She cupped Nyla's cheek softly before turning back toward the kitchen. Mr. Loch was already leading Xander down the cramped hallway toward the sunny sitting room, asking him how he'd found her and thanking him profusely for reuniting them.

"I knew you were someone special when we met by the memorials," he was saying as Nyla finally found it in her power to follow behind them, "but I didn't realize you were a friend of Nyla's."

Mrs. Loch joined them, setting a tray full of sweets and crusty home-made bread with a pot of jam, and a steaming pot of tea on the coffee table in the middle of their small sitting room. Nyla perched herself on the edge of the couch beside Xander, at a loss for words thanks to the flurry of emotion and movement she'd found herself in.

"And just where have you been all this time, young lady?" Mrs. Loch asked, sitting down on the arm of the chair her husband occupied. He wrapped an arm around her, setting a placating hand on her leg.

Nyla smiled softly, dropping her gaze to her lap. "Well…it's an awfully long story…" she started, glancing to Xander and finding him already staring at her with a warm sparkle in his eyes. "But we've all the time in the world to tell it, don't we?"

Xander's answering smile was all Nyla needed, but the gentle reverence in his voice made her heart soar in a way she hoped would never end. "We absolutely do."

ACKNOWLEDGEMENTS

It's crazy to think how I started this journey as a junior in high school and how, over the years since, these characters and this story have not only become a part of myself, but have also taken me on my own journey much like Nyla and Xander have.

When I first started writing *Fire & Flight*, there were many things I didn't know. I didn't have any character names, I didn't have a story or a plot, and I didn't even have an idea of what I was writing. All I had was a girl waking up in a forest that had very little light and leaves of sapphire. She had silver hair and lilac-colored eyes, and it was these few details that became the start of what I would soon realize was a trilogy of young adult fantasy-adventure novels. And the more I ran with this *very* rough first paragraph, the more the world of Tenebris evolved.

While I have many people to thank for their support, their guidance, and their help in bringing these books to life, there's one person who I'd like to take the time to especially thank. Thank you to my high school creative expressions teacher, whose class inspired me to keep writing this story-turned-novel-turned-trilogy. I can honestly say that without your class and your guidance through the writing process, *Fire & Flight* wouldn't exist. Your guidance and advice at the onset of my writing journey has been invaluable to me, and I cannot thank you enough for your help and support in the early stages of my dream to become an author. Thank you, for everything! I hope your own writing is going well!

As always, I cannot thank my readers enough. Any time I felt discouraged during this adventure, I turned to you and the connections we'd made, whether they were online, in person, or if you reviewed/rated my books online. Knowing there were people just as excited about the *Heirs of Tenebris* and my writing as I was became the motivation I needed whenever my self-doubt would creep up, especially as *Winds of War* took me to unexplored areas of my writing. Thank you for taking this journey alongside me and my characters, and also for helping me build a community for my works where we can connect and escape to.

If anyone deserves my undying gratitude, it's my family. All my life they've supported me, encouraged me, and put up with me as I rambled on about a problem in my writing that I couldn't figure out, even though my questions didn't always make sense. Thank you for just bearing with me, but more importantly, thank you for being my entourage. I love how we're *that* family (you know, the kind who will show up for each other and pretend the one we're there to support is famous at her first book signing <3). I still laugh about that, in case you were wondering. I love y'all so much and am so happy that we got to celebrate not just my publication but *all* of our accomplishments together. Thank you for always having my back and for just being awesome in general.

When I first started my publishing journey, the first concern I had was cover design—and art in general. I am so glad I got to work with my amazing graphic designer, Marcella, on not just the covers for the *Heirs of Tenebris* trilogy, but for 90 percent of the artwork inspired by the trilogy too. From the very first graphic, I knew I'd made the right decision in entrusting you with bringing Tenebris to life. THANK YOU, Marcella! I can't imagine how many more ways I can tell you how amazing your artwork is, especially these covers. Thank you so much for everything you've done for this series—I can't *wait* to see what you'll design next, and I just hope I'll have another project that'll need your expertise!

I couldn't have asked for a better team of people to help turn this manuscript into a book than the team I found at Paper Raven Books! I do feel as though I need to apologize for creating delicious-sounding fantasy foods and not being able to provide recipes for them while we were editing *Embers of Eternity*.

As I look toward my next project, I can't help but already miss our banter, your advice, and most of all, the memes and GIFs we shared in our project files. Your guidance and support have meant the world to me, especially as it taught me that it was okay to talk things through and that it wasn't spoiling my novel if I needed help working through something. From my amazing team of editors, to my project coordinators, my formatter, and everyone in the background helping me to polish this series up for publication, your expertise, encouragement, and feedback has meant the world to me. I am so grateful to have had the opportunity to work with y'all!

This may be the end of the trilogy, but I know in my heart that I'll revisit the *Heirs of Tenebris* often. With such a rich world to explore and continue to develop, I hope to find myself writing more about Tenebris and its culture and people and its history in the future. For now, there are other projects calling my attention, including a super-secret project I've been hinting at for years now, probably since I set out to publish *Fire & Flight*. While Nyla and Xander's adventure may be at a close, I'm excited to see where my journey will take me next. Thank you for being a part of their adventure and also for being a part of my own. No matter where life will take me, I know Tenebris is only a book away…or a keyboard!

JOIN THE JOURNEY

Want more from the world of Tenebris? Visit brswrites.com to sign up for my newsletter to receive *Hell's Eyes*, a popular novella penned by the fictional Sir Elliot Thomason, a Tenebrese nobleman and popular author for free!

Let's Connect!

Follow me on social media for insights into my life as a writer, fun behind-the-scenes tidbits, and the latest updates on my author journey!

Facebook: @BRSWritesOfficial

Instagram: @brs_writes

Tumblr: @world-of-fire-and-flight

TikTok: @brswrites

ABOUT THE AUTHOR

Brianna R. Shaffery is a speculative fiction author known for her award-winning young adult fantasy trilogy, the *Heirs of Tenebris*. Always looking toward her next project, Brianna has also written several novellas that can be read on her website, BRSwrites.com.

Aside from her love of literature, Brianna can often be found listening to music while engaged in some kind of craft or whipping up one of her favorite desserts.

DID YOU KNOW THAT READER REVIEWS ARE LIKE GOLD TO INDIE AUTHORS?

For authors, reviews not only give our books some social clout, but they also help readers just like you discover their next read!

Leaving the star rating of your choice and even a line or two about what you honestly thought of the book is a huge boost to indie authors and our book's long-term success. And who knows how many readers like yourself you'll be helping along the way by posting what you thought of the book on retail platforms, your social media, book sites like Goodreads, or on your own blog?

I would be forever grateful if you could leave a review and help me grow as an author.

Happy reading!

Brianna R. Shaffery